D.C. 2002

I.

I.

A NOVEL

———

STEPHEN DIXON

McSweeney's Books

MCSWEENEY'S BOOKS
429 Seventh Avenue
Brooklyn, NY 11215
826 Valencia Street
San Francisco, CA 94110

For more information about McSweeney's see www.mcsweeneys.net.

Excerpts of I. have been published in the following magazines:
Boulevard, Colorado Review, Cortland Review, Florida Review, Glimmer Train,
Hawaii Pacific Review, Idaho Review, Literal Latte, Reading Room,
Southern California Quarterly, Story Quarterly, Sundog (Southeast Review),
Triquarterly, Western Humanities Review, and in the *Pierogi Press Anthology*
and as a chapbook for *Rain Taxi.*

Original cover artwork by Daniel Clowes

Published in the United States by McSweeney's Books

McSweeney's and colophon are registered trademarks
of McSweeney's, a privately held company with
wildly fluctuating resources.

First published in the United States by McSweeney's, 2002

Manufactured in Iceland by Oddi Printing
1 3 5 7 9 10 8 6 4 2
Library of Congress Cataloging-in-Publication Data
ISBN: 0-9719047-0-7

To Andrea Lilienthal and Richard Cantor

I.

CONTENTS

PARIS

HE'D BEEN LIVING in Paris for two months. In a small cheap hotel, two floors above the kitchen of a Chinese restaurant. He came to Paris to learn French, eventually get a job there where he could use the language, and to write. He smelled the food cooking in this kitchen from about 10 a.m. on. Smelled it when he read, studied, wrote or tried to nap, smelled it at night when he went to bed. He always wanted to eat in the restaurant and had checked the menu from its front window dozens of times. Would get hungry reading the things they served. He imagined many times sitting in the restaurant at a small table, ordering three dishes (appetizer, soup, main course) and a large carafe of red wine, eating and reading and looking around the room to see if he recognized anyone he knew and also to see what other people were eating. The restaurant was usually crowed for dinner and half-filled for lunch. Some weekend evenings, people waited outside for twenty to thirty minutes for a table. The hotel was on rue du Sommerand, near the Musée de Cluny. There was a small park across the street from the hotel and he'd sit in it sometimes when he wanted to take a break from his work, and read and watch people go into the restaurant, often carrying souvenirs and books from the museum. There was always lots of chatter and laughing and noises from clinking dishes, glasses and silver coming from the dining room, when the tall front windows were folded open, and when he was in his room, even if his window was closed, the same kind of noises from the kitchen and what occasionally sounded like arguments and barking orders in French and Chinese. A couple in the hotel said they'd been to the restaurant and that the food was very good. A married couple on the top floor, both artists and about ten years older than he, the man Australian and his wife Chinese. They said they'd held their wedding reception there three years ago for about thirty people—most of the restaurant was closed off for it—and since then they'd eaten there four or five times a year and always on their anniversary. For the reception, they said, the chefs prepared dishes that were indigenous to the wife's region and never get on the menu. He said he'd like to eat there at least once before he left the hotel but right now couldn't afford it and didn't see when he ever would. Moment he said that he knew he was fishing for an invitation to be their guest next time they went to the restaurant, but the husband said "Well, if you do hit it rich, and I suppose you know the prices aren't too steep there, make certain you have as your appetizer the marinated crispy fish twigs, as they call it, and for the main course the scallops and oysters in black bean sauce, and ask them not to stint on the garlic but to hold back a shade on the red peppers. Both are divine, and when they're on the menu, we order them every time." He said "I'll make it there some day, if I have to borrow the dough to go. For some reason I have this long-standing fantasy of walking downstairs from my room on an evening when it's teeming outside, going through the hotel's connecting entrance to the restaurant, so I won't even have to carry an umbrella or raincoat, getting a small out-of-the-way table and reading a book I'm excited with while I eat and drink, and then going back to my room for a long peaceful sleep. That's not asking too much, is it?" "Seems reasonable to me," the wife said. "But it's such a friendly, warm place that I hope you go with someone and leave your book behind."

A friend from New York passed through Paris, called him at his hotel and said he'd like to take him out to dinner, does he know of a good place? He suggested the Chinese restaurant. "It's supposed to be one of the best in Paris." The friend said he'd had more than enough Chinese food in New York, and how much better could it be here, especially compared to New York's Chinatown? "My gut feeling is to think it's probably a little worse. When I come to France I want to eat what's regarded by most food experts to be the best cuisine in the world, French." "Chinese cuisine's supposed to be every bit as good as French and a lot more varied, if I'm not mistaken. And Mexican cuisine's supposed to be equal to those two in both variety and taste. It's just that, unlike Chinese food in Chinatown and possibly here, we never see the authentic stuff outside of Mexico." "French, French, we dine French tonight, and with everything that comes with it and which doesn't go with Chinese or Mexican food, like a delicious apéritif and a great bottle of wine. Have you been here long enough to recom-

mend a place, or should I ask the concierge at my hotel?"
They ate at a touristy French restaurant his friend found. In
his head, next day, once again he went to the Chinese restaurant downstairs. "Monsieur," the owner said when he came
through the hotel's entrance to the restaurant, "we have seen
you often in the hotel, said hello to you on the street, but
always hoped one day you would visit us inside here. So near
and yet so far, till today, which is an American slogan, am I
right? The French have one comparable," and the owner
quoted it. By now he knew the language well enough to
understand the saying in French. *"Presque le même chose, je
pense,"* he said. "Table for one, only?" and he nodded and was
seated at a small corner table. He ordered a large carafe of
red wine, had studied the menu on the window earlier that
day so knew exactly what dishes he wanted, took out his
book and read while he ate and drank. The owner would
stop by his table every so often and watch him eat for a few
seconds and then ask how everything was. One time he didn't even know the owner was there till he was tapped on the
shoulder. "Is good, still?" the owner said in English. "Of
course, very good, everything, way past my expectations and
dreams, and they were high and elaborate," he said in
French. The owner said in English "Your French is very
good. You speak almost like a native Paris person now, better than me and I've been here almost thirty years. You must
come once more here, and after that. I will speak in *français*
to be clear perfectly," and then said in French "When you do
come again, the next time, any appetizer on the menu will
be yours with our compliments. You are close to us, almost
like a neighbor, living upstairs, so we don't want you to

always walk past without coming in once. Ten times is all right; eleven isn't permitted." At another small table was a young woman who had moved into the hotel two weeks ago. A ballet dancer, here on scholarship for a year, he was told when he saw her having breakfast in the little dining area off the hotel lobby and asked the desk clerk who she was. At this restaurant she seemed to only be drinking bottled water. He was feeling good, even a bit lightheaded from the wine, and did something he'd never done anywhere before: sent over a glass of wine, from his carafe. She asked the waiter whom it came from. The waiter pointed to him, he waved his hand, she smiled and raised the glass and mouthed "*Merci*," and he raised his glass and they drank at the same time. She's very attractive, he thought, and of course, being a dancer, she must have a beautiful figure. But you don't want to be a pest, so stop looking at her. Later, while he was eating his main course, a waiter put a glass of red wine on his table and said in French "From the young woman over there." He raised his glass to her, she raised hers, he mouthed "Thank you," bowed his head, and they drank. He didn't know wine but the one she sent was obviously much better than the stuff in his carafe. Then he pointed to his table and mouthed—she was from Capetown, the desk clerk had told him that time, so he mouthed this in English— "Would you like to join me?" Her expression said "Why not?" She came over, carrying her glass and the book she'd been reading, and the waiter followed with her plate and bottled water and two dishes of food. They shared each other's food, ordered another main course, got a half bottle of wine after they'd finished their glasses and his carafe.

"You choose," he said. "To be honest, I don't know wine." He asked the waiter for a single check and paid. She didn't want him paying for her, but he said "Next time, if there's one, and only at a moderately priced restaurant, or one no more expensive than this place, it'll be your treat, though I won't hold you to it." They walked around for an hour, stopped at a café for coffee and desert, talked and talked. They saw each other almost every day after that, eventually got a double room in the hotel. A few months later they rented a small apartment some distance away on the other side of the river. A year after the day they met, they went back to the restaurant to celebrate the anniversary. It had closed.

What actually happened was that he lived in the hotel for a year and never went to the restaurant; just never could afford it. Then it closed and a few weeks later it reopened under different ownership as a French restaurant, but he couldn't afford that one either. He'd been working for several months now, teaching English to French businessmen while at the same time editing marketing proposals in English for a French firm that did business with American companies. Both were under-the-table part-time jobs that didn't pay much, so he still either ate in the neighborhood cafeterias or in his room with food he bought at the market.

A cousin and her husband were visiting Paris for a few days, and called him. "Your mother told my folks that you were practically starving here, so I promised everyone that I'd take you out for a nourishing meal." "I'm not starving. And my mom saw me a couple of months ago in New York, so she knows that. What I do is live frugally, since I haven't found a steady job yet. And this city, as you probably found out, can be quite costly." "Anyway," she said, "pick a restaurant and we'll go to it. Being almost a native by now, you must know of a few good ones. And we're on vacation, so money shouldn't be a consideration in whichever one you choose." He said there's a French restaurant in the hotel he lives in. "I've never been to it, but according to people who seem to know, it's supposed to be one of the best in Paris while still being reasonably affordable, and this only in a few months. I've been urged to eat in it before word really gets out what a buy it is for such great food, and the prices go sky high. That's how it can be in Paris, great restaurants in dumpy places." "You know, we've been in France for six days now, and have gobbled down nothing but French food for dinner and lunch and those French pastries and rolls and coffee for breakfast. But I understand that the Indochinese food is not to be missed here, and as second best, and not too far behind, the regular Chinese. We've nothing like Indochinese in Boston, so we're both eager to try some." Main reason he wanted to go to the French restaurant in his hotel was just to finally get down there and see the place. He didn't care how good the food was, though he was sure it was excellent. Based on the menus posted out front, which he didn't look at as much as he did the menus of the Chinese restaurant, it didn't seem any more expensive than that one for a dinner of appetizer, soup and main course and a bottle or carafe of wine. Besides, even if he ever was able to afford the French place, he was less inclined to go to it by himself than the Chinese one, maybe because French restaurants—at least in

New York and the way they looked here—were usually more formal and serious about the food and service, so he'd feel self-conscious reading and sitting alone in one.

His cousin and her husband picked him up at his hotel. They cabbed to an Indochinese restaurant she'd heard great things about, but it was closed for the day. "What's with these people?" she said. "I was told they didn't take reservations over the phone, but that you could always get a table in fifteen minutes, so who would have thought to call on a Wednesday to see if it was open?" There was a Chinese restaurant three doors away and they looked at the menu outside. "So what do you think?" his cousin's husband said to him. He said it seemed pretty good, not as elaborate or unusual as some of the stuff served in the Chinese restaurant that had been in his hotel, and it was also a lot more expensive. "Well, this is that kind of neighborhood. What you never find in Paris is a moderately priced restaurant in a well-to-do area. But the place looks clean, is crowded and lively and the food from the kitchen smells good, which is a promising sign, and we all must be getting hungry, so what do we have to lose?"

When he got back to his hotel room he could smell the food from the restaurant kitchen downstairs. It never had the same effect on him as the smells that used to come from the place when it was Chinese. Those were much stronger and did something to his stomach or nervous system or wherever it did it that made him hungry and want to go down there and eat even when he'd just had a fairly substantial dinner in a cafeteria nearby. He also liked the sounds much better that came from the kitchen when it was a Chinese restaurant. The French downstairs seemed to speak lower and more civilly and he could barely hear them most times and they also didn't make as much noise with their dishes and pots and pans and so on. Or maybe those parts of the kitchen—where the dirty dishes were dropped off and washed and the food was cooked and put on plates and the waiters called out their orders, if they did that—had been totally remodeled and were now farther away from the window two floors below his. Or for all he knew, they might have installed a more modern exhaust system there and didn't even open the window or not as high.

SPEED BUMP

"YOU KNOW, I didn't want to spring this on you, or not at this time. But as long as we're speaking of accidents, even if this isn't the kind you mean, you almost ran over me today." He says "What? What? Say that again. I almost ran over you today?" "I'd say an hour ago, minus a few minutes." She looks at her watch. "No, exactly an hour ago, to the minute. Isn't that amazing? And that I bumped into you so soon after it. Because I looked at my watch then, I don't know why—maybe...well, anyway—and recorded the time in my head, one-oh-two. I was sitting by the Carver entrance, waiting for my daughter to come out—" "What was she doing in school today?" "A group drama class she takes every Saturday for six weeks, not for credit, but given by Mr. Donalson, the theater teacher there. And it was warm inside—I don't think anyone bothered opening a window in the whole building, or maybe they're not air-conditioned— so I went outside. I was sitting under a shade tree on the curb near the entrance when you came tearing through the lot. Yours is a gray minivan, right?" "Yes, dark gray, it almost looks black." "Of course I didn't know it was you or your car when it was first coming toward me. And I suppose, to avoid the speed bump a few feet from where I was sitting, since your head would have gone through the car roof if you had ridden over it at that speed, you suddenly swerved right, where the bump ends and it's only flat pavement, and I literally had to pull my legs in at the last moment or they would have been run over, at least the feet." "It's true. I was driving back from the mall at around that time and used the school parking lot as a cutoff—I mean a shortcut—to Kenilworth." "You were thinking, with that 'cutoff,' that you almost cut off my legs, am I right?" "I don't think so. Just that the words are very close—the two syllables and the 'cut'—but I don't remember seeing anyone sitting on the curb there. I don't even recall a car parked in the entire lot when I was cutting through it." "There were about five, all of them, including mine, parked head-in to the curb on the other side of the entrance from where I was sitting. Don't ask me why we all parked on that side, but we did. It could be that one followed the other and then when the fourth saw the three, he did also, and so on. I only remember those cars because I was sitting for a while with nothing to read or do and had lots of time to look around. I think that you were going so fast that that could have been why you didn't see the cars or me or anything but the speed bump you were so determined to avoid." "Well, I'm certainly sorry that the incident ever happened, and I apologize. I still find it hard to imagine how I got so near the curb you were sitting on—" "I was sitting on it, believe me, for half an hour or more, right where I said." "I know; I'm not disputing that. Nor do I remember driving so fast, but if you say you saw it, then I guess I was, or close to that speed, and I'm really sorry about that too and for the scare or alarm or whatever it might have caused you." "It was pretty scary, but I'm over it," and she picks up her frozen coffee drink, sips it and looks at her daughter sitting with his daughter on the grass about thirty feet away.

He looks at his wife across the small table they're all sitting at. She gives an expression that seems to say "It doesn't sound like something you'd do. Did it really happen?" He raises his shoulders and looks at his wife's friends whom they're also sitting with and they had arranged to meet on the patio of this coffee place. The woman he met when his daughter and he went inside to get everyone's drinks, saw his daughter's friend and her mother, whom he'd spoken to briefly a few times when they were both waiting to pick up their kids at school and things like that, and invited them to join them inside. "Sounds as if you went through something quite frightening," his wife's friend says to the woman when she turns back to their group. He thinks 'Does she have to continue on it? Where's her brains? Can't she see how potentially embarrassing it is for me and that the conversation about it was over?' "But as we were saying regarding our children's proneness to accidents, life for everyone—even kids in a crib—is filled with near-collisions and lucky escapes and it's only the infrequent time when the accident actually takes place and you're affected physically by it." "But it's so odd how I can still hardly believe it happened," he says to the friend. "Again, I'm not saying it didn't, and I'm sincerely sorry and anguished and all that for my part in it, but how did I ever not see her?" "Beats me," the woman says. "I wasn't hiding. I was definitely there, seated, looking around, and I feel—though I don't want to build this into a point way out of proportion to what ultimately resulted, but as long as your friend here is referring to lucky escapes and such—damn lucky not to have lost a foot or a leg, or worse, for that's how close the car got." "I'm really glad it turned out the way it did," he says, "meaning that nothing serious happened except for the scare, which was bad enough," and sips his hot coffee and looks at several people coming out of the coffee place and taking a table nearby and then at his daughter and her friend on the grass.

He works his face into what he thinks is a slight smile and freezes it, as if he's enjoying looking at the girls and content they're getting along so well, while inside he feels awful. Stomach's tense, neck's tight, sweat's on his forehead and running down his back, which, if anyone notices, he can blame on the warm day and that he just happens to sweat more than most people. What he must seem like to the others now, though that's not important, so neither should be the sweating. Glad his daughter's over there and didn't hear what he'd done, though this woman's daughter might tell her, since her mother could have told her during the drive here. Well, all of that he can work out with his daughter and wife, even if he has to lie, and his wife can later explain to her friend that it wasn't as bad as this woman had made out. But to himself: What was on his mind when it took place? What the hell was he thinking of? he's really asking. How could he have been inattentive or oblivious or just plain out of it when he was heading for the speed bump and then after while he was cutting around it? And the parked cars. He honestly has no recollection of them either and he could have crashed into one of those, or did he quickly see them out of the corners of his eyes and instinctively, without consciously realizing it, which is what happens a lot when you drive, established where they were in relation to his car and gave himself plenty of room to get past them? But if it happened with the speed bump and the woman this time, it could happen again with something or someone else, and much worse. He could have killed her or run over her legs and feet, as she said. Right now she could be in a hospital with a leg or two amputated and he could be in a police station or in a police car driving to one. He could be saying to the officers or himself, pulling at his hair while saying it, "I can't believe this has happened. It's horrible. I feel miserable and I'm stupid and reckless and I shouldn't be driving and I'll feel miserable about it for the rest of my life, what I did to that woman, so do what you want with me. I'm guilty and that's it and all I can say is I know what I did is wrong and I'm deeply sorry, as sorry as anyone can be about it, but that doesn't help anything, I know that." The woman's daughter would have found out soon enough in school and run out of her class maybe just around the time the emergency medical ambulance and police cars had shown up. That's what would have gotten her out of the school—got the whole class out. They heard the police and ambulance sirens, wanted to know what was happening outside. There might be a fire in the building, some of them could have thought, or the teacher did and because the school was officially closed for the day he thought the fire alarm system might be turned off, so he hustled his class outside. Or

15

someone could have run into the theater and told them what had happened. "Wasn't it your mother who was so hot in here that she went outside to wait?" So the daughter could have run to the school entrance and seen her mother being wheeled in a gurney to the ambulance or being given emergency treatment on the ground. If one of the woman's legs had been torn off, the medical people would retrieve it. And while some of them would be trying to stanch the bleeding and giving the woman something to prevent her from going into shock, another would be packing the leg in ice or whatever they pack it in today. Because of the advances and successes of microsurgery and limb reattachments the last ten years or so—you read about it a lot in the newspaper—all these ambulances might now have special packing equipment or even a freezer for amputated body parts. The woman would be screaming if she hadn't been sedated yet or the sedation hadn't taken effect or she wasn't unconscious. The daughter would probably be screaming too. He would be standing somewhere near, giving his drivers license number and information like that to the police and saying things he thinks he would: "I did it and I feel absolutely miserable about it and I have no defense or excuse for it: it was the worst thing I've ever done in my life." But suppose—he's thinking, would he do this?—he realized at the time that he'd hit someone—didn't see who it was, so didn't know he'd possibly be identified by the person—and drove, if she wasn't caught underneath the car or in front of one of the wheels—away from the parking lot without stopping? She would have told the police, if she could, who had hit her. Told them at the accident scene. Perhaps just had enough strength to give his name, or his daughter's name, and her daughter would have filled in who he was. The police would be after him by now. They would have first gone to his home. His other daughter, who stayed behind to work on a school science project due Monday and knew where her parents and sister had gone, would have told them where he was. The police might even be here by now and would be questioning him about the accident and saying he'd been identified as the driver who hit the woman. How would they know it was him sitting here? His daughter could have told them what he was wearing and looked like—tan shorts, a dark T-shirt, almost bald, "exactly six feet," he always said he was, which wouldn't help them if he was seated—or they just asked all the male customers of a certain age till they found them or made an announcement inside the coffee place and then on the patio: Is there a Mr. So-and-So here? He would raise his hand, be questioned, say that he had driven past the school at the time they say the accident happened but he doesn't think he hit anyone—that is, if he did flee the parking lot. They'd ask to see his car. He forgot about that and he probably hadn't checked, after he got home, if there was any sign on it that he hit someone. They'd probably find blood, maybe hair and skin and a tell-tale dent on the part of the car they'd say she was most like-ly hit by and he'd be arrested for leaving the scene of an acci-dent and taken to the police station and booked. But if he did stop in the lot after the accident, stopped by choice, which he's almost sure he would—almost a hundred percent sure—the police would probably still bring him in but not arrest him in the lot. They'd politely ask him to accompany him in their car, he thinks, and if he said he didn't want to—though again, he's almost a hundred percent sure he'd go without a fuss—then they'd probably arrest him, maybe even put cuffs on him, and bring him in. And from then on he'd feel, though with a gradual reduction over the years but never where he'd completely get over it, if he had hurt the woman as seriously as he thought he could have, that his life would be ruined and he'd never be the same after the accident, or something like that, but perhaps not as extreme. What he's saying is that it'd affect him as deeply and disturbingly as anything wrong he's ever done and continue to affect him, though perhaps less so over the years, for the rest of his life. That too extreme or exaggerated too? No.

The three women have been talking for the last few minutes about fatigue and several ways to combat it: a certain Korean tea that the woman says gives her quick energy and some leg, arm and abdominal exercises the friend says she does to increase her physical strength. "Let's face it," his wife says. "The worst time in life to cut back on your activities is when you get to around our age, which is really the beginning of the great physical slowdown, when you find yourself suddenly getting pooped over the things you used to do effortlessly. So you have to fight it with all the things you said. A good strong cappuccino helps too."

He thinks Why was he in such a hurry when he drove through the school parking lot? Cutting through it made sense, since it was a shortcut, but he's saying why so fast? Because he'd gone—this is what led up to it—to the mall to buy a pair of running shorts, it so happens—the elastic in the old pair had stretched so much that the pants were slipping down over his waist when he ran—and after he bought the shorts and a pair of shoelaces for his running shoes and was having a cup of black coffee in the mall's food court, as a pick-me-up and just for a break from things to sit and read, he realized he and his wife were to meet her friend at this coffee place in ten minutes and that it would take him fifteen minutes to get home from the mall once he got in his car, another five minutes or so to get his wife and daughter in the car and it was about twenty minutes from home to the coffee place. As it was, when they got here and started apologizing to her friend for being late, she said she only just arrived a few minutes ago and was worried she'd be very late and had thought of calling them but then thought they were already here or at least on the way. The only thing he can say—he's saying, if there's anything to be learned or gained from all this—is that he won't drive as fast when he takes that short-cut and from now on—though he'll see if he ever sticks to this—go no more than ten miles over the posted speed limit on the road. His wife's friend says his name and he says "Yes?" and looks up and she says "So what do you think of what we were saying?" and he says "I'm sorry, what?" and she says "I knew you weren't listening. Off in your own thoughts, where you're probably better off, since we weren't really saying much," and the woman says "Oh, I don't know. They weren't breakthroughs we made, but we were discussing something important." "Truth is," he says, "I was still berating myself for my dumb speeding through that school parking lot, which is maybe what you were discussing," and the woman says "No, and I thought we were over that. I didn't originally bring it up, you understand, to make you feel bad or guilty, although I would caution against traveling through lots of any kind at that speed, even if they appear empty. For your own safety, and of course others, drive slower. But I mostly brought it up to show you something about coincidence. For here I was, minding my own business, the one person on a few thousand square feet of asphalt, it seemed—only visible person. And entertaining these nice thoughts about my family and the upcoming summer and also feeling good because it was so delightful out—soft breeze, cool shade—when a car roars through and scares me out of my wits, and wonder of wonders if it isn't, out of the million-plus people in this city and no doubt half of them drivers, someone I know who I'm then having coffee with an hour later." "I know. Amazing," he says, "amazing."

Later at home he thinks Could she have been exaggerating? Not lying, just exaggerating. Some people do to make their stories better. He doesn't know her well—for instance, if she has a history of embellishing the truth, he'll say—but he's almost sure she was this time. Because he just doesn't remember speeding through the lot. Going about ten miles over what's probably a fifteen-miles-per-hour speed limit for a school zone, okay, but it was Saturday and he thought nobody was around. But why would he speed forty, fifty miles an hour, the way she described it? He means, he had a reason—to get home fast because he didn't want his wife angry at him for making her late and possibly even miss her appointment—but he remembers, not distinctly, just vaguely remembers not going at the speed the woman said. He did turn to the right—not swerve—to avoid the speed bump. But the bump didn't come up at the last second where he had to make a sharp right to get around it; he had intended to avoid it. And because he knew the bump was there long before he reached it, he slowed down. He always slows down when he's about to make a turn. And she described it as if her legs or feet were a few inches away from his car when he made that turn. But the speed bump ends some twenty feet from the curb to make room, he assumes, on regular school days for cars to park head-in. What he's saying is that there must have been plenty of room for him to drive around the bump without getting near her, if he was driving slowly or relatively slowly when he made that turn, since there was no reason for him to get so close to the curb if he could be ten to fifteen feet from it. Scaring her he probably did—this big car approaching the curb for a couple of seconds before making that left turn—but there couldn't have been a moment when she was in any real danger, even if he didn't see her. If she didn't say it was close just to make her story more exciting, then she did it, despite what she said at the coffee place, to make him feel bad, guilty, any of those things. So that's it: she was exaggerating. He'll never know exactly what happened or what their exact positions were in the lot in relation to each other, but he knows the incident wasn't the way she said. He feels better about it now, and he didn't just make up this solution to have himself feel that way. He gets out of his chair in the living room and goes to the kitchen to tell his wife what he thought.

THE SWITCH

HE TRIES TO put himself in her position. She asked that a number of times: "Try. Then maybe you'll change in how you treat me." So in his mind he has her condition. Confined to a wheelchair, has to be helped in and out of bed and often fed. Hands shake, legs hurt. Can't find a good sitting position. Wants to raise his legs but can't so asks her "Would you help me with my legs?" "What do you mean 'help you'? Be clearer. You know the English language well, so use it as if you do. What is it you specifically want?" "Must you always be angry?" "I'm not always angry. True, I'm occasionally a bit miffed, but it's only because I want you to be less vague in what you want of me. Say it once clearly and completely and I'll do it quickly as I can, all of which will save us both some time." He says "I need to have my legs raised on this pillow." "Good, I'll do it," she says, "I always do it. But also, long as we're on the subject, why must you take what I do for granted? A little 'please' and 'thank you' every now and then and even 'I couldn't possibly survive here if it wasn't for you, so I have to keep you healthy, we both do,' and so on, would help, build my spirits a little and show that I'm

23

appreciated." "You need to be told? I thought you knew." "There are times I don't," she says, "although I know you're in pain or very uncomfortable and sometimes you haven't time for simple courtesies and gratitude like that, which I can understand." "So what are you saying? I'm a bit confused." "What can I do for you, is what I'm saying?" and he says "All right, that's very kind and much appreciated. You can do a lot, I'm afraid, starting off with putting my legs on the pillow. I need them raised and stretched out. They're killing me the way they are and it's bad for their circulation to have the feet on the floor or the chair's foot rests all the time." "As I said, will do, and gladly," and she does it and he says "Thank you. That already feels better." "You're welcome, any time. I mean that: never hesitate to ask. Just try to be precise in what you want."

He's in bed, can't get up, wants to get on the toilet. She's sleeping and he nudges her and she says something in her sleep, he thinks, and nudges her again and she says "What is it? Anything wrong?" "I'd like to get to the bathroom." "It can't wait? I'm still very sleepy. I really don't want to get out of bed right now," and he says "I wish it could wait, but I have to go bad. If I don't get to the bathroom, it'll end up a big mess here and then you'll be even angrier at me," and she says "Damnit, when did all this start? When did you become so sick and helpless that you couldn't get out of bed on your own and you became so dependent on me? Sometimes it's a big pain in the ass, I have to say." "I know, but I still have to go, sorry as I am to bother you. I can put myself in your position and see what a pain it is, but it's very important you get me in the chair and wheel me to the bathroom and get me on the potty now," and she says "You don't have to tell me, nor that this will be how it is for the rest of my stinking life." "I don't mean it to be funny. But don't count on it: it'll probably get much worse." She gets out of bed, pulls the covers off him and throws them to the floor, goes around to his side and swings his legs over the edge of the bed and grabs his arms and sits him up and holds him there. "Stable? Not woozy, feeling okay?" and he says "You're a little rough but I'm ready to be moved." "Believe me, what you see as anger and roughness is often the only way I can get the adrenaline going enough to have the strength to move and lift you." She pulls the wheelchair up to the bed. "Don't forget to lock the wheels," and she says "Please, I don't need to be reminded. Let me alone to do what I know what to do and which you should know by now that I do, having seen me do it a few thousand times." She positions the chair so it's right behind her, says "Your arms," and he says "Huh?" and she says "Come on, put them around my neck and hold on tight," he does and she locks his knees inside hers and lifts him and swings him around to the chair and sets him down on it, goes behind the chair and hoists him up by his underarms till he's sitting straight, then gets the chair legs on and puts his feet on the rests. "Jesus," she says, pressing her fist into her back and looking as if she's in some pain, "that last lift almost did it. I wish you'd try to lose a few pounds, since this is getting awfully tough for me," and he says "What can I tell you? Even though I exercise a lot with the stretchies and the weights and don't eat much and I'm not overweight for a person my height and age, I know I'm a load. My pills," and she says "One thing at a time—I was about to get them," and gets his pills from four different bottles, puts them in his mouth and holds a glass of water with a straw inside and he sips. Then she wheels him to the bathroom, unfastens his absorbent pad and pulls it out from under him. "God, it's soaked, but to be expected with all the drinking you do at night." "I don't drink that much. A glass of wine at dinner, maybe a vodka and grapefruit juice before, and no measurable water after six," and she says "You should probably cut back on even that or we'll have to start putting on two pads for bed," and he says "It'd be too uncomfortable to sleep that way. I won't have water after four, then, except for sips of it with my pills. And if I do have a vodka, I'll take it straight." She unbuttons the pad straps, holds the pad by a corner tip and drops it into the plastic bag in the trash pail, which has about four or five soiled pads in it, ties the bag up, says "Phew, what a smell, I'll never get used to it," and puts a new bag in. "Ready?" and he says "I wish—ah, forget it," and puts his arms around her and she lifts him onto the raised toilet seat. "I should have reminded you, but knew you'd complain again if I did, to tighten the seat first. It's loose. I'll keep sliding around on it if I don't fall off it," and she says "I do everything as it is, so I can't remember it all," and without warning lifts him off the seat and back onto the chair and adjusts the seat dial till the seat's tight. "Please tell me when you're about to lift me; don't suddenly grab me and throw me on something. It's scary and I can't straighten my legs first, which would make it easier for you to transfer me," and she says "Yeah, easier. It'll never be easier or easy because there'll never be an end to this. Ready?" and he says "Wait," moves his feet till their parallel a few inches in front of him

I.

and she lifts him onto the seat. "Much better," he says; "thanks." "Anything else?" and he says "Bring the chair closer in case I think I can get myself on it," and she says "Don't even try. You fall and you're on the floor and there goes my back." "Then just closer in case I lean over too far or so I can steady myself with it while I sit here." She brings the chair close, locks the wheels, says "How much time do you think you need?" and he says "Check on me in ten minutes." "Oh boy," she says under her breath, "ten free minutes. I don't know what I'll do with it," and he says "What was that?" and she says "Nothing, just mumbling futilely again; pay no attention to it," and grabs the tied-up trash bag and leaves the room and shuts the door.

Later he says "My legs feel stiffer than usual today and I can't feel my feet," and she says "I guess that means you want me to help you with your exercises," and he says "If you don't mind. But if you're too tired or doing something right now very important to you, like your work, we can save it for later." "No, I can use a bit of a workout. It's not as if I do anything strenuous all day," and he says "That sounds sarcastic but I'll let it pass."

She sees to the kids, cooks all the food and cuts his, cleans the apartment, changes their bed almost every day because he usually wets his side of it overnight, does a wash once a day, pays the bills, does all the driving, shopping and so on. When things go wrong, she handles it. Something uncomplicated breaks, she fixes it or finds someone who can. He says "It kills me that I can't help out more with the kids and chores," and she says "Don't worry, the current state of your illness didn't suddenly appear, so I've grown used to doing

27

everything by now. Though sometimes, true, it seems I've had about all I can take, but those lapses pass." He listens to Books on Tape, naps in his chair, sits on the toilet a lot, tries to do his work but can only put in fifteen minutes or so on it before he gets too tired to continue or is just unable to concentrate. Sometimes, when he can't do what he thought he could, he'll sit in his chair crying or just looking sad and she'll say "What's wrong?" and he'll say "Don't ask. I can't even raise my wrist to my eyes today to see what's the time. I almost feel myself getting weaker and weaker by the hour," and she'll say "You're just more tired than usual right now, possibly because of your medicine, which we should perhaps think about getting a replacement for or cutting back on. I'll call the doctor; but let me make you some tea."

Now she's in the kitchen doing her own work on the small typewriter table by the window. A plank on top of the radiator beside the table serves as a place to put her paper and books and writing supplies and her mug if she's drinking coffee or tea. He's in the next room and feels he has to pee and calls out for her. Door's closed, she can't hear him or is pretending not to so she can finish the line she's writing. He doesn't want to yell her name, which might startle her if she's really not hearing him, so he'll wait till she looks his way. She does in a couple of minutes and sees him motioning her to come in. Still seated, she pushes open the door, her expression showing some disgust at being interrupted, and says "What the heck now?" and he says "I think I have to go to the bathroom again." "You 'think'? You don't know? Tell me when you know, because I can't be the one to tell you when you have to go." "Then I definitely have to go and have had to for the last ten minutes. But you seemed to be working on something important, so I tried to keep it in till you were ready." "Well, that was nice but not very smart, since you probably ended up creating more work for me by already peeing," and he says "I don't think I have, though I don't always feel everything that goes on down there." "Listen," she says "if you haven't peed, then I'll get you on the toilet and you'll sit and sit and most likely nothing will come out, or only a little trickle. Let's be honest: that's how it usually is and most of your pee goes into your pads and pants. Do you want me to start catheterizing you in the morning or afternoon too? If you do, let's get it over with before the kids come home." "It all depends what you want to do," and she says "What I want to do most times is run out of the house and keep running, but I can't; I'm stuck here." "Maybe catheterizing now, if you don't mind too much, would be a good idea, and for the future days whenever we need to," and she says "I should have kept my trap shut," and wheels him into the bedroom, gets him on the bed and catheterizes him. She was taught how a few months ago by a visiting nurse after he was botching half the catheterizations on himself. She doesn't like doing it—the urine smell in the pan, for one thing, and the pain she occasionally inflicts on him when she doesn't do it right or his penis is misshapen in a way where it prevents the tube from going in easily. But he usually says "It's all right, it's half in there, you pull it out and do it again it might even hurt worse, so let's get it over with," and then she has four to five hours where he doesn't have to pee. What she hates most is cleaning up after one of his messy bowel movements on the toilet or accidents in his pants. Not so much cleaning him, which consists of getting him onto the shower stool and letting the shower drench him while she scrubs him with a soapy washrag, but taking off his soiled clothes and cleaning the toilet bowl and seat and often the wheelchair and floor, and worst, the wheelchair wheels. But he only has an accident like that about once a month and the rest of the time is usually able to defecate cleanly into the bowl and do a fairly good job of wiping himself.

He continues to get more feeble. The doctors can't explain it. Well, they never knew much about his disease or could do much for it. They change his drugs, change the dosages of some of the drugs, give one drug a booster, put him through blood tests every three weeks. She takes him to all kinds of therapy and none of them seem to work. A woman comes in to assist her with him a few hours twice a week and he says "Why not have her come in more? That'd take more of the brunt off you and also free up more time for your own work. Some of that kind of help's paid by our medical insurance and the rest we can put down as medical expenses on our income taxes. We need to build that part of our tax deductions up if we want to take advantage of it." She says no matter how much they can take off their taxes, private help's still quite costly. "Besides, the apartment's too small to have someone just hanging around waiting to do something for you. I can do just about everything between stints at my own work and looking after the kids. And they pitch in a little and as time goes on and they get stronger and more responsible and used to your illness, they'll help out a lot more."

Sometimes she throws her back out lifting him off the bed onto the wheelchair or off the chair and onto the toilet, and then she has to call in someone to do it for her for a few days. This goes on for years. If one of the kids isn't around, she pushes his wheelchair up the hill herself to Broadway. "I'm getting too old for this," she says one time while she's doing it. "I'm really beginning to feel my age. Or let's say, taking care of you and especially doing this heavy schlep work is making me feel my age plus ten years." "I know it's tough getting me up it," and he tries propelling the wheels with his hands while she pushes from behind, but she says "Save your strength, though I don't know for what, because you're not helping me out one bit." He once had a motorized cart but his coordination isn't good enough anymore to operate it. Besides, he fell over in it once when it hit a bump and another time when it got stuck in a rut and he broke a bone both times. Sometimes she tells him he stinks, his clothes stink, the wheelchair cushion stinks, she doesn't know how long she can do this, put up with it, maybe it'd be better if he were in a home someplace, for she doesn't see herself doing this year after year for the rest of her life. "I'm not going to live that long," he says, "—I'm certainly not going to outlive you—so I doubt very seriously you'll have to put up with it for more than a few years. But if that's still too long, and I can understand it, though I think if our situations were reversed I'd complain as much as you but would never jump ship, then put me in a home. Unfortunately, that'd deplete our personal savings and whatever money we've put in trust for the kids' colleges, and we'd also probably have to sell the car and cash in my retirement funds."

Sometimes he's the one who says "I can't take any more of this. Not only ruining your life by keeping you chained here, but for me the misery's endless. I'm tired most of the time. I can't do the work I want or concentrate on anything halfway complex for more than fifteen minutes a day. I'm kidding myself big if I think I'll get any work done. I can't live like this and there seems to be no hope that any of it will change," and she says "Believe me, sweetie, that feeling's only temporary. You've had a particularly bad six months, but it's got to get better. There could be a new miracle drug—they're always doing research on them—or the ones you've been taking will really start to work. Or you'll just get better naturally, with the disease receding somehow on its own. Meanwhile, you want to do something less fatiguing and frustrating than what you've been laboring at your entire adult life, write about your condition and how you deal with it and so on, no matter how graphic and revealing, but in the simplest and maybe most artless way you can. Day-to-day stuff that absolutely matters to you, but just what pops into your head, or questions you've been brooding about since you got hit with the illness. Even if you only get a single short sentence or two in a day, though some days you'll be feeling so good you'll get whole paragraphs, it'll accumulate in a few months into something reasonably long and easy to edit. In three months, barring no major setbacks, you could have a hundred-fifty of these sentences. Or a hundred-thirty or -twenty, but that alone would amount to eleven or twelve manuscript pages. Not bad for something that could read or look on the page like poetry. In a year, fifty to sixty pages, or even seventy or eighty, if at times you have a really good run and can work for a few hours. And in two to three years you'll have enough for a short book of these reflections, regrets, brief memories, what-could-have-beens, losses, sudden bursts of elation for the up-till-now taken-for-granted things you realize you still have: your kids, your mind and imagination and ability to listen to books and think about them and put down these words and so forth, all very strong and deep and maybe even naturally lyrical in their simplicity and some of it funny. If that isn't enough, meaning if this different kind of fragmented memoir of American *pensées* doesn't fulfill the creative urgencies in you, write real poetry, but also about your condition and what it's done to you and you can no longer do and so on. Line here, line there, no matter how long it takes, it'll all build into poem after poem. If you only get three to four extraordinary poems out of it for the rest of your life, but twenty to thirty very good ones—and based on your skill with words and demands about art and these experiences the last ten years and your ability to plumb things for everything they're worth, I don't see why you shouldn't—that'll still be equal or more in quality than most poets get their entire lives. Look at the poetry anthologies with three or four poems of many poets and then the collected or selected works of these same poets and think how many really great poems any poet does have. As for the years it took them to write their work, believe me, I've known poets and most are incredibly lazy, so you'll make it up by your drive to get it all down fast as you can, since I don't see you wasting a minute of your working time. If you can't write or type out the lines, work on them in your head one by one and then dictate them to me when each line or two is finished and I'll write them down. Then, every time you want to add a line, I'll read back what you've completed of that poem, and that could be how you'll get it done." He works on a poem the way and with the material she suggested but after a few weeks of about twenty minutes a day on it, which is all he has strength for, he tells her to tear up what he's dictated to her so far: "It's too depressing," and she says "The act of writing or the poem?" and he says "Both; more."

She works out almost every day in the weight room of the local Y for about twenty minutes, develops arms and shoulders that are now as big, since his once substantial muscles have atrophied a great deal the last few years, as his. "Make a muscle; let me feel those things," he says, pressing her biceps that she refuses to flex. "Boy, I'm not going to mess around with you anymore," and she says "I need to be strong to lift you or I'd be calling in the fire department or neighbors every week as I used to." "You never called them in that much, since years ago I didn't fall as much as I do today," and she says "Then once a month, but there were plenty of times I wanted to call for help but thought I'd save it for a real emergency, and somehow the kids and I managed to get you back in your chair or bed." "I like the new muscles and the flatter stomach and bigger chest, except for maybe the neck," and she says "I don't see how you could like most of the rest of it unless you've changed in your sexual orientation, for from the waist up, other than for the softness of my breasts, I look a lot like a well-developed man."

He feels he's become a complete drain on her. The kids too: they help out sometimes but are mostly repulsed or frightened by his illness; maybe it'd be different if they were boys. And when his wife gets angry at him for something like wetting his bed or wheelchair a second or third time in a day or crapping in his pants and without even knowing he did, the kids get angry at her for criticizing or yelling at him and saying things like "I've had it for good with you" and "Every so often, like now, I feel I'd be better off dead" and "Starting from the time you wake up in the morning till I finally have you settled in bed at night, I feel like an inmate in a concentration camp." Then he feels guilty that he's indirectly making things bad between her and them, so he says things like "It's all right; it's so tough for your mommy that sometimes she can't help it, and who can blame her?—certainly not I. I'd probably act the same way as her if she was the one who was sick and not always in complete control of her bodily functions," and they say "No you wouldn't. You'd act nice and try to help out without saying anything."

At times he feels like he should kill himself. "This damn disease has done me in, that's all," he thinks. "I can do less for myself every day. One of these mornings I'll wake up a total vegetable and I won't get any better and then when I'll really want and need to kill myself—when the feeling to do it won't just suddenly pop up and then go away—I won't have the motor control to carry it out, not even to unscrew a container cap or bite it off to get at the killer pills, if by then she'd even leave them around like that." He mentions this to her a few times—"Sometimes I just want to do myself in"—and she says things like "Look, stick around a while longer. You never know what the scientists might find or what somersaults your own body will do to repair itself. Besides, and much more important, the kids love you and need you." "What are you talking about?" he's said. "I'm sure they love me but they don't come to me for anything anymore. They in fact go out of their way to avoid me and now direct all their questions, demands, entreaties and requests to you, and why shouldn't they, since you're running the whole show now and you'll be here when they still need a parent long after I'm gone. "Then I need you, but they really do too, believe me. They're just sad for you now, for they hate to see you suffering and so miserable because of it. I hate to see it too but I can deal with it." "You need me for what?" he's said and she's said "For your humor, intelligence and companionship, and to make me feel good with myself that I'm doing something like this for someone. But also for more practical purposes, like your staying home with the kids when I need to be out."

She takes him to plays and movies and museums, wheels him to coffee shops where they discuss things together or meet friends, reads book excerpts and newspaper and magazine articles and columns and reviews to him that she thinks he'll want to hear. She does lots of things like this, when his illness isn't exhausting her physically, to pep him up and keep him actively engaged and interested in things. About once a month she initiates sex with him. He says once "Honestly, and you must have realized this a number of times, it's little to no fun for me anymore, much as I used to love doing it with you and would want to do it now. But I have no physical sensation down there or in my fingers or maybe only enough to amount to a bit of titillation but nowhere near a completion for me. If I seem to be meeting the minimal demands of lovemaking, then I'm either faking it or it's real but I don't know how I'm pulling it off. It's still visually and aurally pleasurable to see you naked and engrossed in the act, but that only makes things even more frustrating for me. Anyway, if you like, continue to do what you want with whatever part of me you wish to do it with and I'll try to be as cooperative and helpful as I can. But please don't chide me if, as I believe will happen as it has most of the times the last few years, nothing materializes from it." One night, while he's in bed listening to music and she's standing beside him undressing, he says "Uh-oh, you seem to have that look in your eyes again and I don't know what we're going to do about it," and she says "It's true; it's been a while and I am feeling that way. But not to worry, since unlike you before you got sick, and this isn't a dig I've been saving up to hit you with when you made me feel particularly defeated, I can't enjoy it if you're not immersed in the activity and mood too. So let's forget it, since it's not as if it's totally consuming me," and they no longer even attempt to make love, though in bed she often sleeps with no clothes on and her breasts pressed into his back and her groin against his rear end and her hand holding his penis.

"Let me tell you about my typical day with you," she says to him. "It starts off in the morning, once I get the kids off to school, with my trying to get you out of bed into the wheelchair. Sometimes you feel like you weigh three hundred pounds and I don't know if I'm going to collapse while transferring you." "That's because you won't let me help you out." "You can't help me out. There's nothing you can do in just about anything. You say when I've got you sitting up that you want to get your feet on the floor in front of you before I lift, but it takes you too long. I have a million things to attend to, so I can't wait an hour for every little move like that of yours, most of them just to show that you're not altogether dependent on me. And when I've finally got you in the chair and I'm panting like mad from the effort of having lifted this dead weight, I have to get you on the john right away of there'll be a colossal mess and even more work for me to do that morning. Then while you're on the john, I gather up your bed linen and clothes and towels for the first of what will usually be three washes in a day. By ten o'clock I'm exhausted. By noon I'm a physical wreck because of all the things I had to do for you, though I still have my teaching stuff to prepare and once a week for two hours a class to teach and the delusion that I can also get some of my creative work in, all before I have to deal with the kids home from school and other things, but mostly you, for the rest of this afternoon and long into the evening, and almost all of it nonstop. At this pace, and with the chores increasing in number and labor every day, I don't have any doubts about which one of us will kick off first." "What are you talking about?" he says. "You're still in pretty good physical shape and with no major illnesses, so it can only be me." "Why? You get only gradually sicker, while I'll probably have a heart failure during one of these transfers and die on the spot long before you." "Believe me, I'm doing my best to lessen your load and not be such a burden on you, and it frustrates me to no end that I can't do more. But the way I've been deteriorating, which has hardly been gradual the last few years, if I'm not dead in a year I'll consider myself unlucky."

He gets much worse and says to his wife that they should really think seriously about taking his life before he no longer has the faculties to even think about it anymore, and she says "What? Did I hear right? Please, don't ever talk about it, not even as a joke, because it's out of the question your doing anything like that and my helping you do it or just idly sitting by. If anyone deserves to do herself in, it's me; but then who'd see to the kids and you? So I've scotched that prospect a dozen times." He works out a plan to do it. The kids are in school; his wife will be teaching a continuing ed class for a couple of hours at a college nearby. She usually gets someone to sit with him when she's gone for that long and takes a cellular phone with her to call him every hour and in case he has to call her. He tells her not to bother with the sitter this time and also not to call him for the next two hours. He's very tired, just wants to sleep, so if she catheterizes him before she goes he can stay in bed till she comes home. "Leave the reacher and portable phone beside me on the bed in case I have to reach for anything or call you. Also, the front door unlocked in case anything unusual does happen and I can't get a hold of you right away and have to call someone else to come. Not that I'm going anyplace where anything could happen, but you never know." After she's gone a doctor he's read about in the papers and contacted comes to the apartment to help him kill himself. She first gives him a physical examination, takes down a suicide letter he dictates, shows him how to fill a syringe, has him practice the injection on an orange several times till she's satisfied he's got it right and then hands him the syringe he's previously filled and says "We haven't got much time left to do it the way it should be done, so whenever you're ready." "I should use it now like you showed?" and she says "All up to you. If you want to stop, do," and he says "By 'stop' you mean 'not go through with it'?" and she says "That's for you to decide only, and please don't think you've wasted a scintilla of my time if you decide to stay alive. This has happened in nearly half my assist cases, although more than half of those patients asked me to come back a day to a year later because they were now ready to go ahead with it, and all of them did." "I'm doing it. And I'm not saying it's because what you said convinced me. My mind's been made up for a while. It's just that it's very difficult, as I said in the letter I dictated, not to have said goodbye to my wife and children and to have given and received from them one last kiss. But I have to do it while I still have a little coordination and strength left to inject myself, isn't that true?" "Based on my examination of you and the medical records you've shown me and what you say your doctors have said, I strongly doubt your condition will stay the same or improve. But again, the decision is yours alone, including the last remaining deciding factors, and I certainly won't give you the injection myself." "Thank you and goodbye," and she says "You're saying you want me to stay?" and he says "Yes, please, as we arranged, and I thank God that you were able to help me," and sticks the needle in the part of the thigh he points to, pushes the plunger in, keeps the needle in for ten seconds as he was instructed to, pulls it out and drops it into a plastic bag the doctor holds open, and which she then zip locks. He lies back in bed, tries to think of his wife and kids but nothing like that comes, starts crying, then dozes off from one of the drugs in the injection and twenty minutes later is dead. The doctor calls the police. They come with an emergency medical team, try to revive him, call his wife at school—he'd given the doctor the number—and she comes home. The letter the doctor took down and which he dated and signed says "To my dear wife. I'm so sorry for the pain and problems my suicide causes you and the children. I don't want to be obvious and say why I did it (killed myself). But to protect the gentle and helpful doctor, whom I'm sure is known to you all from the notoriety she's received in assisting other suicides, I'll say that I was the one who filled the syringe and gave myself the injection. Of course I'm saying this before actually doing these two things—in addition, I was the one (or will be; however you want to put it) who pushed the syringe's plunger in, or whatever they call that thing (the doctor just told me, but we'll leave what I said as is), all of which was part of the deal I'd worked out weeks ago with the doctor for her assistance. She did provide me with the syringe and its lethal contents, which she openly takes responsibility for as she has in all her other assisted-suicide cases, as well as teaching me how to use the syringe (that she'll be doing right after I dictate this). But I forget where I was in this letter— I'm not feeling at all well today, which is almost like every other day for me the last few years, though a bit worse, which I doubt you noticed before or you probably wouldn't have left—but I think it was about the obviousness of why I'm about to take my own life. Okay: I can't live with my illness any longer and depression over it—what could be more obvious than that? And I was going to say 'a day longer,' but I could live with it another day or even weeks longer but not a couple of months, if you see what I mean. Also, I think I have to say—and not to hurt you, though it might, but just to go out completely honest and say the things that are on my mind at the end and also to relieve you of any guilt you might have regarding this—that even if you hadn't complained so much about taking care of me and criticized me harshly sometimes for some of the things I did, like accidents of various sorts caused by my almost total feebleness, I still would be doing this today but perhaps not as willingly. But I definitely would have done it eventually no matter how uncomplaining and uncritical you were because, of course, I would only get worse, if you can imagine such a thing. So I guess I'm also saying that I can't say your criticisms and complaints drove me to it, but they didn't make it any easier for me to want to stick around. That said, and if I did hurt you just then I apologize deeply, thank you for the care you did give, since I know, as I've told you dozens of times, I think, how tough it must have been for you in so many ways to take care of me and see me endlessly deteriorate. I love you and have loved you since I've known you, though haven't always shown it, but I also have to say that it would have been easier for me if you had helped me out in this or at least been here so I could have said goodbye to you and given you one last kiss and somehow, without disturbing them this morning (if I had done anything like that you would have known what I was up to and not let me go through with it), done the same to the kids. Would I have helped you, which means not bringing in the doctor but just putting some deadly pills in your mouth and holding water up for you to drink them down, if our situations had been reversed? It would have been almost unbearable to, but I probably would have done it. I feel it would have been worse to see you deteriorate any further and go through even more physical and mental pain, though I only would have done it if I was sure this is what you truly wanted. What follows is a brief note to the kids, all of it very sweet and unalarming, I hope, but you be the judge."

His wife grieves, wonders what she could have done to prevent his suicide. "Nothing," people tell her, and things like "Be honest with yourself: he's better off dead. He knew that, which is why he did it, and you, for your own sake, should know that too," but she can't quite come around to think that. A few months later, while she's nursing a glass of wine in the living room late at night, she says to herself "If you were alive you would know it was the wrong thing to have done." Then she thinks "But that's ridiculous, 'if he were alive, he'd know,' so what am I trying to say here? I'm trying to say..." and she stands up and looks at the ceiling. "I'm trying to say," she says, "that you did the wrong thing. Now I'm alone and the girls have no father and they loved you and miss you just as I did and do. And I tried to do my best for you. Sometimes I couldn't and sometimes I failed miserably by some of my actions and what I said, but for the most part I did all right by you, didn't I? The last years of your life were tough and awful and often humiliating and all those things that come with horrible debilitating diseases, but you still had the kids and me. We didn't ignore you. We didn't pretend you were a ghost. We ate with you, joked with you, said goodbye to you when we left the apartment, read to you and still managed to go out to a restaurant about once a month with you and take two-week summer vacations and occasional weekends someplace, hard as all of that usually was for them and me, but we did it because in a way we had adjusted to the changes and wanted you to think that your life had only relatively changed. If you could come back, even in the same condition, even a little bit worse, if it had to be, you wouldn't do that again, killing yourself, would you? I know you wouldn't do it, knowing the effect it had on us, something you probably never even took into consideration until I just spoke about it. But I'm talking too much and maybe too loudly and that might wake the kids."

The kids are very sad at first and then stop talking about it and asking questions about why he had to do it and don't even seem to think about it—at least that's what it seems like to her. But later when they're adults they tell her that their father's suicide was the worst thing that ever happened to them and it altered their lives for good. The only worse thing that could have happened, they say, is if she had taken her life too and around the same time as their father or done it alone while he was still alive. "Why would I? Never," she says. "But what do you mean 'altered'?" and they say it just made them more morose as people, with reduced hopes about life and the future and that sort of thing. "It's hard to explain," one of them says to her during a visit. "But we both agree that although Daddy was sick for so many years and never improving, the way he died and the suddenness of it sunk in irremovably, if that's a word," and she says "Oh yes, it is, and I suppose applicable here."

She eventually meets a man and they become close and he wants to marry her but she first tells him she could only be married to her first husband. "That makes no sense," he says. "He's dead; long dead, in fact. I can understand your continuing to think of him but I don't understand why that or anything else should stop you from continuing on with your life." "I would think of him too much, that could be what I'm saying. I was very much in love with him, though showed him the opposite lots of times, nothing new among long-married couples, so that's not particularly it. So what is it? That I feel too terrible that he died the way he did while I was looking after him. Or if not that, then something else that's stopping me." "That's crazy," the man says. "I'm asking serious questions, so make sense." "Okay, maybe the truth is that I'm afraid—since we're both well up there in years, though you're a little further on—that you'd get very sick and I'd have to do what I did for my first husband and that I'd make some of the same mistakes—not act right to you when you were at your lowest point, for instance—and you'd end up wanting to take your life and maybe succeeding at it, no matter how well I acted to you or what I did." "It could work both ways," he says. "You could be the one who gets very sick and I could do for you what you did for him, but with far fewer mistakes, as you perhaps too self-contemptibly call them. We take our chances when we hook up with someone at any time in our lives, but sometimes it can end up benefiting you in the opposite way you'd think." "Even if it's one chance in a thousand, the risk for me is still too great, for that's how hard it was to take care of him for so long and how terrible the consequences were when he killed himself."

So that's it for the rest of her life. The man stops seeing her, the kids get married, have children, she retires from her job, hasn't the drive to work on her own stuff anymore, sees her kids and grandchildren as often as she can, and then she dies.

THE APOLOGY

"I'M SORRY FOR the way I acted before," he tells his daughter and she says "That's all right, Daddy; I forgive you." "I'm sorry for the way I acted today," he says to his daughter and she says "That's okay, I already forgot it." "I'm sorry for the way I acted this morning," he says to his daughter and she says "Okay, if you say so." "I'm sorry for the way I behaved to you this morning," he says to her and she says "That's what you always say, though not exactly in that way, but all right." "I'm sorry for the way I acted before," and she says "Every time you do something bad like yell or scream at me for no reason, you say you're sorry. But you're always sorry and then you always do it again what you say you're sorry about." "So you're not going to accept my apology?" and she says "No, I accept it," but doesn't smile, barely looks at him, and when she does look at him she does it quickly, and then she walks away. "I'm sorry how I acted before," he says to his daughter and she says "Okay." "I'm sorry for the way I acted before to you and Mommy," and she says "You ought to tell Mommy that. "I did and now I'm telling you." "Okay," she says, "I heard you." "I'm sorry the way I acted last night," he tells his daughter and she says "It was so long ago I stopped thinking about it." "But do you accept my apology?" and she says "Sure." "I'm sorry the way I acted to you in the car," and she says "Why, when was that?" "You don't remember? Because if you don't, I'm sort of sorry I brought it up," and she says "Do you mean when we were driving to school and you yelled at me because I forgot my lunch?" "Yes. I'm sorry I spoke harshly or criticized you in any way over such a small mistake," and she says "You're always yelling, so maybe that's another reason why I forgot about it. I can't tell one time from another." "I don't always yell," and she says "You almost do," and he says "Anyway, not as frequently as you're saying I do, and from now on I'll try not even to do as much as that." "I'm sorry the way I acted to you before," he tells his daughter and she says "You promised you wouldn't yell anymore, and you did, over nothing." "It wasn't over nothing. But I admit I shouldn't have yelled." "What do you think you should do then?" and he says "How should I handle it when I get upset or disappointed at you over something? Not to yell, for certain. To convey in a calm and rational way what's bugging me. I don't know why I continue to do it in that angry way I sometimes have. Anyway, we're friends again, right?" and she says "We're father and daughter and I hope you don't yell at me or anyone anymore. It's awful," and he says "I'll try my hardest." "I'm sorry the way I acted to you this afternoon," and she says "You always say that and I'm starting to almost always tell you that that's what you do. Next time after you yell and you come to me with that face where I know it's for an apology, I'm going to say the words for you." "Don't do that. It isn't nice to mock your father or anyone," and she says "Then don't yell or get so angry at someone where you have to make an apology after." "I'm sorry the way I acted before," he tells his daughter and she says "No you're not. If you were, you wouldn't do it. And I told myself after the last time that I would say those sorry words for you when I saw by your face you were going to apologize for what you did. I wish I had." "I'm sorry about the way I acted before," she tells him and he says "So you knew what I was about to say? And I am sorry, honestly." "You're always sorry and you always do the same thing again, yelling at one of us maybe a day after and maybe at all of us at one time. I should get everyone in the house together now to say that to you: 'I'm sorry the way I acted before.' Maybe that would change you. So far nothing else has," and he says "I'm sorry, really sorry, my sweetheart. I just hope you'll forgive me." "For saying you're sorry over and over for what you said today?" "Both, I'm afraid, if I understand you correctly." "I'm sorry for the way I acted to you last night," he says to her and she says "Darn, I forgot to say it before you did. I'm not going to forget next time and I don't care if you're sorry now, because you always act the same way after you say it." "But I'm really sorry this time," and she says "You said that the last time too and it didn't help things with you. You always yell or speak angrily again right after, just like you did last night." "All right," he says, "I've been justly reproved." "What's that supposed to mean?" and he says "Scolded, put in my place; you know." "I'm sorry for the way I acted before," she says to him and he says "And I accept your apology." "What do you mean? I'm not to blame, you are. I only said it because that's what you always say when you apologize for yelling or something like that." "I know. I was only trying to worm my way out of it, and I apologize for that too." He wakes up and sees a note on his night table: *I'm sorry the way I acted before.* He takes the note into her room—has to wake her up for school anyway—and says, after he says "Dolly sweetheart, time to get up," "By the way, what's with this note? I didn't yell at you yet today or last night. In fact I haven't yelled at you or anyone in this house or talked harshly or overcriticized or done anything like that for days." "It's for the future," she says. *Try not to yell anymore,* her note on his night table says the next day. "I'll try, keep trying, whatever it takes till I get the hang of it," he says to himself, "and especially if it makes her happy," and later wakes her but forgets to mention the note. "Did you read what I wrote you this time?" she asks when she's having breakfast a half-hour later and he says "Oh, yeah, and it's good advice, which I'm following." *You've been a very good boy,* the note says the next morning. *Continue to be one. Rule one: don't yell or curse. Or maybe yell for things like getting a taxi in the streets of New York.* And the next day's note: *Four days and no yelling and cursing at the air and "I'm sorry for the way I acted before." Excellent.* He saw her put it on his night table around three in the morning. She must set her watch alarm to wake herself up. He wasn't waiting for her, just was awake in the dark and she slipped in and put the note there. After she left he closed his bedroom door, turned the night table light on and read the note. "What is it?" his wife says. "The kid's trying to stop me from yelling and cursing and getting angry and so on.

I.

It's working. I mean, the notes. You remember what I told you yesterday about the one she gave." "Who?" and he says "Our younger daughter." "Go back to sleep," she says, "it still must be early and you need the rest." "I'm sorry the way I acted with you before," she tells him the next morning and he says "But I didn't do anything," and she says "I only said it because it was getting too hard to wake up so early to put notes on your bed table while you were still sleeping." A month later he says "I'm sorry for the way I acted to you today," and she says "And I thought you were cured." "I'm sorry, I forgot," he says, "and I'll try not to yell anymore at you or at least not say that silly line again about how sorry I am for the way I behaved." "If you didn't yell you wouldn't have to say that line," and he says "And you've also heard it too many times, am I right?" and she says "Have I ever." "Something seems to have worked," she says a couple of months later and he says "What are you talking about?" "Better I don't remind you, because maybe that's part of what made it work," and he says "Oh yeah, and you could be right, though don't count on eternal success. I'm sort of hopeless." "It worked. Whatever we did, Daddy, it worked," she says a few months later. "I was sitting here reading my diary from more than six months ago and complaining in it about you yelling and cursing and always saying how sorry you are about it and I realized you haven't yelled at me in months. What do you think it is that stopped it?" and he says "I don't know, but it's over and I'm as glad as you." "So we should forget it, not talk about it to try to find out what made it stop, and just let it disappear?" and he says "Sounds good to me, what do you think?" "I'm sorry for the way I acted to you before," he says a few months later and she says "Why, what did you do?" and he says "Nothing. I was just remembering how I used to say it all the time to you and I got a little nostalgic or something over it, so thought I'd just say it even if it made no sense. Stupid of me, right?" "It used to make me so mad," she says, "not just your yelling but also your always giving your apology soon after," and he says "You never told me. If you had, I would have stopped doing both." "I'm very sorry for the way I acted before," she says about a year later and he says "It's all right, as long as you know you shouldn't have behaved that way. But please, sweetheart, try not to act like that again?" "I'm sorry for the way I acted before," she says a few weeks later and he says "Fine, apology accepted, but what got in to you, maybe that's what we should ask." "I got angry at what you seemed to be accusing me of, but I shouldn't have yelled," and he says "The cursing too. Those vulgar words I never heard from you and which sounded awful coming from your mouth." "I can get mad too, though you're right; I was wrong. But you're being honest when you say you accept my apology?" and he says "Of course, what else can I do?" "I'm sorry I acted the way I did with you before," she says to him a few months later and he says "Funny, because I was just going to say the same thing to you, though in slightly different words. We both shouldn't have got so upset, and because of my age and so on I'm much more to blame than you. But let's try not to act that way to each other again, is it a deal?" and sticks his hand out and smiles, she doesn't smile, and they shake. They're talking on the phone years later and she says "Something from a long time ago came back to me today," and he says "How I used to lock you in the refrigerator for days when you spilled your milk while you were pouring it?" and she says "Close. How you always used to yell at me and then soon after say how sorry you were. Till I started leaving notes on your night table every morning that said *I'm sorry for the way I acted to you before*—in other words, the same words you used in your repeated apology to me—which eventually made you stop yelling." "I don't remember that," he says, "my yelling so much or your notes." "Oh please, you have to. Maybe every other day, and it went on for years. Or every week or so or every other. After a while it became sort of a joke between us, but not one that got much of a laugh." "I remember yelling a few times—maybe once a month or every two months for a year, and then later feeling lousy that I hurt your feelings and also lousy for continuing to do what I'd hoped by that time I'd have learned to stop doing. But that's about all the yelling I did to you, and it certainly didn't go on for years," and she says "It did, believe me, you yelled at everyone in the house and probably apologized soon after to everyone in a similar way too. But I think I was the only one who finally got you to stop, with those notes and also by letting you know that you were losing control repeatedly." "I still don't remember it. What I do recall, though, is your sharp temper sometimes and your telling me, after you blew up once again over relatively nothing, that you were extremely sorry and my telling you at least a dozen times something like 'Oh, boy, I've heard that one before.'" "You're making that up. I did get angry at you sometimes, but nothing like what you did to me and it was usually your anger and outbursts that set my anger off." "It's true," he says, "I am making it up. I remember some of what you say about me and my emotional state at the time and I just wanted to forget it. Do you still harbor a grudge over it?" and she says "A little bit. Something like that doesn't entirely disappear, but it's mostly gone." "I'm sorry I yelled at you before," he says to her child years later and his daughter, coming into the room, says "Oh my goodness, I don't believe I'm hearing this," and he says "What do you mean?" and she says "You telling me you don't know?" "Well, some of it, yes," and her son says "What, did grandpa used to yell at you all the time, Mommy?" and he says "All the time? No. Very little, very little. Probably as much as your mother yells at you, which can't be much because that's not what her disposition's like." And to his daughter: "Don't tell him I yelled at you a lot. It wouldn't be fair."

THE ACCIDENT

GETS A WHIFF of it in the living room. Goes into the kitchen and can tell by the smell coming through her study door that she didn't make it to the toilet there in time. "Accident?" he says, and she says "I don't know how it happened. I try to be careful. I'll take care of it, though I need a roll of paper towels." "It's okay, I'll help," and she says "You don't have to," and he says "I know, but let's get it over with. Sooner we get rid of the crap and smell, the better." "Please don't get angry over it. If you can't help me without getting angry, don't come in here." "So what, then, you trying to clean it up for the next two hours? Anyway, I wasn't angry. I was just saying we should get it done quick as we can," and he opens the door. She's on the floor and shit seems everywhere. Flat pile of it beside her, some on her legs and feet, on the raised toilet seat and base of the toilet, and a little on her wheelchair's seat and one of the wheels. Smell is awful. "What a difference a door makes," he says and she says "It's bad enough for me, so no remarks." He gags, walks out, says "I forgot the towels," and he had forgotten them but got out because he couldn't take the smell. "You

55

should've opened the windows," he says from the kitchen and she says "I wish I could, or had thought beforehand to ask you. But it's obvious I didn't know it'd happen, and I don't have the strength and leverage and everything else it takes to open any window here but our bathroom's." "Then you should have shit there, the regular way or the accident," and she says "Do I have to put up with this from you every time? I'm serious, don't try to help me. It'll take time like you say, but I can clean both me and it up myself. And I can see you're going to get excited," and he says "Don't worry, I won't. My initial revulsion, to be honest, is over, and now I'll start taking care of things," and goes in with a roll of towels. "First of all, the windows," and opens both of them as high as they can go. "Now let's get you off the floor, though I don't know to where. The chair, where else, since you're finished using the toilet, I think, or finished having any use for it, am I right? And I'm being serious," and she says yes and he does a quick swipe of the wheelchair seat with a bunch of paper towels, dumps them into the trash container in the kitchen, puts newspapers on the seat— "One step at a time," he says; "don't worry, we'll get everything. Now give me your arms, uncomfortable as it's going to be for a little while," and lifts her up, gets smeared with shit, sits her in the chair, says "Hold on for a second," and gets the raised toilet seat off and goes outside with it, again mostly to get away from the smell, and when he gets back there'll be less of it. Now, should he wash down the seat first or take care of the rest? The shit on his arm first, and in the kitchen wipes it off with wet paper towels. Now the rest. Get it over with. When it's done, she'll be grateful to him.

And do it without getting excited. Because what's the point of getting excited and undoing all the good he does? She and the kids hate it when he goes into one of his tantrums. But the tantrums sometimes help him do things faster, which means getting them over with quicker, and getting it over with now is all he wants to do. But getting excited is just more proof that he's unable to control himself at times, something he should have been able to do ten or twenty years ago; more. So try not to get excited. Just clean her up, the study up, the toilet, everything and all with a little humor or just silence and a stoic face. He goes into the study with a bottle of ammonia, picks the shit up off the floor with some towels. "What a load," he says and she says "You don't have to tell me. I'm glad it's gone." He dumps it into the trash container, goes back and pours ammonia on the floor from the bottle. She says "Shouldn't it have been diluted—ten to one, something like that? Way you did it it'll be harder to wipe up all the ammonia and not only will the floor be slippery but the ammonia could damage it." "Maybe you're right; I was too much in a rush," and gets a glass of water from the kitchen and pours it on the ammonia, gets on his knees and with a bunch of paper towels wipes around till half the floor's been cleaned and none of it feels slippery, then says "We should start cleaning you up," and starts pulling up her shirt and she says "You'll tear it that way," and raises her arms and he takes all her clothes off while she's sitting in the chair. "Excuse me," and he goes outside with the clothes and runs the hose on the worst of them to get the shit off and also runs it on the raised toilet seat, long as he's got the water on and hose in his hand, but for the seat he puts his thumb over the end of the nozzle so the water comes out harder. He wants to wring the clothes before he puts them in the washer but doesn't want any remaining shit on the clothes to get on his hands. Could put on a pair of the disposable rubber gloves he uses when he catheterizes her and also when he cleans out the roof's gutters, but shit's on his hands anyway, though just a little, and on his clothes and legs. So, good: shit. What the hell. Stick your mitts in it and fear or dread or whatever it is of touching it will be over. Not about to try that yet; what comes from dealing with it in the normal run of things is enough. The other stuff would be nuts. Wrings the clothes out and goes into the kitchen and puts them in the washer and then washes his hands under the kitchen tap. Don't run the washer till everything's in. Wheelchair cushion cover, for instance, and towels if he has to use any while cleaning her and of course a washrag or two. "Room's smelling better, isn't it," he says, going into the study, "and my, look how the floor gleams—the water worked," and she says "I wish you wouldn't do all those other things before taking care of me. I feel dirty. And I'm cold with nothing on, and it is uncomfortable. I'm afraid I'll need a shower to get all of it off," and he says "Don't worry, that's the best part of it for me, getting you in the shower. Then I know it's over... at least you're feeling better and even a little refreshed." He wheels her into their bathroom—thinks: What does he still have to do? Washer, things he'll put in it, finish cleaning the raised toilet seat, wheelchair, toilet seat he'll put her on before getting her into the shower, and his clothes and legs and such—and says "Ready?" and she nods and holds out her arms and he lifts her onto the toilet, pushes the chair into the bedroom and says "Okay, here we go again," and takes a deep breath and lifts her up and swings her around to the stool in the shower stall while he moves in little steps toward it and carefully sets her down. "My legs," she says, which are extended stiffly over the ledge of the stall and he says "I know, I know, one thing at a time," and slides her over so she's sitting in the middle, manipulates her legs till they unstiffen and he gets them in, puts the bathmat down and tucks the bottom of the shower curtain between her feet and the ledge. He adjusts the shower nozzle so it's facing the wall behind her and turns the water on. When he thinks the temperature's a good one for her, he says "Want to feel the water first?" and she says "I trust you; you know I like it moderately warm," and he directs the spray to her. He's getting wet and takes his clothes off and rubs soap on a washrag. "I don't like soap on my body," she says, "I've told you that. The water will be enough." "It won't be enough. Only soap and scrubbing can get the tough stuff off. I won't put that much on." He soaps her thighs and calves. "Raise your butt," and she does while holding onto the grab bars and he gets the soapy washrag under her and washes her anus and backside. "Now splash a little," and she moves up and down on the stool while he aims the shower spray at it, and he says "Fine, I think we got it all, or all that's important." He rinses the soap off her legs and just with water and a washrag washes her shoulders and back and arms and armpits and breasts. He gets an erection. "Might as well give you a shampoo, you haven't had one in a week. You can do it by yourself, right?" as he doesn't like washing her hair, especially feeling the bumps on her scalp, and she says "I can't shampoo myself and hold onto the grab bars too. But I don't think I need one," and he says "You do, honestly. Not to malign you in any way, but I sleep close to you and your hair's beginning to smell funny." "That's ridiculous. I'd smell it if I did," and he says "Maybe you're right. But besides, something might have gotten into your hair during the aftermath of the accident—your hair's long—so just let me do it if you can't. And you'll feel better after it also." He squirts shampoo on her hair, works it in, massages her scalp till all her hair's lathered, rinses it, rinses the lather off her body, turns the shower off and while she's drying the top part of her body, he dries her legs. Then he says "Okay?" and she says "My legs," and he gets her feet over the ledge, flattens them on the floor and lifts her onto the toilet. "I'll need the hair dryer," and he sets it up and turns it up and while she's using it he dries himself and dresses, gets the cover off the cushion, puts a towel on the cushion and wheels the chair into the bathroom, checks his dirty clothes and sees nothing's on them that needs hosing down or picking off first and sticks them and the cover into the washer, thinks it's a pretty small load so anything else to go in? Maybe some of the kid's clothes so he doesn't have to do them tomorrow, but doesn't know how good an idea it is to mix them with these, and sets and starts the washer and then ties up the trash bag in the kitchen, as the shit inside's already beginning to stink, and puts it into the trash can outside. I should take a shower, he thinks, and goes back to the bathroom. She's still drying her hair. He looks at her nude, her pubic hair, thighs, breasts, head hair always looks so sweet after it's been washed and blow-dried or dried by the sun and the sort of wispy way it hangs over her face, and he gets another erection. She sees it, looks away and continues drying her hair and he says "Maybe we should use this opportunity. Time, I'm saying, for the kids aren't due back for half an hour," and she says "Okay with me. And I have to say, you handled the whole thing without getting excited once. That was good to see," and he says "I am excited, but I know what you mean. I better take a quick shower first; I got some feces on me. Done with the dryer? I don't want to shower while it's still plugged in so close to the shower stall, and your hair looks fine," and she shuts it off and he puts it away on the shelf above her and then undresses and showers. Comes out and quickly dries himself. She's still on the toilet and he says "So let's go, we only have about twenty minutes, if we're lucky," and then says "Oh no," because he remembers the wheelchair has shit on one of the tires and on the edge of the seat and there's even some on a couple of the spokes, he sees. "This rotten shit. It's everywhere. Look at it on the wheel," and she says "Bring in the other chair to wheel me," and he says "First I have to clean this one—I can't just leave it around with shit on it—and you know how long it's going to take? Twenty minutes at least. I have to get off every trace of it or else it'll get on you, besides stink," and she says "I knew it wouldn't last," and he says "What, not getting excited? Who wouldn't get excited? What was I, born to clean up after you?" and she starts crying and he says "No, I'm not going to also deal with your crying," and puts on his pants and wheels the chair out, bumping it against the wall and door intentionally, and then thinks "If it's on the tire?" and looks down and he did get it on the floor in places wheeling the chair in and out of the room and he yells "Godalmighty crap," and pounds the bed with his fists and she says "What happened, you hurt yourself?" and he says "No, just leave me alone. I've too much work to do to answer," and gets ammonia and clean rags from the kitchen and pours it on the floor wherever the shit tracks are and cleans them best he can, and she says from the bathroom "The ammonia smell again. You using it? If you are, did you dilute it this time? We won't have a carpet left," and he says under his breath "Just shut up, goddamnit," and carries the wheelchair outside and cleans the seat and spokes and tire and leaves it there and wheels the other chair into the bathroom and says "All right, you can't stay in here all day; let's get you into the seat," and she says "You need something over the cushion," and he puts a towel down and she says "And I can get myself in; I don't need your help," and he says "You'll need help squeezing this fat chair through the door. And if you do try to sit in it alone, you could fall and then I'll have that to deal with. Cuts, blood, more cleaning up and attending to, maybe a bone break and then another quick emergency hospital trip that turns into a four-hour wait. Everything, besides you babbling and bawling some more and driving me up the wall and with another day for me gone, another week wasted. Now come on, please, let me help you into here so it can be done with," and puts his hands under her arms and she says "What do you mean 'a week wasted'? I'm the one who can't get anything done," and he says "I know that; I was just raving. Now come on," and makes some movement with his

hands under her arms and she says "This time don't throw
me into the chair. Wait till my feet are firm on the ground
and I'm ready. And put your knees around mine, not
between them or to the side, or I'll cut my legs again on the
chair," and he hoists her up and she says "Don't!" and sets
her down in the chair and she says "I wasn't ready," and he
says "But you didn't cut yourself," and she says "I could
have. And if you keep picking me up like that, I will. God,
how you can turn a good act into an absolutely hateful one,"
and he says "I know, I know, but that's how I am. I can't
stand shit, that's all there is to it," and starts wheeling her
through the bedroom to the living room and she says "Are
you crazy? I'm not dressed," and he says "Oh geez, I forgot,"
and laughs and she does and he says "I'm so sorry for getting
angry, honestly," and touches her shoulder and she says "As
well you should be." "Rub it in, I deserve it," and she says
"Just help me get dressed," and he gets a bra out of her
drawer and helps her put it on, brushing her breasts with his
hands while he does it, and says "I ruined it. I so much
wanted to make love, but like half the time, I did myself
in," and she says "I also wanted to but it's impossible now,
and not only because the kids will be home soon," and he
says "I can understand it. There'll be other days," and she
says "One day, based on the way you continue to behave, it's
possible there won't," and he says "I can understand that
too." He opens her dresser drawer and says "Short-sleeved
shirt or a tank top?" and she says "Either," and he takes out
a tank top because she looks better in those, then a denim
jumper from the closet. Helps her on with them. Brakes the
chair, pulls her up from behind so she's sitting straight, gets

63

the chair legs onto the chair, her feet on the foot rests, bends down to kiss her. "Please don't," and he says "Still mad, right, and who can blame you?" and turns the chair around, wheels it into the living room and gives it a little push to the dining room and says "You're on your own," and she says "Good." He goes back to the bedroom, looks at the bed, imagines them making love. He's put the diaphragm in for her, first spread the cream around on it. He can almost never do the last part, hook it under the cervix if that's what it is: the bone there like a lip. Sometimes though he hooks it without even knowing it. She feels it and says it's fine. But he always has her check, and nine times out of ten it isn't in right and she does the rest. Then he'd get on the bed with her. First he'd have to help her onto the bed. He'd lift her out of the chair and sit her on the bed and then lift her legs and turn her around on the bed till she was parallel to it and straighten her out on her back. Then he'd get on the bed and kiss her, play with her, she with him, not much time spent doing this because they wouldn't have much time, and then enter her, maybe get on his back and help her get on top of him or just roll over on his back while he was already inside her, jiggle around a little, come, clean them both up and get her off the bed and help her dress. Say "That was nice, I'm glad we did it. And imagine, it never would have happened if you hadn't accidentally shit." Or "had an accident." Or "shit by accident" or "crap." Would he have said any of that? Probably would have thought of it and then asked himself "You really want to say that?" and then said to himself "Sure, say it, no harm, really," and said to her "Think of it, we wouldn't have made love if you hadn't had that accident," and if he had said it that way he thinks she probably wouldn't have minded him saying it.

GIRLFRIEND

SHE LIVED UP the block. People said they would get married
one day. "You two are so close. I never saw anything like it
before with such young kids. Would you like to marry her?"
they asked and he said "Sure, why not? When I get older."
How old was he when people started asking him this, or he
started remembering them asking? Maybe six, not quite six.
But they had begun playing together when they were still
crawling, and then only she was crawling, since she was a
few months younger than he. They had lived on the block
since they were born. Their mothers had wheeled them to
the park in their baby carriages and sat or strolled around
there while their babies slept in the carriages or played in
the sandbox, but their mothers were never good friends. If
both happened to be going to the park at the same time,
then one caught up with the other just to have someone to
walk with. Or if they saw each other in the playground right
inside the park entrance, one moved to the bench the other
was sitting on if they were both alone. His mother said she
never especially liked his friend's mother. "Cold," when they
were reminiscing about the block years later, "a real cold

fish, and catty and not too spry in the brains department and forever yakketing about nothing. But she helped me pass the time if I wanted you to get fresh air for a couple of hours and had brought nothing along with me to read. I also thought it'd be nice if you had a young friend from the block, even at that age. And it was convenient to have someplace close to leave you if I suddenly had to be somewhere for something and couldn't find a sitter, and I'm sure same for her." He never knew what his friend's mother thought of his mother. Whenever he went over there, though, her mother would always say when she let him in "How's your lovely mother?" and when he left "Don't forget to give your dear mother my regards." "And my father too," he said a few times and she said "Of course, your father too, though I've still never met him." His mother rarely asked after the girl's mother when his friend came over; usually just "Say hello home." Their fathers had never met, though he could be wrong there. His mother might have introduced them sometime when he wasn't around and his parents had bumped into the girl and her father on the street or at a market or somewhere in the neighborhood. They once kissed, this girl and he. They were playing in the improvised playroom in her building's basement, sent there by her mother because they were making too much noise in the apartment, and they couldn't go outside because it was raining. He thinks they were around seven then, the only year they were in the same class together. "Do you want to have a kiss?" "All right," she said and put out her cheek and he kissed it. He wanted to kiss her lips but he didn't want to force his on her. Then he asked if he could see her vagina.

Asked it a little later, after they had played some more. And he didn't use the word vagina then. What did he use? He wouldn't have known the word cunt. Or pussy. He thinks he said "your slit" or "crack." She showed it. Didn't seem to hesitate. Pulled down her panties till they hung around her knees and held her skirt up with her other hand. It took all of about ten seconds. He said "That's what I thought it looked like." He must have seen his mother's once or twice. When he was in bed, at night, supposedly asleep, he could see the door from where he lay, and she walked past his room naked on her way to her bedroom or stayed outside his door for a few seconds to see and perhaps hear how he was sleeping and he looked at her with his eyes almost closed. Or he barged into the bathroom once and she was standing, drying off after a shower, one foot on the bathtub rim and the other on the floor, or she was about to step into the shower. Or she was sitting on the toilet when he barged in or even standing in front of it and wiping herself, her behind or front. But he wouldn't have been able to see his mother's slit so well because of her pubic hair, unless she had her leg raised, as he said, to dry it or her foot. "There's no hair there," he said to the girl. Oh, he's just making that up and most of what he said and a few of the more specific details. He might have said it, only might have. The incident definitely took place though. He asked, she complied, he looked, she stared at him while he was looking, he said something during or after it or he didn't, she said something or she didn't. In ten, maybe twenty seconds, she pulled her panties up and dropped her skirt. He seems to recall her smiling for a moment while he was looking. Then they resumed playing, and he never forgot it. As for seeing a girl's slit, hers couldn't have been the first if he was seven. On beaches, little girls of one or two or three, running around naked or just with their diapers or bottoms off. He must have looked whenever they did this, and wondered. He thought, after two or three adults told him that he and the girl would probably end up getting married, that this is how people got married. They grow up on the same block, play together a lot, are close for a while as kids, kiss a few times and hold hands—that he doesn't ever remember doing with her, though they must have, if just told to by her mother when the three of them crossed a street—and when they reach a certain age, when she has breasts and his dick gets big and both have hair down there, or just when they're much older and taller and finished with school, people will expect them to get married, and maybe they'll even have to because of all the time they spent together and because they did kiss and he saw her slit, so that's what they do, marry. She had black hair and usually a red ribbon or barrette or clip in it. She had black eyes and people called her Black-Eyed-Susan though her name wasn't Susan or anything close to it. He played with other kids—boys, mostly—but he played with her for his first seven years more than he did with any male friend during that time. He once stood in front of her apartment building—well, he did this lots of times, calling out her name—but on this particular day he called up to her apartment on the third floor with something like "Do you want to come out and play?" She came to the window and waved. "I can't today," she said, "we're moving away." "You're moving to where?" and she told him and he said "I'll see you before you leave, won't I?" and she said yes. So he went home, or to the candy store at the corner to get something—his mother let him be out alone like that at seven years old? Yes—or to another friend's building to see if this boy wanted to come out and play, and forgot about her and a day or two later yelled up to her window for her but she didn't come to it. He rang her bell from the building's vestibule but nobody asked on the intercom who it was. Then he remembered she said she was moving. So she probably moved. Her apartment was probably empty. He didn't see any moving truck on the block near her building the last few days but that doesn't mean it didn't come and fill up with their furniture and things when he wasn't around. It was a small apartment and they didn't have much stuff, so it could have been done fast. Maybe she'll come back to the block one day to say hello or because she forgot something in her apartment and the super's holding it for her or maybe she moved to a street nearby and she'll continue to go to the same public school and he'll see her there. She hasn't been in school for a couple of days, but that could be because of the moving and all the things she has to do in her new place. But she wasn't in school after that and he never saw her again. After a while older people asked about her and he said she moved. They asked if he'd heard from her—a letter or phone call—and he said no but he expects to one day when she gets completely moved in. Later they said he must be very sorry she's gone and he usually said "I guess so" or just shrugged. "Do you miss her?" and he always said "A little. She was my friend, even if she is a girl, and I knew her for a long time." He missed her a lot but that wasn't what he wanted to tell them. He's thought about her hundreds of times after that last time he tried to get her to come out and play and she couldn't. If she had stayed on the block maybe they would have become girlfriend and boyfriend in about seven or eight years, kissed a lot and held hands on the street and gone to movies and parties together and maybe fooled around a little with their bodies, and then become lovers. Gotten married, even, when they were in their early twenties. It doesn't seem to happen much like that in the city but it's happened with some couples. Childhood sweethearts. She was pretty. She's probably still pretty or continued to be pretty for a long time. She was lively and funny and nice and a good sport and she probably continued to be like that too. And he remembers her being a fast runner and a good catcher and thrower when they played ball and very smart, getting some of the top grades in their classes together and always winning or coming in second in the spelling bees at school, something he was good in too but never as good as she. She's probably still all those ways. People's personalities and intelligence and maybe even their motor skills don't change that much, he thinks, unless they get very sick and it does something to one or more of those things. And even if she seemed healthy then, she could have got sick a few years after he last saw her—even the next year—and died at eight or nine or twelve or fourteen. If she had stayed on the block or in the neighborhood, maybe died soon after they had become lovers and talked seriously about getting married one day. He would have been distraught over it but he would have recovered eventually and met someone else. Or started seeing a whole bunch of women for the next ten to fifteen years—seen them one at a time—and then married a girl who looked like her: black hair and eyes, heart-shaped face, freckles and very fair skin—skin so fair she wasn't allowed to stay in the sun for more than a few minutes without putting on a wide-brimmed hat she always carried folded up in her schoolbag or a pocket. The black hair and eyes and freckles and skin were other things that attracted her to him and made him think she was pretty. People would say when he said they actually might marry when they grow up, "You'd marry a woman with freckles?" He said once "Why not, what's wrong with them? I like freckles; they're cute."

REVERSES

IT'S A BAD time in his life. His mother recently died, his wife's sick, his children are ignoring him and occasionally being insulting and difficult. Actually, his mother died almost two years ago and his wife's been sick for several years, and he thinks his kids will eventually come around where they'll be acting pleasantly and civilly to him again, or as much as they did before. He wonders if his wife will ever get better. If she'll even stabilize to the condition she's in now. He's thought of his mother every day since she died, sometimes many times a day: things she said, things they did together and with his father and brother and sister and then with his own family. Most of the times when he thought of her, she was smiling. Occasionally, she was staring off vacantly. Most of her life when she was with him she was smiling or looking at him kindly. The last years of her life she was bitter. But he could usually get her to laugh and she could get him to laugh, or at least smile, too. She said, intentionally, clever and funny things. His work isn't going well either. He does it all right but he just isn't interested in it anymore. Hasn't been interested in it for a few years, but this year has been the hardest it's ever been to conceal his lack of interest. He's sixty-two and has eight and a third years left till he can retire. He can retire when he wants, of course, and his department would probably be happy to see him go—a much younger person could be brought in to replace him at half his salary and benefits—but eight and a third years from now is when his younger child, if everything goes as expected, graduates college. So he needs to keep his job because his employer pays half his children's undergraduate college tuition, and they're both planning to go to some very good expensive schools. But it's a struggle for him to get through it every workday and also through the work he has to do for it at home, and he gets no satisfaction out of it. None, or little, very little. The car hasn't been running well either. He's taken it in lots of times the last year and had to wait around for hours a few times, or rent a car for a day or two while the garage tried to figure out what was wrong with it. They only have one car in the family. Not "only": he's chosen to only have one. He doesn't want to take care of two cars, and besides, his wife isn't well enough to drive anymore—her eyesight and motor coordination and she can get tired so fast—and he doesn't want his older child driving yet. He fears for her on the road. That's another thing. He was in a car accident two weeks ago. He was in the passenger seat of a neighbor's van, helping him cart an old stove and some other heavy things to the county dump. He didn't see what happened. He was reading a book he held in his lap and his neighbor was listening to a call-in radio show. The accident occurred in the other driver's lane. His neighbor said that's because the guy was originally in their lane, and his neighbor, seeing trees a few feet away to their right, darted into the clear lane on his left to avoid hitting the car. But at that moment, the neighbor said, the other driver corrected himself and shot back into his own lane. The other driver said their van was in his lane all the time and came straight at him and there was nothing he could do to avoid the accident. The police didn't cite either of the drivers because it was raining and there were no tire or skid marks and it was one person's word against the other and no real witness. Anyway, the two cars collided head on, more on the passengers' sides than the drivers'. The next thing he knew his neighbor was screaming "Oh no, my goddamn van," and the other guy shouted "Your goddamn van? My new BMW! I haven't put five hundred miles on it." The drivers were both out of the car and he was still in his seat and figured he'd been knocked unconscious from the impact for about thirty seconds, because that's—his neighbor told him later when he asked—how long it was between the time they crashed and both drivers were out of the cars and screaming and shouting. Air bags and the belts saved them. His neck and shoulders still hurt from the accident but not enough to make him want to see a doctor or stop him from going to work or doing all the things he has to around the house. He was shaken up, had to take tranquilizers the next few days to get to sleep. Gets nervous driving now, goes much slower than he should. Drivers honk at him from behind, and when they finally pass him on the left they look at him the way he used to look at drivers sometimes when he felt they were going too slow. Another thing is that his wife's been saying lately that when the kids want something or feel they need to tell them something, they only go to him, and treat her as if she doesn't exist. He says "I always tell them to go to you first for almost everything like that, or the two of us together if we're at the table or in the same room," and she says "It's because I've become physically weaker than I was and they think I'm unable to make a decision anymore or perhaps can't even register what they say," and he says "That's not true and you know it. I'm sure it's only something they're going through. Or maybe they're trying to pit one parent against the other for some reason. Or they think you're the stronger and more judicious one while I'm easier to finagle and a soft touch, so the one they obviously have a better chance with. Consider yourself lucky they're not coming to you more for the time being, because look at the ballbreaking way they've been treating me recently, no matter how much I give in to their pleading and demands." A bottle of olive oil fell out of a kitchen cabinet yesterday and broke and it took him a half hour to clean up. A small thing, but big at the time and which made him yell "God almighty, can nothing go right?" Because just an hour before, the bathtub drain was clogged when he was taking a shower, and he had to use the plunger for a good ten minutes till he got the hair and gook out. And the frame of his glasses cracked the night before that, and the previous morning to that a pot of soup he'd made for the next two to three days spilled on the stove when he was carrying it to the blender. Also small, but upsetting at the time, and so much work cleaning the insides of the four burners, and the waste. "Not another thing," he yelled when it happened. "What is it, a goddamn curse on me?" The cat's been throwing up just about every other day the past week. Enough. But he has to take care of it almost every time. He yelled out last night "Kids, someone come and clean up the vomit your cat made." Or he just sees the mess, as he did the two previous times, instead of the cat chucking up in front of him as it did yesterday, and yelled for the kids to deal with it, and one or both of them will say "You don't have to yell, and why are you always blaming us for things?" "Then please, just clean it up without any more fuss," he'll say calmly, and most of the times they don't. They're busy. They're sleepy. They're not feeling well. They've homework. They're doing a school report or project due tomorrow, in their room or on the word processor in the dining room. They're watching their favorite TV show of the week and tonight's isn't a re-run; they'll clean up the mess during the commercials. They've a friend to meet at a movie theater he promised to drive them to, and they're already late. They're on the phone getting the homework assignment they missed or involved in a very important call and they've only been on for two minutes. Phone, word processor, TV, they all stink, he thinks, plus most movies, and ought to be abolished. He said something like that at the dinner table a few nights ago, and his wife and kids looked at him as if he were crazy. If he said to the kids "Listen, cut the crap; just do it," they'd say why does he always have to curse? Because doesn't he tell them not to? He knows he'll have to take the cat to the vet with one of the kids tomorrow or the next day. His wife will insist on it, saying it could be something serious that can be cured with a single visit. Sit in that smelly waiting room for an hour with animals barking and hissing and crying and scratching and tearing at the carriers they're in and most of the other people there blathering about their pets. Nothing will be wrong with the cat, but the visit will cost him around a hundred dollars, and they're short of money. Even his personal work at home when he finds the time to get to his desk because of all the chores he has to do beforehand: nothing's coming out right and hasn't for days and he feels everything he's done for weeks is crap. But he has to get to work. He says to his wife "I got to go now," and she says "I know, and you don't look too happy about it." "I'm not, but what else can I do? I wish I had thought of doing something else with my life thirty to forty years ago, which would have helped me to retire sooner. But a little too late for that, right? So I'm stuck." "It's not that bad, is it? You've done plenty of good things with your time, and look what we've got," and he says "I really haven't the time to talk about it." He kisses her goodbye. His briefcase, he thinks. Forgot it last week and only realized he did when he got halfway to work. Should he turn back for it, he thought then, or continue to drive to school and give some excuse to his students why he can't return their papers and then try winging it through class for most of the two hours? and drove back. He gets his briefcase, checks that everything's inside, kisses his wife goodbye again and leaves. The car won't start. Figures. Is he going to get upset? he thinks. How can he after everything else that's happened? So there's something he's gained from this recent run of bad luck, some success. He tries starting the car again, then goes inside and his wife says "I know, I could hear," and he says "See? Just what I figured. I didn't tell you I was thinking that when I went out to the car, but I swear to you I was, and this time it really seems to be dead." He calls up the local service station and asks that they pick up the car, either by towing it or jump-starting it here, and do what they can to get it working again. "If it needs a new motor or something like that, don't tell me; just push it into a ditch and bury it and send me the towing and burial costs," and the owner says "I'm sure it won't turn out to be that bad." "Maybe we need a new car," his wife says when he gets off the phone, and he says "We can't afford one, but you're probably right." He calls a taxi service and asks to have a cab sent right away. "To save time, I'll be waiting at the head of my driveway." "Wish me luck," he says to his wife, and goes outside and waits. Cab doesn't come. He goes back home and calls the taxi service. "One of our cabs broke down," the dispatcher says; "another can't be located. A third just went off for the day and the rest are on breaks or have long trips to the airport and train station." "Why didn't you tell me this when I first called?" and the dispatcher says "I didn't know it at the time except for one of the airport rides." "Ah, come on, what do you take me for? Cancel my order, I'll get to work some other way," and calls a friend at his job nearby and is told he's home sick today. He calls his department's office and asks the secretary "Are there any graduate students around who have cars?" and she says she doesn't see any and wouldn't know which ones have cars anyway. "You'd ask. You'd see a grad student and you'd say 'Do you have a car?' If one does, then you'd say I'd be willing to pay, since they always need money, a good amount to have him drive me to school now. But what's the difference. Please put a sign up on my classroom door that I'll be about thirty minutes late and that no one should leave. I don't want to make up a class on some other day." "I'll take the bus, that's all," he says to his wife. "Call another cab company," and he says "The one I called is the only local one, and I'm tired of relying on someone who probably won't come." "But the buses run once an hour or so and you don't know the schedule. I'll call for it." "Okay, please. No, I can call, I'm not helpless," and gets the bus information number out of the phone book, dials, and the line's constantly busy. "I'll take my chances then," and walks the half mile to the stop. He sees a bus approaching his cross street when he's about fifty feet away from the stop. He starts running; the briefcase is keeping him from sprinting. "Hey, wait, hold up, don't go," he yells. The bus passes the stop. "You saw me, you bastard," he shouts, "you had to," shaking his fist at it. The bus stops about two hundred feet away, backs up while he runs to it. The door opens. "Sorry I made you run," the driver says. "I didn't see you till one of the passengers said you were there." "Thanks," he says. "If you had gone without me, I would have been miserable."

THE PARADE

WHERE TO BEGIN? There were always the smells. He'd wake up and the cooking smells were already pervading the apartment. He'd be in bed and would smell some of the food cooking. He'd be asleep and suddenly there was food in his dreams. He'd wake up and know it was Thanksgiving Day and there was the Macy's Day parade to go to. That's what he and his friends called it and for a few years they actually thought that's what it was called. The parade would pass right up the block. He'd say to his brother in the next bed "It's the parade today," and his brother would say, if he was awake, "So what? Let me sleep." "But you'll miss it," and his brother would say "Don't worry, I'll be up in time for it. And if I miss it once, no big deal." "But you won't want to miss it even once. I know you'll be sorry," and his brother might mumble something into his pillow like "Leave me alone already," or "Don't open the blinds when you get dressed," and go back to sleep. He'd get out of bed, wash up and dress, and go to the kitchen and see his mother in a housedress and apron, cooking. "I could have got up later to start this," she'd say. "But you know me; get things done

83

before they do you in." She ever say that? Something like it perhaps. And it sounds like her and what she'd feel: concerned that the cooking smells and noises might awaken her family when they could sleep late. He'd have a quick breakfast, maybe shove a slice of dry bread from the breadbox into his mouth and drink a glass of milk. "Is there anything I can do to help you before I go?" he'd say. He wouldn't say that. He should have though, every time. Maybe he said something like that once in all the years he left for the parade early and his mother was cooking the holiday dinner, and he's sure she said "No, have a good time, I'll be all right. I've the whole day to get things done, though I wouldn't mind if you set the table for me later this afternoon." Then he'd kiss her goodbye and leave the house. The apartment. The building. They lived in a five-story brownstone on a side street between Columbus Avenue and Central Park West, about halfway between those two. He once told his friends "I'm the king of the block because my building is exactly halfway between Columbus and Central Park West and my parents own it." "What about the building across the street from yours," someone said, "which is also halfway." "The north side of the street is more important than the south, since it's further up in the city. So if there was a kid in that building and his parents owned it, he'd only be a junior king, or just a high prince, but subject to me." "And your brother? Why isn't he the king then? He's older than you." "He had the position but gave it up, and I'm next in line, just like they did in England." He runs up the street to Central Park West. The parade's supposed to start at 8:30, it's always at least ten minutes late, and it's now almost exactly eight. He's to meet a friend at eight o'clock on the corner and from there they're to go to 77th Street to watch the last of the balloons being blown up all the way. Last night they watched two of the balloons start to get filled— it can take all night, one of the men manning the helium tanks told them. His friend isn't there. Is he sure it's eight? The kitchen clock said three minutes after eight when he left the house, but maybe it was wrong. But his mother always keeps that clock five minutes fast, not a minute sooner or later, and it's electric. He waits for around ten minutes, then runs to 77th Street. Two of his friends are there. They suddenly get so close that they only want to be together and are planning to leave him out? "Why'd you leave without me?" he says to his best friend, the one he was supposed to meet. "Leave where?" the boy said. "We were to meet in front of number 7 there—seven-seven-seven, don't you remember, for triple good luck?—and you weren't here so we started walking around." They see Santa standing beside his sled and smoking a cigarette. Members of two marching bands tuning up. A few majorettes high kicking and twirling and tossing up batons, one of them catching hers behind her back. Some clowns talking together and laughing at what seems like a joke. A couple of floats with costumed kids on them waiting impatiently for the whole thing to start. Then over a bullhorn a man says "Okey-doke, folks, let's have a parade," and blows several blasts of a whistle into it and the different groups on this wide side street start assembling. Santa stomps out his cigarette and checks his beard and bangs in a pocket mirror. One of the bands gets into formation and the clowns walk to Central Park

West. The kids on the floats are smiling and screeching as their parents say goodbye to them. He and his friends run to their favorite viewing spot near the northwest corner of 75th Street. Not many people there so they can get right up to the police barricade and can even sit on the curb if they want and watch from there. The parade lasts about forty minutes. "Much shorter than it was last year," his best friend says, something one of them seems to say every year. "How many balloons they have, five? Last year's had six or seven and all were better inflated." "At least the weather was good," he says. "Last time, what'd it do, rain or snow? And the one before that it was so windy the balloons were bouncing off the lampposts and the people holding the ropes could hardly hold on. I was hoping one would fly away." Then he goes home. Or he goes with his friends to the park and goes home for lunch. Or stays with his friends till late afternoon. Or they go to a movie in one of the theaters on Broadway in the eighties but first buy a knish or hotdog each at a deli nearby, and then he goes home, feeling starved. Relatives are visiting for a couple of hours. They came in from Brooklyn to see the parade and the store windows downtown, and as long as they were in the city... Turkey's in the oven or out of it but still in the pan. His mother roasts it in the oven for about five hours. First at a very high temperature for half an hour, turning it over on its side every ten minutes and then leaving it sitting up. Then at a low temperature till about two hours before dinner, when she takes it out and covers it and lets it continue to cook in the big pan. They only use that pan on Thanksgiving since that's the one time of the year they cook turkey. The pan's tough to clean. Crust and grease. He's been given the job to clean it a few times with a wire brush and steel wool and soap pads, something he hates doing. He pours the juices left and bits of whatever they are into an empty coffee can. When the grease can, which is what they call it, is filled, the last person to use it will tape the lid down and stick it in the garbage. He never does a good job cleaning the pan. His brother often has to take over, gets it cleaned a little better because he's stronger and scrubs harder, and then his mother will usually say "Though I don't like leaving anything out with food in it—you know me and my fear of vermin—let me soak it overnight." In the morning she'll finish cleaning the pan before anyone else wakes up and will store it for the year way in back on the top shelf of what they call the cleaning closet. They'll have a number of guests for dinner. Aunts and uncles and their children. Friends of his parents. Sometimes patients of his dad who are single and were going to stay home or eat alone in a restaurant. Years later he invites a girlfriend. Did this a few times, girls who didn't have dinners to go to or the ones with their families were earlier that afternoon. Once a Finnish girl he met in Denmark—not a girlfriend—who was now studying in New York. They have the dinner in the dining room for one of the three times they eat there during the year. The other times are for seders, where they also have guests, though he doesn't think he ever invited a girlfriend to one, and the meat is always roast chicken and brisket. They eat the rest of their dinners in the breakfast room on what they call the breakfast room table. He once asked his mother why the room (and thus the table) was called that, maybe asked it a few times, but forgets what she said. Something about light and English, he thinks. Also, that if one has a dining room, then the other room that has a smaller dinner table is called a breakfast room, since that's where you'd normally have breakfast. So he does remember why it's called that, or rather, what his mother answered about it. They only ate breakfast there on Sundays though. His mother would cook eggs and onions in a small enamel pot rather than in a frying pan. She'd sauté the onions slowly in butter till they were soft, then add the beaten-up eggs and keep stirring it with a fork under a low flame. Some of the eggs, after she scooped out the pot onto a serving plate, would stick to the pot, so something else he or his brother had to clean. But this one they were able to clean easily with a single soap pad. Also, slices of lox and a chunk of kippered salmon, they called it, though maybe that's what it's actually called. And cream cheese and bagels and seeded Vienna rolls. Or is it creamed cheese? He could check by looking at the cream or creamed cheese container in the refrigerator, which they frequently referred to as the icebox even if they never had ice delivered to their home. Other apartments did. He remembers the ice truck parked on the street. And the rubber apron, he thinks it's called, on the iceman's shoulder when he delivered these huge blocks of ice. The tongs too, of course, for moving the blocks of ice around on the bed of the truck and probably for some other things. When the iceman was in a building delivering ice, he and his friends would sometimes chip off pieces of ice from the blocks and suck on them. The iceman caught them at it several times and would usually say something like "Beat it, you kids, you're cutting into my profits. You want ice to eat, take the pieces already lying on the floor." But all the other days his family ate breakfast on the even smaller table in the kitchen alcove, though he doesn't think they ever called that area anything. He and his brother and then his sister ate breakfast there before they left for school. He also ate lunch there (his brother too, though at a different time) when he came home for about forty minutes around noon. Well, ten minutes to get home, ten to get back to school, so about twenty minutes to eat his lunch. A sandwich and glass of milk and a couple of carrot and celery sticks would be waiting for him on the kitchen table, and a paper napkin folded in half. His father ate breakfast at the table after the kids left for school, though sometimes their breakfasts overlapped. If that happened, one of the kids had to move over if he or she was sitting in their father's regular seat. Half a grapefruit and a boiled or scrambled egg and a slice of toast with jam or butter and a cup of coffee with milk and sugar. When grapefruit wasn't in season, stewed prunes and cream, or sour cream and bananas. His mother only had black coffee for breakfast. She drank her first cup standing up while preparing and serving food to her children and husband. After they were gone, she'd sit at the kitchen table reading yesterday's newspaper and having a second cup of coffee and her first cigarette of the day, something he saw when he stayed home sick from school. Used to fantasize, when he was fourteen and fifteen, about the girls in drum majorette costumes when they passed him in the parade and especially when they high kicked and did splits. Or right into his young twenties, who's he kidding?—women and girls in brief costumes of any sort and their legs exposed. Started fantasizing about bringing a girlfriend to the parade, which he never ended up doing, and hugging her from behind, from the time he was sixteen. For a few years in a row he used to meet at the parade, not by any prearrangement or anything, an old friend of his brother's from the neighborhood who had become a philosophy and religious studies grad student. After the parade they'd go to the Cherry restaurant, it was called, on Columbus between 75th and 76th Streets and over coffee and English muffins have long interesting discussions, he'd call them, rather than conversations. He looked forward to meeting up with the guy there and their discussions after more than he did the parade. Then the guy didn't show up for a couple of years, so he figured he got a teaching job out of town somewhere, or something changed, because the guy seemed to like the discussions as much as he did. Once, in his mid-twenties, and back home for the Thanksgiving holiday, he saw his former best friend with a child on his shoulders, watching the parade from their old spot near 75th Street. Well, he always caught the parade from that spot; he doesn't think he ever saw it from anywhere else. His friend was now living upstate, was visiting his folks for the day, had been married a few years and had another kid on the way, which was why his wife wasn't seeing the parade with him, and was a printer. So he began fantasizing about being married and coming in with his family for the long holiday weekend and staying with his folks and watching the parade with his kid on his shoulders. When he was twenty-eight he did have a kid on his shoulders at the parade. For a few months he lived with a woman and her child in Washington Heights and volunteered to take the girl to the parade. But after ten minutes of it she got spooked by the crowds and clowns and balloons and animated floats and wanted to go home to her mom right away. He didn't even have time to stop off at his folks' down the block, though he would see them that night for dinner but went alone. The woman didn't like his parents. Besides, she said, her daughter would associate their neighborhood with getting scared and probably start crying hysterically the moment she got out of the subway station. Twenty years later he took his first child to the parade when they were living in New York for the year. His wife liked the parade—used to go to it with her father when she was a girl, though downtown—but said she'd take advantage of their being out all morning and sleep and maybe get some work in if he stayed away till after lunch. The side street between Columbus and Central Park was so crowded that they had trouble getting up it. He hoisted his daughter to his shoulders because he thought she'd get knocked down and maybe trampled by people pushing past. When they got to his old spot he couldn't find a place to watch the parade. Nor for his daughter to see it from his shoulders, as there were three or four rows of people in front of him with kids on their shoulders, and his daughter was very young and small then and couldn't see over the other kids' heads. He finally got her to the curb, all the time saying to the people he asked to move, "Don't worry, I'm not trying to squeeze up front; just taking my little girl there, but I'm coming right back," and told her to sit there till the end of the parade when he'd come get her. When he was a kid there was never that number of people watching the parade. The crowds might have been two deep at the most on the building side of Central Park West and just a single line of people on the park side, even on the nicest days. The police let you duck under the barricades and cross the street anytime you wanted so long as there was a break in the parade. When he saw the parade with his daughter, the police kept you back unless you had a good excuse, such as you wanted to join your family across the street, and you were only allowed to cross at the corner. The parade seemed a lot longer that day too, with about twice the number of balloons and bands and celebrities and floats. And there was more publicizing on the floats and the banners in front of each balloon for different TV shows and Broadway musicals and new movies, but his memory might be wrong on that. Also, the marchers and bands didn't seem to stop to do their routines for the crowds as much as they used to. After the parade, he and his daughter stopped off at his mother's. He wanted to take her out for a late breakfast or early lunch, but she didn't want to leave the apartment because of all the cooking she had to do for dinner. He had suggested they all go to a restaurant that night, one that specializes in Thanksgiving dinner, but she wouldn't hear of it. The only guests would be he and his family and her sister. All his other aunts and uncles had died. Her friends had died too, or moved away and she never heard from them again. His cousins hadn't come to her Thanksgiving dinners for more than thirty years. His father had been dead a number of years. His sister, too, shortly before his father. His brother was living in Minnesota and only came to New York in

June, unless business brought him, and had his mother out there a few weeks every year. He wishes his father had known his wife, seen his child, seen him as a father. He's glad his mother did, with both his children. Now she's dead too, and they don't have turkey on Thanksgiving, since his kids are both vegetarians and his wife doesn't care for the meat and most of the trimmings, and he only watches a few minutes of the parade on television. His kids watch the whole thing. It's become a tradition for them, waking up early for a non-school day so they can see the parade from nine till noon. He used to pop into the master bedroom where the only TV in the house was and once said "Look, there's West 77th Street, two blocks from where I lived. When I was a kid—" and his younger daughter said "We know, you saw them blowing up the balloons and Santa waiting around for the parade to begin and one time smoking a cigarette. How come we never get to do that?" and he said "We only lived in New York as a family for one year, early in the marriage when I was on sabbatical, and you weren't even born yet. Your sister was and old enough to go to the parade on my shoulders and actually see those things coming down the street, but she says she doesn't remember any of it. Imagine not remembering one of those giant balloons looming above you." "Look," he said another time, "Central Park West and 75th Street. I recognize the two apartment buildings—the San Remo and the one directly north of it—the red one—whose name I can never remember. The Kenilworth, I think; yeah. In front of the Kenilworth is where my friends and I always watched the parade." They said he'd already told them—"It was almost like a religious rite, you said"—and that they just want to watch the parade. Then a commercial might come on—lots of commercials. Or a goofy announcer wearing a funny winter hat, or one supposed to be funny, and talk about the parade so far and what's to come. "The whole parade's done for television now," he said, when the kids were watching it another time. "Before, when I was a boy—I know, you've heard that phrase before; when I was a boy. But I was a boy and the parade then wasn't endless, as this one seems to be, or on TV. At first, just because there wasn't much television around except on an experimental basis to the few hundred households in the city that could afford a set or maybe build one themselves. And when I reached my teens, I suppose, and the parade started to be shown on TV, I still never bothered to watch it there, since I was seeing it live on the street." "It's all good," one of his daughters said, "even if it's only on TV. And what choice do we have? We'd love to go to New York to see it. Why don't you ever take us if you think seeing it like that is so great? We have a place to stay." "The trip takes twice as long by car during the Thanksgiving holiday, same with the drive back if we left on a Sunday. I once drove in from Baltimore when I was engaged to your mother and she was still living in New York, and it took eight and a half hours." "Did you go to the parade that time?" his younger daughter said, and he said "I don't think so. It was so late when I got in that Wednesday that I probably slept later than usual the next day. Anyway, by then the crowds watching the parade had got too large for me, so I waited till I had my own child and was living in New York before I went again. I think I only put up with it that time because I thought your sister would enjoy the parade. And she seemed to, though I couldn't see her till after it because I was standing way in back, and I also wanted to drop in on your grandma. Though I have to admit that I did, up into my early thirties, I think, get a little kick out of the parade in a cynical way. Making snide or funny remarks about almost every float and celebrity that passed. And the more I didn't recognize the celebrity or balloon character or theme of the float, the more distant I felt toward the parade, along with a kind of perverse pride that I was so out of touch with popular American culture. But that's just another reason why it wouldn't be such a great idea to go to New York and see the parade with me. I'm afraid, despite my attempts not to, that I'd ruin it for you." He doesn't think his mother ever saw the parade from Central Park West, or at least not since he was a boy. Sometimes when he came back from it right after it was over, she'd be standing in front of their building in a housedress and sweater, and if it was raining or snowing, in a coat and holding an umbrella. "Did you see the parade?" he'd ask and she'd say "A little of it, but only from here." And one time: "The balloons, mostly, and a very tall float with a trapezist flying around at the top of it." "Why didn't you go up the block to see the whole thing? It would have taken you a minute." She said she didn't want to leave the oven alone when it's on. "You know what could happen." "So you turn it off for an hour, what's the harm?" and she said "I also wasn't dressed for it, and just seeing the balloons from here was satisfying enough. You can get quite a different perspective of the parade, these enormous figures suddenly appearing between the tall buildings at the corners and because they're in a wind tunnel or something, being blown about. If I was a photographer I'd take several pictures of it." His father used to got to Central Park West to see the parades on the nice days, getting there a minute or two after it began. He always took a newspaper with him and would fold it in a way where it became a long strip and read·it when nothing in the parade was passing or coming. Several times he waved to his father at the corner and then maybe he'd go up to him for a minute. "How do you like the parade so far?" he asked and his father usually said "It's pretty good and a great day for it. And you?" "I like it. I'm with my friends," and his father usually said "So stay with them. I got a good spot here where I can see it just fine. When it's over, I'm going to Cake Master's or Bloom's, so come home if you want a fresh Danish or hot bread and rolls." "The parade must have been better than ever," his mother, standing in front of their building, said a few times when he came right home after. "The excitement of the people walking down the block from it, and all the children look so happy." Sometimes he saw his brother and sister at the parade with their friends. Then his brother stopped going to it and would sleep that day till noon. "The parade's become so boring and repetitious," his brother said. "With one new balloon a year and that one looking suspiciously like the one it replaced from the previous year except for a different nose and maybe the addition of a tail. I've also got fed up with the endless intervals between floats and things, so being forced to look at and smell the manure in the street from the police and cowboy horses that passed." His sister began going downtown to see the parade, either at Times Square or in front of Macy's. "How can you see anything there and enjoy it?" he said. "It's got to be so crowded." And to his brother: "How can you not go to it? It's the best thing about living where we do, halfway down the block from the best parade in the country and only two blocks away from where they blow up the balloons? People come in from other cities to see it, I hear." The last Thanksgiving turkey dinner his mother made was when he and his family were living in New York for the year. "It doesn't make any sense to prepare such an elaborate meal anymore if it's only going to be for my sister and me," she said. "Just two people, carving and eating a turkey alone, no matter how small a one, and those birds can only be so small, is depressing." He tried getting her to take the train to his city for the Thanksgiving holiday after that. She said "Why, would the trip down there be any easier than if you made the trip up by car? Both ways, it's the biggest holiday traveling time of the year, the newspaper said, so you're smart for staying put. I plan to broil your aunt and me a thick veal chop for dinner; we won't be the only ones not eating turkey that night." At the last turkey dinner at her apartment, with just his family and aunt, she said "I think I got too big a bird and made twice as much stuffing and creamed onions as we needed. Though remember when we used to have a dozen or more people over for Thanksgiving and I'd put a twenty-two or twenty-three pound turkey on the table? Al, the head butcher at the old Gristede's down the block, used to say I ordered one of the biggest turkeys out of all his customers." He said "Once even a twenty-five pounder, I remember. I was so proud of the weight that I boasted about it to my friends." "How big is twenty-five?" his daughter asked and he said "Just a little lighter than you, I think." "No," his wife said. "She weighs thirty-one pounds." "So, she's too big to fit in the oven then." His daughter started crying. "That wasn't a smart thing to say," his wife said. "It wasn't smart or clever, you're right. I'm sorry, dear," he said to his daughter. "Daddy's very sorry," and tried to stroke her cheek but she moved away from his hand. "Two of your cousins visited today," his mother said. "They were in the city, came to the neighborhood especially to see the parade, and dropped by for coffee and a chat." "That must have been nice. Did you see the parade?" "How could I?" she said. "I was cooking all this." "You could have taken a break for an hour. But really, I should have stopped in beforehand and we could have gone to it together. I should have called last night, in fact— sometime, yesterday—to tell you I'd be picking you up. But then you probably wouldn't have gone to it anyway, even if you had consented yesterday." "Yes I would have," she said. "I've always wanted to see it from the parade route. And when I finally had the chance after you kids were out of the house and my turkey dinners and responsibilities got much smaller, it was always one thing or another that prevented me, and I also didn't feel very comfortable going to it alone. Your father would have gone with me—he loved that parade. But by then he was too sick to, which was a new responsibility but not one I couldn't be an hour away from, so we watched it on TV." "I'm sorry then; I should have called. Next time we're in town for the holiday, whenever that'll be, you'll go with us. Maybe by then we'll have a sec-

I.

ond child, one small enough…but I won't say it." After that he called her a few days before each Thanksgiving and asked if she was going to the parade; she usually said "Maybe this year I might." And then he called on Thanksgiving Day and asked if she had gone to the parade, and her answer was always no.

DETOURS

I'M SITTING HERE with my shirt off, typing on my typewriter, wondering if I should write this in first person, a
form I haven't used in a while and don't like much. It's cold
in the room—it snowed late last night and this morning,
apartment doesn't get enough heat and the wind comes in
off the river through the windows and I haven't insulated
them yet with masking tape on the seams and newspapers
and rags stuffed into the cracks between the windows and
window frames. My shirt's off because I came back from a
jog about ten minutes ago and the shirt was wet with sweat.
But I don't want to get up and get a shirt in the other room
because by the time I sit down again I could lose my train
of thought. I was just passing through this room—the
kitchen, which faces the river—well, all the rooms do—and
not passing through. I came in here to tear off a piece of
bagel from out of the bag the bagels are in and stick it in
my mouth and then take a shower, and saw the typewriter
table by the window and thought—and the typewriter on
top of it, of course, and I never did get to the bagel bag—
I'd give it a shot and if nothing came of it after a few min-

utes, or more than a few but until I gave up on it or I got too cold—and if it was just the cold I'd quickly get a shirt from the next room and run back here and resume typing and I doubt in that short time I'd lose my train of thought—at least I'd tried. The first person's okay, I suppose, or feels more natural for me than it has in years, but I should still—because I'm more comfortable and seem to have greater freedom with it—do this in third. So he's sitting here typing with no shirt on and wondering about the way he acted last night and if it'd be good material to write about. It's certainly been on his mind since it happened— he's talking about his behavior—where he even had trouble sleeping because of it. Third's not turning out as well as he thought it would—feels a bit stiff—but maybe because of the sudden shift from first, so he needs a little more time with it. The trip in—they have two residences he probably should explain: a house they own in Baltimore and a rented apartment on the Upper West Side of Manhattan that they sublet as often as their landlord permits them so they can afford to keep it for their three to four weeks and several weekends a year in New York and in case their older daughter goes to college here in a year and a half, which she's talked about doing, and wants to live in it—was full of tie-ups and long waits at the numerous toll plazas and lots of slow traffic and one major detour, but he was good about it. Meaning, he dealt with it much better than he usually did. No snarling and cursing under his breath and blaming this and that, like the toll plazas for not letting the cars through free during this holiday period so there wouldn't be five-mile backups and his wife and kids for taking so much time getting ready that they set off later than he'd planned and he had to drive half the trip in the dark. Even made jokes about the long trip and recurrent delays while he drove (he forgets some of the things he said but he knows they laughed at his remarks several times. Oh. One was "Anybody see me getting upset by all this? No. Though don't count on it being a sign that I'm a changed man"). And when the detour from the Jersey Turnpike (he'd learned from its driver's advisory radio band that all the exits heading east between 13 and 18 were closed and at a rest area, where he went to look at the big wall map it had and decided on an alternate route, that there'd been a car chase and shooting and accident involving a truck and several police cars) took them through Staten Island and over the Verrazano Bridge to Brooklyn and then the Battery Tunnel to Manhattan, he didn't gripe once. Said things like "Bridge looks pretty, lit up like that, doesn't it?" when it first came in to view, and "Look to your right, that Waldbaum's supermarket; it's as big as a jumbo jet airport hangar," and pointed out streets in Staten Island and Brooklyn where it seemed most of the rowhouses on them were gaudily decorated with hundreds of Christmas lights...anyway, it was a successful trip for him personally, he could say. But when he was home for a while—after he'd unloaded the car with the kids, got his wife and the cats and all their stuff upstairs, told the kids how helpful they'd been just now and good they were during what he knows was a long arduous trip and asked everyone what they wanted at the Mideastern takeout place and put the car in the garage and got the food and had a drink and they'd eaten—he blew his stack. Doesn't know where it came from. Said things he of course never should have. Just exploded. One moment he was calmly slipping a pillowcase on a pillow and the next he was saying "Goddamnit, is there no end to this freaking labor? I'm fed up with it. When's it going to stop? I don't have the frigging energy for it anymore; I just want to rest." Screamed, cursed, banged a table with his fist, threw the pillow against the wall above the double bed he was making, said "Tell me—you're all looking at me as if I'm crazy and way off base—but tell me why we had to leave the day before Christmas eve. Why do I always give in to every demand each of you makes? We could have left yesterday. The car could have been packed and ready to go when the kids got home from school, and we wouldn't have faced anything near to what we did today. But no, they had to spend the last day at school with their friends because they wouldn't be seeing them for ten days. And you," he said to his wife, "agreed with them that it was fair what they were asking, even though we both knew today was a wasted school day because nothing would be taught. So of course the highways are going to be jammed. Of course everyone and his uncle's on the road going to God knows where on what's got to be the second heaviest traveling day of the year. Of course some nutty trucker's frustrated by the traffic too and rams some cars and gets chased by the cops, which they probably did on the shoulders, and shot up by them which causes havoc on the Turnpike for about fifty miles. And of course Manhattan's crowded with last-minute shoppers on every block and there are major tie-ups and backups and no letup in traffic all the way from Baltimore to New York." His wife told him to calm down, get control of himself, and the kids said "Please, Daddy, do what Mommy says," and he said "Calm down, sure, and get control," and picked up a couch pillow and threw it at the same wall and it bounced off it and knocked over a table lamp. Both the shade and glass stem of the lamp, or whatever the part's called that's between the base and the bulb, broke. This made him even angrier. Maybe first person was better off after all. Try it again. "Always something else," I screamed, and thought why's all this, when I'm so tired— and maybe that was why I blew up, or it contributed to it— got to happen to me? "And the lamp was my mother's. She had it for sixty to seventy years. The shade I can see it breaking—it got brittle. But the stem part, or whatever it's called, survived all the balls my brother and sister and I threw around the house and everything else in that time, and here I break it after not even two years," and got on my knees and started picking up the glass and pieces of shade. "Sweep it up, don't touch it with your hands," my wife said, and I said "I just want to get the damn thing over with," and cut myself. No, I don't like the way most of that came out. The I and my and me. Stick with third. "I can't believe it, now this," he said, and went into the bathroom and washed the cut and looked for the box of Band-Aids. "Where are the Band-Aids?" he yelled from the bathroom. "I know we had a box of them last time we were here." He came out with his handkerchief wrapped around the cut and said "You kids use them all up?" They said they hadn't touched the Band-Aids, except for maybe one or two of them, and why did he always have to yell and blame them for everything? He was nice before but they knew it wouldn't last. "Not so," he said, but didn't know what he meant and turned away. His wife said to him later when the kids were reading and listening to music in their room "You're lucky they're not frightened of you, the way you rage." "What are you talking about?" he said, though he knew. He was just too ashamed to discuss it, and went into the kitchen to make himself another drink. One of the ice cubes he was taking out of the ice tray fell to the floor and he said to himself "Don't let this get to you, just pick it up," and he did. He was sitting in the kitchen with his drink, looking at the lights across the river while listening to the Mass in B or St. Matthew Passion on the all-Bach festival on the radio, when he heard his older daughter say goodnight to his wife in the living room. A few minutes later the younger one said goodnight to her too and came to the kitchen door and said to him "I suppose you won't want to read to me tonight." He read to her every night. "Sure," he said, "now?" and she said "If it's all right," and he went into her room, sat on the radiator cover at the foot of her bed, kept the floor lamp very close to him so the light wouldn't disturb his older child, who was in bed staring at the wall of books across the room, and read softly from *Kristin Lavransdatter*, the novel he'd been reading to her the last month. He wanted to stop a couple of times and tell them he was sorry for the way he behaved before, but didn't have the heart to. The heart? Whatever he didn't have. Anyway, it was too soon to apologize to his oldest daughter. She'd probably continue to look away from him, or keep her eyes closed if she was facing him, and act as if she hadn't heard a word he said. When he came to the end of the episode he was reading he looked up and it seemed both girls were asleep. He said the younger one's name. Her eyes stayed closed. He'd have to go back a few pages tomorrow night to the point where she dozed off. He shut the light and kissed her. He felt he'd been slightly forgiven by her when she asked him to read. Or maybe she only wanted him to read to help her get to sleep, and part of the problem of her getting to sleep might have been his yelling at her. She'd said lots of times "I can't sleep for a long time if you haven't read to me." Then he helped get his wife into bed and positioned comfortably. "Can we talk about what went on before?" she said. "And more than just frightening the kids, though that alone's worth a good talk," and he said "Please, not now, I couldn't. I know what I did though, so don't worry about it." "You're the one who should by worrying about it," and he said "I know, don't rub it in." "It's not that; I'd never rub it in," and he said "I know that too. Just another senseless thing I'm saying, forgive me, but let's drop it please, at least for now?" "Fine," and she turned over and went to sleep. He read in bed, *The Magic Mountain*, only five pages but long dense ones, a new translation, couldn't get through the old one, too English or artificial or something, couldn't read any further tonight this one, too many things on his mind. He was disgusted with himself. Everything was wrong, felt wrong, he felt terrible about what he did, which is how he always feels after he acts that way. He doesn't know what to do about it but he has to do something because he blows up like this about once every two weeks. He should probably go into therapy, his wife would love that, but he doesn't want to because he doesn't like therapy for himself. Then at least speak to a therapist about it once or twice, his wife's, because wouldn't that be better than repeating the way he acted? Sure, but if he could stop it on his own it'd even be better. He should try. He has. But try much harder. Because he failed a few times it doesn't mean he can't succeed. In other words, it's not impossible. Tomorrow you can start acting differently, focus on what you're doing more and catch yourself before you pop off. For instance, what did it today? Could have been a whole bunch of things that built up to the explosion. Getting the house set for their almost two weeks away from it and the family set for New York and all the anxieties that go with it in getting off on time. Packing for his wife, loading the car, cleaning the house, because he likes to come back to one that's tidy and clean, doing three loads of wash and folding all the clothes and putting them away because the kids weren't around to help him, assisting his wife with a number of things, and the light timers and more. Tried to write for an hour and nothing came out, or something did but nothing good, so that could have been part of the buildup too. Also had to pick up the older girl at school and bring her home, then the younger one at her school, and before that you had to critique several student manuscripts and papers and go to school and leave them by your door for the students before they went on vacation, and write several recommendations and photocopy them and fill out the forms, most of which you could have done the day before, all the time looking at the clock or your watch, wondering if you had time. Then you had to take care of the car, get the handbrake fixed and the car filled with gas, which wasn't anything. Then got the

kids. That was the chronology. Home, school, cars, kids.
And they had to do this and that before they could leave,
which got you angry but you held it in and didn't even give
it away with your face how you felt, just kept saying things
like "Please, girls, we're running late, so let's get a move on.
Mom, me, and the cats are ready, and I want to drive in the
daylight for as long as I can because driving at night and all
those headlights strain my eyes." And you did so well in the
car: joked, laughed, made fun of your anger on previous
trips, said "Look at me now; not bad, right?" and stayed that
way the entire drive. Everything went well, in fact, except
the traffic. Forty miles from New York, about twenty miles
farther away than you expected, you picked up the
Columbia University radio station playing all-Bach twenty-
four hours a day for the next ten days. "There it is, I can't
believe it, and almost what I come in most for during the
Christmas holiday. I have to send them a contribution,
something I know I say every year around this time but
always forget to, so when I get home someone remind me,"
and held your wife's hand a little while you drove, massaged
her neck a little too and she smiled warmly at you and said
"Um, that's nice, feels so good," and you thought tonight
you'll make love while the kids are asleep in their bedroom,
but first you'll have to fix the couch up as a bed and
rearrange some of the furniture; the sub lessees, who'd
moved out today for twelve days—part of the sublease
deal—had probably changed the place around and forgot
where everything originally belonged. Around then, or
actually ten to twenty miles before, you saw the turnpike
advisory sign flashing and tuned in to the 1610 AM signal

and a man's voice—you could barely make out what he was saying, there was so much static and crackling and music overlapping from another station, so had to listen to the message several times—warned of a big tie-up ahead. Police have blocked off all turnpike routes going east between exits 13 and 18, and so on. Delays up to two hours in some places. Motorists—or did he say "travelers"?—are advised to seek alternate routes. You found one, after looking at the map and speaking to several truckers in the next service area, but it was bumper to bumper on it till you crossed the bridge into Brooklyn, and you got home more than two hours later than you thought you would when you started out. But you never complained once, didn't even feel like complaining. You were enjoying your continuing good mood through all these setbacks. Garage you usually parked in was half-empty—you were a little worried there would-n't be a space for you. Falafel place was still open—you were afraid it'd close at ten. When you were carrying the takeout food home you told yourself "Damn, you really did it; I'm so freaking proud of you. Didn't rant, gripe, act sullen or bitch under your breath once, and for the rest of the night, now that you're out of the car, it can only get better. Just look how your mood affects everyone else's. May this be the start of a major change in your disposition and your behav-ior to your family. Control's the word. Though calmness, patience and resignation first—take it as it comes, don't jump the gun—and then control if things really start going against you." An hour later, you blew up. Could it have been that you were tired by then? Were you tired at all? Certainly a little, and your eyes hurt, though fatigue usually makes you more placid and agreeable. And this morning, while everyone slept and after a night where you slept badly, you felt miserable about yourself, and still do. You wonder how any of them could ever forgive you. Not "ever," but for the next few days. You were uncontrollable, bordering on the insane. And to act like that the night before Christmas eve, no less, when the kids—you forgot this—traditionally put a few of the wrapped presents on the drop table in the living room and tape their old Christmas stockings to the folded-down leaf and decorate the top of the table with ornaments and tiny Santas and a foot-high plastic Christmas tree they take out of the shoe bag on the linen closet door, where all these things have been stored the past year. Could it have been that you were upset by the deteriorating condition of your wife, who was quite tired and weak by then—though she slept most of the trip—and looked it? No, there's no excuse for what you did, and don't try to find one for it. So that's that and now you sit, writing this, shirt off, suddenly feeling a bit chilled, you'll have to get a shirt and some socks on soon, looking outside, snowed overnight, Riverside Park looks so beautiful covered with it, people walking their dogs, someone in the street on skis, a father—or you assume he's the father—pulling his kid on a sled, you envy him, he for sure didn't have the night you did and his family doesn't feel toward him now the way yours must to you, or will when they awake. But what's the purpose of this thing you're writing and hurrying to finish? No other purpose but to get it out and down on paper and to think about what you're writing and to read it after it's written and in future days for it to remind you of what you did yesterday and how you felt about it today and also for you to perhaps get something from what you did last night that might end up being more than just a reminder of how you acted and felt, even if right now you don't think it's much, if anything at all.

CITY

THERE WAS A girl in college he once kissed on campus. He can only draw her up, doesn't remember her name. Doesn't think he ever saw her other than on campus. Maybe at a luncheonette nearby, but that's all. A subway school, a city campus. Went up there by subway, went home or to work after school by subway. Or when he was in evening school, which he attended for three of his five college years (and nobody there seemed to call it "night school"), to school after work. It was usually dark when he got out of the subway station closest to school after work. Then he had to climb up a fairly steep hill to campus. He could have avoided the hill by switching subway lines at the Columbus Circle station, but that usually took fifteen more minutes to get to school, even with the easier walk. He was usually tired in his evening school classes. He cheated on a test a number of times then because some evenings, after he got home from school, he was too tired to study. There was a guy who had the same class before his. A survey course in American literature; he knew the guy from the previous summer when they worked as waiters in a Catskills resort

113

hotel. The teacher gave the same test to both classes. And this guy, in the ten-minute break between the two classes, would tell him the questions he remembered, and if he knew the answers to them, then the answers. But the girl he kissed. Not a girl. Around nineteen, twenty. He walked her from the main campus building where the cafeteria and student union were to the building her class was in. It was night, so he had to be in evening school then, as she was, and at the door of the building he walked her to, right in front of it, they continued to talk, hold hands and then kissed. More than once that time, he doesn't remember. She lived in Brooklyn, an hour away from school by subway and bus. Sometimes more than that if she had to wait a long time for the bus, which happened often, she said. So he never dated her. The trip out to her place just seemed too long. Only saw her on campus and at the nearby coffee shop and, he now thinks, at a very cheap luncheonette-style Indian restaurant once a few blocks from school. "Oh no," he remembers her saying when she told him how long it takes her to get home from school, or something like this, "I bet that's going to make you think twice about coming to Brooklyn to see me one day." He forgets what he said but it was probably something like "I don't think so; why would it?" Then one night he was supposed to meet her at the school cafeteria for dinner and she didn't show. He missed the first ten minutes or so of his class waiting for her, then ran to it. He called her from home after. She said she quit college the previous day, was looking for a better job than the one she had, one with more of a future in it for her, and that she wouldn't be seeing him again, and he said "You mean at school," and she said "No, ever, unless we accidentally bump into each other. You see, I've been dissatisfied the way things have been going for me and I want to completely change the direction of my life. Besides, you didn't want to travel all the way up to the Bronx," he now remembers she lived in, somewhere past Pelham Parkway, "so what could I have meant to you?" "I'll go there," he said, "now that I can't see you in school. Tell me when. This weekend?—fine. I'll take a book with me for the train. Two books, even, if the trip's as long as you say." "Oh thanks," she said, "you certainly know how to make a girl feel wanted," and hung up. He called her a few days later and she said to do himself a favor and not call again. They only knew each other a few weeks. When she was twelve or thirteen she was an actress and even had one of the leads in a Broadway revival of *The Children's Hour*. "I played the snitch, if you can believe it." But she grew to hate working on the stage. "Going out for roles, then the sometimes ignorant but always self-centered and invariably wrong-headed people you have to work with when you do get a role. And how many years can I do it before I'm too old for this part, not quite right for that one, longer and longer hiatuses between plays. And then what will I end up with: a secretarial job at best. Or maybe a part-time acting coach, which is why I'm at City: to study for a more practical profession, one that pays well and there's always a demand for," though she had to work thirty to forty tedious hours a week as a dental receptionist, she said, while she was studying, since her folks were not only sick but poor. He forgets what she was taking at school and what profession she was aiming for.

Graduate school after she gets her B.A., he remembers. Apparently, all that changed. Or maybe it didn't and she went back to City after he graduated, or to another city college. He forgets how their met. He doesn't forget what she looked like; that's easy to recall. He pictures himself standing opposite her in front of that school building where they kissed: she was relatively short, maybe five-three. Cute as hell, even beautiful, with long dark hair, heart-shaped face, dark eyes, full lips, small nose, thick eyebrows that joined above the bridge of her nose and which she was told that if she wanted a career in theater she'd have to pluck an inch gap in the middle, a pleasant intelligent voice. The voice of someone who had taken speech lessons to improve her diction and get rid of any accent. No fake voice though. At the time he thought it might be nice if she became his girlfriend. But it seemed like she didn't want to be rushed, so he told himself to go slow: lots of talk, little holding of hands, every now and then a soft kiss, and then finally a date off campus on a day they didn't have classes, and if possible where they'd meet in midtown and maybe where she could stay overnight in a friend's apartment in Manhattan, if she knew anyone there. Deep down, she said, she was a conservative prudent girl when it came to relationships, though she had had a couple of stage flings. That meant she'd slept with a few men already, though she never said so, and he wanted to eventually sleep with her too, but knew that'd take awhile. Now he remembers how they first met. She was sitting at a table in the school cafeteria, reading a book, but a serious novel, not a textbook, a big long one that she was almost done with, judging by the page she was on. Dickens, he recalls; *Our Mutual Friend*, or was it *Bleak House?* He remembers that she started one of those right after she finished the other. He was a reader too, but not of Dickens, or not since high school and only the ones he was required to read for English, and he liked girls who read. If a girl didn't read—if she couldn't talk about books with him—he didn't see her, at least after the first date, even if it seemed she'd be willing to put out. He immediately thought she was pretty. She seemed kind of short though—he was six feet and usually felt uncomfortable if a girl he was walking with and had a romantic interest in was much shorter than he—but when he finally saw her on her feet—he thinks it was the next time he was with her—she turned out to be not as short as he'd thought. Seen her a few times before, so he could have had that "short" thought then—always sitting alone at the same out-of-the-way table and reading a book while eating a real dinner and drinking tea. Knew it was tea because the string of the teabag hung over the rim of the cup or was wrapped around the spoon on the saucer. He does; he remembers all this. He wanted, those times before, to sit down at her table, but never had the courage. This time he told himself to stop wanting to sit down and just do it before some other guy comes, sits at her table, gives her a line, they start talking, she likes him, they start meeting every time here, and that finishes it for you. So he sat. But before he did he stood at her table holding his tray and said "Is this...excuse me, but is this seat taken?" She looked up, smiled, said no, looked back at her book, he sat down, took the soup and roll off the tray—those two were just about what he always got in this cafeteria, plus a glass of water.

They were the cheapest filling things to eat, and the food at the steam table, though not expensive, wasn't very good, and it was too late to get a sandwich made and the ones premade and wrapped in wax paper or Saran Wrap were usually on white bread, which he didn't like, and somewhat soggy. He sat there a minute eating his food and drinking the water. Then he took out a novel he always carried with him—it was probably by Turgenev or Dostoevsky because for his first two years of college, and he thinks this incident happened in his second year, he almost only read Turgenev and Dostoevsky when he read a novel—and read while he finished his soup and roll and probably the crackers that came with the soup. Looked up a few times and she was deeply absorbed in her book while eating her dinner and drinking tea. Then he thought "Do it. You probably won't have another chance because next time you ask if the seat's taken or you just sit down without asking, she'll know what you're up to and might mind it. And if she wants to speak to you she will, and if she doesn't she'll let you know someway," so he said "Excuse me, but that book you're reading..." not knowing what he was going to say next about the book but hoping she'd start talking about it, and she said "Yes?" and stared at him and he said "What kind is it? It must be very good, if just by the intense way you're reading it." "It's just a novel," and held it up for him. "Not one of his best, but I'm a habitual reader, and I finish everything I start if I get beyond the first thirty pages. If you detect intensity it's mainly because I want to race through it so I can begin something else of his," and he said "I never finish books I don't like, unless they're for school," and that's how the conversation started. There are lots of things he should have done in his life that out of laziness or fear or over caution or timidity, he didn't. One was this: he should have asked her out for a date and then gone to the Bronx to have that date. Showed up at her door, met her folks, gone with her someplace, brought her back to her door and kissed her goodnight, or whatever they would have done by her door or inside her apartment if she had invited him in, and then gone home by bus and train. She was really very sweet and bright and interested in things intellectual, and she had had an adventurous life so far, and to him an attractive one, since he liked it that she had worked in theater, and she was around his age and they would have made a good pair. She kissed well too. And he liked her soft looks, and the way she was built: slim and shapely, with nice legs. She must have had a fairly strong body and was maybe even muscular in places, which he liked, since she said she'd studied dance seriously for many years as a kid and still took a modern dance class once a week, and from a former boyfriend she had learned judo and how to box. So he should have dated her—he's saying, not just once to the Bronx but many times. But at the time all he saw in his head was the long subway trip—it really had nothing much to do with his playing it slow with her because he thought that's what she wanted—and then the bus ride from the subway station to her neighborhood and the three to four block walk from the bus stop. Although on nice days, she said, but only during the daytime, she liked to walk from the subway station to her home, which took about twenty minutes if she kept up a brisk pace. And then what would they have done in that part of the Bronx, which was mostly six- to seven-story apartment buildings—block after monotonous block of them, was how she described it. So they would have had to go to a livelier part of the Bronx, by bus and maybe even also by subway, and then he would have had to take her home and then return to his own home in Manhattan, which by that time, because of the reduced service late at night, would probably be an hour and a half trip if not more. It's possible she knew someone from her acting days who had an apartment in Manhattan she could have stayed at after one of their dates, or a friend from school or work who lived there and could have put her up, though she once told him he was just about the first person at City she'd said more than boo to since she started going there that year. But their relationship, or whatever it should be called, never got that far for them to talk about her staying overnight somewhere in Manhattan, though it was something he probably should have considered then if he wanted to go out with her. Anyway, he regrets he didn't pursue things with her, because for a short while—maybe a month, maybe more—they got along well and seemed to be attracted to each other and neither of them was seeing anyone else at the time. As for romance between them, there was only some holding of hands and maybe some hugging and a few nice words, and that kiss. He remembers not only where it happened but exactly what the front of the building looked like. That building, with its rough-hewed black or dark gray stones and white mortar, in the neo-Gothic style, if he's not mistaken, is still there. At least it was up until ten years ago when he visited the college to speak to a friend's class and told the friend, who had to meet him at the security booth at the main entrance to the campus or else he wouldn't have been allowed in, "There's the building"—when they passed it—"where I once kissed a very lovely young woman when I was a student here in evening school, and it doesn't seem to have changed at all in more than thirty years." He assumes it was fall when they kissed, probably after Daylight Savings Time had ended, since it was dark out and they were wearing coats or heavy jackets, though it wasn't that cold yet, just chilly, if he remembers. And also fall because she had only attended school for a couple of months before she dropped out and she had no doubt started at the beginning of the academic year. And because it was dark and they had just walked from the cafeteria where she had probably had dinner and he had had his soup and roll, it was around seven or eight o'clock, which was when most of the evening classes started. After they kissed he remembers they held hands awhile and he thinks they looked at each other without saying anything or smiling, and then she said she had to go to class now and he probably said he'll see her or he'll call her, and she went into the building and he went to his own class thinking that was good that kiss; this little thing with her is turning into something.

AUTHOR

HEADLINE ON THE *Times*' obituary page says "Joshua Fels, 76, modernist author of abstruse, labyrinthine novels, is dead." The obit covers three-quarters of the page and includes a critique of his work by the paper's cultural affairs editor, a list of his novels and years they were published, and excerpts from some of them. A large photo of him—slim build and chiseled, craggy face—sitting at his writing desk in a polka-dot tie and what looks like a tailored suit, holding a lit cigarette and facing the camera but looking away. The caption gives the year of the photo, "when his literary reputation took a sharp rise." That was the year his third novel came out and won both major fiction prizes, but can't be the year the photo was taken. His hair's dark and full and he looks no more than forty, while when I. met him that same year his hair was gray, not as full, and he looked his age: 52. Critics, literary scholars and well-known serious fiction writers are quoted. He's called immensely inventive and virtuosic, a novelist of vast range, complexity, erudition and wit, with a masterful use of language and an audacious, original style. Arguably, the greatest American writer since

Faulkner, one critic says. Maybe since Melville, another says, "and it's conceivable partly because of the difficulty of his work though mostly because of his brilliance, that he'll become one of the most influential novelists we've ever had." Fels lived in London and Martha's Vineyard the last ten years, the obit says, and is survived by his fourth wife, three children from his three previous marriages, several grandchildren, and a sister in Buffalo, NY. His first novel, "which weighed in at a dense 893 pages of only seventeen paragraphs and no chapters," was universally panned, except in England, but quickly developed a cult following. Despite this underground success and the many printings of his book that resulted from it, he didn't publish another novel for twelve years. All his books are now in print and have become contemporary classics. He recently completed an interconnected story collection, his editor says, which is longer than anything he's written and is the most innovative and demanding work he's done, and it'll be published at the end of the year.

I. met Fels more than twenty years ago. He was going with a high-school teacher in a small town on the Hudson about twenty miles from New York, and she invited him to a party there on one of the weekends he was staying with her. He was introduced to the host, who asked what he did. "Well that's a piece of luck for the party giver," the host said. "Josh Fels is coming. Lives down the hill, and as far as I know you'll be the one other person here who tinkers on a typewriter that way and knows something about literary publishing. I should remember to introduce you, or maybe you know him." I.'s girlfriend asked how come she didn't know Fels lived in town, and the host said "Probably because he's sworn all his friends and the local real-estate agents to secrecy, so, shh, don't breathe it to anyone beyond these walls or we might lose him. I assume he doesn't want fledgling writers pecking on his door with manuscripts, and other unwanted encounters that hotshots like him must face. Even in the one interview he's given, when the question of his residence came up he said 'Just say a village along one of New York's main fluvial arteries where none of the streets are named, everyone has an unlisted phone number, no one comes to his front door if he's not expecting anyone, and a couple of residents have illegal guns.' I was surprised myself when he accepted my invitation. I think he only did because his wife's been out of town for two weeks, he's deep into the beginning of a new novel, and he wanted a short break from his solitude." "Getting back to what you asked me," I. said. "I'm of course familiar with his work, though I don't even know what he looks like, since he's never had an author's photo of one of his books. (He checks the obit photo credit; "Judith Fels," maybe one of his wives, or even a daughter or his mother, but not his sister, since the obit gave her name as Phoebe. But how'd the newspaper get it? Anyway:) "I'm sure he does that so he won't be recognized by complete strangers," the host said. "It hasn't reached the point where fans are tearing his clothes off for souvenirs when they learn who he is, but just by his having alluded that to me, I bet it's come close to it." "Yeah, maybe that's the reason," I. said. "Why, what else could it be, other than a strong dislike to being photographed?" "Who can say if this no-photo and -show and rare-interview business isn't just another way of drawing attention to your books. Not a unique stance today but one that's come to be respected for serious writers and much written about. But what do I know? Although I'm no fledging—I've been flapping my writing wings hummingbirdlike for more than fifteen years—I've never had a book published. But since my first book, if and when I do get one out, will have an author's photo on it, I'll never again be able to hide entirely from the public. At least not for the next ten years after that, unless I lose all my hair because the reviews are so bad or my face is disfigured beyond repair for some reason—let me think of one: distracted by a part of a new story I'm going over in my head, I walk into an electric fan." "Funny. Now, if you don't mind, tell me what you think of Fels' work. Sure, we all know he's celebrated and revered for his novels—I don't know if I pronounced that right: ear, ev—but I'm interested in what another experienced writer has to say about them. And be frank now; I won't be telling him one way or the other what you say. Not because I won't value it but because I know that what people think of his fiction—critics, book reviewers and scholars especially—is the last thing he wants to read or hear." "His work? It's good, of course; it's really good." "That's it? One word sums up thirty years of work? Which books particularly do you or don't you like, and then what parts of those books particularly? Form, structure, style—isn't that what writers talk about when they're not talking about publishers, agents, advances? Not Fels, with that last unnecessary crack, and probably not you either, but do you like his style, for instance? Does he as a writer move you, bore or excite you, do other things like that to you?" "I've read all his books. There aren't many in number but there are a lot of pages. Though I admit that some parts of his stuff I quickly flipped through, but I do that with lots of writing and especially long books. But his work, summing it all up, is very intelligent and his style is interesting at times, and his dialog's tops. As for the form and structure, I don't know; they seem to work. 'Architecture.' I'm sure his is good also, but I really don't know what the word means when it's used about a work of literature. Look, I'm not good with the language of criticism. Critical language. Whatever they call it. I'm a meat and potatoes reader, you can say, when it comes to fiction. I just know that if a work hits me, I keep reading it, and if it excites me, of course I feel it, and if it overwhelms me—meaning, it's so powerful and original and readable that there's almost nothing I want to do but read it, which doesn't happen often—well, the reaction is obvious: I'm overwhelmed and I read it every chance I get and never flip through or skip, no matter how long the work is. That's not how I feel about any of Fels' work, though. His is good, maybe very good; he's probably an important writer." "But not a great or an excellent writer, you're saying, the way some distinguished critics and all those honors and awards have built him up and portrayed him?" "Excellent, great, very good, good; he's close to all of those at different times, maybe. Excellent in some ways and just very good to good in others, but never less than good, which is saying a lot. Or maybe a few passages and a page here and there are a little less than good, but you could say that about any writer, I suppose: Ovid, Shakespeare, Joyce, Proust, Dickens for sure—all those contrivances and coincidences in his work and the occasional inflated language, even if they were the accepted conventions then. As for Proust, I actually haven't read enough of him, or let's just say not all that much of him, or maybe even I'm saying I've read all I want to of him, at least for the time being, for I find him fluffy and fussy and a bit boring. 'Spun sugar' I call some of it, which comes from a line in one of the first three *Remembrance* novels, I think—no, it'd have to, since that's all I've read of his, and only half of the third. But that lack of appreciation, or you could call it understanding—the lack of—could come from my own limitations, and he really is great, as Fels might be, though right now, from what I've read, not to me." "You mean both of them?" the host said. "Really, what writer can be called great except Shakespeare and Keats and Virgil and Tolstoy and I guess you gotta throw Joyce in there, and a couple of others?" "Plenty more, I'd think, but I get what you mean. Have a good time, and speak to you later. Hey, where'd your pretty gal go?" I.'s girlfriend had long ago left them to speak to some other people and get a drink, and also, he was sure, to get away from his babbling about literary matters. "Just because you write fiction doesn't mean you know literature," she once said. "You rely on gut feeling too much and come out sounding uninformed, if not lowbrow and bitterly envious." He'd forgotten also that she'd done her master's thesis on Dickens' readings in New York and loved that writer's work, every contrivance and line. He said what he did about Fels because he wasn't going to say nothing or what he really thought of the work. Forget even the possibility of greatness regarding Fels or some lack of his own understanding, was what he thought then and still believes. No writer's great if you have to have postgraduate degrees in seven different disciplines to understand most of his work. Besides, saying what he really thought would have been impolite and made for a somewhat uncomfortable evening after and no intro to the author, probably, and he wanted to meet him if it came about without him pushing himself on Fels or urging the host to introduce them. Just to see what he was like and particularly how a writer handled such fame, but not to get in good with him for any self-serving purpose. Fels wouldn't like his work, even if he did, for some reason, get to read it. In fact, even if Fels, if they had gotten to speak, had asked to see some of his work, he would have begged off, saying something like "Really, I want to spare you, and I also know how busy you must be with your own writing and all the things that go along with it, but thanks." If Fels had insisted, saying something like "Come on, I like reading unpublished manuscripts of younger writers," and he wouldn't have said this, but also "As an established writer who's had his share of good breaks, I almost feel duty-bound to from time to time," and then "and it's possible I can do something for you with my book editor and agent, providing I like it, of course," he would have said all right, and taken down his address, but he doesn't think he would have sent him anything; their work was just too different. (Kafka, he thought right after the host left him, he should have mentioned him and probably even Chekhov and Gogol and, though this would have sounded silly and naive, Homer, whoever he was, as other great writers.) Fels' fiction—and I.'s opinion on this deepened over the years—was extremely erudite, witty, well-crafted and tricky, etcetera—fiction of the fifties, I. called it, even when it was written in the nineties—and he did his research, that's for sure; probably spent a year or two per book just on that—while I.'s research consisted mostly of making sure the streets and dates and such were right, if he was writing about a real city and time, and to call a thing by the right word or term, such as "athletic bag" for the bag you carry your gym equipment in (he'd called a sports store to make sure, or are they called sporting or sports good stores or athletic shops? For that one, if he wanted to use it in his fiction, he'd go to the category section of the yellow pages). And despite all the modernist moves or fixtures or whatever they're called, in Fels' fiction, such as self-reflexiveness and periodic lists and longueurs, a word that'd be in Fels' work but not I.'s, he was a bit old-fashioned as a writer, with long introductions to scenes and plenty of atmosphere and description and explaining and the plot going from A to B to C and so on, though I. still had a tough time staying with it because of the density of the prose and lengthy sentences and enormous paragraphs and unconventional punctuation and devices like quotation marks within quotation marks within quotation marks and sometimes seven- or eight-person dialogs with no attribution for each line of dialog most times and everyone sounding alike. He was also a humorous writer but not in a way I. liked. That smart-alecky almost upper-crust English tongue-in-cheek cheeky humor, and he also seemed like a misanthrope in his fiction, with just about no character likable or sympathetic in any way. (Come to think of it, not Dante, Cervantes and Rabelais on his "great" list either, since he found them to be imaginative cold fish with flashes of compassion and, for the last two, humor that he thought mostly cartoonish and slight.) Oh, he's not explaining himself well. (And what about Montaigne and Sophocles and most of Yeats and Camus and lots of Conrad, Coleridge, Dostoevsky, Swift, Blake and Defoe?) Or to put it more plainly (and enough with this idiotic list, particularly when he quickly wants to sack Swift and say "lots" instead of "most" of Yeats and "almost all" of Blake, and he forgot somewhere in there to put in Bernhard, Beckett, Eliot and Wordsworth), or just in a different way: Fels' first novel was two to three times longer than it should have been, or that's how it felt even if he couldn't finish it, though he did go back to it several times to try. Didn't even get through half of it, though that was still more than four hundred packed pages, but he could tell, by flipping through and periodically dipping in to the rest, that it wasn't going to pick up. So what's he saying? That the language in it was arched, artificial, pretentious, smug—most of, he's saying—and the story was plodding and the book as a whole seemed intent on being labeled a masterpiece when it was actually a big bloated tiring boor. (He knows he said he was through with the list, but how could he leave out Horace, Catullus, Whitman, whoever wrote "Ecclesiastes" and "Job" and "The Song of Songs" and certain early passages of the Bible?) Now he remembers a photo of Fels in the *Village Voice* more than thirty years ago. He even remembers where he was when he read the article the photo was in. On his fold-out bed in his crummy one-room apartment on New York's Upper West Side. He even remembers the rent: eighty-six dollars and two cents, and ten dollars a month for gas and electricity. He had to stick the rent check through the slot in the landlady's mailbox and slip the ten dollars in cash in an envelope under her apartment door. She said she'd rather keep it a secret why she wanted a check for one and cash for the other and in the ways she wanted them given to her—he remembers saying it'd be easier for him to pay both at once and in the same monetary form, preferably the teller's check—but it probably had something to do with taxes or separating the business expenses from the rent or just part of her eccentricity. He also wasn't going to make a big deal of it, since that was a very low rent and charge for utilities even then. Anyway, Fels had been part of a literary symposium at Judson Church downtown. (More than likely, I. had a glass of wine on the night table when he read the article, and a small plate of celery and carrot sticks, which he almost always prepared for himself when he drank and read in bed during the afternoon, and a sour pickle he'd slice up if he had one around. And it had to be the afternoon, or early evening. He never read a newspaper in bed late at night because he didn't want to go to sleep with newsprint ink on his hands or have to get out of bed to wash them if he felt himself falling asleep. And if he did have a glass of wine by his side, then it had to be late afternoon at the earliest, since he never started drinking alcohol of any sort—and still doesn't today except if he's taken out to lunch by his editor or agent, let's say, and then, just to be polite or to unwind, he'll have a single glass of wine—before five or six p.m.) The photo seemed to have been taken from

the rear of the audience or maybe even from the front row of
the balcony, for there were many rows of people between the
camera and the front of the church and he could barely make
out the faces of the people on stage. The article singled out
Fels as one of the discussants—a rare appearance in public,
they called it, and a rare photo of him, the caption said.
Maybe Fels had made that one of his stipulations for partic-
ipating in the symposium: that the photographs of the panel
be taken from so far back that he wouldn't be recognizable
in them. Even at that time—it was several years after the
first novel had come out, the one with few reviews and con-
tinuous small reprintings and finally major appreciations in
important intellectual journals—he was already something
of a literary celebrity in New York or at least had a cult following there and probably on many American college cam-
puses, as well as being a best-selling author in England and
Europe. He remembers now when he first heard of Fels. A
writer friend a few years older than I.—they'd met in '61 at
the only writers' conference I. had ever attended, one they
both got full fellowships to or they never would have
gone—had told him about Fels' first novel and was flabber-
gasted he'd never heard of it, since it was one of the three or
four best novels written since *Ulysses*, and that includes one
or the other of Kafka's two best posthumously published
novels and the big one by Musil and the last half of Proust's.
I. wanted to read it and the friend said he'd have to buy his
own copy, if he could find one in a store, or borrow it from
a library, and for that, if the 42nd Street branch didn't have
it, he might have to go to the Widener or Library of
Congress, because the friend would never loan his own rare

first-edition hardcover in a million years.

But what's he going on about? I. isn't his initial ("I am not I.," he's tempted to say, but that's not the person he's writing this in) and Joshua Fels, it should go without noting, isn't the name of the writer whose obituary he read today. He had met this writer who died yesterday (checks the obit and sees it was yesterday and not some day before, so it was probably written a while back and just the latest details had to be added) about twenty-five years ago (reconstructs in his head—not "reconstructs" but pinpoints or something a whole bunch of factors—now that had to be the first time he's used that word, as was "reconstructs," which he ended up not using—to determine the year they met, and it was exactly twenty-five years ago) and in the way he said (girlfriend, summer, party at a town on the west side of the Hudson about a half-hour's drive from the city, host he spoke to at the door and what they said, or did he first speak to him beside the swimming pool in back, or was that just a small manmade fishpond with goldfish inside?). But the question's still: What's he getting at with all this? Something about memory, he thinks, and how events just seem to pop back from some buried spot when the mind's been triggered by something like an obituary of someone you knew or were acquainted with in some way, and also about being a young writer (actually, not so young; thirty-eight, but still, with five or six book-length manuscripts by then, no book published after trying to place one for around fifteen years) snubbed by an older well-known writer and how he felt about it and what it meant to him, if those two aren't the same thing. Oh, stop with the crypt of memories swinging open and all that. Fine, then what? Simply this: he finished something yesterday—okay, a short story—wanted to start something new today—story, novel, two-page short-short: what did he care? A fiction of any length—even a play if it was possible—because he gets agitated with himself and grumpy with his family if at the end of the day after the one he finished a fiction he still doesn't have something to work on the next day. In other words—but he thinks he explained that okay. So he woke up knowing he was going to try to start a new work today (he's still on winter break from school so has more time than usual to write), made his kids breakfast and drove them to their schools, prepared his wife's breakfast (all he'd have to do later is heat it up) and a salad for the family for tonight's dinner, made his daily mug of miso soup (broth, really, since it's just boiled water, heaping teaspoon of miso and a little grated ginger. Supposed to be good for the prostate, he read in a *New York Times* science article a few years ago, but just get on with this), sipped the soup or broth while reading today's *Times* in his easy chair in the living room (perhaps he should have said that the paper's delivered and he went out to the end of the driveway to get it right after he made the kids breakfast, since he doesn't want to chance driving over the paper when he takes them to school—and papers, for they also get *The Baltimore Sun*—nor chance that his neighbors, who live in the only house up the hill and share the driveway, drive over them), turned to the obituary page (that last parenthetical sentence could be clearer, and he knows it's going to take work), the first section he looks at after reading the headlines and a few paragraphs of what seem like the most important articles on the front page (and settle for "soup," as "broth" seems too weak a word for his miso drink and soup is what he calls it), and saw the obit of Fels, he'll probably continue to call him (the name has no conscious double meaning and seems like an apt one for the type of guy he was and his patrician background), dropped the paper on the floor (soup was finished and the tea kettle was just about to whistle), and going into the kitchen to put the miso mug in the sink and pour the water for his coffee (he'd set up the two-cup drip pot with coffee grounds last night because he likes getting a jump on his early-morning chores: kids' and wife's breakfasts, water and food for the cat, tonight's salad, getting the newspapers, several other things like shaving and calisthenics, and sometimes he even prepares his wife's breakfast and his miso soup, minus the water, the night before and refrigerates them, and sometimes the entire salad, washed and dried and in a bowl with a damp dish towel on top to keep it fresh, or just washed and in the dish towel and next morning he'd cut it up into the bowl and then put the towel he used to wrap the salad in on top) he thought he'd try to write the first draft of a story about his encounters with Fels at the party and also what it was like (for one reads plenty, or let's say a lot's been written about starting-out writers but not much about one this age) to be a not-so-young-anymore unpublished writer, except for around ten stories in mostly little to very small magazines, and while he was pouring the water a first line came to him which he wanted to jot down soon as he finished pouring because it seemed a good one to start off with, one that would lead to another one and so on, and which he might forget, but forgot to: "Headline in the paper today said

'Famous Innovative Writer Dead,'" got his manual type-writer and a stack of paper off his desk in the bedroom (wife was sleeping stertorously—a word a student of his wrote in a story last week and he said in class "What the heck you using a word like that for? It sounds like a sleeping dinosaur. 'The husband was snoring in bed,' or 'The husband was in bed, snoring,' or 'was asleep, snoring, in bed,' or something like that, but don't get so goddamn—I was going to say 'goshdarn,' but that would have seemed so fake coming from a person like me—fancy, and I'm saying that for all of you"—and the room was dark because the curtains were still closed, so did this as quietly and carefully as he could because he didn't want her to wake and ask him to help get her up now), set the typewriter and paper on the dining room table, went back to close the bedroom door and then the louver doors separating the living room from the hallway outside the bedroom, brought in his mug of coffee, got his pen out of his pocket and put it on the table, forgot to get his Ko-Rec-Type tabs off the desk but that's all right, he thought, this will only be a first draft or however far he gets in it before his wife wakes up and calls for him, sipped some coffee and started to type.

He could have done that so much more simply: he fin-ished writing something yesterday, wanted to start writing something today, saw the obituary and started to write.

Even simpler: "...wanted to start on something today," and the rest of it.

So what did it feel like being snubbed by that writer? He really didn't care, if he remembers correctly, thought noth-ing of it then, it now comes back to him, even laughed about it a little later to his girlfriend—"You won't believe the way Mr. Bigtime Famous Author just high-hatted me," and when she said "What'd he do, not that I'd know who he is unless someone pointed him out to me. That him, the handsome natty one in the blue blazer and Topsiders?" and he said "Yeah, he moored his sailboat in the driveway. We were introduced, all very nice and chummy, and he treated me like an enormous lump of elephant dung, something he wanted to get away from fast for all the obvious reasons," and she said "And to name a few?" and he said "My size, origin, the ugly sight of me, of course my smell, and that if he lost his balance or was feeling a bit tipsy he might fall in to me." But high-hatting elephant dung? Doesn't work. And better to just write what happened than say, before he says how he felt, what happened. That doesn't make much sense and he forgets what he intended to say with it, though if he analyzed the line he's sure he could figure it out and say what he'd intended, but just move on.

Fels arrived at the party (I., he'll continue to call his main character, since he has to call him something or he'll get him mixed up with Fels or someone else), actually heard people around him say "Fels is here." "Someone says she just saw Fels at the food table." "You know who's at this party? Fels. I'd heard there was a possibility of his showing up, but I never thought he would. A fantastic writer even though I only understand every other line he writes and am not even so sure about that") and tried not to smile—no, that's not fair; he just didn't smile—or show any expression but an uninterested one when the host grabbed I.'s arm (I. was walking past, didn't know the guy talking to the host was

Fels but had been on the lookout for him, figuring a writer might look different than the other people at the party) and said—this was by the swimming pool or fishpond—"Joshua, I'd like you to meet another writer, someone relatively new to our little community," and gave I.'s name. They shook hands. I. said "It's a pleasure, sir." No, he wouldn't have said that. He probably said, since it's something he almost always says—a fair guess: nineteen out of twenty times, and for the past thirty years, when he's introduced to someone the first time—"Nice to meet you," and smiled. Fels said "Thank you," or something, the no-smile blank look, and turned around, seemed to be searching for someone, seemed to locate that someone in a crowd of people at the bar nearby, which was where I. had been heading, excused himself to the host, didn't look again at I., and headed for the bar, and I. said to the host "Vel, dat vuzz a fine how-do-you-do if I ever hurd one," and the host said "'Why, what's wrong?" and I. said "Nossing, vat could be wrong? I got my gatkers on backvards? I don't sink so, it don't feel like it, but maybe I'll get to talk vit him later, if I could only lose dis accent furst," and the host said "Yeah, what is it with the accent, though it's a very good one, whatever kind it is." Then: "See you later, gotta do my host-mosting," and left, and I. watched Fels. Fels asked the bartender for a drink, then was spoken to by one of the guests and looked at this man as if he couldn't place him. Still, he smiled, then laughed, got his drink and clinked glasses with the man and then with the woman next to the man, and talked to them for a few minutes, or let's say he was still busy talking to them, smiling and laughing and patting the man's upper arm, when I. looked away. Point is:

that encounter was all by accident. Fels—I. could tell by his reaction to them from the start—didn't know who the hell these people were, though they for sure knew who he was, or at least the man did, and they had probably even sought him out once they'd heard he was here. I. imagined the conversation while he was looking at them. "Mr. Fels"—"Please, we're at the same party and were invited by the same people, so call me Joshua" —"Joshua, then, all right, though it isn't easy to, but Joshua, we—I mean I—I mean both of us, my wife and I, since we've both read you (so the wife did know who Fels was), simply want to say how much we admire your work and that we'd like to drink to you and your next book, which we hear is close to being finished," and Fels: "Thank you, but tonight the less said about my work, past, present and future—" and the man: "Of course, anything you say, sir," and Fels: "And please no 'sir' either, if you also don't mind, and I hope I'm not being too demanding. Even though I'm invariably older than almost everyone I converse with, that 'sir' address always makes me feel bloody ancient," and the man: "Really, we understand, and I'm terribly sorry," and Fels: "Now look at me; I've put you on the defensive. Please, let's get past these weary time-consuming civilities and social empathies and talk about something more important, which would be anything but my work," and the man or woman: "Whatever you wish, sir—excuse me," and they all laughed and started talking about other things: the town, weather, what they're planning to do this summer (it was a Fourth of July party, I. now remembers, and the host even set off an elaborate fireworks display near the end of it, one that could probably have been seen from across the river), what work the man and woman do, a book either the man or woman had read and which wasn't Fels', they want to assure him, so don't think they're going to violate his request not to talk about his work... . Later, I. was heading for the bar and saw Fels there asking for a drink. I. thought it's obvious the guy doesn't want to talk to me, but that shouldn't stop me from getting a drink when I want one. When Fels got his drinks—a glass in each hand—and turned around and saw I. a couple of feet from him, he quickly looked away and excused himself past some people. That cinches it, I. thought. All I was going to do was nod hello but he wouldn't even give me time for that. Maybe he thinks that because I'm a writer I'll want to talk about writing and from that I'll get around to asking if it'd be too much of an imposition for him to read one of my manuscripts or we'll start talking shop and I'll ask if he knows of a good literary agent or book editor I can send my work to, and what about his, "Do you think he or she would be interested in looking at something from a writer who considers himself a serious one and who's never had a book published but has been trying to for close to fifteen years?" Or maybe it has nothing to do with me, I. thought. Give the guy the benefit of the doubt. Maybe he told someone a minute ago that he's getting a refill at the bar—"May I get you one too?"— and he'll be right back, and considers himself a man of his word. Is a man of his word. He hates people-hopping at these parties, he could have told this person, and much prefers sitting to the side with someone and having a long deep conversation on a subject they both know something about or one he up till then knew little about but learned from this person and found very interesting. (Just thought of some more for his list: Dickinson, Murasaki, probably Baudelaire, Melville and Rimbaud, and if Euripides instead of Sophocles then Sophocles just a rung below, and of course Chaucer if he didn't already have him on it, and at the bottom of the greats, Céline, Celan, Mandelstahm, Hamsun and Undset, and okay, Dostoevsky.) That was the last time I. saw Fels. When he and his girlfriend were leaving, the host said to him "Did you and Joshua ever get to talk?" and I. said "I don't think he took to that idea very much, or maybe I'm mistaken, but no, we never got around to it, though not because I went out of my way to avoid him. I did get to see what he drinks. Margaritas if you have tequila, gin and tonics if you don't. I don't know what he would have drunk if you didn't have tonic," and the host said "We always have tonic, even in winter, and limes. But that's unfortunate you found him that way, and I'm surprised too. I know he can show a steely exterior to semi-illiterates who practically boast they don't know a book from a brick. But to most people, once you get to talking to him, he can be a puppy inside, and someone whose fame hasn't affected him one whit. He left before my great fireworks display because he has to rise early tomorrow if he's to meet the deadline he's set for himself on his new book. His publisher has spring-listed it the third year in a row and Joshua doesn't want to disappoint them this time." "That's a concern I should only have," I. said, "plus about a tenth of the handsome advance I'm sure he got and also a publisher who'd be so forgiving and indulgent. I guess they must want the book a lot so don't want to say anything to lose him," and the host said to I.'s girlfriend

"He kidding me?" and she said "I think not."

There was a second time, he now remembers. At a book party in a huge rare and used bookstore in downtown New York. The writer of the book also managed the store and got the owner to host the party with his publisher. A couple of hundred people must have been there, mostly writers, editors and agents. Eventually the place got so crowded that someone stood at the door, only letting people out. "Fire regulations," he kept shouting; "we're way over capacity," though when a prominent writer appeared at the door, and this might have happened a number of times, he said "For her I gotta break the rules and let her in, which I'm sure the rest of you waiting will understand." I. had done a lot of browsing in the store and got to know the manager that way, so was invited but told to get there early or he might not get in. He was living with the same girlfriend in an apartment a few blocks away, but she'd gone to St. Louis with her daughter to visit her maiden great-aunt who was quite old and sick and planning to leave most of her inheritance to them, and whom she hadn't seen for many years. New paragraph? He met a woman at the food bar. They were both reaching for the stuffed grape-leaf tray, their hands collided, he said "Sorry," and withdrew his hand, she said "No, you first; your hand was there before mine," and he said 'Wouldn't think of it; please." Anyway, she got a leaf, then he got one which turned out to have no rice or anything in it. "Look at this; oily and empty. I'd complain to management except he's the one the party's for, so shouldn't be disturbed at such an event with something this trivial. Besides, I should feel lucky to be here at all with such an illustrious crowd. It's like a magazine pullout or two-page spread of who's who in writing today. You must know the kind, where all the writers are lined up in rows and at the bottom of this spread are their names, best-known book titles, most prestigious honors and awards, and what size advance their last book got." "Were you in one of these photos and I'm showing my ignorance in not knowing who you are?" and he said "Not by a long shot, and that isn't because I don't write or have never been published. To me it's such an asinine ignominious thing to be part of, a group literary photo. I wouldn't have posed in one even if by some rare chance I'd been asked." "So you're a fiction writer who's probably had a book out recently from a small publisher, with a small printing, small to no advance and barely a review." "You nailed the nose, lady, except for the reviews. There were none, but then it's only been around for six months. The best thing I can say about the way my first and only book came out is that I didn't have to pay to get it published. And you, a writer?" and she said "Married to one." He asked "Who?" and she said "I could easily tell you, or you could play match-the-writer-with-his-wife, but you'll have to scout the room first." "Henri Michaux," he said without looking around, and she said "Wrong continent, I know he's not dead, and he is one of my all-time favorites, like my husband. But why'd you say him?" "I wanted to try out my pronunciation of his name." "Joshua Fels," and he said "Oh, I don't know him though we did once meet, but really no more than a handshake. And if I hadn't met him, your match-the-spouse game would have been virtually impossible, since I hear he doesn't sit or stand for photos or anything for a book jacket like that. That must be why, since I'm sure they asked him, he wasn't in the recent *Esquire* spread on American writers. Though maybe he also wasn't in it for the same reasons of asininity and whatever the second one was that I gave. It was at a July 4th party two years ago. You might have been there too and we were never in the same room or the same area outside together." (All that could have been done much quicker. Just should have said: "Two years later he was at..." Or better: "They met again, he now remembers. Two years later he was at a big crowded book party in New York, though he first got to talking to Fels' wife. She was about twenty years younger than Fels, very pretty, lively and smart." Or no description of her. And she was actually beautiful, and tall and slim and well-built; he at first thought she was a fashion model. But just: "...to talking to Fels' wife.") "I didn't know Josh then; we only got married this year. But I know the party you mean. The Abramowitzes. We like that town so much that we bought the house from his ex-wife after she got it as part of their divorce settlement the year before. They hold it every July 4th; we were at the last one. Fabulous fireworks. I'm curious, though, and it's not something I can very well talk about yet with Josh's friends and our neighbors, what your impression of his ex-wife was, if you met her. I never have but I understand she was quite witty and attractive, and Josh said that unlike me, she loved parties." "Really, far as I could make out, he seemed to have come alone. In fact I'm sure of it, because I remember something about being told his wife was out of town for the night with their child and that was why he'd be able to get up early the next morning to write. No, what am I talking about, that's actually me and the woman I live with, but tonight. She flew to St. Louis with her daughter and tomorrow I get to have an uninterrupted day of work." (Best to skip all that and go back to "...talking to Fels' wife.") He told her where he'd met Fels and she asked what his connection to the hosts was. "The woman I'm with now in New York used to teach high school in that area and had a small rowhouse in town, which she still owns and we go to almost every other weekend. In fact if you're living in the house Mr. Fels had then, you've probably driven past hers a number of times." He gave the street. "Sure," she said, "I pass it a couple of times a day at least." Just around then Fels said to her "Enjoying yourself, darling?" But before he came over to them, I., out of nowhere, said "I know this has nothing to do with anything we were talking about—and if you think I'm hogging your time or you just want to move on to see who else you may want to speak to, please say so—but I've been curious lately as to who certain people involved with or interested in literature think are the greatest writers since Creation, and that should include not only poets and novelists and such but, if their styles warrant it, essayists, historians, philosophers" ... all of which, of course, he never said. Though for about thirty seconds he thought it a different way of getting in a few of the names he might have missed, but got the timing screwed up. She could have said "For starters, Milton, Goethe and Flaubert." And he could have said "Milton should be an obvious choice, but I could never read him for more than a few pages without wondering where I was in the work or feeling a bit stomach-sick or sleepy. As for the other two, and maybe Stendhal, though you didn't mention him, I might agree with you. But please," he would have said if he had actually asked her this—and there's always a slight chance he did and then for more than twenty years forgot he had even thought of it—"because I can imagine what your husband would think of such a ridiculous question, if it's at all possible, forget I ever asked it." But to go back: "Just around then Fels said to her 'Enjoying yourself, darling?'" or used her first name, which I. forgets and will probably never remember, since the names of the first three wives aren't given in the obituary and "Toba," the surviving wife, can't be it, since it's such an unusual name that when he saw it in the paper he would have remembered it. She said yes and that she's been having a very nice conversation with this man. She apologized to I. for having to ask his name again or maybe they hadn't exchanged names till then, and said "My husband, which you must have guessed, Joshua Fels," and I. said "Nice to meet you," and they shook hands. "We've already briefly met," and Fels said "We have?" and gave that look of "This certainly comes as news to me," and I. said "Not tonight but a while back," and she said "That's right, at the Abramowitzes', I forgot to mention it. Not only that, dear, but his close woman friend has a house a short distance from ours, one we pass regularly in the car," and gave the street name, which I. also forgets. "We should have them for drinks one of the next few weekends when they're staying there," and Fels said "Good idea. You make all the arrangements, though check with me beforehand to make sure I'm not previously engaged," and smiled at her or something and walked away without looking at him again. I. wanted to say to her "Listen, we'll forget about the drinks, but nice try, for it might've turned out okay." Or "Christs, I don't care if he is your husband, but that's the second damn time—we're talking two for two, lady—he's given me the big brush-off while I was standing next to him. What is it with the guy? Can't he just say, if he wants to beat it away fast, 'Nice to meet you, goodbye'?" Or "God, what a freaking—excuse me, and I'm actually holding myself back—snob. Talk about being dismissed? And almost you too for suggesting we visit. He wants to see my girlfriend and me about as much as he wants a crippling case of stomach cramps this very minute." Or—But forget it. "So," she said, "let me have your woman friend's name and her phone number up there," and she wrote it down in a little address book. "This is terrific and a wonderful stroke of luck meeting you here. If I pass by your house and see the light's on—it's dark otherwise, am I right?—then I'll know you're around and I'll call you. Yours is which of those rowhouses?" and he said "Facing them, one on the extreme right with the abandoned refrigerator on the porch." "I'd love to get to know a congenial young couple in the area who are also literary and artistic," because he'd told her his girlfriend's also a printmaker. "In town, Josh seems to know mostly lawyers, doctors and people who move around other people's money, several of whom are quite as literate as doctors and lawyers used to be but reluctant to talk with us about what they read. It could be they're too intimidated by Josh's book reputation to discuss literature in front of him and that he seems to have read every serious piece of writing ever writ-

ten, but I don't think you'd act to him that way. And one
weekend evening soon would be ideal, since Josh is busy all
week writing or doing other literary business and only starts
to unwind on Saturdays after five. Now you should circulate, covertly provoke 'And what do you do?' questions
about yourself, spread your name around and get your book
and future projects known. I'm not an expert on it—all the
reapings Josh gets seem to drop out of an envelope into his
lap—but I bet you'll never have a better opportunity than
here to get the publishing and book-reviewing and
grants-giving world interested in you. I'd spread the word
about you myself, but I'm not familiar with your work. I
will be, though. Who was it who said 'Any writer'—I'm
standing in for Josh with this saying, and I know he'll back
me—'who doesn't buy another writer's book is either
pathetically penurious or a cad'?" "Kipling, it sounds like,"
he said, "or maybe Galsworthy or Wilde." and thinks
"Kipling; good, especially three or four of *The Jungle Book*
stories, but not great."

Fels' wife never called. Did he expect her to? Sure, why
not? She seemed sincere about it and too smart and meticu-
lous to forget. Repeating their phone number twice to make
sure she wrote it down right. Fels must have said when I.'s
name came up for drinks at their house "I'm really
chock-full of writer acquaintances and friends, darling.
Maybe when one of them drops dead we can replace him
with this young man as they do with members of the Arts
and Letters Academy, and you did buy his book." But what's
he being so rough on him for? Fels might have said he's not
in the mood to meet anyone new now (hasn't I. felt that way

a number of times?), pleasant as this young man seemed and he's sure his woman friend is. And he has a book section to finish and another one to research and write, so he wants—for the next twenty years, he'll say, and he's only being facetious about this by half—to keep his social obligations down to something he can control. "But you want to see them so much? Just say I'm overextended right now and offer my apologies, and then meet them at a local café or pub. Because you know what can happen if we have them here. It'll be interesting for all of us up to a point. And then, after some trepidation, they'll invite us in return, and I wouldn't want to possibly hurt or offend them by saying no, just as I don't want this invitation thing to snowball. Best, I'd say, to appear insincere from the beginning by not phoning them as you had planned. You run into him again and he brings up the matter about the lights on in their house and that was the signal you'd established that they were there, you say that for some reason you thought they were in the city and the lights were on to ward off burglars. Though why am I putting these narrow-minded thoughts into his head, as if either of them would ever think you insincere? Simply don't invite them and let them supply the reasons why, which I'm certain will be nothing short of magnanimous: 'Fels might not be well.' Or 'He's known for being somewhat unsociable and a bit of a loner, so let's not take it personally.' And the one I'd think the young man would empathize with and respect the most: 'He's busy with his work, just like I'd be if I had the time and could afford it.'" A few months later, while reading a book on the porch of his girlfriend's house (James' short stories: brilliant mind but the writing quite turgid and stodgy), I. saw Fels and his wife drive past in an open convertible, Fels in the passenger seat and looking as if he was holding down his hair with his hand. After that, he saw Fels' wife drive past alone a couple of times, staring straight ahead. If she had looked his way, he would have waved.

Now remembers another time he met Fels, this one a quickie. The following spring or summer—anyway, it was warm, shorts and T-shirt weather, and it couldn't have been the following fall, for by then he and this woman had broken up. Fels coming out of the small market in town, carrying a bag of groceries and I. heading for the store. I. said hello and Fels looked up, didn't smile or nod, gave no sign he recognized him, kept walking, stopped at a bicycle leaning against a wall, divided up the groceries into the two baskets on either side of the rear wheel and threw the empty grocery bag into a trash container, unlocked the bike and pedalled off. "Damn, you got me again," I. said, Fels too far away by now to hear him, and I. hadn't intended him to. And then wanted to yell in a funny Russian accent like the guy on a comedian's radio show more than forty years ago—the Mad Russian the guy was called, on the show for less than a minute each week—"How do you do? *How do you do? How do you do!*" but thought "Don't. He'll come back indignantly and say something like, and maybe even give some indication he knows whom he's speaking to, 'Was that gibe supposed to be meant for me?'"

And another time, this one a real meeting, and he thinks the last time he saw Fels. Thinks hard and thinks yes, the last. I. was married by then and his wife had known Fels' third wife. Or maybe she was his fourth and the one he was married to when he died was his fifth and the obit had the count wrong. That can happen when you don't list all the names. But the wife after the one I. had met at that book party in New York, that he's almost sure. I.'s wife and she had been in the same women's college, only the woman was about three years ahead of her and had tutored her in some subject or another. No, that's not how it went. Then why'd he think it? It just came to him and he thought it was right and was even going to say "some subject like calculus or astronomy or Chinese." So where'd they know each other from? A dinner party that Fels and this woman had given in their apartment in New York. (Wait a second. —No no, forget that, the chronology's right. The book-party wife and the one before her lived with Fels in the Hudson River house. Then Fels lived with the dinner-party wife in New York City and no doubt another place, and Fels and his fifth wife lived in England and Martha's Vineyard and probably some other place, or maybe at the end he was living alone in these places but he and the fifth wife hadn't got divorced. But how could I. have forgotten that his wife, a year or so before he knew her, had gone to this dinner party and met Fels? He just forgot, that's all. Completely slipped his mind and was replaced by something he didn't know he was making up.) His wife had been taken to the party by a well-known English poet, more well-known today for his essays and critical books and translations of Greek tragedies and Scandinavian plays. But at the time—I. remembers reading about it around then and for a few years after in newspapers and cultural journals—it was said he stood a fair

chance of getting a Nobel and that he was reportedly short-
listed for it once or twice. Some of his poetry—is this necessary? Maybe none of the stuff about the poet is, except to
show how I.'s wife got to the party, but just finish the
thought because maybe something will come out of it. I.
thought some of his poetry was vigorous and exciting for its
sensuality and ferocity and honesty and even the brutal or
just vehement way he spoke about art and poverty and
women, especially his two previous wives, and so I. would
say he had five or six exceptional poems and he loved the
guy's clarity but overall as a poet (and he never cared much
for literary criticism, and a good translation of a play
shouldn't be too hard if you know the language or have
first-rate literals) he wouldn't call him great. There, that's
something what he hoped he'd land on by continuing with
it. The poet used to see I.'s wife (of course, before she knew
I.) for about two years every time he came to the States on a
reading tour or university lecture or week's poet-in-resi-
denceship at one or just to see her and his American publisher, which meant they saw each other about four times a
year. She also spent several months in London with him
once. She even thought they might end up getting married
then. But the guy was a philanderer, even when she was living with him, and drank too much and often got angry and
insulting when he did and sometimes violent—not hitting
her; just throwing around chairs and books and breaking a
finger when he slammed his hand through a headboard—so
she decided better to just see him occasionally till she was
seriously involved with someone else, and only in New
York. The party, though. But one more thing about him,

now that it's in his head. The last time the poet called her—this was a few months after she and I. had met—I. answered the phone and said she wasn't home and who should he say had called? and the poet gave his name, but his full name rather than the two initials and surname he used for his published work, and asked whom he was speaking to and I. said "A friend of hers," and the poet said "Just looking after her plants and cats?" and I. said "No, I live here now, so those are only two of my household duties when she doesn't see to them," and the poet said "By living there, and please don't think me presumptuous or snoopy, does that mean you're not simply renting a spare room to help her out with the rent or borrowing a couch and some linen for a week or sleeping on the floor for a few nights?" and I. said "That's right; our clothes hang side by side in the bedroom closet and with her approval I've commandeered her bottom dresser drawer," and the poet said "Well, that's a damn pity for me. But I think it's wonderful for her and I wish you two the most brilliant future together. Tell her I'll try calling again next time I'm passing through, and perhaps I can take both of you out to lunch." (New paragraph? No, just that will do.) The two women (Fels' wife and I.'s future) sat next to each other at the dinner table. That's it: they discovered they'd gone to the same college, though Fels' wife had graduated a few years before I.'s had entered the school, and they talked for hours about their teachers and courses and interests and poetry and translations and theater, and met once after that for lunch and had a lively time together then too. Then something happened—I. forgets what. But he does remember she said she never saw Fels except at this party and he barely said a word to her other than "May I get you a drink?" and later "May I refresh your glass?" so involved was he with other people, particularly the poet, and she also got seated at the opposite end of the long table from him, though he seemed like an engaging fellow and extremely funny, had everyone around him laughing and even breaking up at things he said. "I almost wished, though I was enjoying myself plenty at my end of the table, that I'd been seated closer to him because of all I was missing. I also found him to be very attractive, looking at least fifteen years younger than someone there said he was. How old is he now?" "Did he drink a lot?" I. remembers saying then, and she said "I didn't notice, and in what we were just talking about, why's it matter?"

So where was he? He really went off then. The last time he saw Fels. Right. The last time was in front of FAO Schwarz when it was still on 58th Street, he thinks, and Fifth. I. and his wife and their first child (not even ten months then but standing, though at the time seated on I.'s shoulders) were outside the store around Christmastime when they saw Fels and his dinner-party wife heading toward it. I.'s wife saw them first, and of course I. wouldn't have known who the woman was, and said "Look, Joshua Fels and his wife, what's her name?…darn, it'll be embarrassing if I can't remember it," and he said "I don't know, which one? I only met one of them, the second or third or whichever one she was—I know she wasn't the first—and I forget her name too. You of course mean the one you had dinner with at their apartment before you met me," and she said "Got it," and called out the woman's name just as they were about to enter the revolving door. They turned to her—several people on line behind them said something, so they stepped out of the way. The woman waved to his wife and said something to Fels. He made some kind of hand motion—I. didn't, and still doesn't, know what it meant; sort of throwing up one hand, but as part of the same motion one would make if he were throwing up both hands, if that's clear—and she came over and Fels looked at the door spinning fast with nobody inside and then opened the regular door to the side and went in. The two women kissed. I.'s wife introduced him and their child. Fels wasn't in the lobby. Or else I. couldn't see him among all the people there—anyway, he wasn't standing by the doors and windows there, so he might have gone inside. The woman said "My goodness, look at this gorgeous thing and those blond locks. You lucky stiff. I wanted one so much. But Josh already had so many that he said one more would break his back. Literally, he meant too. That he was too old for carrying them on his shoulders; that grandchildren were much lighter for that." I. said "I'm getting too old for it too, I think," and set his daughter down. "Upey, upey," she said, raising her arms, and he hoisted her back up. The women talked about things they'd done the last few years. A photography book on doll furniture the woman did; a book-length translation of poetry his wife did. Oh yes, the woman saw it. Teaching; people they both knew; the poet: he's doing fine, Josh sees him more than she does, but he seems to be writing less poetry and more about it these days. "If we're going to talk some more," I. said to his wife, "don't you think we should go back inside the store? It's probably getting too cold for her," pointing up to his daughter, "and I don't think she's old enough yet to know how to complain about it." "It's not so bad out," his wife said, "and she's bundled up like a bear against the cold." "If he really thinks—" and his wife said "No, she'll be fine." Did he say that—of course also for his daughter's sake—but to get inside and maybe see Fels and be introduced to him again and they'd talk? Was that what his wife was trying to prevent because she sensed that Fels didn't want to talk to anyone (not coming over with his wife) and she knew I. wanted to talk to him? No, that couldn't have been what she thought but probably was what he did. "Oh, look, hubby shows his illuminated face," and she waved to the store, and there was Fels, ceiling light beamed directly on his head, behind a lobby window, looking at them and pointing to his watch. Come join us, her wave now said. He threw up that same hand again, the left. He a lefty? I. still didn't know what the motion meant though. Maybe something like "I don't want to. Why do you insist on doing things I don't? We're wasting time. We will be wasting time. (Reverse those. First time: "will"; second: "we're.") It's always the same. You want to, I don't. You want to (hand shoots up again), I don't." But get to the point with all this. Really isn't one. He's recounting the last time he saw Fels. Putting in almost everything he remembers about it. Not to prolong but to describe. Why? Seemed the right time. And while remembering, finds himself remembering more. Things he didn't know he remembered, had never thought of or not for years. The illuminated face: new. She actually said that, or words close. New too: ceiling light beaming on Fels' face but mostly onto the top of his head, turning his gray hair bright blond which, I. thinks, it must have been when he was a young man. Wasn't wearing a hat that night? (And it was night, did he say that? Or dark, around five or six.) Probably not. Or he was, he now remembers—a fedora of sorts—but took it off, no doubt, when he went into the store. But "to the point," so speed it up. They were introduced. (Obviously—but maybe not so "obviously," since they ((the two women and I. and his kid)) could have gone into the store—Fels came over. Actually: same "they" were approaching the store when Fels left it through the regular door and headed for them.) Introduced. Fels' face? Just get on with it. Shaking hands. "There's absolutely no reason why you should remember this, but we've met before (I.)." "Oh, have we (Fels)? I've an atrocious memory for such things, growing worse with age for it and everything else. It's also been the kind of strange, hectic day that would contribute even further to my memory loss." All right, Fels' face: dyspeptic (a word used fairly commonly in Fels' fiction, along with pudibund and conundrum and fatidic, spelling literary fake) when he walked over, and aloof or put off or bemused, except for quick on-and-off smiles appearing solely around his mouth, while he was there. So, was the description worth it? Again, hardly, and slowed this down even more. "Harrying's what the day's truly been like (Fels' wife). And then, after all that happened earlier, which Josh would kill me if I revealed so much as a part of"—"No. I wouldn't, dear; though perhaps a small mutilation"—"to want to come here to buy presents for his grandchildren and buck the mobs outside and in?" "I love my grandkids (Fels to her). Sometimes more than I loved my own children when they were kids, something I'd like you to forget I confessed. But are children just getting sweeter and smarter with each generation, and if so, where does that put mine when we were kids? In the precociously know-nothing ogre class like our parents said? So I'm saying that almost anything's worth bucking to prevent their disappointment come Christmas day if they arrived to find us giftless (still only to his wife)." "In fact (I.), about what I was saying before, we've met twice, not counting today or seeing you in the local grocery store in that town you lived in upstate." "Twice, now (Fels)? My poor memory's really going to get a workout from you and look shot. When was all this?" I.'s wife's glance said she thought I. was about to say something sarcastic about the previous brush-offs, and not to. But I'll fool her (I. Oh, go to regular tags. Getting "thought" in this way looks too clumsy). I'm going to act respectful and maybe even a bit obsequious, he thought, and in no way allude to those two times when he practically spit on me. All right: no more than ignored. "The last time was at that Strand bookstore book party for the manager of it," I. said. "I think it took place just a little before that terrific relatively short novel of yours came out." "That party," Fels said, "is almost a total blank. If we stand here for thirty seconds more with no further mnemonic elbowings, it'll be completely erased. I'm sorry, it's not you I forget, or want to, but the entire affair. It was loud, overcrowded and a horrendous ordeal to get to the bar. But I do remember thinking throughout it, and it's conceivable this thought nudged out the rest, of all those beautiful old books and bound galleys and reviewer copies being ruined by spilled drinks and dripping dips. What a dumb idea that was, having a party there." "You're probably right; I didn't think of it that way. The first time I met you, though, was a couple of years before that. Around the time you were finishing *Recapitulations*. A July 4th party at—I forget their first names, but the Abramowitzes, near where you used to live, or for all I know, still keep your house." "I've been to their parties a number of times on that holiday." Fels said, "so by now I can't distinguish one from the next. They all have a minimum of a hundred-fifty people at them and end the same way: lots of rockets ejaculating in the sky and a final big bam!" "It's true; this one had that too, and was pretty crowded. But there's a third time, I just remember," I. just now remembers saying. "At the Academy and Institute of Arts and Letters' May ceremony and banquet, where you were being inducted into whichever one of those two is the more august body and I was getting an award in literature." "Could that be right?" Fels said. "I've only been to one of their events, when I got that same literature award a hundred years ago. But I never showed up for either of my inductions, so you must have me mixed up with another older writer." "Truth is, I wasn't being serious about it. Just a case of—my professed literature award, I mean, if I'm even using 'professed' right there, and I've no idea why I brought up that induction business—of 'don't I wish.'" "I see," Fels said, "I see, or think I do." "I was wondering also," I.'s wife said, "since I don't think I ever heard you mention that award and certainly not in that context. But what I still can't quite grasp is what made you bring it up now." "As I said," I. said, "a don't-I-wish, which is no doubt as close as I'll ever get to it. But that's not enough?" He looked at her and the others. She was shaking her head, Fels was looking off at the traffic, and Fels' wife was staring at him and then did some movement with her face that seemed to say "Don't look at me; I don't know." "Okay, what can I say," I. said to his wife. "It was stupid, clearly stupid. So excuse me, but I have my bad-joke and low-intelligence moments too. Hey," squeezing his daughter's hands, "even through the mittens I can feel her little fingers getting frozen, so we should go." "Yes," Fels said, "don't let the child catch a cold. Goodbye, my sweet darling," he said to her, and kissed one of her hands and said to his wife "Did you ever see such a doll?" and nodded to I. and his wife and headed for the store. Fels' wife said "I don't want Josh to go in alone. He'll get peeved at me if I can't find him and he has to hunt for me through the place," and asked I.'s wife for her phone number, said "I don't have to write it down, I'll remember," and waved goodbye to them and their daughter and hurried after him.

THE SADDEST STORY

IF HE WERE to write his saddest story, this would be it. It wouldn't be about a young child dying and the surviving parent suffering deeply because of it. It would be about an elderly parent dying, one who'd been taking care of its seriously disabled child for years, and the child feeling helpless now because it wouldn't have anyone so caring as this parent taking care of it anymore. Also because of how close the father and daughter (the parent-child relationship he knows best, so the one he'd be able to make the most believable, he thinks) had become since he'd started taking care of her. (What their relationship was like before, so long as it was a healthy one, wouldn't matter in the story.) And that the daughter had once shown so much promise as an artist and thinker and was so lovely and good and was surely on her way, before she became disabled, to doing great things in whatever work she went in to and to becoming a wonderful parent herself. The father would be about eighty-six and the daughter about forty-four when he died. The mother would have died about twenty years before. The daughter's condition came about from a car accident she was in when she was nineteen. Nineteen or twenty seems right: two to three years before she would have got out of college and gone off on her own to some job or to graduate school, and a number of years after she'd first shown such tremendous potential if not gifts. It wouldn't make much difference who was responsible for the accident unless, of course, the father was. But he wouldn't want to lessen the sadness of the story by complicating what caused the accident and injuries and resulting disability. So, just another very bad car crash. She hit a car or her car was hit by one or skidded on ice or an oil slick and she lost control of the wheel and crashed or her car turned over and perhaps rolled. Or a skiing or bicycle accident or even one involving diving—she liked to dive into pools and higher the diving board, better she liked it—and she was a terrific diver too. But something where, once she left the hospital, she was confined to a wheelchair and then a hospital bed at home and was never able to take care of herself except for the most minimal things: chewing her food or saying or indicating what she needed or wanted. In other words, an accident that injured her severely and a condition that never would kill her so long as she continued to get special care, something, he thinks, only someone who loves you and is always with you can do for fifteen to twenty years, and only at home. First, though, both parents would take care of her at home for a few years. They'd learn what to do and would become as good at it as the professional nurses who taught them. Then the mother would get sick and the father would end up taking care of both of them, in separate bedrooms, for a couple of years, and then the mother would die and for the next twenty years or so the father would take care of his daughter alone. But why bring the mother into it, and in this way? Not to make the story sadder, since he doesn't think it would be sadder for the father to first lose his wife and then for the daughter, who also lost her mother, to lose her father too. Or maybe it would be sadder, since it'd be terrible for a daughter to lose both parents and to be left so helpless. Maybe even sadder if she quickly lost them one after the other, or even at the same time—a car or plane crash. Though maybe not, because one of the ways of making this story so sad, he thinks, is to show how close the father and daughter got before he died, which would take many years of his looking after her alone. And also for the daughter to grow accustomed to her father's help and protection and love, and then to be left without anyone like him looking after her. The mother would be in the story so he could avoid the contrivance, he could call it, of the father being the sole parent when his daughter suddenly needed such special care. In other words, to avoid him taking on the responsibilities and duties of looking after her so soon after she got out of the hospital. Because most men, even the most caring and dependable of fathers, would have a tough time adjusting to it, wouldn't they? He thinks so. Which is why he has the mother in it: they'd do the work together awhile, with the mother, in fact, taking on the major load. Then, by the time the mother got sick, the father was as good at taking care of his daughter as she was, and in some ways—lifting her out of bed, for instance (and maybe there aren't any others), even better than the mother, but only because he was stronger. And then, when the mother died, the task of looking after his daughter alone would almost be a cinch in comparison to taking care of the two of them at once, and the prospect of looking after his daughter for the rest of his life or hers (if he stayed healthy) wouldn't seem so hard. Anyway, he'd read novels, stories, newspaper and magazine articles to her. Plays, poetry and essays too. He'd in fact act out all the parts in the plays sometimes. He'd cook whatever she liked, if she could eat it. He'd explore macrobiotic cooking if he thought it could improve her condition somehow. He'd hold a straw to her mouth from a glass or mug so she could drink. The father in the story would be doing all this, he's saying. Watch TV and videos with her. Listen to the news or music on the radio or music on a CD player if she wanted him to, because sometimes she'd want to do that and other things alone. The daughter in the story, he's saying. What else would the father do for her? Plenty. Make her laugh, or try to if the situation was right for it at the time. Or just do what he could to make her as happy and comfortable as she could be. Take her to museums—wheel her in her wheelchair or take the public bus which has a chairlift or drive her to them in a special converted van he'd buy to transport her in her wheelchair. To stores and malls and parks and into the country sometimes and restaurants now and then if she didn't mind going to them—in fact, only if she wanted to go and he knew she wasn't doing it just because she thought he wanted to get out. He'd ask friends of hers along if she still had some and she wanted them to come or just one. Concerts and recitals and movies in movie theaters, and so on. He'd also, of course, wash and dress and feed her. Clean her up after her bowel movements, catheterize her as often as she needed.

He'd do everything for her, he's saying. The father would. He'd have help from people sometimes—aides—but he'd do most of the work. The less help the better though—he wouldn't like having strangers around, particularly during the times when they had nothing to do and would be in his way—so only when he was sick with the flu or something or very tired and needed relief or when she wanted someone else to talk to or read to her, and so on. But the father would never leave her alone in the house with one. At least not after a certain incident that he'll put in the story. The father had gone to a play she didn't want to go to—"Much as I want to see it," he could have her say, "I always think people are staring at me rather than the stage, which is why I like movie theaters better: the audience can't see me"—and left her with an aide for a few hours and she was mistreated: thrown too hard into her wheelchair when she was being transferred from the toilet and then cursed at and threatened when she complained. "You tell your father what I did and I'll come back here when he's not home and beat you black and blue." That'd also give the father and daughter some idea what it'll be like for her when he dies. And it would have to be a daughter in the story. If it were a son there'd be less chance, he thinks, that he'd be mistreated that way or sexually molested or even raped by people taking care of him, or maybe he's wrong. Anyway, the father-daughter setup does seem to him to be—well, he doesn't know quite how to put it—but a potentially sadder one than father-son or mother and son or daughter, especially when the father would be more than forty years older than his daughter. He'd also make her an only child so there'd be no one else in the fam-

ily to look after her. If she did have aunts and uncles, he'd
have them live so far away that they'd be of no help to their
niece and brother or brother-in-law, and maybe the only
time they'd be in the story would be when they came to his
funeral. Cousins? No, cousins would have their own families
and immediate concerns and so would be too far removed
from them or busy to be of any practical use, even if they
lived in the same city as the father and daughter. But having
married cousins in the story could make it that much sadder.
He might have them visit her once and she'd see again, or
just more acutely, since her cousins would be around her age,
what she had missed out on in life: husband and children,
though he doesn't want to milk the situation, so he might
not put that in. In the end—when the father's dying, he's
saying—he'd have the father and daughter see each other a
final time. Maybe there wouldn't be any funeral scene and
this would be the last or next to last one in the story; he'll
see. The father would be very sick by now. Had had several
operations, was considered terminally ill by the doctors, he'd
be on painkillers—morphine, even, but in smaller dosages
than the doctors wanted to give him, since he'd rather go
through the pain than not be able to recognize his daughter
or speak coherently to her. The father would ask to be taken
from his hospital room, where he'd be dying, and wheeled
into her room in a nursing home. That's where she would
have been brought, and where she'll probably remain for the
rest of her life, after he got too sick to look after her. He'd sit
in his wheelchair by her bed. (Or he might have it where
they'd both be sitting in wheelchairs or the father in one and
the daughter in a comfortable easy chair by her bed.) And

hold her hands and kiss them and maybe kiss her feet, if she was in bed, and, if she could reach over, her face and head and say he's so sorry he's dying—not for himself, since he's lived a long full life and had a wonderful wife and the dearest of daughters—but for her, because now who will look after her the way he did? (The father would be thinking at the time that he's deeply worried about what will happen to her and also to the money he's leaving to take care of her, but won't say it.) He tried to stay alive as long as he could. All this would be in actual dialog, not paraphrased. He tried to keep healthy, is what he's saying, the father would say. He'd stopped drinking years ago, or at least cut his cocktails down to one a night and his wine to one or two glasses at dinner, while before—before she had the accident, he'd say—he used to have two to three cocktails a night and knock off half a bottle of wine during and after dinner. Of course, he was a lot younger then, he'd say, and, paradoxically, felt he had less to live for, if she gets what he means. He wouldn't have all that in the story. Just: He almost completely—"I almost completely stopped drinking in order to stay healthy and take care of you as long and well as I could." He also walked a great deal and jogged a mile a day to stay in shape, he might have the father say—though only when he thought she'd be all right at home alone or with someone, the father could add—and ate the right foods or as close to the right ones as he could, and worked out daily on the multi-station exercise machine in their basement so he could continue lifting her when he had to. Off the floor where she had sometimes fallen. In and out of the bathtub or onto the special stool in the shower if she had the strength to hold on to the

grab bars there when he gave her a shower or bath, and he
never once felt anything sexual to her. He wouldn't have the
father say that but he would have him think it. Though the
father might ask that last day (and intentionally ask it in this
oblique way) how full a life did she think she'd had?—this,
after he'd say how full he felt his had been with his family
and work. And then hope out loud that she'd had before the
accident something like the deep physical and emotional
closeness with someone as he'd had with her mom. He could
have the daughter say to her father "Close to it, I guess,
though in intensity, not length. But if you don't mind, I'd
like to keep that part of my life to myself," and the father
could say—well, he could also say, but wouldn't, "I hope it's
not that you're anxious about telling me. In a few days or so
whatever you tell me won't even exist in my head, and not
because my memory went bad"—something like "Of course,
anything you want, my darling. And you know I only asked,
in what I admit was an oblique or roundabout way, so I'd
know and could take pleasure in the fact that you'd done
some of the things just about every human being—oh, you
know what I mean, so subject permanently closed," and he'd
try to laugh and by laughing, make her laugh. If she did,
maybe then he'd say "Although you needn't have been anxious about telling me if that's what it was that held you
back. I don't mean to appear morbid, but whatever you
would have told me would be gone from my head in a few
days with no retrieval or trace." And then he'd feel so
weak—at some moment when he was in his daughter's room
that day—that he'd ask to be taken back to his hospital.
They wouldn't be in the same nursing home. (Or maybe he'd

have to place him there if an editor, let's say, pointed out the implausibility of someone in the father's critical condition being allowed out of the hospital for even a couple of hours to say goodbye to his only child. But if the daughter was unable to go to him in the hospital because of her condition? He's sure he could get away with it if he made the father adamant and convincing and showed there was no way for the daughter to leave the nursing home at the time and he also had someone on the hospital staff recognize the importance and urgency of the father's visit and help loosen the hospital's rules.) So they wouldn't need to be living in the same nursing home. It'd be too contrived, the father and daughter ending up in the same place, no matter how big a building or medical complex. And they'd know that this would be the last time they'd see each other. He'd cry and she would and she'd say "But I'll be all right, Daddy. I swear I'll be okay and able, in my own way, to look after myself, so please don't worry," and he'd say "And I'll be okay also, so not to worry about me either. But know that my greatest sadness ever is now happening to me, and that's that there's no chance I'll get better and resume taking care of you (and he'd be thinking but wouldn't say "and leaving you to the mercy of others"). Though my greatest happiness ever, or at least equal to the days or weeks after your mother gave birth to you, is that I've been able to look after you all these years." (This would have to be the first time the father told his daughter this in the story. And where it's possible the father hadn't even alluded to it before, since it'd be a more powerful story for it to come out here than anyplace else. He'd also have the father think, while he was saying it—before or after, he means—that though he knows it'll make her even sadder, he needs or needed to get it out and tell her and somehow feels it'll comfort her once he's gone.) "I've been a good father though, haven't I?" the father could say and she'd say yes. "And you've been," he might have the father continue, "—no, it goes without saying (since the father would have already said it in the story), since I've said it many times before, the most rewarding thing to ever happen to me in my life." Soon after that, or perhaps right at that moment, he'd show signs of being too sick to be with her any longer and would ask someone to help him leave, or even without asking he'd be quickly wheeled out and he might even die on the way back to the hospital, but he'd be dead in a day. She'd be told—an administrator from the nursing home would come in to give her the news—and she'd say nothing, close her eyes and think something like now she's alone. She doesn't know what she'll do. She won't have him to help her anymore or just around to cheer her up and be with. She's almost powerless to look after herself and see that people take care of her well. She told him she'd be all right to make him feel better, but he must have known she was only saying it for that. She's so sad. She can't stand it. There's nothing to go on for. She wants to die. This would be the end of the story. He can't think of a sadder one, which means a sadder situation than this. When two people, not one—a father and daughter, he's saying—are so saddened by their permanent separation, and where there's really no hope left at the end and just more sadness to come. Why he'd want to write it though, he doesn't know.

SHOE

THIS HAS WHAT to do with anything? He'll see. It started while he was driving his older daughter to school. His younger daughter looked so grown-up in skirt and high-heeled shoes last night, he said. Those weren't high heels, she said. They're platform shoes. "Platforms; okay. But that reminds me of a funny story. Actually, not so funny. But something I probably haven't thought about for more than thirty years. It concerns high-heeled shoes. You interested?" "Depends if it's interesting." And then in the short trip he told her the story. A friend wanted to hook him up with what he said was a very good-looking intelligent woman. I., around thirty-two at the time, said he hated going on blind dates and his friend said he promises this one he won't regret. So he asked the friend to call the woman to see if she'd mind I. calling her. "Don't build me up or anything. I don't want her disappointed that way if she does agree to see me." She told the friend to have I. call her. So he did, they spoke for a while and seemed to get along and have several similar interests, and made a date to meet for coffee. The woman was as attractive and smart as his friend had said. She was beautiful, even, and pleasant, and had a love-ly slim figure. So they had coffee, a good time talking, he walked her back to her apartment building and in front of it he said "Would you mind if I called again?" "Sure," she said, "that'd be nice." He said "Why even bother calling? Maybe we could arrange right now to meet for dinner or a movie sometime or anything else you might like to do." "Sure," she said, "when's good for you? I'm not busy Friday." "Friday, then," and they shook hands and he went home—he was living with his folks till he saved enough money from his job to afford to get his own apartment—and started fantasizing: beautiful woman, great figure, gorgeous legs, very smart, cheerful, terrific sense of humor and interested in so many of the things he was: books, music, theater, art, certain movies; even opera. He saw himself kissing her goodnight at her door after their first real date; they'd decided to see a movie. She might even invite him in after that kiss, then more kissing and maybe some petting. She seemed modern, uninhibited, so who even knew if she wouldn't suggest they go to bed after a lot of kissing and petting, or they just ended up in bed, neither of them suggesting it, most of their clothes off in the living room, the bedroom the next natural place to go to. He didn't tell his daughter any of that. Nor that he went to the woman's building that Friday at the time they'd set. A brownstone, not far from his parents' building. Rang her bell in the vestibule. No one answered. Rang it several times, waiting a minute between each ring. It was ten min-utes or so after he was supposed to be there, so what the heck's going on? he thought. Someone was coming down-

I.

stairs from the second floor. A woman but not her. He thought she might object if he just walked in while she was walking out, or kept the door from closing, so he said when she opened the door "I've an appointment with Susan Geller, third floor, and her bell doesn't seem to be working, excuse me," and slipped past her and hurried upstairs. He found her apartment and rang the bell. No answer. Rang again and knocked. "Susan, you home?" He heard someone walk quietly up to the door; it sounded as if she was bare-foot or in slippers. He forgot to mention he'd come with flowers. He didn't know why he brought them. He thinks she expressed an interest in flowers the last time, that she was raised in the country and how much she missed flowers not being right outside her front door this time of year, so he thought they'd please her and, let's face it, get him in good with her. Of course that was the reason. Anyway, he said "Susan, that you? We had a date tonight, don't you remember?" "Oh...gee," she said, tsking. "I'm sorry; I forgot." Just then someone from far off in the apartment—a man—was saying something I. couldn't make out. "Shh if you don't mind," she said, "I'm talking." The man got a little angry in his voice and said something about solicitors and canvassers and for her to do what he always does to them through the door and that's to cut them off fast. "Is there a guy in there with you?" I. said. "What kind of stuff is that? We were supposed to go to the movies right around now." "Listen," she said, "I'll have to break the date. Please call me tomorrow and I'll explain." "Call you tomorrow? You crazy? Go screw yourself," and he threw the flowers at the door and left. What he told his daughter was that he was once inter-

175

ested in a woman when he was thirty. Dated her a couple of times, or maybe just once, but with a little coffee date before the first real movie one, which is when—after it, at her door—she told him she wasn't interested in seeing him again. "All right, that happens, you can't expect every woman you want to go out with to want to go out with you or continue to after the first or second date. You're lucky, in fact, if one-third of the ones you like or are attracted to—or at least that was my ratio, or maybe a bit higher, since I didn't always go for the ungettable—have the same feelings for you. But I did like this woman and was sorry she didn't want to see me again. And even though nothing ever happened between us, I couldn't get her out of my head and even suffered a bit of heartsickness over her. She was so beautiful and smart and funny and lovely, that I thought she was perfect and I would have died to have something happen between us. Then, a couple of weeks later, when I'm still pining for her and even thinking of calling her for a date, though I never believed she'd go out with me again—and I should make this short so I can get the whole story in before we get to school—I see her on Broadway in the theater district. I was looking for a job and she was working as a publicist for a movie director, though I think really as his factotum—someone who does a lot of different menial jobs for someone—who was casting then for a film he was going to direct in New York. A big name too, I remember, though I forget it now. She was standing as if frozen next to a building and not looking too happy. I was about to go over to her and say something like 'What a coincidence'—not, that we were both unhappy, me over her and she I didn't know what yet, but of meeting her—when her expression changed to anger and then as if she were about to explode, and her body started jerking. She was struggling, it turned out, to get one of her high-heeled shoes—this is where the high heels come in—out of a sidewalk grate it was stuck in. You know, the long thin heel part wedged between two of the bars. First she tried jerking it out with her foot still in the shoe. Then she took her foot out and tried pulling the shoe out by hand. Finally, she squatted down and tried pulling the shoe out with both hands, but nothing worked. I thought 'Should I help her?' Then I thought 'After what she did to me?'" "Why, what'd she do that was so bad?" his daughter said. "She didn't want to go out with you. That's all right, isn't it?" "Of course, and what I immediately thought too. So I started over to help her, if she wanted me to. But just then she got the shoe out—she never saw me, you understand—but the heel part separated from the rest and stayed stuck in the grate. That did it for her, and she raised the bad shoe over her head as if she wanted to throw it someplace. Oh, I don't know if I remember all that exactly, but something like it, and then calmed down, I think she tried dislodging the heel part from the grate again, couldn't, and walked lopsidedly to the curb—because she only had one shoe on, you see—and stuck out her hand for a cab. People were staring at her walking in this funny way and then standing there, one side of her a few inches higher than the other. She was fuming again, so nobody dared, it seemed, to say anything to her or help get her a cab. Me, I ducked aside because I knew she'd never want to know that someone she was acquainted with and had been introduced to by a fairly good friend, even someone she probably didn't think much of—I'm sorry, I don't mean to flail myself like that, but that's what I felt then and still do—had observed all this. Then a cab came, she got in and drove away, and that's the end of the story. And right on time too," as they just then pulled into the school driveway. "But what was your reason for telling me it?" she said. "Shoes? Or that's what started me going. So maybe it was just that seeing her looking so awkward and even buffoonish, though that might be too hard a word for it—her foot stuck in the grate at one point before she pulled it out of the shoe and then hobbling to the street carrying the broken shoe, and with a briefcase and in a good suit—sort of made me feel better and helped me get over her from that moment on. Because I never again thought of her in a romantic or even a positive way after that." "Why didn't she take the good shoe off and walk in her feet on the street? And how come she didn't put the broken shoe in her briefcase, if it wasn't too stuffed up, so she wouldn't look silly? But that's mean what you said, using her trouble and then her being embarrassed for your own benefit like that." "You could be right. And also about the shoe in the brief-case and walking with both feet instead of a shoe and a foot. I don't know why she didn't do either of those. But you're definitely right about my wrong attitude at the time. What I should have done then was help her get the shoe out of the grate, if she would have let me, and why wouldn't she have? Or at least the heel after it had separated from the shoe. A shoemaker could have put the two parts together easily, I'd think, while without the heel she probably had to throw the shoes away or just hope that a shoemaker or the store she bought the shoes at could send away for a new heel, not to say all the time she must have spent cabbing home to get another pair that day or to a store to buy a new pair. And think of the money she could have saved if I had retrieved the heel, and certainly the whole shoe intact, which is what I should have thought of then instead of taking pleasure in her predicament. Also, for whatever it would have been worth, she would have thought better of me too." His daughter smiled, as if she liked that he thought she was right, and he kissed her goodbye and she got out of the car. "You have your lunch?" and she said "You asked me that when we left." "Right, I did, and besides, I can't even remember the last time you forgot it. So I'll see you at two-twenty. Don't be late, because I have a class at three," and she waved and went inside the school. Driving home, he thought he wished Susan had seen him staring at her while her foot was stuck in the grate and then when she tried to get the shoe out and hobbled to the street and later when her cab pulled away. No, he did the right thing by making himself invisible. It was enough the incident got him over her, and who needs revenge? He heard from that same friend about a year later that she moved to L.A. and got a good job in publicity for a movie company. Then he never heard anything about her again or even, he thinks, thought of her till he was in the car with his daughter.

THE ERROR

How to explain his behavior? They couldn't go out to celebrate his wife's birthday on Thursday because he had to
attend the graduate diploma ceremony and reception that
night. So they went to a restaurant in the city the next
night, he and his wife and their two daughters. It was on the
top floor of a museum; their table was on a balcony with a
beautiful view of the harbor. There was a party going on
below in the museum's courtyard. Lots of loud music,
sounds of people having a good time, clinking of dishes and
silver and so on. Occasionally, for some reason, a couple of
firecrackers going off, or what sounded like them.
Normally, that'd disturb him, and also the loud music. But
he found it exciting. "It's lively down there," he said; "it's
like New York. They're helping to celebrate Mommy's
birthday." "Her birthday was yesterday," his younger
daughter said. "But we're celebrating it tonight," he said.
"Surely you knew I meant that. And that's not a reprimand,
I want you to know. Just my way of informing you how
much I know how you think." "But I wasn't thinking like
that," she said. "Okay, you weren't," and he raised his wine

glass. A very good wine too, The cheapest red on the wine list but still the most expensive bottle he'd ever bought except for a champagne for their fifteenth wedding anniversary two years ago. But champagne's champagne, so it doesn't count as a wine. "To Mommy," he said, "and many more." "Many more what?" his younger daughter said. "Birthdays, birthdays; don't tell me you thought I meant glasses of wine or mommies." "You should say exactly what you mean then; that's what you always tell me. 'To Mommy on her birthday, and many more.'" His wife raised her coffee cup of wine. Because of her illness, she had trouble holding a glass, especially a wine one with a long stem, so he'd asked the waiter for a cup. The kids raised their water glasses and they all drank. He'd wanted them to order soda or iced tea or lemonade or Shirley Temples, but the older girl said, after checking the menu, that the first three were too expensive and though Shirley Temples weren't on the menu, it was a drink for children. "Then get a Jackie Coogan," he said. "What's that?" and he said "Something nonalcoholic that's close to a Shirley Temple, I think. Maybe it's just a Shirley Temple for boys but with the ice cracked or jagged instead of whole to make the drink seem tougher." "Then I certainly don't want it," she said, "because it's still a kid's drink." "Anyway," he said, "what's a few extra dollars?" "Five or six dollars for the glasses of soda is more like it, and maybe seven dollars with the tip and tax." "So?" he said, but thought seven is a lot for just two sodas and probably free refills—God only knows what the Shirley Temples would cost, and you rarely get free refills on those—and water will do them fine. It has ice and a lemon slice and straw in it too, so it's special water. "I'd have a sip of your wine if you'd let me," his older daughter said. "You bet," handing her his glass. "And you too, if you want," to his younger daughter, but she said "I hate wine. I don't think I'll ever get a taste for it," and he said "I got mine when I was twenty. I was traveling by myself through Europe, hitchhiking or going by cheapest bus or train, and was in Rome," but he'd told them the story of being the only customer for lunch in the only restaurant open near the student house he was staying at and being given a complimentary glass of wine by the owner. That wasn't his first wine but the first time he liked the taste and when he started drinking it with his meals. It was also so cheap. "So what happened there?" his younger daughter said, and he said "Oh, I've told you the story. I got to like the wine, when it was like a hundred degrees out and everybody else was siestaing, at a little outdoor restaurant with the tables on this narrow cobblestone street. *Una quarto caraffa di vino rosso, per favore*, or something, I ordered every day for lunch—the big meal in Italy. And sometimes I also went there—well, I was only in Rome about a week—but for dinner because they were friendly and acted as if I were an old customer and they let me read as long as I wanted to after all my dishes but the wine glass and carafe had been cleared. In other words, they didn't give me the bum's rush, as my dad liked to say—hustled me out because I wasn't buying anything anymore—in the bum's case, because he isn't going to buy anything—so I thought it a good place to go." "That's so sad," his younger daughter said, "eating alone all the time." "Ah, I was young and wanted to travel around Europe and none of my American friends wanted to, and I eventually hooked up with someone in Denmark about a month later. And it was a good learning experience—that I could eat alone and almost enjoy it. I also got a lot of reading done this way." His daughters had salads and an appetizer each as their main course. He'd wanted them to order more. "There's really nothing else for us here," the older one said. She was a vegan, the younger one a vegetarian. He and his wife had appetizers and a main course each plus a salad between them. Two desserts for the four of them after, but the vegan would only eat the berries she took off the top of the fruit torte and rubbed the cream off with a napkin and washed in her water glass. He had a cognac at the end of the meal— "What the hell," he said. "We've spent so much already, what's another million?" He'd started off the dinner with a martini made with black vodka. "What's that?" he asked the wine steward, or just the person in charge of providing the wine list and serving all the alcoholic drinks, who'd suggested it. Told what it was, he said "Sounds interesting, and good for you, all those filtering processes, but probably very expensive," and she said "Because I'm introducing you to it, I'll give it to you for the same price as the house vodka," which, he now realizes, is something like, but really not that much like, the story of his first complimentary wine in Rome. The drink was very smooth and he had his wife sip it and she smacked her lips and said "Doesn't burn like martinis usually do, the three or four I've had in my life. It's pretty good." "Want one? I'll drink it if you don't finish it," and she said "I'll wait for the wine." And so the evening went. Beautiful night, ideal weather for sitting outside; even, for about fifteen minutes, classical flute and harpsichord music from the courtyard—it sounded live. They'd learned it was a prenuptial party for a movie director and rock singer, though the wine steward didn't know which was the male and which was the female. "I do know," she said, "and I hope what I say doesn't offend any of you, since it's meant purely as a fact, they're of two genders." Ships and boats and barges passed in the harbor, one boat with about—or maybe with so many sails and being quite long it should be called a ship—seven to eight sails, the front ones billowing. This was Baltimore; the water was the Patapsco River, he's almost sure, which he's also almost sure flows into the Chesapeake Bay. Then the check came. He was astonished, a word he's rarely used for anything, at what the dinner cost, and that was without the tip. How'd it get so high? he thought. Did the wine steward or whatever she was charge him the regular price for the black vodka and did the waiter also make a couple of errors in totaling it up and perhaps charging them for a main course they didn't have? He checked the check and the vodka didn't seem unusually high and everything else seemed correct. "I knew it'd be expensive," he said to his wife. "We both knew it before we made the reservation. But I'm literally astonished, a word and action I can't remember using or having about anything in my life." "How much?" she said. "Oh, I had to have used it and felt astonished a few times, but never about a restaurant check I had to pay." "How much?" and he silently mouthed the figure—"without tip but with tax," he said aloud. "Wow. Anyway, it won't break us, and everything was delicious." "And for a good cause too. No, that's not an appropriate word for it; but your birthday. Happy birthday, sweetheart," and he kissed her. His younger daughter had brought her camera and took a picture of them kissing. "Do it again," she said; "you moved, and I want this to be a real art shot." "No chore at all on my end," he said. His wife smiled at him. They kissed.

"I'm going to check the answering machine," his older daughter said moments after they got home. And then: "Two are for Mom and one's for either of you. I skipped the messages, so don't think I listened to them." "Who even questioned it," he said, "and why would it matter if you did listen?" and went into the bedroom. The two for his wife—from her mother and then her father, though they lived together—were for her birthday. Both said they couldn't get hold of her yesterday and apologized for not calling earlier today. The third call was from a friend of theirs. "We waited till we had… You were supposed to… Excuse me, I think I drank too much waiting for you, which may end up being the best side-benefit of this. You probably forgot that you were to have dinner here tonight. It's now ten past nine. (He had his hand to his forehead already, was thinking "Oh no, I couldn't have.") We gave it an hour and a half, assume something went wrong, hope everything's all right, and we're sitting down now to eat. Talk to you soon." "Oh God," he said, "what a disaster." He looked at his pocket planner—it was on the windowsill above his writing table in the room and had probably been there for a week—and opened it. In today's space: "Kagens, dinner, 7:30, kids invited." What the hell does he have this damn thing for if he doesn't use it? he thought. He went into the kitchen. "You won't believe this," he said to his wife, "but

Eli left a message that we were to have dinner with them tonight." "That's terrible," his older daughter said. "And you see? I didn't know it. You can tell by my surprise." "All right," he said, "all right. What are you going on about?" "Was it supposed to be at a restaurant?" his wife said. "Worse, at their house. I don't know how I could have missed it. I had it written down in my pocket planner—" "Your what?" she said. "My little black book, the long narrow one, for every day of the year—you've seen me look at it and write in it, and I thought that's what they're called. And I had it written down—'Kagens, dinner'—and probably the time too—7:30—but for Saturday, I'm sure." "Saturday, that's what I remember you telling me weeks ago, or whenever you and Eli arranged it. But I thought at a restaurant and that we'd talk with them tomorrow as to which one and what time. Is it possible they got the day wrong?" "Hardly. It's just like me the last few weeks to screw up like this. Too many fucking things to do for one person—excuse me, sweetheart," to his daughter; "but to do and think of and remember and plan and execute and everything, besides my regular work. It all, goddamn, falls on me," and she said "Okay, I know you work hard and take on most of the family chores, but don't suddenly make it seem my fault because I can't do what you know I can't do, in addition to ruining what we all agree was a wonderful evening." "But if I am responsible, for whatever outside stuff caused it, and I'm not blaming you, or even if nothing caused it and I'm just a first-class screw-up, what a thing to do to such nice people." "I'm sure they'll understand," she said. "Just tell them that we both thought it was for

Saturday, and that you even had it written down as such, and that should do it." "What a thing though," he said. "To prepare dinner, probably an elaborate one—you know them. And to set the table, no doubt with their best silver, china and glasses. You've seen how they set it when they have guests. Tablecloth, candles, the works, or special placemats, which always look ironed or brand new, and cloth napkins with napkin rings. And unusual appetizers with the drinks before, always one with polenta because of your wheat-free diet, and a tapenade she makes. And then while some of the food's cooking, or because of me, burning, or maybe not so bad as that, but to wait around an hour and a half for us? I just hope other people were invited. But by what Eli said, I don't think so." "Why, what'd he say?" "He didn't mention other people, so it's more what he didn't say." "Anyway, as I said, it's still possible it wasn't your fault." "No, it was terrible of me. I'm to blame. I hate hanging people up, making them wait, doing anything like that. I'm always on time with people. It upsets me to be even a few minutes late and I can't remember the last time, if it was only me who was going to meet someone, when I was. I respect people too much for that—their time, making them hang around places they might not want to be at for very long. Though in this case—their home—it's different. But you make a time, and it's not something like a major unexpected traffic tie-up that's slowed you or the babysitter showed up an hour late—that was in the old days—then you meet it. So, I'll just have to explain best as I can. Too late to call them now though. I will bring up that business about Saturday and that I wrote it down in my appointment book—I'm sure I did—and just the possibility of their getting the days mixed up, but all that in the morning."

He called the next day, got their answering machine and said "Eli, Henrietta, I'm so sorry. I had it down in my appointment book for Saturday, same time, 7:30, and that I'd let you know about the kids only if they were coming, which I think was supposed to be our arrangement regarding them. I'm sure the dinner wasn't for Saturday, but is there any possible chance it was? I don't know why I'd have it down for Saturday, but I feel so bad if I got it wrong, which I'm sure I did. We're both very upset over it, and the kids have been berating me for being such a dunce, and they're right. Listen, can we try to make it up to you by taking you out to dinner tonight? Cecily too, of course, if she wants to come, and we'd love it if she did, though tell her I can't promise that our daughters won't be doing something else tonight. So let me know. And again, my deepest apologies for this terrible, awful, dumb—I don't know what to call it. It'd seem that any word like the ones I used would be too good for it. Maybe 'contemptible' best describes my blunder. Bye."

He went into the dining room and said to his wife "I called their home and left a message on their answering machine. They could be out sailing. Wouldn't you think that's what they'd be doing on such a beautiful breezy Saturday? What better kind of day for it," and she said "You're probably right. So they'll call back later." "I just thought of something. If they are sailing, would they have planned an elaborate or just any kind of dinner for guests the previous night? Don't you have to be up early for sail-

ing and maybe stay away from too much drinking the night
before so you can have an extra clear head and your stomach
won't be woozy on the water and things like that?" and she
said "Neither of them is much of a drinker, and they've had
us over a couple of times the night before they went sailing,
and one time even before a big round-the-isle race or something." "Anyhow, I just thought. But I'm sure that they're
also this moment, or sometime around, or at least did so earlier this morning—during the drive to the boat club they
belong to, most likely, if they did go sailing—talked about
what a nincompoop I am...how about that for an old word
but with an apt meaning for what I was?" and she said "And
I'm sure, if they went sailing, they talked mostly about boat
preparations and a possible race today—I think they race
almost every Saturday they sail, some longer than others.
And during the race, or just on the boat if there wasn't a
race, concentrated, as serious sailors do, solely on the race
and their sailing." "You're no doubt right there also, but I'm
sure last night's fiasco came up sometime too."

He could hardly think about anything else the next few
hours. How could he have done it? To make that kind of
mistake when he had the information right in front of him
if he had only taken the time to open his appointment
book? Why didn't he think the Kagen dinner was one day
this weekend, or at least coming up, and look? How they
must have felt, and so on. He went over what led up to it.
When he accepted the Kagen invitation for Friday, he
thought he was taking his family out on Thursday. Then, a
few days ago, so about three weeks after he'd spoken to Eli,
his chairman asked if he was going to the graduate diploma

ceremony and reception. He said he wasn't planning to—he wants to start getting some of his own work done and he really can't stand those insipid speeches and the endless summoning of students to come up to the stage and receive their diplomas—and she asked if he'd go, since she wouldn't be able to. She'd been asked to stand in for the dean of faculty at some function in Washington that evening. She doesn't know why the dean can't go to this other function; something about being overextended himself. And honestly, she said, it's good for the students to have some of their faculty at the diploma ceremony and even at the reception after, though she'd never insist they go to them. He said "I agree with you, but I've gone to them for years, and it's my wife's birthday that day; we were going to go out. You can't ask someone else?" and she said she already had and maybe she should have said this first: Would he please do it as a personal favor for her? So he told his wife they'd have to celebrate her birthday another night, and she said "Is Friday okay? It's a much better night; the kids don't have school the following day." He said "Looks clear to me—I can't think of anything—but you don't think the kids might have something planned with their friends on Friday?" "Even if they do," she said, "and it's a little early in the week for them to already have weekend plans, I'm sure they'll want to celebrate my birthday with us. And if we tell them now, that'll head off their making any plans for Friday." He said "We could always go on Saturday if they already have something very important to do on Friday, or if one of them does," and she said "If only one of them has something very important to do, I think she can break it. But since it doesn't really matter to me what day we have my birthday dinner, Saturday's fine too." He didn't write anything in his appointment book about the birthday dinner for Thursday or Friday. He'll remember, he thought, or his wife will, without him having to put it in the book. He also didn't write in the ceremony-reception for Thursday either, since it was only a few days ago he was asked to go to it and he was sure he'd remember because it was on his wife's birthday and had replaced her birthday dinner. As for the time of the ceremony, he didn't think he had to write that down either. He knew, from having gone to about ten others, that it started at six, so, as he'd done the last few times, he'd hold off getting there till quarter of seven at the earliest to miss some of the opening statements and speeches.

He called the Kagens a few hours later. Their daughter said her mother just called from the boat club to say they were finished sailing and after a quick lunch, would be heading home. "Listen," he said, "when you next see them, or if you're going to be out, then please jot down a note about this, tell them I called again and how sorry I am about last night. You must have heard what happened," and she said "Just that you were expected for dinner and didn't come." "Well, I'm mortified at what I did, totally embarrassed and horrified and everything else. I take complete responsibility for it. I was the one who accepted your parents' invitation and I'm the one who keeps the appointment book too, and even though my appointment book says the dinner was for tonight, Saturday, I'm sure it was for Friday as they said. Of course that's too much to write down or tell them, so just say how bad I feel." "I don't know why you're so upset over it," she said. "It seems like a simple innocent mistake. I'm sure they didn't mind." "Thanks, and you're no doubt right. And this must sound peculiar to you, but the whole thing still bothers me a lot."

Henrietta called about two hours later. "Thank God," he said. "I've been dying to explain things to you." "Believe me, last night's long wait was about as comfortable and enjoyable as it could get. Sometimes, as you know, little accidents turn into wonderful experiences. We had drinks and hors d'oeuvres outside and talked and listened to music and Eli pointed out several constellations and stars and showed me how to find them. Then we sat down for dinner, though a much better one than we'd normally have for ourselves. Eli had this very good wine he was saving just for the four of us, but we'll try to get the same bottle for the next time we meet." He said "As I think I said on your answering machine or to Cecily, I'm totally distressed by it all. I've never done anything like it before—not even close," and she said "Then you've led a much more sheltered life than anyone we know." "No, a careful one. I make sure these things don't happen. That's why I'm so surprised it did. My appointment book says Saturday, but I know that's wrong. Still, somewhere in the back of my head I seem to remember Eli saying Saturday, so Saturday's what I put down. But he had to have said Friday and I only heard Saturday. Or else his accent had something to do with it, though the two words, other than for the 'day,' sound nothing alike." "Look, it's possible he did mispronounce the words—even I sometimes still have a bit of trouble understanding him—or that he actually told you to come Saturday by mistake. He's human—like you—and can flub speech and botch up dates and write down the wrong word, so don't worry about it a second more; it's not important enough to. Anyway, he's off to Tel Aviv tomorrow, we join him next week, we'll be there for a month and then trekking through Turkey the rest of the summer, so we'll catch up with you at the end of August." "Okay, see you then. But please tell Eli that I know he didn't make the mistake, or any of that business with the accent before, and that it had to have been my fault entirely. Oh boy, though, how it's killed my day." She said "What can I say? The incident was forgotten by us when we sat down to eat, other than for our concern that something might have happened to one of you that prevented you from coming and even calling to say you weren't. And I forgot to tell you—see? I make mistakes too. We can't take you up on your generous offer for dinner tonight, as Eli still has a mess of business to attend to and packing to do."

Eli called soon after. "Don't think I'm saying this to make you feel better. But when Henrietta said you were almost sure the dinner was for tonight—she mentioned a memo book—it suddenly struck me that you could be right, even though she said you later retracted it. Our calendar—I'm referring to a tattered sheet of scrap paper we tape to the refrigerator door for the month—says Friday. But I've made the same error with words dozens of times before. Said 'tall' for 'short' and 'up' for 'down' and 'moon' for 'sun' and 'Friday' for 'Saturday,' though in this case it was probably 'Saturday' for 'Friday.' Henrietta didn't tell you I do this, or you never heard me? Most times I correct myself immediately, but this time I probably didn't, and look at the consequences." "No, I never heard you do it." "You mean you don't remember me doing it, because it never amounted to anything. But it's become a family joke. Usually the opposite of words but sometimes just something very close, like the sun and moon switch. And one time, to my great embarrassment, 'autopsy' for 'biopsy' which I said to someone that my mother-in-law was going in for. It's a problem I have with English; with Hebrew, it's rarely happened. So I'm sorry for what I put you through. Sorry too that you saved Saturday for us and now we can't get together. What I'm most sorry for is that we opened the bottle of wine we were reserving for last night—it had to be drunk young and in two months it would have had whiskers, so I doubt I'll be able to reproduce it for our next dinner with you." "Something seems a little fishy with your story," he said. "You sure you're not just saying it, after what I told Henrietta, to get me off the hook, and I didn't mean that as a joke. Even if 'Saturday' is what I remember you saying, I'm willing to believe that either my hearing was bad or I imagined it." "Honestly, I can almost remember, when I invited you, making the same kind of verbal mistake again but for some reason not correcting it on the spot. Because of that memory of it, vague as it is, and my history with word transpositions and opposites and the like, I'm just about convinced now it was my error and not yours." "It would certainly be nice to believe that. Not to make you look or feel bad, you understand...but you know what I'm saying."

Henrietta called half an hour later, his wife spoke to her and later reported what she said. "We really regret what we put him through—you have to tell him that. Though it was so sweet of him to take full responsibility for what Eli did. And he does finally believe it was Eli's slip and not his own mistake, right? I should have told him straight off that Eli does that more than occasionally with words, 'contraption' when he means 'traction' and so forth, but never with such disastrous results."

"I do remember them saying 'Saturday,'" he said to his wife soon after she told him what Henrietta had said. "Eli saying it, I mean. But you don't want to say you're absolutely sure about it—I of course mean 'I don't want to say it'— because that's sort of insinuating the guy's losing his memory or going nuts. People are very sensitive about that—the memory thing—and occasionally frightened of it, especially when they get to around Eli's and my age, though he's about seven to eight years younger, wouldn't you say?" "Ten, maybe," she said, "though maybe less." "But also, you know me," he said. "Minute a mistake's made and I'm somehow involved in the matter, much as I believe I wasn't at fault I suddenly start assuming I was, don't ask me why, meaning don't ask me why I start to assume that." "I knew what you were saying," she said. "But that sort of contradicts what I was saying before about being sure I heard 'Saturday' as our dinner day, but you get the gist of what I'm saying. I feel sure I'm right but then become less sure when someone else is convinced he's right, and then I get almost completely sure I'm wrong when the other person keeps insisting he's right. When he won't even budge an inch, in other words. Oh, it's possibly not even that, but close enough. I'm having a hard time finding the right words now, I don't know why." "The whole incident; it's disturbed you that much. That has to be it. You were tossing and turning in bed last night, which is unusual for you. Over your worry about it, I'm sure. I don't know how you slept through it." "It did worry me. But as I told Eli, or was it Henrietta? No, it had to be Eli: I feel such better about it now that he's sort of confirmed I did hear what I thought I did and that he has this ancient history of verbal mistakes, as he calls it—the switching or reversing of one word for another, but only in English." "I've never heard him do that, have you?" and he said "I think so, once or twice. But I could be wrong, since it's not something I think one would remember except if the person did it repeatedly—several times in a single conversation or encounter with him. Anyway, at least everything's resolved, and I really do feel a lot better. Infinitely better, I can even say." "Good," she said, "because were you ever miserable."

Now he thinks "What a stinker I am to make Eli think he was the one who got the days mixed up and because of it had put me through so much." He wants to call him and say it actually was for Friday that he had asked them for dinner—he found a little notation on the inside cover of a book he was reading which he remembers scribbling right after he accepted the invitation: "Kagens, dinner, Fri., 6/18, 7:30", but thinks that would make them suspicious he knew all along the dinner was set for Friday but was too embarrassed to admit it so he made them think it was their mistake, or Eli's, mostly, and now he feels guilty about it. He gets his appointment book, blacks out the reminder he wrote for yesterday, with a different-colored pen writes in today's space: "Kagens, dinner, 7:30, kids invited," and puts the book on top of the dresser next to the phone where he knows he can find it, since he often loses it.

"I still feel lousy about it," he says to his wife that night. "What happened with the Kagens, I'm saying, even if I'm almost a hundred percent positive it was no fault of mine." "Then don't feel lousy," she says. "I'd say that to you even if it was your fault. What I'd also say is for you to come to terms with it, that it doesn't help to continue to dwell on it, and to just try not to make the same mistake again. As for when we next see them, we should make certain we say nothing to make them feel guilty about it, which I don't think they will. They're reasonable and sensible people who know that everyone makes mistakes. They, you, me and the world at large." "That's what Henrietta said to me, almost in those words. And when I said to you that I was almost a hundred percent positive, I meant that I think there'll still always be a little feeling in me that I was the one who got it wrong." "After what Eli told you? It doesn't make sense." "You're probably right. No, you're definitely right. I should just drop it because it's obvious the incident's finished."

THINK

WHAT'S THERE TO say? He did it again. Said he wouldn't; promised her. "I won't, that was the last, never again." But he can't keep his word. That isn't the expression he wants. Can't keep himself from repeating his mistakes. Not all of them. Oh, he doesn't know how many of them—the percentage of them, he means. A third, he'll say; a third seems reasonable as a figure. Can't keep from making the same mistake on about a third of the things he does that he thinks are mistakes. That's not a bad way of putting it. It's fairly accurate, in fact. But how can he avoid repeating these same mistakes? The ones he does about a third of the time, and not just to his wife. He doesn't know. He's tried almost every trick. "Every trick" isn't the exact expression he wants but it comes fairly close. And it's obvious here he's trying to avoid saying what he did to his wife that brought all this up, though why he's doing this isn't quite clear to him.

Maybe he should try this. He's lost his credit card three times in the last, oh, he'll say six months. He retrieved the card all three times when he went back to the place where he left it (and which forgot to give it back to him, he can also say). After the third time, when he got it back from the man behind the store counter, or was it a restaurant? Does it make a difference? Maybe it does if there's some correlation between forgetting to get your card back and the type of place you left it at (and which forgot to return it), but he's getting away from what he started out to say, and that was that…what? Has to go back. No, think what it was, a test of your memory, and he thinks and it doesn't come back. So he goes back, reads it, sees what it was. After the third time he lost his credit card, though that time, even if the information isn't important for what he thinks he's trying to get across here—then why's he putting it in? Because that's what he often does. One of the mistakes he can't keep himself from repeating? Possibly. But where was he? He's not kidding. Lost it again. And don't even try to remember what it was because it'll be faster to go back, read it, and continue. Which he does. After the third time he lost his credit card…well, it was in his apartment building lobby and he was speaking to the doorman, Emilio. Actually, he was waiting for the elevator and Emilio was first reading a book behind the window in the little room the doormen sit in when they're not hanging around the lobby or in front of the building or sitting in one of the two lobby chairs…and they're not called doormen anymore, are they? They hold open no doors. But they watch the entrance to the building to see who comes in, and in this building—through a monitor near the elevator that can be seen from both the lobby and the little room—the entrance to the building's side door as well. So perhaps they are doormen in that respect. Which might, for all he knows, be the original meaning of the word. They guard the doors. Though tenants have a key to get into the side entrance, if someone tried forcing his way through that door or was accosting one of the tenants at it, the doorman would, if he was watching the monitor, see it and do something. Leave his front-door post perhaps and go to the side entrance, or call for the super or one of the building's porters. Though he doesn't like that word, that is what they're called, the guys who clean the lobby and hallway floors and pick up the garbage. Anyway, Emilio was sitting behind the window in the room that houses the building's intercom system and has cubbyholes for each apartment and shelves for packages to be left or picked up, and he—I.—was waiting for the elevator. Had just come in from the outside, I. had. Had about twenty minutes before got his credit card back from the restaurant or store he'd left it at the previous day and only about an hour before had discovered was missing. Discovered this when he opened his wallet to put in two twenty dollar bills to replenish the cash there, and saw—he often checks for his credit and ATM cards and driver's license when he opens his wallet—that his credit card wasn't there. So he called the store. No he didn't and it was a store, he now remembers, the last place he'd used the card and which he'd bought some phone equipment at. Hustled right over—it was about ten blocks away—and got the card back. Was extremely happy about that. Especially that moment when the woman, it was, behind the sales counter said "Yeah, we have it. We would have called you if we knew where to get you, but the salesman who took care of you remembered you didn't want to give your phone number and address for our computer file."

"I don't like junk mail, that's why. Fills up the mailbox when we're gone with information about stuff we don't want or need, and stores tend to sell their address lists to other places," and she said "We would have put in the computer not to if you had told us. Can I see your driver's license or some other like ID?" He returned to the building, still feeling very good that he'd got his card back, and Emilio was there. I. said hi to him (he'd come on duty since I. had left for the store), pressed the elevator button, then turned to him—I. doesn't quite know why this is but sometimes he likes to tell people things he doesn't think at the time they'll be interested in; maybe just to be friendly—and said "I just got back from getting my credit card where I forgot it yesterday. Radio Shack, on a Hundred-eighth? That ever happen to you?" "Never." Emilio said, "not once since I started them, maybe twenty years," and I. said "How do you avoid it? I've lost mine three times this year alone." And Emilio said "I always make sure to get it back. I think; I remember; I concentrate my mind on the card from the instant it gets out of my hands till it comes back. And not just back in my hands either. Because, you know, you can put it on a counter or table someplace for what you think's only a few seconds and then forget it there too—but until it's in my billfold." "So you use a billfold. Maybe that'd help; I use a wallet," and Emilio said "Billfold or wallet or even only in my pocket, though a pocket it can fall out from and a wallet's too small for me for all the things I carry. My point's that I never lose track of it in my mind once till I have it back." "That's what I'm going to do from now on," I. said. "Keep my mind focused on the card till it's back in my wallet. I think I always do that but it's obvious I don't a few times. From now on, as a reminder, I'm going to think or say to myself 'Think Emilio' every time I use the card." Emilio laughed. "Glad I can be some use to you." "You don't know how much. 'Think Emilio. Think Emilio.' It'd be better if your name—better because I'd remember this memory device better—was just one syllable. But it's two—no, it's four—and you gave me the idea, so I'd like to use it if you don't mind." "Why should I? I'm glad to give it for such a good purpose. Losing my credit card and not knowing it was in a safe place I could get it the next day would be terrible for me. I'd worry about it all night." "Same here." Elevator came a second time and I. said "Thanks," and got in and went upstairs, or rather, to the seventh floor where the apartment was.

So what was he saying? He was saying, he was saying that he'll use some trick or device or motto or watchword or guideword or something as a reminder every time he makes or is about to make one of his other kinds of mistakes. Mistakes with people, not with things. Mistakes such as he made with his wife before. In other words, to avert the mistake before he makes it or stop it before it's completed. Something like "Think what you're doing." That's all right but too long. He knows his memory, his memory isn't very good for something like a long reminder. Better to keep it to one or two words as he does now with "Think Emilio" every time he uses his credit card. How about, then, "Think Emilio" for mistakes with people too? Seems to have stuck and it's certainly worked. Hasn't lost or even come close to losing his credit card the last couple of months. But he ought to have a different reminder for the mistakes he makes with people like his wife and kids. "Think mistake" then? No, he's not sure why, but no, it won't stick, he just knows it won't, though maybe it should be something that begins with "think." As with his personal ID numbers, or whatever they're called, for his ATM and phone cards, all of them—he has three: two ATMs for the two cities they've residences in and one phone card—are as close to being the same PIN, it is, as he could get them. If he had three very different PINs he wouldn't remember them as well, especially because he doesn't use them that often. In other words, though he's not sure he wasn't being sufficiently clear there, if he chooses something close to the "Think Emilio" reminder he's been using for a while he might have a better chance of remembering it. "Think Em"? No, doesn't make sense, though would have in place of "Think Emilio" when he first started using it—three syllables shorter. But the truth is that even back then he would have remembered "Think Emilio" better than "Think Em" because it was from Emilio that all this reminder business started from. "Think reminder" then for people? It isn't quite right but if it works, it'll do, and it makes a certain amount of sense. So, from now on, every time he's about to act crossly to his wife or kids: "Think reminder." Or about to blow up over something she's done or he has to do for her when he's busy with something else and doesn't want to stop or when something like that happens with one of the kids or some accident, after a whole slew of other things, by one of the cats and he's on the verge of saying "Godalmighty"—something like this—"will this crap never end? Why does everything have to constantly screw up? What the hell's wrong with things? What in God's name am I, cursed? This freaking life is a joke, a trick, it's the worst, that's all it is, hours and days of useless doings and stupid duties and hard work with a few good moments to an hour tossed in every now and then to give you the illusion...to make you believe that...to fool you into thinking it's possibly worth living," and so on, think "Think reminder." Rather, say it to yourself, or even out loud if you're by yourself, or even out loud if you're with someone or even with a group of people—it'd be worth it, wouldn't it, if it stopped you from starting another horrible scene and making an even greater ass of yourself? Someone asks what it means, say "A warning to myself. When I feel I'm about to explode or act unpleasant or hateful again to my wife or kids or anyone else and sometimes even to the cats, I say, for a reason that's not really logical but I settled on it a while ago and so far it works, 'Think reminder.' Without it, stupid as it is, I'd be a fool."

He goes to his wife—she's in the same room and chair he left her in, the situation he didn't resolve when he thinks he could have; instead he blew up and stormed out—and says "I apologize." "Oh great," she says, "after the damage has been done and left to fester so long it's almost become permanent. You ought to think more about the harm you do sometimes and how it affects people and what you look like—especially people who are closest to you and thus most hurt by your outbursts—and the impression you make while you're doing it and also the foulness you leave behind." "That's why I came back to you. And why it took so long, because I've been thinking. I not only apologize for what I did and know how it and other things I do like it affect people and what I must look and seem like while I'm doing it, but I've also devised a way to stop myself from acting like that again," "And what is that?" she says. "It's to say," he says, "and you can ask why I settled on this phrase but I'm not sure it'll make any sense to you after my explanation, just as in some ways it doesn't make much sense to me though I still think it'll be effective…but what was I saying? I'm sorry, and I'm not kidding, or stalling, but what was I?" "Why you settled on a phrase that's going to stop you from blowing up at me, and I hope also at the children, again." "That's right. Exactly what I meant, thanks. And the phrase…damn, what was it? I didn't mention it already?" "No. All you said was…you were going to say… I forget, suddenly. Probably because I don't, by now, after all your previous efforts to overcome your fits and bullying flare-ups believe anything will work for you, so I'm just not taking you seriously," and he says "I can see why you'd think that and be depressed by it also, which you didn't say. But this new tactic, what I have in mind, will work. It started with 'Think Emilio.' Regarding my credit card. Losing it? Our doorman? You know what I mean." "Emilio's reminder to concentrate on your card when—" "'Think reminder'—thank you. And sounds as if it makes no sense, right? But that's the phrase, what I'm going to use from now on to prevent my awful behavior. I forgot it this time. But you know it, or heard it, and I'll write it down someplace. Maybe even several places. Keep one of those written-down reminders with just 'Think reminder' on it in my wallet and another on the refrigerator and a third tacked above my writing table and a fourth taped to my desk at work, since I could forget where I keep it if I only have one, and you also couldn't recall the phrase." "This is what you came in to tell me?" "That and to apologize," he says, "and also that I know what I've been doing and how it affects people, etcetera, and the goon I must look and sound like while I'm doing it. But 'Think reminder.' I'll think or say that to myself or even aloud if it doesn't sink in any other way, and it should stop it or start to." "Knowing you," she says, "I think you need more than a facile reminder to change. Something considerably more drawn out and functional, like therapy." "I knew you'd say that. But a phrase will do, after a few repeats of it, as it has with my credit card. My problems only seem irremediable without professional help till I start doing something about them, or something that can work. This one won't be fixed overnight but I'm hoping it'll be quick. Will you at least accept my apology?" "All right," she says, not smiling, "and now please help me with my feet? That's what I asked when this whole business started and you immediately—" "I know what I did. I thought I had—well, I did have something I was about to do then, but I can see your feet are more important. That they were stiff, and are probably even worse now, and hurting you. I have to tell you I never got to do what I felt was so urgent to—never even started, after I stormed out—because I was so upset at my treatment of you when I could have just done what you asked in the time I spent mulling over my lousy behavior." "That's true and a character insight I've never heard from you." "Thank you," and he gets on one knee and takes her left foot. "This one worse than the other?" and she says "Both the same." So he works on her feet. Spends a half-hour doing what she says needs to be done to them. "Leave it to me," he says while working on the toes of one foot. "Before, it probably only would have taken me fifteen minutes for both feet and you would have been grateful and cheerful to me after. Now it's taking twice as long because I didn't give them immediate help when they needed it. And maybe also, as you more than once pointed out, they got even worse because of the emotional stress I caused you, or something like that, so no matter how much time I work on them you'll still be angry with me. Am I right?" and her eyes are closed and were closed while he was saying this, but not with a look of satisfaction or pleasure, and she nods and shrugs her shoulders at the same time, meaning what? he thinks. "Anything else you want?" he says after she says "That should do it," and she says "No; thank you; just this time put my feet down gently please?" and he rests her feet on the foot stool and goes into the kitchen where his typewriter and typewriter stand are to do what he wanted to before he blew up, but when he gets there he forgets what that was. Let's see...something about...did he jot it down anywhere? No. So think, think, but nothing comes. Some words that were in his head. A sentence, but a short one. An ideal starting-off line, he thought then, because he can recognize one when it comes, and which he felt would have a good chance of building into a first draft of a complete work. But it's not coming back and most times when that happens without him having put the line or thought down, it's gone for good. Best, then, to do something else though not necessarily something with so much drama. Huh? What's he saying? He doesn't know and doesn't know how the line got into his head. He thinks he got that last thought right but he probably didn't. His mind just doesn't seem to be working well now, so for the time being give it a rest.

He lies down on the bed in their bedroom. He was going to say "his bedroom," but then it's also hers, one dresser and small closet for the two of them, the bathroom they share, and so on. Wait a minute, doesn't he have his two residences mixed up, one his wife's old student apartment in New York and the other their house? The bedroom in the apartment, where they stay lots of weekends and sometimes weeks at a time and twice in the last fifteen years for half a year when he was on sabbatical, is the one the kids sleep in. He and his wife sleep in the living room there on a box-spring bed that doubles as a couch during the day. The kitchen with the typewriter and stand is in that apartment also. Now he's in their house two hundred miles from New York—all right, a little town (it could even be called a village) in Baltimore County, what's the harm in saying it?—which has three bedrooms, the master one and one each for their kids, and a kitchen much larger than the New York one and which has no typewriter or typewriter stand. Doesn't have to, since the table he types on in the house is a long one in their bedroom. Typewriter's the same, though, since he carries it from place to place. But how's he explain the scene in the apartment building with Emilio and the lobby and elevator and, just before, the kitchen with the typewriter and stand? Emilio, etcetera, happened three months ago during his winter break when they were staying in New York for two weeks. The kitchen scene is just a mistake he'll correct by changing the room to the master bedroom. For about a minute there he thought he was stuck. So, after he takes care of her feet he goes into their bedroom, sits at his work table, line doesn't come back and he gives up on it and gets on the bed, puts three pillows behind him—he and his wife each sleep with two pillows, so one of them is hers—wipes his eyeglasses till the only thing obscuring part of his vision is the scratches in the four lenses, grabs off his night table the book he's been reading, and reads. This is good, he thinks, a few pages into the book. Not the book but his feeling. The book is only okay and has been 'only okay' and sometimes a lot less than that since he started reading it, which he has to do for one of his classes; when he selected it, having read it about ten years ago, he thought it would be much better. What he meant before was that he feels good. He's brought peace back into the house. Or let's say "his marriage," and did he? Well, something like it or gravitating toward it. He's so sure? Well, he thinks he is, but go over it: he was the one who blew up and disrupted things and he patched it up, or sort of did, and he isn't even upset that he lost an opening line that he's almost sure would have grown into something good that he could have worked on for the next few weeks or more. "Think reminder." Has to remember that every time he feels he's about to blow up or act in any way like that again to his wife and kids. "Think reminder," or even quicker, "Think peace." No, he started with "Think reminder," it's in his head, he's already remembered it—he did just now, didn't he?—so keep it rather than start with something else.

He reads some more in bed and finds himself drifting

off. Good time for it too. Well, it's also a good work time for the same reasons: kids out of the house, place quiet, and he's smoothed things over with his wife, or for the most part, so no self-damning thoughts in his head. But read some more, see if you really want to nap. Reads a few more lines, eyes start closing, body feels relaxed, even a bit of tingling in his fingertips and toes. He's drowsy all right. Takes off his glasses, sets them to the side on the bed, lets the book rest face down on his chest. He naps, doesn't know how long—clock on the dresser is facing away from the bed. Someone must have moved it. Could only have been one of the kids, when she was on the phone or just trying to make a call, not realizing she was moving it from where it served a purpose facing the bed. That happens. People absent-mindedly diddle with things when they're on the phone. He does it too on the dresser with two ceramic frogs and a turtle someone gave him—three different people, actually—which usually sit on top of his wife's jewelry box. But he never does it with the clock, or rarely, and if he does he's sure he always turns it back to the bed again. So what's the time? and he takes the book off his chest and rolls over to get up and something snaps underneath him. "Oh no," he says. He knows what it is and that he's broken off or cracked an important part of it. Every part of it, in fact, is important. "I am such a dunce," he says, "I can't believe it." Take a peaceful nap, break a pair of glasses, he thinks. "Think glasses" he should have gone into his nap with or said several times before. Or just put them—of course this would have been better—on the night table, and in their case, if he knew where it was. He looks: one of the sidepieces has come off. He can't see the extent of the damage—if a screw came out of the hinge of the sidepiece, for instance, or if the sidepiece broke off—without his glasses, so he gets an older pair from the night table—an earlier prescription, but he can see out of them—puts them on and sees that the sidepiece broke off and the frame part above one of the lenses is cracked. This is the third time he's done this the past year, though one time when he left the glasses on the bed he sat on them and broke both sidepieces and the frame. "In fact, I am such a dunce that I really can't think of anything more to say about it," he says. Now what's he mean by that? Who cares? What's the difference? The point is he broke the frame and it's going to cost him to replace it. But if he did want to answer that "What's he mean by that?" question, he'd say: he doesn't quite know. The "quite" there meaning he thinks he knows a little but not enough to explain it. So what does he know that's a little? That he forgets and forgets and forgets and never seems to learn from his forgetting. Or put more simply: ... No, that's it.

He goes to the kitchen and says to his wife "Chalk off another seventy-five to a hundred bucks from our savings, because I just rolled over on my glasses while I was taking a nap. Or really, after the nap and while I was getting off the bed to look at the clock—to see how long I napped and also what time it was—and broke them again. The frame, not the lenses; then we'd really have to go into hock." "I'm sorry," she says. "But you have a couple of usable old pairs if you can't wear the broken one now, and consider the new frame you'll get as a necessary medical expense, so tax-deductible." "And you know what? I never did find out what time it was.

What time is it? I think I also forgot where I put my watch when I took it off for some reason earlier today and now I'll probably have to spend ten minutes searching for it." She looks at her watch and is about to tell him the time when he glances at the clock above the sink and says "Oh; and I didn't nap long at all." "You should make up a reminder for those kinds of possible forgetful actions, as you did so successfully for your credit card. 'Think case,' or 'Think put the glasses in a safe out-of-the-way place' when you take them off. As for your watch, just 'Think where I left the watch,' though the last two would be a bit long to remember." "A bit long?" he says. "Can you even remember what either long one is just a few seconds after you said them?" and she says without seeming to think about it 'Think put the glasses in a safe out-of-the-way place' and 'Think where I left the watch,' in addition to saying 'though the last two would be a bit too long to remember.'" "That could be them," he says, "and also the last part, because I forget. But your memory isn't that much better than mine; just much better today," and she says "I also said, before I said 'Think where I left my watch'—and I'm only saying this to test my own memory—'when you take them off' and 'as for the watch.'" "That I remember," he says, "though you messed up on an article here and there." "What would you say to 'Think safe' for your eyeglasses? Easy. Two syllables. To be used every time you take them off in bed. As for the watch... ah, you should probably only work out one problem at a time." "I'll say the 'safe' one next time, if I can remember it. It's a good thing I'm married to you. You give me lots of useful ideas, and for other reasons too, of course." He kisses her. She lets him but

213

looks at him warily before, during and for a little while after the kiss, as if she doesn't know quite what to make of it. Actually, he's not sure she looked at him that way while he was kissing her—his lips on hers—since his eyes were closed.

FOLKS

HOW TO EXPLAIN his parents' behavior? They were in the back seat of his old VW bus, acting like young lovers, he could almost say. His mother's head against his father's shoulder. Both with their eyes closed, I. in the front seat driving. Folks in the one row of seats behind him. Middle seat had been taken out so he could carry things like his father's wheelchair folded up, though that he could store in the narrow luggage space behind the rear seat, so the opened wheelchair when he tied the bottom part down with bungee cords so it wouldn't move. With his father in it, of course. But this is getting a bit muddled. To him, so it probably would to just about everyone else. Something about his folks' behavior, he'd started out saying, so get back to it.

He was driving back from dinner at his brother's house in Connecticut, his folks in the rear seat. His brother had rented a house in Westport for the summer and I. had rented one in Old Mystic, about an hour away from Westport, for his folks and himself. His mother had first said he should spend the two months there alone: he could use a break from them and all he does at home. Besides, she said, she doesn't like the country much: mice in the house and bats and biting bugs outside and nothing really to do but look at nature and compare sunsets and take long walks on dusty roads and be driven to a market and read till your eyes get bloodshot, but he told her he wouldn't go without them. His father had Parkinson's disease and diabetes and I. was the one who mainly walked him for exercise and gave him all his insulin shots, and he wouldn't feel right being away while she was taking care of his dad in the city and she knew she'd never become adept at injecting him since she was afraid of needles. "We'll plant a vegetable garden and watch the animals steal from it. Why should you stay in the sticky city when you can be in the sticky country? Though the nights are bound to be a little cooler, for the hot ones it'll be like the old days when you had to rely on natural breezes and your own sweat and fans." "Does the house have adequate screens?" she asked. "Do you know if all the cracks and holes in the basement are plugged up and the locks on the outside doors work?" and other questions, most he couldn't answer because he'd never seen the house, only had a description of it. But he eventually convinced her, and his father went along with just about everything they wanted to do; he'd become easy to persuade since he'd gotten Parkinson's, when before he was often unbudgeable and domineering. So they were driving back from his brother's. Ride actually took about an hour and a half—this was the second time they were doing it—since the bus could never get above fifty miles an hour except going down hills, and going up fairly long hills, no more than thirty-five. I. would have liked a few days alone in the country—a week, even; two, three—but, as he'd told his mother, it couldn't be. His brother couldn't take his folks in even for a night. He had a wife and three kids and a large dog and several smaller animals and the house he was renting, more like a cottage, had two small bedrooms and no screened-in porch and there wasn't enough room anywhere else for all the kids to sleep; the oldest boy was already sleeping on the living room couch. How'd I. get the farmhouse? He'd met a writer—a woman twelve years older than he—at a film screening two months before, they began an affair, using her pied-à-terre in New York, and she suggested he rent a house near her for the summer and bring his folks with him; she owned a studio in the town she lived in and they could have their trysts there. She was married and her husband knew she had "other relationships," as she called them, "but doesn't seem to care nor carry on any of his own. That's been the state of our marriage for five years. We sleep in separate beds, though for appearances in the same room. Make love no more than four times a year and always at my initiative—all of a sudden, you could say seasonally and even after I've had consummative sex with someone else that day, I get these pleasant undeflectable stirrings and wake him up and tell him to move over—and only stay together for the sake of our girls. Once they're both in college, we're divorced." She lived in Westerly, Rhode Island, about twenty minutes from Old Mystic, maybe more; he never made the trip. She looked in the houses-for-rent sections of the local newspapers, found this one for him, the rent seemed within his means, she said, but she'd cover part of it if he couldn't afford it all plus utilities and his parents didn't chip in (she and her husband came from old-line money and she also did pretty well with her writing), so he rented it. Day after they got there she called him and said maybe it's not the greatest idea to carry on so close to home and her discerning daughters, and he said she's probably right, it was different when they had the freedom of her pied-à-terre. She offered to send him a check for the first month's rent, since it was she who had pressured him to take it, and he said no, coming here was the right move: his folks haven't had an extensive vacation for many years and he can use the quiet and lack of distraction to finish a work he's been on awhile. So she's out of the picture. She said in that call she hoped to resume their friendship, as she called it (she wouldn't even meet him for coffee in a café that summer) when he got back to the city, and he said "Who knows, because by then you might have a new male friend you'd rather be with or a solid prospect of one," and she said "We'll see, but I won't write you off and neither you me."

So, I. in the car driving. Looked at his folks through the rearview mirror. Father's head against his mother's shoulder now; they were holding hands on one or the other's lap. This is the way he remembers it. Her other hand holding his father's thigh or knee. Their eyes were open. His father was smiling slightly, seemingly to himself, and because of the Parkinson's, he thinks, the smile was frozen. His mother just looked content. "Everything all right back there?" he said. "What do you mean?" she said. "Everything okay, the two of you comfortable, seat not too hard and the ride smooth enough?" "Very comfortable, soft and smooth," she said, and smiled. "For an old buggy this car still has good shock absorbers. Are they still called that? It's been so long since I had anything to do with a car, I wouldn't know." "Suspension system, maybe; though I think 'shock absorbers' is fine. I know as much about it as you do, but probably less because you drove a lot longer than I." Her smile widened; his father's stayed the same. Hers for her love of him, his father's just of someone feeling good for the time being. I. could see his folks through the rearview mirror, even if it was around eight-thirty or nine, because it was early July so still light. "I can say the same too," his father said. "And that's...?" I. said. "Very comfortable, like your mother." "I'm glad. You look like two lovebirds back there." "We are two lovebirds," his mother said. "I can second that too," his father said. And then something startling happened. No, that gives it away. Something he didn't expect, then. That too, a giveaway. Well, it's already been given away, so just say it: his father kissed his mother's lips. She saw his face coming and closed her eyes and they kissed. I. had a little difficulty keeping his eyes on the road and watching them in the mirror. His father's eyes were closed too when they kissed, he thinks. After they separated they both smiled and then his mother stared at his father for a few seconds, seriously, he remembers, and then rested her head against his upper arm and his father held her hands with one of his hands and the other was around her shoulder. No, couldn't be so if she was resting her head against his upper arm. Maybe she rested it there and then when he took his arm away to put around her, she rested her head against his chest. They stayed that way the rest of the trip, or if they moved around and then back to that position, he didn't see it. When they'd got about halfway to the farm-house, his folks seemed asleep. He kept looking at them in the mirror—it was dark by now so he only caught glimpses of them when there were lights from the road.

So, how to explain their behavior that time? While he was driving and after they kissed and then seemed to be sleeping, hands still held, his mother against his father's chest, his father's cheek, he just remembers—he has a clear picture of it—resting on his mother's head, he said to himself something like Where's all this coming from and why now? After he parked by the farmhouse, he said very softly "Yoo-hoo, lovebirds, we're here." Then a little louder "Hello in there, you gotta get up." They awoke at almost the same moment. He wasn't looking at them in the mirror now; he'd turned around to look over the seat. Of course he'd have to get out and go around to the side door of the bus and help his father out. First he'd get the wheelchair from in back and unfold it and set it up—cushion, rubber pad on the cushion and hand towel on that—and then help his father out of the bus and into the chair. "Boy, that was a fast ride," his father said while I. wheeled him to the house and his mother held open the door. "Because you slept," I. said. "Oh, I wasn't sleeping. I was resting quietly with my eyes shut, enjoying every second of the trip. Your mother has a soft head to sleep on. I say that as a compliment. It felt soft." "I slept," his mother said. "The ride was very nice." "Very nice," his father said. "I can even say I had one of the nicest days of my life today," she said. "That so?" I. said. "I don't mean to sound stupid or provocative or anything, but how come?" "Just being with you all and the way everyone and everything cooperated and went so well." "Your mother's right." his father said. "And plenty of it has to do because of you, so thank you, son." "Son?" he said. "What the heck's going on? You never called me that." "I used to call you it all the time when you were young." "Did he?" he asked his mother. "I don't recall," she said. "We're talking about a while ago. But if he says he did, why not believe him? My memory isn't as good as it used to be but your dad's is as sharp as ever." "What I said," his father said; "your mother's right." "Would you like a cup of coffee," she said to him, "or water or soda?" "It's a little late for me to drink anymore," his father said. "I'm almost ready to go to bed." "That's right, I forgot," she said. "Do you want to get started?" "I'll take care of it, Mom," I. said. "You just take it easy." He wheeled his father to the stairs, walked him up to his bed-room—his folks slept in separate rooms in this house. Sat him on the bed, took off his pants, got him on the commode they bought for the room, since the one bathroom was downstairs. Dumped the urine into the bathroom toilet, came back upstairs and took his father's shirts off and put on his pajama top. I. thinks his father always slept that way from the time he first got married and maybe before; *that* he never asked but the part about the marriage he did, or his mother once told him. That was it: "Since we've been mar-ried, whenever I buy him pajamas I have to give the bottom part away." "Who would take it?" I. asked and she said "Nobody, of course, I'm sure not even Goodwill. What I was really saying was that I use them as rags." Then he helped his father to lie down on the bed and put diapers on him, though his father hated when he called them that.

221

"Anything would be better; the name of the make, for instance—Chux." "So, goodnight, Dad," he said, covering him up. It was a nice night, cool, breezy, dry, and the air smelled good; someone from one of the houses or the farm nearby must have mowed the grass or done whatever a farmer does to get that smell. "Want the night-light on, off?" "Keep it on. And please get your mother for me. She'll come in anyway later on to see that I'm okay, but I have to tell her some things for tomorrow." "Sure," I. said, and kissed his father's cheek, said goodnight again and left the room and told his mother his father wanted to see her. She went upstairs, they talked—I. couldn't hear what they were saying and wasn't listening—and then went into her room and back into his father's room and shut the door. I. went outside for a walk; he didn't want to hang around. Looked up at the sky—it wasn't a great night for stars—and then didn't look anywhere, just thought. So this is how it ends? Sometimes? They'd fought for so many years. Almost every day a fight and usually when his father came home from work, and usually at dinner. No, that's an exaggeration. But twice a week at least, it seemed, and sometimes bitter arguments where they shouted at each other, called each other names, but never came to blows. Never even raised a hand to each other or even threatened to strike or hurt the other. His father threw money at his mother a number of times; his mother threw a fork or spoon to the table or floor and left the table during dinner several times, sometimes in tears, usually not; just angry. Slamming of doors. A few times one of them leaving the apartment and not coming back for an hour or two. Even an argument a week ago that almost turned into a fight. But I. stepped in and said "Come on, will ya, stop, you know I hate all that stuff," and they shut up, looked away from each other, didn't say anything to each other or him for a couple of hours, but at times when they could have and it would have been normal to. So why that night, he thinks, were they so warm to each other? It have anything to do with his telling them the week before that he hated their arguing? Doubts it, for he'd done that lots of times before. The day, like they'd said? Well, there'd been others as good as that one. A few, anyway. The weather, a combination of all those things and more? Could be, but he could never know for sure.

He took a long walk, along the road their house was on, through a cemetery, around the general store, which was closed—it closed at five—past the closed collectibles, usables and antiques shop, which he looked in the windows of for a few minutes, then along another country road till it connected to the one their house was on. The light in his father's room was out, when he got back. His mother's bedroom light was on. She was probably reading. He saw this from the front of the house. He looked up to see if more stars had come out; they hadn't, or he didn't see them, and no moon either. He went inside and poured himself a vodka over ice and sat down to read. Maybe things will go as smoothly as this for them from now on, he thought. He hoped so. It was wonderful to see. It made him feel good for them and himself. He wished, of course, it had been like this all his life.

CANDLE

So how's it that she's sitting next to him in the car? She's in the passenger seat, he's in the driver's, and he's on the expressway driving home from work. Suddenly he looked—sensed something was there; thought for an instant it was a shadow or sun ray or paper of his that had blown onto the seat—and saw her, holding a handbag to her waist and staring out the windshield. Her lips start moving as if she's talking, but the noise from outside's pretty loud and he can't hear her—both windows are open; it's a warm day and he rolled them down right after he got into the car. Also, the radio's on, and he turns it off and rolls up his window almost to the top and says "What's that you're saying, Ma?" "Oh," she says, turning to him and smiling, "I'm kind of sorry you did that; I was enjoying the piece. You always had a way of getting the best out of a radio—a magic touch, it must be. Every time I've been in a car with you and you switched on the radio, or at your home, beautiful music came out without you even moving the station dial and at a perfect sound level if you pressed a button rather than turned a knob." "It's not magic; just luck the station happened to be playing music you liked. As for my not dialing around till I find the right station, I'm afraid I'm the one in the family who controls most of what plays on the car radio and radio in the living room, I think you're talking about. And I always keep the dial tuned to the classical music station in the city or the Washington one you can only pick up in the car. And the sound level, which automatically goes on when you press the on/off button rather than turn a knob—when it's that kind of radio, I'm saying—is the same you last had it at before you shut the radio off. Anyway, probably more than you wanted to hear about it, right? But to get back to what I was asking you, what were you saying when I didn't hear you before?—ah, I guess it doesn't matter now," and she says "I wasn't saying anything. That action with my lips moving and not even a hum coming out is a habit I developed when I got very old and which I've no control over, you haven't noticed it before? But now that I have you here, tell me how you're doing?" "Me? You know, fine as ever, always fine, fiddle as a fiddle, as I used to say as a boy, you once told me." "You got that expression from Dad. He said it the right way, and you tried imitating him when someone asked how you were and said it the way you just did, 'fiddle-fiddle, drum-drum.' But how am I, you should be asking," and he says "Of course, I'm asking, I've certainly been thinking about it, because I most deeply want to know," and reaches across her to pull out her seat belt and buckles her in. "I don't need this harness, do I?" she says. "I'm not a child and I've never been in an auto accident in my life, as a passenger or driver," and he says "It's the law; I could be stopped." "In that case, I'll submit to it, since I don't want to be the reason for you paying a fine, not that I wouldn't pay it for you if there's any money in this bag." "What I'd also like to know from you—well, lots of things, as you could imagine, but this one almost the most—is how you got in the car?" and she says "Quite simply, I wanted to be near you, so here I am. I've tried many times but it never worked. You happened to be driving when I tried this time, and I obviously turned out to be successful for a change. But this car; it's so small; how can you and your family and your wife's wheelchair and everything fit in it? What happened to your van?" and he tells her about the head-on collision he was in a month ago and that this car, because he had no car-rental provision in his auto insurance, was the cheapest one he could rent, though prefacing it by saying "Before I give you this explanation, so you won't get alarmed I want you to know that nobody was hurt."

No, this is awful, he thinks—going nowhere, sounding flat-footed, if that can be used as a critical term, but he wants something with his mother in it. That's what he sat down to do. He was going through the living room to the kitchen—wanted to get a grapefruit from the refrigerator and cut it into quarters and eat half of it (probably while leaning over the sink so he wouldn't drip any juice on him)—when for some reason, seemingly out of nowhere he could say, though if he looked around the living room he bets he could find something that made him think of her—the two to three small photos on the mantelpiece of her with his kids, for instance, which he might have caught a glimpse of—the thought came to him to put aside what he was working on then to do something about her, and he went back to his bedroom to start it. And "Ma"? When did he ever call her that? Maybe never. Or so long ago he can't recall it, because since he was six or seven or eight it's only been "Mom." Never "Mother," except as a joke a few times when he said it to her in an exaggerated upper-class accent, nor "Mama," though that too he possibly could have called her when he was very young, and most likely did. It might even have been his first word, as it was his daughters'. For even that last day: "Mom? Mom? I'm so sorry, Mom. But you must get better, I know you're going to get better, so rest now, rest, Mom, everything's going to be all right, I swear." This is what he wants: where she suddenly appears, they quickly get the miraculousness of her being there out of the way: "I don't know how it happened either," she says. "'I'm not knocking it, though, since it gives me the chance to see you and you the chance to do something for me I very much want done." He asks what; she says "It's not my place to say." He says "Come on, Mom, don't stand on ceremony, as you liked to say. You want me to do something for you and we don't know how much time we have together here, so just spill it," and she says "Maybe if you tried to guess, because I still don't think it proper for me to come right out with it." He says "'Proper'? What kind of word's that for what we're talking about? I'll do whatever you want me to, because I know anything you'd want would be within rea-son, but you got to let me know what it is," and she says "Please, dear, let's not argue over semantics now." He says "When did we? Oh, the 'proper.' Okay, here's a good guess. You want to see your granddaughters," and she says "That'd be very nice, I can't tell you how much that would mean to me, but it'd be too frightening for them, and it wasn't what I had in mind." "Then I give up. I was always bad at guessing games unless I got help," and she says "Do you know what today is?" "The date? November 14th. Is that the old Armistice Day? No, that used to be the Eleventh. It's your birthday; I knew that." "You're fibbing me again. You don't want to hurt my feelings, but you needn't be concerned about that." "Okay," he says, "I forgot. But the day's a little more than half over with, and less than that if you consider when I get up and then go to bed at night, and I would have remembered by the end of it. I remembered your last two birthdays long before the day was over. When I woke up, in fact, the first time, or soon after—when I was having my first coffee, I think, which I do after I get up and exercise—and both times I drank to you at dinner, which I would have done tonight, and then talked about you at the table with my family," and she says "It's been three years, if you're counting today's as the third, since I stopped commemorating them, one could say, though that's not important. All right: I'd like a memorial candle lit for me, my 95th birthday, or anniversary, just as I did for my parents and your father and sister every year," and he says "Isn't my remembering your birthday, or anniversary, and thinking and talking about you a lot that day, enough?" and she says "It probably was for your father, though I still did it. I'm more of a traditionalist on this matter, so for me it isn't enough. And it is something I would have done for you, though I'm thankful it never came to that, whether you had wanted me to or not." "Okay, easy enough to do, I suppose, and if it pleases you, it's more than worth it," and he drives around—so he had to be in a car or van or to have eventually got in one—not to his town, which wouldn't have any twenty-four-hour candles like that, but to another town a few miles away near where they used to live that has several Orthodox synagogues and a couple of religious-articles stores and even the supermarkets in it, or the one he shopped in, had those candles in its kosher foods' section. He goes to that market—before he left the office he called home and his wife gave him a list of groceries to buy, so while he's there he'll get that out of the way—and chooses a candle that once the wick burns down he can clean out the glass it came in and use for drinking. He goes home, puts the groceries away and makes himself a drink and gets dinner started—most of it he already prepared that morning—and puts the candle on a metal plate on the mantelpiece and lights it and says to himself "Look, Mom, I have no prayer or blessing. There's one on the candle glass but I can't read Hebrew well, and it would sound odd to the family saying it aloud too, but this one's just for you." Ah, what am I doing, he thinks, talking to her like that? A few minutes later his younger daughter says "Who's the candle in the living room for, Grandma?" and he says "You knew? That's great. I thought I'd have to do a lot of explaining to everyone about it. How'd you know it was for her?" and she says "She used to have them at her home for your father or somebody, or she did once when we were there, and this is around the time of her birthday, isn't it?" and he says "That's right; today; very good." "Won't the glass break from the flame?" and he says "It must be very strong glass, because I'll tell you, it's hot. Don't ever touch it. You can feel the heat when you get near. It's a nice glass too, if you can picture it without the wax. After it's burned down and the glass is cleaned—probably in the dishwasher, next time we load one, just to make sure all the wax is out—we can use it as a water or juice glass," and she says "Don't ever give it to me. It must be bad luck, or I'd think of Grandma and would get sad." "Then if nobody will use it, I will. Maybe for my one big drink at night. Like a jelly or jam glass—I like the way they feel in the hand—though those I don't see anymore." After dinner his wife says "What's with the candle?" and he says "Why else? My mother." "It could also be for your father, for all I know, since I never saw you light one before. It's the anniversary of her death?" and he says "Her birthday; she died in May." "That's what I thought. But aren't yahrzeit candles supposed to be lit on the day the person died, though I guess it doesn't matter?" and he says "I'm not sure; you may be right. Yeah, I think you are, but you know, the two calendars are different and I'd think if you really wanted to do it right, you'd go by the Jewish calendar. And how do you go about finding her birth or death date in the Jewish calendar, or even go about getting one of those calendars? Oh, a synagogue would most likely have one, but I never go in them, and a religious-articles store for sure, but those places give me the creeps. Anyway, the way I'm doing it is the way she did it for my dad and sister and her folks. Maybe she faced the same problem with the two calendars, but she lit the candles on their birthdays according to our calendar. It's possible their birthdays meant a lot more to her than the days they died. I'd think so, but I never asked." His older daughter comes into the living room while he's reading in the easy chair and she doesn't say anything, just stops at the coffee table to look for a minute at a magazine on it and then goes, though she has to have seen the candle—it's so bright. When she walks past him again, he says "Did you notice the candle, sweetheart?" and she says "Where? No, what candle?" and looks for it and sees it and then looks around the room and says "What beautiful shadows it's giving off." "They'll probably even be better when all the lights are out. It's for Grandma, her birthday, or anniversary—birthday should do; anniversary I always think for weddings or big events—her 95th," and she says "That's very nice of you to think of doing that."

THE PICKLE

HE WRITES AND writes and writes and nothing comes out.
Oh, plenty does, but nothing of any worth. So he writes
some more and some more and some more, and still the
same thing. Lots of words come but words seem to fail him.
Clichés, though, don't. Words and clichés, same situations
or similar ones, people talking and acting and reacting the
way they've been doing a long time in his work or close to
it, things he's done, things he's done something very much
like, things he doesn't want to do but finds himself doing
and knows he'll have to cut, things like this: crap, bilge,
blather, fakery, self-imitation, pushing it, meaningless
words, lines, pages, but all in one paragraph. So he takes a
break and then starts again, writes and writes and writes and
it's the same thing, it's nothing, it's worthless, it's familiar
stuff, it's, it's…it's hopeless, that's what it seems like,
though he knows it isn't. He's been in this position before.
He was going to say situation but he's already said situation.
But first he was going to say pickle. So why didn't he say
pickle? Because it really isn't a pickle and saying pickle
would be saying it just to, well, not ingratiate himself with

whomever sees this, though that was what he was going to say and is probably what he means, but to…to just sound amusing and appealing and maybe even winsome or endearing or something. There, an obvious example of the pickle he's in, when it's obvious he's just padding this thing and can't even find the right words or substitutes for them so he doesn't have to repeat the ones he's just used. He should take another break, it's obvious he should, and he does and comes back and writes and writes and writes, lots more pages, lots meaning seven, eight, nine and all of them with almost no space left at the foot of the page and margins on the sides, and these and the rest of the ones he's done so far today he knows will be discarded later. Discarded meaning junked, dumped, not torn up but just crunched in his hand and dropped into the trash can under his work table, or just collected and dropped into the can without being crunched, and tomorrow, or whatever day he empties the can—probably tomorrow, for it's quickly getting filled—he'll take the can to the kitchen, take out all the paper and stuff it into a shopping bag with old newspapers and magazines and other things made of paper for the recycling pickup every other week. Nothing's coming out, that's why. Out of what he's doing at his work table, he means. Nothing funny or deep or emotional or real or dark or strong or intelligent in any way. But more important…but he forgets what he was about to say. That's right: more important, or equally so or almost, nothing that engages him is coming out, much as he hates that word the way it was just used. "The work engaged me." Oh dear, did it? "What an engaging work," and so on. He knows there are less pretentious words for it, but what's he supposed to do, waste more time flipping through the thesaurus or some other word book for something he's not going to use? Drop it again, take another break, take lunch—have it, he means—and he does, even if he's rarely eaten lunch since he doesn't know when and this one isn't what most people except perhaps Asian Buddhist monks would consider lunch: a mug of miso soup with some thin seaweed strips and a little ginger grated into it and a plain unsalted rice cake and mug of green tea, all brought to his work table, though from now on, to simplify things, he should call it a desk. So he's by his desk and sits and writes this and some more in between soup sips, constructing the sentence that way so the sits and this and sips would hitch, though for what purpose, and particularly that inaccurate added-on hitch, isn't clear. Oh, he knows, what's he talking about? For the effect or affect, he likes to say and probably has said somewhere else on other pages. But that's so...so...not silly or superficial but something along those lines, and isn't it, after all the times he's gone to the usage section of his reference manual for this problem, about time he was able to distinguish those two without thinking of it? Yes, without question, for he feels like an idiot sometimes when he realizes he used one or the other incorrectly in conversation—in print, of course, while he's writing it, he can just go to the reference manual again—but he's not going to do anything about it right now. Why not? Because he doesn't feel like it, for one reason. He's doing something more importunate (he doesn't think he ever used that word before, in conversation or print, so where the hell did it come from, though he's not quite sure he used it correctly) and who says he has to deal with it immediately? Maybe after this is done...Ah, it's done, just give up on it, since it doesn't seem to be going anywhere, or for the time being stop, maybe take a longer or just a different kind of break by walking around the block. That sort-of rhyme wasn't intentional. It just came, and it makes sense as something to do if he wants time away from his work so he can think about it, except that he doesn't live on or near a block anymore. Did till about seven years ago when they moved to this rural suburb where no part of it that he's familiar with is rectangled or squared by streets. When he leaves the house through the kitchen, which of the two exits they have is the one almost always used—the other through the living room opens on to a broken step and tattered doormat and overgrown weeds and, it seems half the time, thick mud and is about thirty feet from the driveway and carport—he can either walk down that driveway to the neighborhood's main crossroad and go left or right at it for about half a mile to one or the other of the main arteries in the area, or make a right when he leaves the carport, which the kitchen door opens on to, and walk up his neighbors' private road that passes the side of his house, cut through their property—it's huge and they've given him permission to anytime he wants though said to use a flashlight at night because they won't be held responsible if he falls and breaks a bone—and once through the woods that border their backyard, get on a street that connects to another street that winds its way down the steep hill to one of those main arteries which eventually hooks up with the crossroad that runs past his house. Is there a good reason why he went into all of that?

Can't think of any and he had nothing in mind when he started out with it except perhaps...no, he was going to say something about the way things connect—thoroughfares, in this example—and how that connectiveness or whatever you want to call it acts as a sort of completion, but that's something he just this moment thought of and really doesn't work. Description, then? A different way of laying out the area he lives in? Like the last one, he only just thought of it, and as an explanation for putting in all that street and road business, when he really gets down to it, it doesn't make much sense. Oh, just leave the house already, and he does, through the kitchen, but first says through the door of his wife's studio, which is right off the kitchen (as is the dining room right off it but with an archway between them rather than a door): "I'm going for a short walk, is that okay?" and she says "Take your time, everything's fine here...I'm settled," and he says "You sure? You're strapped in?" and she says yes and that's when he leaves (after he says "Then goodbye"), up the road about twenty feet and then thinks no, and not because this is the way he usually goes when he sets off on one of his solitary walks, long or short, and which he does on an average of once every two weeks, but because...because this time...well, he just doesn't feel like starting it with a steep climb up the hill, and turns around and goes to the end of the road, which connects with his driveway near the crossroad, and thinks left? right? which way should he go? Right leads to one of those two main arteries...wait a minute, he's almost sure he didn't picture the layout of the driveway and crossroad and private road very well. When you enter the private road from the crossroad you can either go up the hill to his neighbors' house or, ten feet into it, make a sharp right to his driveway, which pulls up alongside the carport, or, if you want to back into the carport, you drive up his neighbors' private road about seventy feet, though he supposes—no, he knows—it's partly his private road also up to the end of the carport, since his neighbors once showed him real estate documents to support their claim that he was responsible for paying half the repaving of the road up to the end of the carport. That should do it. So: left, right, which way should he go at the crossroad? Right leads to one of the two main arteries and he'd have to walk back from it unless he wanted to circle around to the other main artery—he doesn't because he doesn't want to leave his wife alone that long—a walk of about three miles. So he goes left—right also isn't as picturesque a walk and is also at the start a lot hillier. Walks on the left side of the road, feels good, air's fresh, sky's clear, and there's a pleasant smell of something burning: a lit fireplace in the air. He of course means a lit fireplace somewhere. Reaches the main artery, goes left, passes the first street because its incline's too steep, goes left at the next which is also steep but not as much as the street he just passed. In this neighborhood, it seems, you really can't take a walk anywhere—a circular walk, meaning not doubling back—without going up a big hill. Oh, this is getting worrisome—worrisome; what a word—his inability to say almost anything clearly: the descriptions and then his interpretations of them, he means, and even what he just said doesn't sound right. But stop worrying. Just get on with this, see it to the end, and if there's nothing there or nothing to work with, chuck it in the bin. Now that one he likes. He walks up that second street, stopping twice to catch his breath…sign of age? You bet. Let's face it, he thinks, you're getting old, or let's just say you're not as strong physically as you used to be, no matter how much exercise, weightlifting and jogging you do, because ten years ago you could have taken this hill without a stop. Maybe not jog up it without stopping, as you could have ten years before that, but walking briskly up it you definitely could have done. Well, you still can sometimes—not briskly (though part of the way you probably can), just without stopping—but not as often as you could have done ten years ago or even five. So? So, nothing. He walks up that second street to the top, where it joins with the first street he passed. In other words, the two streets meet at the top of the hill, the second street ends and the first continues on, which is what he does on it after stopping to catch his breath at the top. What a complicated or just poorly worded way of saying he's now walking along that first street. He reaches his neighbors' long stretch of property, goes through the woods at the widest opening, cuts across their yard—no lights on in the house; both must be at their jobs downtown and their dog's probably inside—goes down their road to his carport, enters his house through the kitchen, and that's his walk. "I'm home," he says through the door of his wife's studio," and she says "Hi, that wasn't long." "Well, it was just to…you know, take a breather. Anybody call?" and she says no. "How're you doing?" and she says "No change from before, thanks," and he says "Good. Need anything?" and she says "No." "I'm here if you do, but if I'm in back, just

239.

yell," and she says "Okay. You bump into anyone or see anything interesting on your walk?" "No, nothing eventual
happened; I mean, eventful. And not a soul. Nice and quiet;
way I like it. Almost the whole area to myself." It's true, he
thinks, putting the tea kettle on for coffee, he didn't see any
people on his walk except in a few cars and a delivery truck
when he was on the main artery for a short time. But not
one car passed him on the crossroad and streets. He didn't
even see a dog, though heard—so it wasn't entirely quiet—a
couple of them barking behind bushes he passed and one
time one snarling and scratching at the fence it was behind
as if it wanted to tear through it to attack him. He also saw
a dog sitting in the front seat next to the driver of the car,
though first thought it was a person. So how long does he
think he walked? Far, he means. About a mile. He calculates
while waiting for the water to boil: half-mile down the
crossroad, first that hundred feet to it, then a half mile or so
on the main artery and streets up the hill and to his neighbors' woods, then two-hundred feet across their property,
maybe even more, and another hundred down the private
road, so altogether more like a mile and a quarter. Not
much of a walk. Why'd he add that? Not that not much of
a walk but the whole thing as to how far he went and his
calculations? Water's about to boil—he can hear it in the
kettle—but he suddenly doesn't want coffee or tea. Doesn't
know why he added it; it certainly wasn't interesting or necessary in any way he can see. It just came and he put it in.
Words just come and they come and they come and he still
has nothing to really show for it. So he's home now and he
at least does feel refreshed from the walk and he forgot while

he was walking why he started out on it. So, why did he? Well, he... Not just to take a break. He thinks it was to try and come up with something to write about when he got home. He's almost sure of it. No, he's sure, he's positive. An idea for something that could materialize into something. But it didn't happen. Did he even take a pen and pad or loose piece of paper with him in case he wanted to write something down? Feels his pants pockets, feels something in the right side pocket that feels like a pen, and puts his hand in. Yes, he did; pen and folded-up sheet of paper. Doesn't remember putting them in. As a memory exercise, try to, and he shuts his eyes but nothing comes. Something of course does—that photo-negative-like image of the room's window he was looking at before he shut his eyes, moving in quick short jumps to the right till it disappears and then immediately starting the same hopping motion from the left, dark panes outlined with light frames. As he said, like a negative. So, what did he think about while walking if it wasn't about what he'd originally taken the walk for? The dog behind the fence, he remembers thinking. And dogs in general: why almost everyone in this neighborhood seems to have a dog or two, most of them behind underground electronic fences. But the one behind the real fence...is this really important? Just finish the thought. One behind the real fence: hoping it wouldn't get loose. Not that he wouldn't have stood where he was and shouted for it to stop or go back, and if that didn't work and it looked as if it wanted to attack, kicked it in the head. It's true, he thinks now, he would have, or something like it. Maybe held up a stick if his shouting didn't work, and if the dog still didn't back off, swung it at him, and as a last resort, brought it down on its head. Plenty of sticks around, he remembers from the walk, even along the main artery. Probably as a result of the gale-like winds a week ago, or maybe around this time—late fall—branches just naturally snap off trees and break into smaller pieces when they hit the ground. And then he'd ring the doorbell of the house the dog came from and tell the owner what he did, and if no owner was around—what? Leave a note under the door written with the pen and paper he had with him, and his phone number. Or maybe just run home and call an emergency vet service to care for the dog, saying he'd pay—he'd even meet them there—that is, if the dog didn't get up after he clubbed him and scoot away—though later try to get the money back from the dog's owner because it had tried to attack him. He'd do all that? Just about; he's not just talking. That's the way he is. When he was a kid and right into his thirties, standing up against much bigger guys if he had to, never backing off if threatened except one time with a knife, never starting anything himself, or rarely, but getting excited by a good fight. And more recently? Well, the last twenty-five years, with his mouth mostly. No, only. But if something happened where words didn't work and he had to protect himself or someone else, and he's still pretty strong because of his daily gym work but does have trouble with his wind, he'd jump in and try to finish it quickly: headlock till the guy cried quits, or a couple of well-aimed punches, maybe one to the groin. And a woman and baby seen through a living room window, he now remembers from his walk. She seemed to be helping it to stand or walk. Now that's something—nothing to write about later but to tell his wife—because...or maybe it is something to write about; he'll see...because he remembers that while looking at the woman and baby, and it was only for around twenty seconds—didn't want to get caught peeping—and he didn't think this while looking at them but when he resumed his thought, he means walk, he thought of when he did the same thing with his kids, letting them go finally and catching them if they started to fall. He loved those years. Holding his girls so they could stand and walk, later their little hands in his when they were walking, and his wife walking then too, always holding her hand on the street if he didn't have to hold the children's, everything so much lighter and easier. Memory now, one he's had many times before: carrying his older daughter in a Snugli in the Whitney Museum, maybe his favorite memory other than when his wife gave birth to her while he was in the birthing room. Really, looking back, he can't think of any two better. Why? Well, the birth one sort of goes without saying, doesn't it? Forty-five and his first child? Something he wanted for around fifteen years and twice came close to having—proposed and would have married just to have the babies but both women ultimately chose abortions and then dropped him—and after all the complications his wife had in the hospital right up to the moment of delivery? That one was easy. But the one in the Whitney? He doesn't know why. They were alone; it wasn't an unusual day or event. His daughter was what—three, three and a half months, four? Calculates: born middle of February, they were in New York on his winter break, so that's about right. Her face against his chest, head just below his chin, one of his arms always around her, or actually supporting her from the bottom, since he didn't trust the sling she was in. Walked across the park, he thinks, probably after visiting his mother on the West Side, no doubt holding the wool baby blanket around her with his other hand because of the cold. But the really memorable part: walking through the various museum rooms, kissing the top of her head and exposed cheek, talking softly to her while she slept, about what he forgets, and her light breathing and heaving. What else from today's walk? Plane overhead, number of crows squawked from trees as he passed, bunch of geese—not a bunch but a what?—flying in formation not too far up. He's sure they were geese by their honking, but maybe they were ducks. Anyway, he's back and didn't come up with anything on his walk to write about that he can see. The woman and baby? Doesn't think so. Tells himself to sit at his desk—he has a little time left, and his work, he means his wife—he doesn't know why he keeps making that kind of mistake—seems okay. "So go, vamoose, sit, work, work," he says out loud to himself, and what's the Russian word for it that he knows from his wife and is sort of a joke between them when either of them knows the other isn't doing what he should be, which is working… "*Rabota! Rabota!*" and his wife says through her door "You referring to me, sweetie?" and he says "No, just giving myself marching and work orders while I still have the time; sorry. Everything still all right?" and she says yes. Good, he thinks, good; everything's okay, so no more excuses for delays. Because maybe something's there that wants to come out—thinks this while going to

I.

his room—or will come out when he starts typing. Gets to his desk, sticks paper into the typewriter and starts to type and types and types and types and nothing really comes from it. He reads and rereads it and it's nothing. Tried using the woman and baby after all and his reflections on his own life that came from it, and it was nothing. The long walk, up the hill and down and thoughts that came from it: nothing. The snarling dog behind the fence, a scene showing what he'd do if it got loose and tried to attack him; nothing. Meaning nothing usable, nothing he'd want to work on later, nothing he likes or that excites. Nothing he finds funny or powerful or deep or moving and other things like that. Original. Nothing original ... for him, he means. So, give up on it already; no, give it one more shot. Puts paper into the typewriter, places his fingers above the keys. Thinks he must look like a pianist about to play; also because of the intentness of his face. And he once did play the piano, when he was in his teens. Totally self-taught. Can't remember getting as involved, for the first fifteen minutes or so each time he was at the piano, in anything more. Right from the first time he sat down on the piano bench in his family's living room—of course he'd sat down on that bench other times, but this time it was to play—and started tinkling and running his fingers up and down the keys and then banging away and to his ears it sounded something like serious music. Serious music, classical music, to him they were the same and the only music he loved. And the more he played, the more it sounded like that kind of music. Did this for several years, all stuff he made up in his head as he played or had made up in a pre-

245

vious sitting and was now reworking or that he'd heard on a record or the radio or in a movie and which he'd add to. Lots of chords and heavy foot pedaling. Almost everything in C major, and he rarely used the black keys. His father often called it a racket and asked him to stop, so he tried not to play when he was home. His mother, who played occasionally from music books, said some of his compositions were soothing and sweet and did he want to learn to read music so he could write them down? His brother and sister had both taken piano lessons and liked his playing sometimes, though other times said it was busting their eardrums and the same tune over and over again driving them nuts and he should think about giving his fingers and feet a rest. Sometimes he even sat down at the piano at parties. A couple of times someone sat next to him on the bench or leaned on the piano to watch him play, and then left in a minute or two without saying anything. He knew they had expected better. He remembers thinking a few times he was fantasizing he could play well, he wasn't even a good amateur, so why did he persist? Because he got things out of himself from the piano he didn't in any other way, and sometimes he hit on something that sounded like an original melody and which was sad or strong or rousing and moved him, and that that could happen one time in ten was enough for him to continue to sit down and play. He once consented to take lessons his mother would arrange for him. The teacher said the first day "You say you already play, so let me hear," and after he played for about thirty seconds: "No no, it's a nice simple tune you have there, but everything else is wrong." He showed him how to sit at the piano and spread his fingers and place them on the keys and where to put his legs and what to do with his feet and what a sharp, flat and clef are and gave him musical notes to copy in a staff book the next week and a scale and short children's piece about a milkmaid and pail to practice for his next lesson, but he didn't go back. Knew he wouldn't, two minutes into the lesson, and walking home he felt guilty his parents would have to pay for it. Never had another lesson in his life. Once dated a music major in college who said she'd teach him the basics of piano playing in a week and he said he thinks that'd take all the fun out of it and he's always been a lousy student anyway. Anything in any of that? Doesn't feel like it. Sometime while thinking all this he took his hands away from the typewriter and put them on his lap. He's done for the day, he thinks. Gave himself a chance, didn't he? Did; many. Tried on and off for at least two hours. Wasted a lot of paper, though to be honest most of it was the clean side of photocopies of finished manuscripts he didn't need anymore or last-draft pages he didn't complete. Face it: it's not going to be one of those times he leaves his desk knowing he has something to work on there. Because that's all it is, right? A place to go to alone and something to do. No. Though maybe later, after he returns from work, meaning his job that pays. But probably much later tonight, after he gets home and makes dinner for his family and they eat. But night's usually the worst time to write. By then he's had a vodka and something, more likely two, and a couple of glasses of wine at dinner. Besides being tired from the job that pays and then cooking dinner and cleaning up after dinner with his daughters and it just being so late, considering that he gets up at 6:15 in the morning, in a long day. Tomorrow, then. Tomorrow, after some school work he'll do at home, looks clear, though he never knows what can come up. His wife might want him to do some things for her; there might be more school work than he thinks. But now he has to pick up the kids and right after that drive to work. He puts the cover on the typewriter, straightens up the desk, dumps the hundred or so pages he wrote today into his wastebasket. Okay, not a hundred. Maybe fifty; maybe not even that. Count them, what does he got to lose? It'll take a minute and might be interesting. Some writers count the words they've produced in a day, he can start counting the pages he's thrown away. Gets the pages out of the basket, stacks them and counts. Thirty-six. Year he was born, although he sees no significance in that. Just mentioned it because for a moment it struck him and he thought maybe, maybe it might lead to something in his head he could jot down or set to memory and later use on the page. Something about coincidence or his birth, or both. His mother liked to say that unlike with his brother and sister whom she had by normal deliveries, minutes before he was born...but he has to go. Dumps the pages back into the basket, flips his sneakers off, empties the pockets of the sweat pants he's wearing for the jeans he'll wear to work, quickly undresses and dresses, puts on his shoes, makes sure he has a handkerchief—feels his pockets; doesn't, so he gets one out of his dresser bag. He means drawer. He was thinking one line ahead. Gets his bag, which already has his school things inside—it's really a canvas briefcase, given to him by his daughters for his last birthday—and knocks on his wife's door. "Who that there?" she says. "I like that," he says; "I'm going to use it one day if you don't mind. It's I. I'm leaving to pick up the kids, and after I drop them here I'm heading straight for work," and opens the door. She puts down the notebook she was writing something in, and he kisses her. She says "See you later." He says "That a poem you're writing?" and she says "We'll see." "I'll call," and he leaves. He tried, he thinks as he drives to his daughters' high school. He tried and there's nothing much more he can do but that. Tomorrow, maybe something, if things work out. He's ready, he's open for it, so no reason why they shouldn't if he actually does find the time. The end of that last line an intentional sort-of rhyme? Yes, but not the following line. So, enough? Yes again. This one goes into the trash too.

AGAIN

HE MEETS HER at a dinner party. Did that he doesn't know how many times. Meets her walking up a building's stoop to the party. Meets her while resting on his way up the brownstone's stairway to the party. Meets her in the apartment building's elevator going up to the party. Meets her outside the door of the party where she's taking off her snow-wet boots and changing into shoes. Meets her coming out of the one bathroom at the party which he knocked on repeatedly because he had to pee badly and thought the person inside was taking too much time. Meets her on line at the buffet table where they're both helping themselves to food. Meets her at the drink table which he followed her to so he could introduce himself. At first she doesn't take to him at the party. At first he doesn't think that much of her. Later—after they've known each other a while and been spending almost every night together—she tells him she didn't like his cockiness and crudeness at the dinner table at the party. When she first saw him while they were having drinks before dinner she didn't think by his expression and clothes and speech that he could be too intelligent. She

251

thought he'd come to the party with a woman so she tried ignoring what she felt were his flirtatious glances at her. She changed her mind about him because of a certain remark he made at the end of the party and which she forgot when she recounted the incident to him. When he volunteered to clear all the dinner plates off the table and acting like a professional waiter brought in all the desserts in one trip and then the coffees and teas. When she went into the kitchen for aspirins and overheard him wittily critiquing a much ballyhooed serious play she also thought was trite and way overrated. When he caught up with her at the front door as she was preparing to leave and started in how he'd wanted to speak to her all evening and got very funny when he said he'd get on his knees to help put her boots back on if that's what it'd take to give him another two minutes with her. When someone at the table asked if anyone knew what *celeri-rave remoulade* was and he gave a recipe for it using silken tofu and went into the time fifteen years before when he first had it with regular mayonnaise at an open-market stall in Paris. Later—on their first date or after they'd been seeing each other a week or a couple of weeks or a month or more—he tells her he didn't think she was interested in him during most of the party because she kept turning away every time he looked at her. He thought she actually didn't like him for some reason and even thought him a goof because he was wearing old chinos and a short-sleeved polo shirt on a freezing day, while all the other men at the party were in dress shirts and sport jackets and suits. He tried not to pay much attention to her as a tactic to somehow pique her interest in him, for right from the moment he saw her at the party he was bowled over by her good looks and nice body and soft intelligent expression. He ignored her through most of the party because he was trying to figure out the best way to approach her and was afraid he'd immediately ruin things by saying something stupid or foolish or making some kind of bumbling move. What he really thought but never told her was that he wasn't the least attracted to her at first and in fact for about half the party found her somewhat stuffy, overformal, fakely gracious and with conventional ideas and views, besides wearing a silly-looking Russian or Polish outfit that made her appear frumpy and which clattered when she moved because of the metal beads or balls hanging from the skirt hem. He became attracted to her sometime into the party and doesn't know why. Something to do with seeing her in profile smiling, coupled with the way the lights in the room, familiar as this is, made her blond hair shine. That she had what seemed like real blond hair and light eyes and very fair skin, a combination he always liked, and that an hour into the party he was already a little high and feeling a bit sexy. The way she laughed openly and loudly at someone's remark, then caught him looking at her from about ten feet away and covered her mouth with her hand, dropped her smile, and for a few seconds stared somberly at the floor. How she looked beautiful to him in a mirror she wasn't looking in, when he hadn't thought her good-looking before, and he thought it's just a trick of light and glass and when he looks right at her she won't look as good, and he did when she moved out of range of the mirror and was facing his way and she was just as beautiful. He suddenly started noticing her curves—buttocks, breasts, long slender neck—and when she sat, the nice shape, length and muscles of her legs. How so many men at the party, including some of the married and attached ones who had come with their wives and girl-friends, were playing up to her, competing for her attention, asking what they could get her from the food table or bar, and if they weren't in the group around her then darting looks at her from the side, and he knew there had to be something about her he wasn't seeing or hearing to rate all that. He looks at her standing and bringing a glass of wine to her lips and he imagines her lying on her back in bed, knees up and legs slightly parted, that intelligent soft smile, her long blond hair let loose and spread around her head and—if the light's right—looking like a halo, arms reaching up to him to bring him down. He gets her phone number from the host as he's leaving the party and calls the next day. He calls the hostess the next day and says "That very lovely woman at the party in a white blouse and black skirt with little red flowers on it and whose blond hair I'm sure, if she let it down rather than the way she had it knotted at the back of her head, would be quite long, maybe down to her waist. What I'm saying is I've misplaced her phone number she gave me, so do you have it and also her name which, because I might've had a bit more to drink last night than I should've, I suddenly forget?" He calls the host a couple of days after the party and says "There was this very pretty young woman at your party, a Russian scholar I think she said she was, or maybe I only overheard that. Average height, long blond hair, broad forehead, blue or green eyes and very intelligent face? Well, unless you're involved with her in some way that wasn't evident to me or thinking of becoming involved and want me out of it, could you give me her name and phone number or at least tell me how I might get in touch with her?" After she leaves the party he gets her name and the approximate area of the city she lives in from one of the men she talked to a long time and who seemed to know her from before, judging by the way they greeted and spoke to each other, and looks up her number when he gets home. There's one listing in the Manhattan phone book with her unusual last name and common fore-name, and the address is nowhere near where the man said she lived, and he calls her the next day. He tells a woman she was talking to at the party and who seemed to be a friend of hers that he found an expensive fountain pen of the blond woman in the Russian outfit soon after he'd talked to her and she left and wants to get it back to her but doesn't know her phone number or address and, now that he thinks of it, her name either. The woman says "How do you know it's hers?" and he says "Because she was holding it when she was about to write her name and phone number down for me, but got distracted by something and then I suppose she just misplaced or lost it." "Give it to me. I'll be seeing her in a week. I'll phone her tomorrow and let her know you found her pen, and if she needs to get it sooner, I'll run it over." And he says "There's something else I wanted to tell her about—a teaching job at a New Jersey college that I think she'll be interested in. It's tenure track and easy to get to by that Path system tube." The woman gives him the phone number and name and he calls the next day. He says "You don't know me but you might remember me from the party last night. I was the guy…well, maybe I shouldn't direct any more attention to it than it deserves, but the one in the short-sleeved striped polo shirt. I was told it was going to be a simple informal party. And that shirt is, unfortunately, inappropriate as it is for this weather, my best, but anyway, I wanted to speak to you but could never get the chance. There were…well, you were always busily engaged with someone or even several people at once, mostly admiring men, and I didn't want to bust in, and when I next looked around you had left. I got your phone number from a friend of yours at the party, someone I also don't know and whose name is…I forget, but I hope you won't mind too much that I called." He says "First of all I want to assure you I'm not a telephone crank or masher or some guy trying to sell you a newspaper subscription or cemetery plot or anything like that, but a friend of the host whose party we were both at last night. As you can see this is extremely awkward for me, but I hope you'll hear me out. If it becomes too uncomfortable for you too, please, anytime in our conversation and without warning if you like, hang up, and I promise I won't call again," and gives his name and says why he's calling. "Hello." he says. "We were at the same party last night and I think you lost a watch that I found." "Excuse me," he says, "I've never done this before, phoned someone I only just saw at a party the previous night and whom I was never proper-ly introduced to or had even spoken to a few seconds, but you were always immersed in conversation with other peo-ple that I felt it'd be futile to try to speak to you and that I'd try my luck the next day." He first speaks to her at the front door when she's about to leave the party. She's putting

I.

on her coat, he goes over, helps her with her second sleeve, she says thanks but what she really needed help with were her boots, he says if he had only known, she says only kidding and they start talking, seem to hit it off, he asks her to stay another fifteen minutes so they can really talk, she says she has to get home to finish up some work for tomorrow, he says may he call her sometime? She says she doesn't see why not, he says then he'd need her name and phone number, she gives her name, spells it out and gives him the street she lives on and says she's in the phone directory, he says now she's making him work...only kidding, and gives his name, they shake hands and she goes. He wonders, when he leaves the party ten minutes later—didn't see any reason for staying, now that he'd met her—if she was leveling with him about her name and street. Sure she was, because why else would she have spelled out her name? Only to make it more convincing? No, it doesn't make any sense. If she didn't want to see him she would have told him straight off. Still, he's not sure, and he goes into a bar, asks the bartender for a drink and the Manhattan phone book if he has one, looks up her name and she's in it on the street she said. He has another drink, thinks while drinking it should he call her to try to arrange a late-night meeting now or something for tomorrow? No, she's busy, or tired, he might slur from all he's drunk tonight and she'll sense or know he's high and wonder if he's a problem drinker or if he has to get high to call her; she'll remind him she left the party earlier than she wanted to do important school work at home and he should have more regard for her time; she'll think he's showing just a bit too much eagerness to see her tomorrow by calling

257

tonight and wonder if he's a little odd. So he'll say right off "I know it's late and you're probably working, so please excuse me. I only wanted to speak to you a minute more to find out if you'd like to meet sometime in the next week, since I didn't know if I'd get you tomorrow—you might be out." If she says "Meet when?" he'll say Tomorrow?" but maybe that would also be showing too much eagerness, so instead "Any day you're free but tonight." But best not to call at all, and he thinks about having another drink, then thinks Don't get so bombed, because you are now a little woozy, where you'll be hung-over tomorrow and not in great shape to call her. He goes home, is so excited by the prospect of calling her in the morning and seeing her soon that he has trouble sleeping, wakes up several times to go to the bathroom or jot down things he'll open their phone conversation with. In the morning he throws away these notes, thinks What the hell was he thinking with them where he'll sound so programmed and rehearsed that she'll see through it in a minute, and waits till a few minutes after noon to call her. She isn't in and he doesn't leave a message on the answering machine when it comes on, wanting her to think that the first time he reaches her is the first time he called. He tries a few more times that afternoon and because he now knows the answering machine goes on after the fourth ring, he hangs up after the third. He works a little at his desk, reads, exercises, goes out, takes a long walk, browses in a bookstore, does a little grocery shopping, gets home around six and calls her. He forgot about the answering machine but hangs up the moment it comes on. He calls again at seven and then at eight and she answers the phone.

"Hello," he says, "it's me, from last night," and gives his name and hopes he's not calling her at a bad time. "Not at all," she says, "and it's nice to hear your voice again," and they start talking. He first speaks to her while they're walking downstairs from the party. He saw her leave and he quickly grabbed his coat and left without saying goodbye to the host. She's nearly down the second staircase by now and he says from the top of it "Miss, excuse me, but miss?" and she turns around and points to herself questioningly and he says "Yes, yes, you, wait up please," and runs down to her. He says he's been meaning—first he says hello, his name and he knows this is unusual and possibly even scary, his yelling from the stair landing and chasing down after her like this, but just hear him out a second and if it at all upsets her he'll go right back upstairs, even if he's got his coat and was thinking of leaving anyway—to speak to her all evening, then when he saw her leaving he thought this would be his last opportunity, so, to be quite honest, he hustled after her, and he's sorry if he startled her and for everything else. She says she wasn't startled and isn't in the least frightened though she is surprised by his actions and she'd really like to talk to him but she has to hurry someplace, she's already very late. But if he wants—because, honesty for honesty, she's sort of noticed him too—not "sort of" but just noticed him—and even entertained the thought of going over to him at the party and introducing herself, since she felt that's what he wanted to do but something was holding him back—why doesn't he call her tomorrow or sometime, and gives her phone number and name and he writes it down in his memo book, first says just give it to him, he'll remember it. No, to play it safe he better write it down, because if he forgot it he'd really be ticked off at himself, though he's sure he could then get it from the host. They leave the building and walk down the stoop and he says maybe they're going in the same direction. If they are would she mind if they walked together or took the bus or whatever she wants to take? She says she plans to hail a cab right outside here and she's so late for this other function that she'd prefer not even taking the few minutes it might take to drop him off if he was going her away. He says he understands, it's okay, sees a free cab coming, says should he get it for her? but she's already in the street signaling it down, smiles and waves goodbye to him and gets inside and the cab drives off. He first speaks to her when they're walking downstairs from the party with several other people he doesn't know. The host had said a few minutes ago to the thirty or so people at the party "Folks, I'm sorry, and don't be alarmed, but I'm suddenly not feeling well. Nothing serious; probably just the opening salvos of a one-day stomach flu, though if one of you discovers me dead tomorrow you'll know it was something more. But I'll have to ask you all to leave so I can tend to the bug before I collapse and then get to bed. And nobody worry about cleaning the place up. A professional's coming in tomorrow to do it." He says to her on the second stair landing "This is funny—excuse me, I should've given my name first," and gives it, "...but the two of us leaving at the same time, when the truth is," and he speaks very low, "I've been meeting to mean you...I mean—oh, you know what I mean, though what a time for a verbal blunder—but I didn't know how to go about it, to meet you." "You go up to that person if you're at a gathering like the one we were at where everyone was invited, and introduce yourself. And don't be concerned about the transposition of words before; it's an easy mistake to make when they're alliteratively so close." "Of course you're right," he says, and speaks very low again as they continue downstairs, "but you were always around lots of people or engaged very deeply with one and I thought you'd think I was a simpleton or interloper if I tried insinuating myself in that way," and she says "Why? It's the universally recognized breaking the ice. It's totally acceptable clumsy human behavior, if it isn't done rudely. And even if you have to barge in a little to make the initial contact, it's okay. Anyway, hi," and gives her name and he says hi and gives his name again and sticks his hand out to shake and she says "I hope you don't mind if I don't take off my glove; it's not easy to get on while the other hand's gloved," and they shake. They go to a nearby restaurant for coffee and dessert with a few of the people they walked with downstairs, and he gets her phone number there. He starts talking to her in the foyer as they're getting ready to leave the party, goes to the elevator with her and eventually gets her name and phone number and permission to call her while they're waiting for it. When it comes and the door starts jiggling but doesn't open, he says "Not that I want to scare you, but do you think something could be seriously wrong with the elevator? It took so long to come, now the door doing a dance, and we heard what sounded like an elevator alarm bell go off for a few seconds." She says "I'm for chancing it, since I'd rather not walk down twelve flights," and the door opens and she steps inside and says "You coming or do we say goodbye here?" and he goes in. "Somebody was probably holding the door open for someone else for a long time," she says. "Or filling the car with boxes or groceries and then taking them off at his floor. And in doing one of those, accidentally leaned against the bell, but because he was a tenant, knew how to turn it off. But it seems to be riding smoothly and I'm sure the door will open in the lobby without a snag." "You're no doubt right. A good positive attitude, the opposite of what I usually have. Just that I wouldn't want anything to happen to us now that I have your name and phone number and am planning on calling you in the next few days." And she says "That's ridiculous," and looks as if she really thinks it is. "Maybe you should give me that paper with my phone number on it," and he says "Too late, I already swallowed it, and I know I was being silly. It's called first-association nerves," and she says "I'm sure it is, and of course I was only kidding before too. There, we've landed and not even a bump. If you have nothing more important to do now, like to go for coffee someplace near?" and he says "Sure, that'd be great. I want to say 'more than I hoped for,' but I don't want to start ruining things for myself." "Actually, tea for me, since it's late and coffee can be hard on my stomach at this hour, but we can get both in the same place," and he says "Tea's a much better idea, you're right again, though I don't want you to think I'm always so agreeable. For me, unless I have to drive home from a party that I had a bit too much to drink at, and I'm not saying I have a car or that I'm a big drinker. Just hypothesizing or hypotheticizing or something...what is it with me with words sometimes? I ask you: how do I get myself into these linguistic spots? Five in the afternoon—I think that's where I left off—is about the latest I have coffee." He walked her to the subway after the party and calls the next day. First he introduced himself when she was putting her boots on in the hallway outside the front door, said he was about to leave too and would she wait a minute so he could say goodbye to the host, because he'd like to talk to her some more, and she said "I don't know; I really have to go," and he held up a finger signaling one minute—he'll be one minute? just another minute of talk? he didn't know what she thought—and ran into the living room and said goodbye to the host—"I have to be quick; somebody's waiting for me at the elevator," and the host said "Who? You stealing my guests?" and he said "Yes, or trying to; very pretty; blond; Russian or Polish shirt; you know her"—and ran and then slowed down and walked fast to the front door thinking she'd probably left, but she was there, hat and gloves on, coat buttoned up, looking as if she was wondering why she'd waited, and he said "Thanks for waiting; I hope I wasn't too long," and looked for his coat among all the others in the hallway closet and on the closet floor and chair near the closet—"Oh Jesus, where the hell is it? My coat," he said to her, "it looks like a half dozen others," and found it, checked the pockets to make sure it was his, slipped it on and they took the elevator downstairs. Outside, he said "How are you getting to wherever you're going?" and she said "Home; I've work to do; by subway," and he said "Mind if I walk you to it?" and she said "If you'd like." While they walked and talked he thought she's as wonderful as he thought she'd be; better; she's smart, lovely, pleasant, good sense of humor, she's too much to ask for, too much, it's almost hopeless, somebody with so many great qualities? Surely she has to have a troop of suitors and someone special, but he thinks she came alone to the party, is alone with him now, smiling nicely, waited for him, though it seemed impatiently, seems interested in what he's saying, laughed at some of his lines, so he'll give it a shot. She directed their walk to the uptown entrance of the IRT subway and he said "You going uptown? I'm going uptown too, but I don't want you to think I'm just saying that to ride with you. Ride the subway uptown with you. Only kidding. Oh, I don't know what I'm saying, excuse me. Half the time, I mean. And I'm sure two-thirds of the people in Manhattan live uptown from here, though of course only about ten or so percent of them on the West Side. You on the West Side?" and she gave her avenue and cross street and he said "Me too," and gave his street. "By the way, in case you're worried about catching the next train, I'm listening for it, so if one comes you can dash downstairs. You have a token?" and she said "Yes, in my glove." and he said "Because I have a few extra in case you didn't. Actually, if you'll be all right riding home alone, and it must be getting cold for you standing out here," and she said "I'm dressed warmly for it, how about you? Because you only have on a skimpy shirt and coat," and he said "Thanks, I'll be fine. Though as I was saying, I'm close to Central Park West, so the IND is better for me"—he could make, and she must know that, the change at 59th to the IND, but he didn't want her to think he was too eager to be with her, he'd already given too many signs he was—"so if you don't mind

I'll take that line home. Though if you want someone to ride with you because of the hour, I could always change at Columbus Circle—59th, if you're taking the local all the way up," and she said "I could. But I don't mind riding alone, and I've something good to read." "Oh yeah, what? Which reminds me," and he patted his coat pocket, "—just checking to see my own book was there," and she told him what book she was reading and he said "Never read it but I've been told I should. A little classic that got away from me. And don't worry, I'm still listening for your train," and she said "It's all right, I can miss one. I have a book, remember? Even if I do want to get home. Have to, you can say, as I've a ton of work to do for tomorrow." "Then, would it be all right—this is the next step, and I'm sure you knew it was coming—if I phoned you sometime this week? Of course I'd have to have your phone number. If it's in the book, tell me—but only if you don't mind my calling—and if I have the right spelling of your name in my head," and gave it and she said "You're way off. And I don't know about your calling me. Oh," and she put her hand over her eyes, expression he could make out under it and from her mouth that she was doing some hard quick thinking, "oh...oh why not?" Took her hand away and said "You seem okay, sane, so on, and I don't mean to put it in that flippant way, because I think it would be nice to meet you, for a coffee or walk," and gave the number of her building—"You remember the avenue I'm on?"—and spelled her last name. "There are several variations of it in the phone book. This one isn't even cross-listed, there are so few of us in Manhattan—just me and my parents and uncle and a distant cousin—so I doubt you would have found it." "Well good, I got everything I need, so I'll see ya," and stuck out his hand to shake and then said "Actually, why don't I ride with you? I'll make the transfer at 59th and that'll save me a two-block walk aboveground to the IND now." "Fine with me. I didn't mean to suggest I prefer reading to company, although I often do." During the ride uptown they talked about their work, schools they went to, some of their interests, a particular piece of music she heard at a concert the other night and which he also likes, where they know the host from. He stood up as the train was pulling in to 59th and said "So I'll call you, and I have the right spelling now," and intentionally misspelled her last name and she said "Two e's, an i, no o—you don't think you should write it down or perhaps take my phone number?" and he said "Just joking again, sorry, and I don't want you to think I've a paltry memory," and the doors opened and he smiled, she did, and he got off. He wanted to wave through one of the windows after the doors closed, but she was pulling a book out of her bag and didn't look up. "All right, you made your point, I'm nothing to you, nothing," he said when the train started moving and she was already reading. "Pretty please, just look at me, maybe a facial squeeze? Just joking again, sweetie; no need to worry about me. I'm as sane as you said and also intemperately clean and I love your face and voice and body and can't wait till I next see you. What else do I want? You said a mouthful. Dumb? Oh boy, is he. Good thing the train's noisy and you can't hear him." Calls her two days later. Calls her three days later because he wanted more time to think if he should call her. If he calls, he thought, they'll probably make a date to meet this week or the coming weekend. She seemed fairly interested. The book—going for it so fast—that didn't show any interest. But really, what did he expect her to do once he got off the train, look around for him and wave? They'd said their goodbyes in a way: he joked, they smiled, doors opened and he left, and as far as she knew (if she thought of him a second after) he was heading for the stairs or already on or up them to get the uptown IND local. If he calls, he calls, she might have thought, and they'll take it from there; he doesn't call, no great loss. There are always other guys and he didn't seem especially bright. She'd think that? He didn't know. But the truth, let's face it, is that he came across as less smart than he thinks he is and his humor, what there was of it, felt forced and constantly fell short. But she did tell him how to get her phone number and was even ready to give it. He should have said yes, give it to him and he'll quickly write it down. But he had to make that stupid joke about paltry or faulty humor. Another instance of his rather unattractive, he thinks, self-maligning. Anyway, he thought, he's certainly interested in her. Body, etcetera, and going to bed with her, just as he said to himself after the train was gone. And on their first date or meeting or whatever you want to call it they'd take a walk if the weather wasn't too rainy or cold, so a short walk if it was. Or just meet someplace for coffee or a drink or have dinner at a simple place which he'd want to pay for—though he's almost sure she'll insist on paying her share—even if he doesn't have much dough. And then he'd walk her home or take the bus with her or put her in a cab, and while he was in front of her building or in its lobby if it had one, saying goodbye or goodnight—and not put her in a cab but help her flag one down or just walk her to one—or before she got in the cab or he got off the bus he'd say would it be all right if he called again? Or "That was fun. Would you like"—or better: "That was nice"—"to see each other again?" And they probably would, he thought, the next week or in a few days, unless things didn't go well for them for some reason that first date or she told him something like she's involved with someone else and up till now didn't realize how much and seeing him again would only complicate matters and be unfair to him, though the chances of that happening were pretty small. But if they did go out again it'd be to a movie or museum, he thought, or for dinner, if they didn't on their first date, or lunch or for a walk if the weather was good or coffee or a drink, even if they did that their first date. And he'd see her to her building after or to a cab or ride with her on the bus, and if it was to her building he wouldn't ask to come up and she wouldn't invite him up. He'd just say at her building or in the lobby or by the cab she was about to take or on the bus before he got off "So I'll call you in a couple of days," or she'd say "How about if I give you a ring later this week and we'll arrange a time to meet," and he'd say "Sure, that'd be great, I'd love it," and give his phone number and they'd meet a third time. Maybe at her apartment for dinner, probably not at his, though he's a pretty good cook. But he didn't think she'd want to come to it that night when they'd probably start kissing and maybe petting a little. She'd want to be in a position where she could say to him "This has all been quite nice but has gone a bit fur-

ther than I want it to right now, so I'm afraid, before it gets
too uncomfortable and difficult for both of us, you better
go, though we'll see each other tomorrow or whenever you
want." If they did have dinner at her apartment that night
he'd bring a good wine and fancy dessert and special appetizer he'd buy at a fine delicacy shop in his neighborhood,
thinking he could be the big sport, since she was providing
what would no doubt be a terrific dinner, and especially
when it might end up or even help get them into bed
together. But they probably wouldn't that night. They'd
kiss and touch each other a lot, he'd ask to sleep with her,
she'd say it's an attractive idea but she doesn't feel it's the
right tine for it yet, they'd make arrangements to meet the
next night, or the one after, and that'd be when they'd first
make love, probably after going to a movie or the theater or
out for dinner or just someplace for a drink or snack. Then
they'd see each other steadily—almost every day and
night—and talk on the phone the days they didn't meet,
and in time get married, he thought, and think about having a child. They'd live together before they got married;
her place, probably; his was a bit seedy and too small. But
not for long—six months, maybe; a year—because he was
already in his forties (she seemed to be about ten years
younger than he), so if they were going to have a child—and
he wouldn't marry anyone or he thinks even go out with
someone very long unless he felt sure she eventually, if
things continued to go well with them, wanted to have a
child—he'd want to have one soon after they got married
and maybe start one a month or two before. All to explain
why—or this was the main reason, he thought—he waited

three days to call her. He wasn't sure he wanted things to go that far, which he felt, just from their one quick encounter at the party—or at least for him—it could. Or she calls him four days after they met at the party. He hadn't called her yet because he felt he needed more time to think if he wanted to go out with her. Her looks, he thought. He wasn't sure if he liked them or if he even remembered what they were like. She also seemed a little heavy—he'd always preferred slender or even slim but well-built women—so maybe there was a predisposition to overweightness in her family and which would really show up after she had a child. She also seemed a bit pretentious, even something of a pedant, a type he never got along with or liked. But he could be wrong about most of it, right? He'd been drinking at the party—a lot more hard stuff and then good wine than he normally drinks at night—and they'd only spoken to each other for about ten minutes, so just call her, he thought, for what's one short date? It could be in the afternoon, just for coffee or a beer. And she had to be intelligent, he felt—he definitely remembered good speech, a big word or two and a reference to something literary—and it was usually interesting hearing about a person's life for an hour or so and even briefly going into his own history with someone new and talking about what he likes to do—when she called. He says hello, what a nice surprise and that sort of thing, and by the way, how'd she get his number? and she says from the host of the party, who else? "He was the only one there who knew us both, I think. But I didn't want to tell him the real reason I wanted to call you, which is if you'd like to meet for coffee or a walk today, so I said you had loaned me an expensive fountain pen when I needed to write something down and I'd forgot to return it to you. If he ever asks you if I called, that's the story line I'd like you to take." Or she looked up—she says this—his name in the Manhattan phone book. "It's an easy enough name to find—there doesn't seem to be more than two spellings of it—and how many in either spelling could there be with your fairly uncommon first name?" Or "You gave me your last name—even spelled it out twice, though it's a fairly common name and there's only one way to spell it as far as I know—and said you lived on the West Side." Or "You introduced yourself with your complete name, neither one is difficult to spell and I overheard you tell someone you lived in the West Seventies between Columbus Avenue and Central Park West. So I called Information, gave your name and said your building number is probably between one and sixty on one of the blocks in the West Seventies, and got your phone number, simple as that." Or "Let me refresh your memory, for I fear you did a bit more tippling at the party than you remember and no doubt some more after I'd left. You started passing out a card with your name and phone number on it to all the women at the party except the one tending bar," and he said "Yes, that's me all over. I do it at almost every gathering I'm at and am always running out of those cards but oh, the largesse." Or "I told you, when you said you'd like to call me and asked for my number, that there's been some serious trouble with my phone—it must be a cut cable someplace, because my entire building has the same problem—and that I'd have to call you from outside, and asked for your number and you wrote it down," and he says "Now I remember; thanks for reminding me. But what I'd also like to ask—and don't get offended, since I'm only kidding around with this—is what took you three to four days to call? I've been hanging around my phone a lot of that time and had just about given up," and she says—she says nothing; she just laughs and he says "Great, we both got a sense of humor; that's a good start, don't you agree?" and she says "Good start of what?" and he says "A phone conversation, that's all. What did you think I meant?" and she says "I really can't say," and he says "You really can't say because you don't want to—are being polite—or you really don't know?" and she says "Excuse me, but I'm slowly losing what sense of humor you said I had," and he says "Don't worry, I'll clam up. Let's just make a meeting time and place for coffee or a drink this week, what do you say? And believe me, there was nothing provocative or to provoke or anything like that in that last remark about saying, I swear," and she says "Listen, I'm reconsidering—" and he says "Don't reconsider, please. Honestly, it's just that I'm a little nervous and thus awkward with first phone conversations with someone I'd really like to see, so let's just meet, what do you say—I mean, okay?" and they make a date to meet at a coffee shop in her neighborhood the next day. She sends him a letter. "First, it's entirely possible, for any number of reasons, that I have to recollect for you who I am. We met two Saturday nights ago at a surprise party for Barbara Holski which, unfortunately, I was too late in getting to to be in on the surprise and I had to leave before the big cake and other delicious desserts were brought out. We spoke for a few minutes as I was leaving and you asked for my phone number. I gave it, you didn't call, and I thought perhaps you had a change of mind about calling me or lost my phone number. If it was the former and you still hold to it, you needn't read on. Yesterday I asked our mutual party host for your address. I didn't want to ask Barbara, since she wasn't the one who invited you and, from something you said, I thought our mutual party host (MPH) would be a better bet to know how to reach you than her. I also could have got your phone number from our MPH, but I didn't want to call you about the matter I'll soon raise. I thought that would seem a bit too forward on my part and also be somewhat hard for me to take if you didn't recall who I was. For my own reasons I didn't tell our MPH the real reason I wanted your address. So please, if you two speak to each other soon—although I gathered from our MPH that you're not as close as you were at the artist colony last summer where you first met him and Barbara—don't let on that my wanting to give you pertinent information regarding a job offering I told you of at the party and you said you were interested in wasn't the truth. (Ten-second contemplative pause. Then: benign expletive to herself of the oh-hell kind and returns to writing letter.) Oh, go on and tell him, why would I care? Our MPH isn't a prig. I'm sure he wouldn't even be curious if I told him I wanted your address so I could go to your apartment to speak to you about something a lot more personal between us than what I actually want to say to you in this letter. Which is: if you'd like to meet, as you said you would when I was leaving the party and which I assume was the reason you took my phone number, please give me a ring. (You don't, by chance, have

some other mysterious, recondite numerical reason for taking people's phone numbers and which has nothing to do
with calling these people, do you?) If I don't hear from you
after you receive this letter—and our MPH was sure this
was your address, since he said it's where he sent the party
invitation, though it could have been forwarded to you if
you had moved (but in that case, so would my letter), I'll
simply accept that you had that change of mind I referred to
before (we'll forget my idiotic notion of numerics) and
that'll be the last you'll hear from me. Most sincerely," and
she signed her first name. He wrote back: "Thanks for your
very funny letter. You couldn't have known, but I love
receiving and opening letters as well as reading and writing
them. Unfortunately, I'm corresponding with no one now,
so your letter was especially welcome, though I have corre-
sponded with seven to eight people at once and with two of
them, till recently, I exchanged a letter a week. One of my
former correspondents is the son of a woman I used to live
with in California for a couple of years. He's a teenager now
and I suspect writing letters became too much of a burden
for him, creatively and perhaps emotionally. Or else he saw
no point to it—he even expressed this, I now remember—when we could far more easily talk on the phone. Out
of sight, out of postage, I suppose, but from my end of it the
cost of the calls has become so high that I have to keep the
number and length of them down. Truth is, I don't think
he'd mind if we dropped the whole connection thing altogether: that I'm part of a past that's getting dimmer and
dimmer to him and ever less important. As for the rest of
my correspondents: one died, another's living in an area of

the world without postal service, a third was asked by her fiancé to stop, and a fourth correspondence I had to end myself, since she always included a fairly long piece of her fiction she wanted me to critique. That leaves two or three others, whose letter-writing—for no reason I could see except perhaps they also died, God forbid, or got very sick or were so misinterpretably hurt by something I wrote that they couldn't even ask me if what they read was what I'd meant and also wouldn't respond to my inquiries—suddenly ceased. I realize, regarding you, that it's slightly absurd corresponding with someone who lives a short subway ride away and when the cost of a local call is pretty cheap and I'm also perfectly ambulatory (all the others lived from fifty to ten thousand miles from the 72nd Street/Broadway subway station). But, if it's not a chore for you in any way, please write back at least once, telling me some more of yourself or of anything, including what a stupid discursive letter you just received. I've often thought that part of a person's personality can only come out in letter-writing, which I don't think is true for talking on the phone. I'll answer your letter (postcard, note, line) the same day, and then, after I feel sure you've received my letter—what do you think's the maximum number of days it takes for a letter to go forty blocks uptown on the same side of the city: three?—I'll put aside my desideratum to start a new correspondence, and call. "She calls him the next day. "Hi, it's me, your remissful correspondent. Thought you should know, and not just because the New York post office gets an unfair share of brickbats, that your letter got here much quicker than you thought. But the real reason I'm calling—and I thought it silly to write you, just as you said—is that if you want to meet for coffee or something for an hour, we'll keep it to, let's make a time." Or she doesn't call him so soon after the party. Said she would but didn't. He doesn't have her phone number though knows how to get it. But figures: if she wanted to call, she would, and if she lost his number, she'd know how to get it, so don't be a schlemiel and call her. He could just imagine: "Hi, it's me, the guy you met at Barbara Holski's birthday party, fellow with the…no, I don't want to make a joke about it, it'll only make me look bad, but something regarding a short-sleeved striped shirt and not an umbrella?" "Who?" she'd say. "Where? What? Oh yeah, the shirt. But the umbrella? Listen, I don't mean to sound rude or anything. But I'm very busy at this moment, and for reasons I'd rather not go into I have to get off the line now. And since I feel it's best to be direct about these matters, it's probably not a good idea to call me again." Then she calls in a month, maybe it was even more, and doesn't say why it took her so long to call since she took his number and he doesn't ask. He just says—well, first he says "I'm sorry, who?" and she gives her name again and says where they met—"Oh yeah. Hi, nice to hear from you, how're you doing?" and they talk. Have a good conversation, plenty of laughs and some interesting ideas and observations exchanged and expressed, and he asks and she says "Sure, that's why I called," and they meet. They have a good time together that first date (coffee, a short walk)—both of them say it—and shake hands when they part on the street, with the understanding he'll call her sometime that week. Does, in a couple of days—wanted to call her the night after their first date but she didn't seem the type who'd want to be pushed that fast. Better, he thought—since it did take her more than a month to call him and she never said why and he didn't think it'd be prudent to ask—to call her the next week, even, so she wouldn't think he was that eager to see her. He even thought: give it two weeks before you call, but he didn't want to chance her meeting another guy in that time. They go to a movie and after it to a restaurant for a light dinner and drinks and then start seeing each other every week and then once during the week and once on the weekend and then it's almost every day. This takes about a month and a half since they started seeing each other. In a couple of months they're sleeping together. He wanted to sooner. Tried a couple of times to get her into bed and she said the first time "I'm just coming out of a relationship, so give me more time." And then: "Listen, try to be more understanding. I was in deep and long with this other man and at the end hurt bad, so I still need more time. Sleeping together at this point might not seem like 'jumping in' to you, but it would to me." The first time, he said "Sure, what am I doing? I got carried away. Take as long as you want. It's just nice being with you and I wouldn't want to ruin it for anything." The second time, he said "It's getting a little tough for me—frustrating's the word. Very frustrating; my balls are beginning to ache. But I understand and won't make a big deal about it or try to force you on it again, I swear." They kissed a lot during this time and petted a lit-tle—mostly her breasts through the bra and she rubbing his back under his shirt or backside through the pants—and then she'd ask him to take his hand away or would take it away for him, saying something like it was getting a little bit too much for her, and other than for those two times, he didn't try to push it. When they first did sleep together it was very simple. They'd gone to a movie, were in her apartment sitting on the couch as they often did at the end of one of their dates, he drinking a beer or brandy and she an herbal tea or some wine, the two of them kissing. This time he put his hand on her thigh and began stroking it and when she kissed him harder, slipped his hand under her skirt and stroked her bare thigh and then moved his hand to her panties and just left it flat against her hip a minute to see if she'd take it away and then slid it onto the crotch of her panties and began rubbing the part where he felt hair. She's not objecting, he thought. Either she doesn't feel his hand or she doesn't mind. She was rubbing the back of his neck up and down, something she'd never done, and her eyes were closed he saw when he opened his and she had that dreamy look of someone in the midst, he could say, of love-making, but his take on it was probably a mistake. Anyway, he thought, he made a big step tonight in eventually having sex with her, going further than he ever had with her, and when their faces separated, he said—though he didn't want to say anything; he wanted to resume kissing and get her back in that dreamy mood and put his hand inside her panties and feel around and then rub her down there—"I know, you want more time. It's okay, I'm okay about it if that's what you want," while he kept picking the bottom end of her panties up with his finger and letting go with a slight snap, and she said "No, it's fine now, everything's finally worked out in my mind. You couldn't tell by what we were just doing and from what we talked about before?" and he thought Before? What did they talk about? and said "I suppose, but so what do we do now? I don't want to go ahead with anything unless you do," and she said "And I don't want to direct things. We should both agree on what we want to do. For starters, perhaps, like to stay the night but not on the couch?" which he'd done a couple of times when their evenings ended very late and once when she had a bad stomach flu and thought she might need him to help her. He'd actually looked forward to it: lifting her off the bed if she felt too weak to herself and helping her to the bathroom and holding her head over the toilet and maybe even kneeling her on the floor in front of it or picking her up off the floor if she fell and while doing any of those sneaking a peak under her nightgown, as he hadn't even seen her breasts yet, and maybe also getting what'd seem like an innocent feel in—he was that hard up. He said "So long as you're not taking the couch this time and giving me the bed," and she hugged herself and said "It's getting chilly. The building always turns down the heat around now," and kissed her finger and put it on his lips and got up and they went to the bedroom. In four months he sublets his apartment and moves in with her. "We love each other, we love each other," he says to her when he's moving in some of his things, "hurray." "I love living with someone I love and who says she loves me, and, you do too, don't you? and don't say no or even equivocate," and she says "Yes, no, yes...I'm teasing you. Yes, you letter-writing fool, in spades," and he says "Letters? From me? When have I ever written you them?" and she says "You write them to lots of people, so

why not me? I love receiving them, keeping them, reread-
ing them, or would if they came from you, especially if they
included a poem about us or really anything but one just for
me." So he sends her a letter once a week with a poem in it
about his love for her and her body and voice and their love-
making and walks and talks and evenings out and in and the
sounds she makes in her sleep and what goes through his
mind while he watches her play the piano or work at her
desk or sit in her Morris chair and read or holding her hand
in a movie theater and for a few seconds when it's very dark
in one kissing her and other things and when she gets the
mail from downstairs with one of his letters and he's home
or he gets the mail and hands her his letter she says "Please
go into another room or walk around the block and maybe
have a coffee outside, my darling, because I want to read this
when I'm absolutely alone." When he comes back or out of
the room, where he's been typing or reading, she always says
something like "That was beautiful, thank you, I could
never write letters to you like that when we're living so
close or show you my poem so soon after I wrote one." In a
year he gives up his apartment. "But hey, don't think it a
big sacrifice on my part or anything smacking of a major
commitment to you, since that place, small and shabby as it
is, was never cheap. Though it's true—here comes the serious part—I love living with you and don't see how it could
ever end, what do you think?" and she says "Ditto. No
major sacrifice having you take half the bed, bedroom closet and rent." About a year later he says "Want to get married? I do." They're in an Indian restaurant, their favorite
one in the city because it's so friendly, inexpensive, close and

good and they can bring their own wine and beer, and they've just ordered. She's in a green crewneck wool sweater. He said "Don't you want to take that off?" and she said "No, I feel a bit chilled," and he said "I hope you're not coming down with something, because this place is almost too warm." Her hair's brushed out over her shoulders and he can smell herbal shampoo or conditioner or both, so she must have washed it in the last hour or so. He wasn't home when she did. He'd entered the apartment, she said when he said hello and kissed her, "Want to eat out tonight?" and he said "Sure, great idea, where do you want to go, our favorite?" and she said "Just what I was hoping you'd say." "Yes," she says, "and you mean married to you, don't you? Though let's think about it some more. We don't want to pledge ourselves, eat our chana masala and kofta, and next day or so change our minds." A few days later he says just as he's about to go into the kitchen to his tiny typing table to write so she can read his newest letter to her he'd just brought upstairs (the letter saying only that he's run out of ideas and things to write about so soon after the last one, so his future correspondence, he thinks, will have to start coming every other week; the poem mostly about his suggestion of marriage the other day and how giddy it'd make him if she said yes and what her expression was like when he'd proposed (("A beautiful not-too-surprised look/ the kind that comes to the end of a book/ of the imagination and thinks/ 'Is this all there is/ or what did I miss?'")) and then how they just ate dinner (("Maybe it was my disappointment or fright/ that you didn't in a wink say aye/ or maybe the restaurant had a substitute chef that night/ but all the food tasted bad")) and later went to bed without making love (("As if my eyes had never cried/ come be my bride for life/ and right up till the time/ I wrote this poem/ we never spoke of it again"))), "Oh, by the way, before you go in there and I forget, any further thoughts regarding my marriage talk?" and she says "Why, how do you feel about it? Still on? I know I am," and he says "Then it's a deal?" and she says "About getting married to each other, yes," and he grabs her and swings her around and kisses her and punches his palm several times while he says and shouts "I don't believe it. I just don't believe it. I'm gonna get married. We're gonna be married. People are gonna say 'How's your wife?' and I'm gonna say 'Fine,'" and runs to the liquor store up the block and buys a cold bottle of expensive champagne and starts to run back but slows to a walk because he doesn't want the champagne to explode when he opens it, and they finish off the bottle while they talk about what kind of ceremony and reception they want (simple, in the apartment, they'll do most of the cooking, thirty or so of their closest relatives and friends, by a rabbi if that's what she and her folks would like and maybe her concert-pianist friend to play a bit of Bach before the ceremony begins and anything she wants to play after) and set a wedding date for three months when the school he's teaching at is on spring break, and that night they start making love without her inserting a diaphragm and in the most efficient position possible, she's read, to conceive. "Stay in deep as you can for a minimum of three minutes," she says soon as he's through ejaculating. "That's what's advised as much as the pretzel we've turned ourselves into." They have a child nine months later. "I think we hit it the first shot," he said when they learned she was pregnant, "or the next morning," and three years later another child, and never once in the twenty years since they started living together did they think of separating (they told each other this), although they were at each other's throats plenty of times (he a lot more than she) and several times after a particularly bitter argument they didn't talk to each other for one or two days. "It's been pretty good so far," she said on their tenth anniversary (in a Japanese restaurant; kids with them. Drinking "the best saki Japanese merchants are allowed to export," their waiter said. She was dressed in a black outfit and white sneakers, since neither of them or their children could find her black shoes, and wearing the string of amber beads he'd got her for their engagement. Her hair brushed back and smelling of conditioner and shampoo; about an hour before he'd gone into the bathroom to pee while she was sitting under the shower in the bathtub—they lived in a house by now and one of the kids was in the other bathroom—and saw her applying the conditioner). "Damn good, from my viewpoint or from where I'm sitting," he said, "and I'm not talking about our darling kids," stroking their faces and heads. "No, neither of those sounds quite right, and they in fact sound stuffy, but you know what I mean," and she took his hand and kissed it and said "As these two are my witnesses, I do."

But the party he met her at she was in a wheelchair. He didn't know she was in one when he first saw her; thought she was in a regular armchair. He'd just come into the apartment, was holding his coat and didn't know where to put it, as the front closet was completely filled. There were even a couple of coats and mufflers on the floor of it, which he picked up and tried to find hangers for but there were none nor any room to put the coats on other coats, so he left them on a chair next to the closet, the mufflers on top. He looked around for the host; not only to say hello but to ask where to put his coat. He didn't want to leave it on the chair. He had a feeling it'd end up on the floor, get trampled on or put someplace where he'd have trouble finding it. That was when he saw her sitting across from a couch in the living room, talking to a few people. He was immediately struck by her: face, hair, smile, intelligent expression, wide forehead, simple attractive outfit she was wearing, no lipstick or any makeup it seemed, and what looked like a good body: nice-sized breasts and narrow waist and flat stomach—her legs were obscured by someone else's chair—and she was speaking animatedly and her voice had a lovely clear tone to it and sounded bright and pleasant. The host came into the room and they said hello and he said "Thanks for having me, seems like a nice crowd," and asked where to put his coat—the host said "On the bed or chair in the bedroom; I doubt there's room left in the coat closet, though you can always try." "By the way," he said, "that woman over there," bobbing his head toward the woman in what he thought was an armchair, and the host said "Which one, the dark-haired, Beth, or the stately blonde?" and he said "The stately," and she gave the woman's first name—"I believe that's it, or close. Came with Beth, and with so many people getting here at once, we were introduced too quickly. No, it has an 'a' at the end of it, so two syllables, and as for the last name—don't ask or you'll have me stumped. But you know

Beth, right?" and he said no and she said "She's lovely, and brilliant; a Russian scholar. I think her friend is too. You two would have so much to talk about—Russian literature, samizdat, émigrés; Beth's specialties and field. Here, let me introduce you, but first get rid of your coat," and he did and slipped into the bathroom right outside the bedroom to make sure his hair was combed back and collar was right and to check his nostrils, which he'd thought of doing, but forgot, before he left home for possible hairs curling out of them; it'd been about a month since he looked. Saw two in one nostril and pulled them out with his fingers, then checked his ears. Five to ten hairs in each but not in a clump. He looked inside the medicine cabinet for any kind of scissors—hair, nail, cuticle, regular, even sewing, which he checked the drawers underneath the sink for—but there were none, and grabbed hold of some hair in one ear and pulled hard, a few came out but made his eyes tear, so he thought just live with it and went back to where he last saw the host, but she wasn't around. So go over to Miss Stately without her, he thought; no, don't call her that, even to himself; it's stupid. So what was her name? Something with an "a" at the end of it, but the host said it too fast or he wasn't paying attention. But he doesn't need anyone to introduce him. Though maybe circulate first, don't show he's in such a rush to meet her, as she might have seen him come in and turning his head to her a few times while he was standing there holding his coat, and get a drink. He got one—Scotch on rocks with a little water, since it was a drink he could never drink fast and he didn't want to be even a little high when he spoke to her, flubbing over his words and maybe seeming to her like a lush or jerk, and walked around with it, said hi and hello to several people he passed but didn't know though nothing else to them, put the glass to his mouth but it was empty without him even realizing it—he didn't spill any, he hoped—and got another and some crudités off a side table—carrots and celery sticks, a cauliflower floret, no tiny white radishes, which he liked but they'd make his breath stink—but skipped the dip that went with them because he didn't want to risk any of it dripping on him or the floor. Then he wiped his fingers that had held the vegetables so they wouldn't be wet if he shook hands with the two women, stuck the cocktail napkin into his pants pocket because he didn't see any other place to put it, and went over, smiled at them as he sat on the one available space on the couch across from them, said hello to the man and woman he sat between, who were looking around the room and nodded pleasantly at him, and leaned forward and said "Beth, you don't know me and might even be a bit startled—surprised, really's, the word—that I know your name. But our host gave it to me and said I should introduce myself to you and your friend, whose name, I'm afraid—she was in the midst of doing something—she didn't give...something about things in common and so on. I'm sorry, that took me so long to get out," and gave his name, the friend gave hers and this time he concentrated on remembering it, and Beth said "We all already know mine. Maybe I should say 'Elizabeth,' my given name, to get equal recognition," and they laughed, the couple on the couch too, and he shook hands with the two women. "Nice to meet you. And very nice to meet you too," he said to the friend.

That was when he saw—well, he saw it the moment he sat down; actually, as he was squatting over the couch, preparing to sit down while carefully holding his glass so it wouldn't spill—she was in a wheelchair. He didn't want to ask her why she was in one. Seen other people make that mistake. "Break a leg skiing this winter?" "I only wish it were that. No, I went into elective surgery for a relatively minor problem and the surgeon severed a nerve and I'm stuck with this for life." Or once: "My brother's in a wheelchair now too. Tripped over his mutt and sprained his ankle bad. Something like that with you?" "Not quite," it finally came out. "Bone cancer." Later, when he was getting them a plate of crudités with a little side dish of dip, he asked the host "Do you know what's wrong with her that she's in a wheelchair?" "No I don't," she said. "She's so healthy-looking, I doubt it could be anything serious." Later she stopped him when he was on his way to the bathroom and said "I think I was being much too sanguine about her condition," and told him what she'd learned. The three of them started talking, but after awhile he was almost only talking to the friend. Beth of course noticed it, and maybe even wanted to encourage it, for she excused herself, saying there was something she had to do and when her friend asked what, she said "Personal, in the pantry," and she'd see her later, and left. "It wasn't anything I said or did, her leaving, was it?" and she said "Why would you think that?" and he said "Well, it couldn't be anything you said or did. And the suddenness of her move, the ellipticness...ellipticalness...damn, whatever the word is in regard to her personal pantry remark," and she said "She probably just got an urge to meet and mix and perhaps also wanted to give us a few minutes together. I don't mind, do you?" "No, why would I? But it was nice talking to her," and she said "Then I'll call her back," and he said "No, it's fine." So they continued to talk. How did she find him at first? "What a question," she said. After they'd been seeing each other a few weeks he asked it, "just for the record," and she said if he really wants to know, she found him that night kind of skittish—"Skittish?"—"Jumpy, nervous, hyper something, overly self-conscious, awkward, compulsive and a bit more chatty and self-referential than I feel comfortable with. The truth is, you kept steering and domineering the conversation, less when Beth was there, possibly because you sensed she wouldn't sit through it." "You think that's why, that first time we all talked, she got up and left kind of abruptly?" and she said "Did she? That I don't remember. Anyway, I let you steer and domineer, when you and I were sitting there alone, since I'm not very talkative when I first meet someone. Although I was a lot more so with you than I usually am with a man I've just met and who seems reasonably interesting and whom I'm not unattracted to. But, to counterbalance all that, I also found you peppy, charming and legitimately funny." "Not intelligent?" "Somewhat, but it didn't stand out," "Charming? Me? You've got to be the first woman to say that, or to my face, anyway, or behind my back where I could overhear, and maybe the first to ever think it other than my mother, who almost always thinks everything highly of me—to build me up, you know. So she at least says it; I doubt if she really believes it. But what about how I first found you?" "You already said—some of it a half-hour after we met, once Beth left—and encouraging you to reprise it would only be dibbing for compliments, unless you changed your mind or weren't speaking the truth." "I wasn't. It was all said to get you into bed and my hope was that night, but it didn't work. No, that's not true and was stupid. Forget I said it. That night I only had holy thoughts of you." He found her from the start very intelligent, in a way so much more than he, that he thought she wouldn't be interested in him, and also composed, soft-spoken, personable, desirable, stimulating everything like that, and again, so beautiful that he didn't see how she could ever get interested in him even for more than a thirty-minute chat. Articulate, deep. Every little and big body part. Nose, ears, eyes, forehead, breasts, etcetera. Mouth, teeth. Sexy, the rest. He could go on. Fingers, cheeks, hair, shoulders, neck. He couldn't see her rear because she was seated. But judging by her flat stomach and small waist, and she wasn't in an outfit that was cinched there to make them appear small and flat, and that her buttocks didn't spread over most of the cushion she was on—he saw this when he got up to get them more crudités and himself a drink—he guessed her bottom wasn't overlarge. Legs, he could tell, since they were covered to her ankles by her skirt, but the bulge her thighs made through the thin cloth indicated they were solid but not wide, and her ankles seemed normal if maybe a little swollen. But that, he thought, could be because she was sitting in the chair so long and something to do with circulation, for all he knew. None of which he told her. He remembered sniffing for smells, though, to see if she was sitting in her own piss, and not smelling anything but the food coming to the buffet table and already on a couple of people's plates. So he told her what? That he'd been thinking of her...but how'd he even get into talking of that? "I've got to tell you something. You might not like it—I swear it's not bad, or all depends how you look at it, I guess—but I'd still like to tell you unless you object before I say anything." "What is it?" "That means I'll have to tell you," and she said "All right, go ahead; I can't see any harm." They were still sitting wheelchair: couch. Beth hadn't come back. The piss thought came later, after he'd learned what she had. His hand was on her knee. The couple had left the couch at the same time, so they were probably together but he didn't see them speak once to each other, and no one else had sat down. He'd put his hand there without realizing it, and when she looked at it—it seemed unfavorably—he jerked it away. "Sorry. I'm always, you know, touching people's shoulders and waists when we're going through doors or I want to let them pass, and if I'm sitting across from someone and close enough, often the knee." She spread her hands out over her knees; that was when he first noticed her fingers: long piano-playing ones it seemed, without a ring. The buffet table at the time didn't have anything on it but silver, napkins and a tall stack of plates. "Don't you want something to eat?" a man said to her when people were helping themselves at the buffet table. "Not right now," she said. "Would you like me to fill up a plate for you? I'll tell you what they have and you can tell me what you like." "It's okay. I'll go myself when the line's shorter." "You don't want to miss out—neither of you. The good stuff's going fast, and I checked with the caterer and the very best specialties there's only one platter of." "I'm sure that whatever's left will be sufficient for me, but thank you very much," and looked at I. and he thought what, what? For she had this look she hadn't had before that suggested she wanted to stay here with him and he felt funny because he wanted to believe it but also didn't. That was about fifteen minutes after he said he'd been thinking of her…his actual words were he'd had his eye on her from the minute…what he actually said was he couldn't take his eyes off her from the moment he got to the party and was standing there with his coat over his arm and saw her sitting here…did she mind him saying this? He would if he were her, he said, but he wouldn't if she were saying this or something comparable to it to him. "Really," she said, "such a long prolog to what you started out to say. Maybe you better forget the rest of it. The food aromas are becoming so strong that I don't know how long I'll be able to concentrate seriously on anything but them." "That's not the reason, of course," he said. "Of course it isn't. Excuse me, but please don't pretend to be blank. We were doing quite well and at a comfortable pace till you ventured into your had-to-tell-me talk. Why don't we resume where we left off? Or anyplace not focused on me, since I forget what we were talking of. Unless you feel unduly chastised, and that it was especially uncalled for, coming from someone you just met, and would rather not have anything more to do with me." "No no, everything you said is right. I can be such an impulsive schmuck. So, what do you know: our first argument." "What are you talking about?" She looked angry. "You see?" he said. "Just what I said: impulsive, schmucky. But I was only doing it to prove it to you. No, that's a lie and I'm getting myself in deeper when I absolutely don't want to. Forgive me. But one more blunder or asininity like that and you should cut me off for good. Or maybe you already have. Listen, this doesn't—what I'm about to say, I'm saying, and don't wince, because it isn't at all focused on you—this doesn't mean anything but what it says, and that's that I have to go to the bathroom." He didn't have to but felt they needed a short break. Then when he came back in three to four minutes, if the bathroom wasn't occupied and he got right in and out of it; even if it was occupied, he wouldn't have to go in because he didn't have to pee—maybe the mess he just got himself into would have blown over. And he actually headed to the bathroom, through the crowd in the next room and was about to enter the hallway to the rear of the apartment when the host stopped him, grabbed his arm and said "Got a second?" and led him out of view of the woman and told him what she'd heard. He'd said to her just before he left "Now don't move. And I'm not being facetious and certainly not malicious or anything like that. I really do have to make in the pantry and I'll be right back. Of course, if you feel you have to go—away from here, I'm saying, and again, I wasn't making any joke or pun—the damn coincidences of language just seem to come at the wrong moments—then you should do what you want and maybe we could talk after." "Is that very serious?" he asked the host. "I mean, I've heard of it but don't know anything about it, not even how it's spelled, or know anyone who's ever had it. Because to me...well, she looks so healthy and strong...I thought maybe she had something like a sprained leg or fracture she was still healing from. At worst, a slipped disk, painful but not permanent." The host said "It can be serious. And because she's in a wheelchair, it probably is, at least now," and told him some other things she knew about the disease. He said "I can only hope hers isn't serious—she's such a nice fine person, though of course for anyone in that situation. But now I really gotta get to the john," and went into the bathroom, peed because he'd probably have to in half an hour and the bathroom might be tied up then, and thought while he was inside—checked his watch and thought "Oh my God, I've been away five minutes already"—what is he getting himself into this time? He's already committed himself way more than just coming on too strong. He means by that? But suppose he really wants to go out with her? He does want to, at least once. So he goes out with her once, what's the problem with that? No problem. Though suppose she has a physical problem he finds difficult to deal with on that date? Oh come on, by now she must be so used to her illness and how to deal with it that she'd never put someone in a position like that. She'd take care of everything beforehand, be prepared for any eventuality and deal with it discreetly, see that nothing out of the ordinary, in other words, would happen while they were together. She wouldn't just...anyway, she wouldn't. And he'd push her in her chair if he had to, up and down curbs and such and in and out of a restaurant, if that's where they ended up going. On their first date, if she had trouble moving the chair herself—that is, if she was confined to a chair all the time, because tonight's confinement might be just a temporary setback—sure, why not? Get in back, push, find a curb cut, down that, up the next, and a restaurant—she must know the ones in her neighborhood, which they'd probably stick to for their first meeting, that are easy to get in and out of and move around in. So, one date, that's it, or all he should think about, because he can't back out now—wouldn't be right and it could end up hurting her: "Sure," she could think, "once he knew what I had, he changed his mind"—that is, if she wanted to see him even a single time. There was a good chance—maybe even a very good one—she didn't. He could go back and she might not be there. She might even have left the party by now. Got tired suddenly—her illness—or discomforted about something—her illness again—she felt she could take better care of at home, and asked her friend could they go? Or she left alone. She might be able to get around that independently. Called for a cab and was down-stairs already or on her way down in the elevator and the cab would come and she'd be able to get in it on her own or her friend would most likely go down with her to help her into the cab and the cabby or her friend could fold up the chair and put it in the trunk. She was probably able to stand, just not for long. Walk, even, most times, on her own or with a cane. Just tonight might be a particularly bad night for her, but tomorrow or the day after or so she could be out of the chair and walking everywhere after that, with certain limits of course. Till the next relapse, or whatever the host called it, when she'd have to use the chair again a lot. But all that was something he felt he could deal with their first date. If she'll go for it, he thought. But now get out of here before she decides he's never coming back and he may even have left the party without a goodbye. That wouldn't make her feel too good. He washed his hands, made sure his hair was down again, for it had a habit of popping up on the sides, which with his balding front gave him a sort of clownish look, and left the bathroom, wanted to get another drink but didn't want to spend the time getting it—the crowd around the bar was large again, people getting wine to go with their food probably—and anyway, he'd made enough mistakes with her already that he didn't want to chance getting even higher than the little he was, or sleepy, which is what wine often did to him, if he wanted to switch to a drink that looked more sociable and was less alcoholic. She was smiling at him as he approached. Good sign, he thought, for a nice sincere smile—glad to see him, it seemed—though he bet all of hers were. The couch was taken by three people eating off plates on their laps. Same with the chairs around her. And all these people with glasses of wine or bottles or glasses of beer at their feet or on end tables. She had a plate but no glass, it seemed—the one she'd been drinking from must have been taken away—and was feeding herself all right but having a tough time keeping the plate straight on her lap. "Good, you got food," he said. "Looks good too. Sushi, other Japanese stuff; great. But you sure the plate's safe there? I don't want to nose in, but it's not a bit unstable?" "I have no other place to put it." "I might be able to find you one of those fold-up trays or a small table, if there's one. Or I'll hold the plate for you while you eat." "No, I wouldn't like that," she said, looking cross now. Oh damn, he thought, another careless remark. Well, he was only trying to help her, but he should use more sense when he does, and now how does he get out of it? "Thank

you, I'll manage," she said, that smile again, so maybe she
was trying to get him off the hook, "or I'll get food later
when I'm at a real table. Why don't you have it?" offering
him her plate. "I've barely touched it—in fact, just two
sushis and a noodle—but you'll need fresh silver." "I would-
n't mind; I'm famished," taking her plate. "Forgot to eat
breakfast, which is nothing unusual for me, and I don't
mind using your fork. Though I'll look around for a chair so
I don't have to eat standing up." He thought: he could sit in
her lap, how about that? But he won't say it because he
doesn't know what that'll bring. "I think I have that solution too," she said. "This gentleman—Ronald is it?" and the
man in the middle of the couch looked up from his plate and
said "Ron, and excuse me, I forgot. I got too taken with the
food." "Ron only wanted your seat till you got back. I told
him I was saving it for you, though I thought you'd come
back with food for yourself, you were away so long." "I had
things to do," he said, and "No, sit, sit," to Ron; "really, I
don't mind eating and standing," wanting her to think him
gracious. "Deal's a deal, man," Ron said, getting his drink
off the floor and standing. "And I'm done anyway, or with
this round. Food's great," and left. He sat down and said
"Wouldn't mind a little wine myself. Can I get you one
too?" and she said "Please don't leave again. This time I
doubt I'd do anything to save your place for you," and he
said "Sure, and I don't need the wine, though food always
tastes better with it. We can get a drink later, if you like."
"Sure," she said, and he thought then it's sealed, or something is. That what he want? He already said, at least for one
date. They talked while he pushed the food around with his

fork. Meat, which he didn't much eat—fishy sushi and that dish, what's its name again? with long cellophane noodles and a variety of vegetables and thin slices of marinated beef. But he didn't want to start anything about how he hadn't had any kind of meat but a bit of fish and half a chicken salad sandwich in months—saw a whole skinned animal torso, he thinks a calf, carried into his neighborhood supermarket on a pole by two men before the store opened and that did it for him—so had a couple pieces of each. Later he'd tell her, if they went out for dinner. But for all he knew she might feel the same way and was given a plate of food by someone like that man before who saw her just sitting there when almost everyone else was at the buffet table or eating, saw it was meat and didn't want to make an issue of it so ate a little, and that could be why she handed the plate over to him. About music, but how'd that subject come up? He was rapidly tapping his fingers on the bottom of his plate while deciding what to eat from it and she said "Do you play an instrument? Often, people who tap like that, do." "No," he said, stopping, "just, extemporaneously, the plate. But do you?" "Used to play piano and was taking lessons from a concert pianist up till three years ago. First my hands stopped cooperating, then the feet. Actually, the feet first, so till the hands became too enfeebled to play I only chose pieces where the feet weren't needed." Then she told him what she had. He didn't ask; she just came out with it. "I've got." "That so?" he said. "I've heard of it and figured you had something. How much can you get around by yourself?" and she said "You mean in the wheelchair?" and he did but thought oh no, not again; what do I say to get out of this one? Dumbhead, dumbhead, because her expression seemed to suggest it was a totally inappropriate question, and he said "No, just, you know, anyplace. Do you get around? I meant. Concerts, opera, museums, movies? Take advantage of the city like I almost never do except an occasional movie, which I invariably bitch about, so I'm not really a good one to go with, and a walk across the park to the Met when I need a break from my work," and she said "Not as much as I want, but I used to a great deal. Maybe I've just become too busy." Taught two humanities courses a year at Columbia and was on a postdoctoral fellowship she was surprised he'd never heard the name of. "No, that's not right of me—I apologize—because why should I think anybody would know of it other than someone planning to serve a life sentence in academia?" Also wrote poetry and he asked and she said yes, a few, though not in great places but the only ones that would take them. He ate another piece of meat, thinking when he put it in his mouth that it was a black mushroom, and had to admit to himself he liked it, just as he had the two other pieces he intentionally ate before, and finished the rest of it on his plate while she told him some of the magazines she'd been in—he'd asked before he stuck his fork into what he thought was a mushroom—and books she taught in this semester's humanities course and he thought he might even go back to eating meat again but on a semi-regular basis, because why be a phony about it?—he liked it and especially this beef and a small amount of it each week can't be that bad for you—and that he also might go back to the buffet table for more. "Impressive magazines to me," he said, "and sounds like a great course. I'd love to hear your ideas on those books, though a few I haven't read but would probably start to. Can I get you anything at the buffet table? Maybe something other than what was on this plate, since you hardly touched it," and she said she was taking a new experimental medicine every other day and had lost most of her appetite as well as some of her hair because of it and probably shouldn't have even had the few sips of wine she did. "Your hair? No, it looks too thick and rich; you couldn't have lost any." "Anyway, I can be a drag sometimes when it comes to eating and drinking. Unfortunately, the medicine must come first, but thanks." Just then Beth came over. He didn't know how he hadn't seen her since she left, but maybe that was an indication of how absorbed he was in the conversation. Or she came over about a minute after that medicine-comes-first remark—they'd started talking about Ovid's *Metamorphoses*, which she'd taught this semester and he'd just read for the first time ("I'm gradually making my way through a lot of the classics I haven't read")—and said to her "I'm afraid I have to steal you away, cookie," and pointed at her watch. "I know it's still early and you're having a good time, but it's already half an hour past the time we said we'd be there, and from what they said our presence is needed." "You have to go?" he said. "I'm sorry. And you haven't really eaten yet," and she said "There'll be plenty where we're going, not that I'll feel like having anything more there than here," and he said "Then we should get together some time. For talk, coffee—your books for your course and stuff," and she said "If you'd like," and gave her address and spelled her last name twice. "There's only one of me in the book—you can imagine, with such a complicated name—and two of the three with the same last name and who live on West 83rd are my parents." "And the fourth?" and she said "The fourth?" and he said "The other person in the directory with your last name," and she said "God, I can be slow, excuse me. It's been looked into. My father, who lost his entire family in Europe, is always on the alert for possible newly discovered relatives, no matter how distant. He called this fourth name the first year it appeared in the Manhattan directory and the man was in no way related to us and didn't even know what country his father's family had emigrated from and hadn't a clue what the name meant in German." She said goodbye and stuck out her hand to shake and he said "Let me see you to the door first," and got up and she said "That's very nice but there are some things I have to do before I go, besides other goodbyes to make." He shook her hand and said "Listen, when I call you...ah, nah, forget it," and she said "'What?" and he said "No, another dopey attempt at a joke again, and I don't want to make myself look worse than I already have," and she said "What are you talking about? We'll speak," and looked at Beth who, already behind the wheelchair, pushed her through the living room to the back hallway. He got himself a drink, wondered what she had to do—something personal probably, but that was her business—and sat on the couch, his back to the living room, since he didn't want to catch her eye again and do that ridiculous smile and wave and moving mouth routine. "Hello. Goodbye. I don't know what my wave means and I'm not really saying something and the smile's automatic." He do the right thing before? he thought, sipping his drink and staring at the floor. Good, sitting here could be used to think out some things. He actually going to see her? Didn't just say it and maybe even meant it at the time but won't call? He could do that? Got cold feet when he realized how sick and incapacitated she probably is? If he doesn't want to see her should he still call but say something like he's sort of involved with someone or he's too tied up now with his work and he'll call her soon as it's done? A deadline, he could say? No, those are ridiculous lies she'd either see through and get more hurt by than if he hadn't called at all or she could say "Why's that"—to either—"have to make a difference? Do what you wish, but I think anybody can find a little free time. We had a pleasant talk, we could continue it over a coffee, which is all I was thinking of anyway." He still attracted to her? What if he became more attracted to her—enamored, even—and she in some way to him? Why jump so far ahead? Jesus: one call, a single date, take it from there, because what's the big deal? And she's expecting him to call and he thinks he wants to see her again a lot. Does he? She was nice, she was bright, she was lots more that he likes, and that she's in a wheel-chair and maybe can't walk and possibly other things wrong with her shouldn't change it that much. Love stuff, that's a different story. But again, why shoot so far ahead? There are other things though, right? He wouldn't feel a bit uncom-fortable just walking on the street with her if she was in a wheelchair? Less so pushing her if she had to be pushed, because then he'd be behind rather than alongside and doing something useful. Alongside, two or so feet above her, leaning in lower and closer every so often while he walked so he could hear her and she him over the traffic noises, he might feel somewhat self-conscious or just, well, something like that. Oh come off it. You're with someone, she happens to be in a wheelchair, you make certain accommodations for her, so is it just a matter of what other people you don't even know think? Passersby, or people you do know whom you might meet? Truth is, most would only be thinking good things about it, the few who thought anything at all except "Oh, what a pity this poor pretty young woman in a wheelchair if it's something permanent," but he wouldn't be doing it for that either, of course. And he did go through it with his dad. True, his father. Last two years of his life. He was the main one to push him, for by the time they got him to accept the fact that if he wanted to get out and around he had to be in a wheelchair, he didn't have the strength to push it himself or the coordination to operate a motorized one. As he said before: up, down, in, out, "See a curb cut coming up?...Watch your feet, lady...Excuse me, please, coming through, coming through." If things go okay their first meeting they can continue seeing each other awhile, even if he started something with someone else. Though maybe not. But for now, once a month for coffee or dinner. Or every other week, or not so systematically prearranged as that, because then she might think he was only doing it out of some kind of duty. Or for a movie or play or museum or something to do with music: concert, opera, even a ballet. He in the seat next to the empty orchestra space set aside for her wheelchair. Or she in the aisle, he in the seat right beside her—that is, if it's difficult for her to get from her wheelchair into a regular seat. So it's done, yes? Don't even think anymore about it. Have another drink, or maybe just a glass of wine or beer. He'll call, they'll talk and see what they want to do, if she still wants to meet. If she leaves the eating arrangements up to him: dinner in a relatively inexpensive Indian or Japanese place, as he'll want to pick up the tab. If she insists beforehand on paying her share or dividing the bill in half, then maybe a better restaurant. If she picks the place he's sure, since he couldn't have looked well off to her by any stretch and she's only a little more than a grad student herself, it wouldn't be a very expensive one. And it's still possible she isn't always in a wheelchair. Tonight might be the anomaly, or for the last few days. Couple of days ago or so she suddenly wasn't feeling secure on her feet, he'll say. This, the host said—though she didn't claim to be an expert on the disease; just stuff she picked up from a friend who has it—could go on for weeks or just days. Then she's back on her feet with a cane or even without one, maybe a trifle worse off than before it started, or using a walker, even one of those with wheels. He'll just have to see. Of course what he hopes for, he thought, is that she recovers completely from this latest attack, as the host called it and if that's what it is, and walks on her own without any assistance, or close to it. He stayed at the party another half-hour, walked around, had a selection of desserts and a semisweet dessert wine, which was so good he had two more glasses of it, at the dessert-wine table chatted briefly with a few people about nothing, really. The two or three women there he thought, by their looks and something they were giving off, he could get interested in seemed pretty much tied to their men, and said goodnight to the host and left. In bed at home, while reading, he decided he'll call her tomorrow morning, and because it'd be Sunday, no earlier than eleven. After noon would be better, he thought, putting his book down again—but only a few minutes after—since she might get to bed late tonight and also need to make up for a shortage of sleep the last week. For the next week he thought of calling her every day but something always stopped him. Mostly: maybe, because of her condition, it just wouldn't be a good idea. If he did want to get involved with her, he thought—if it reached that point, he's saying, for it has been almost two years since he saw a woman steadily for even a few weeks and he hasn't been to bed with one for months—what were the chances of anything really developing between them? For instance: for the last few years he's been wanting to get married (it's true he doesn't make much money, so in that respect isn't much of a catch) and have a child right away—he was forty-two and didn't want the age difference between him and the kid to be that great—and she might not want to conceive or carry one because it could make her illness worse. That's what something he read about it said. He'd checked a book on it out of his neighborhood library—had gone there to see what was on the new-release fiction shelves—and saw her disease in big yellow letters in the title of the book on the subject in the new-release nonfiction section next to the fiction one: *A Guide for Patients and Their Families*. He read through enough of the book to know that if she had the worst kind of case of it or that was where she was heading, and about twenty percent of those who have the disease are in that category, it would definitely be a major problem for him and probably scare him off. Visual and hearing loss could be a problem too for people with the disease. Constipation, incontinence, just getting on and off the toilet and dressing and eating and swallowing, though she seemed to see and hear all right and hold her fork okay and had no trouble getting her food down, little she ate that night. He once even had the phone receiver in his hand and was about to dial her number. She has to know something's wrong that he didn't call, he thought. If it did end up where they went out several times and kissed and fondled each other one night and then wanted to go to bed together, how would they do it if she was, as so many people with the disease are, the book said, partially paralyzed or unable to move or maintain control over certain parts of her body? If she was in the wheelchair, and he cant see himself kissing and fondling her while she was in one—kissing her deeply, he means, but fondling her in any way—could she just lift herself off it onto the bed or use some device like a board to slide herself off and then back on? Or would he have to lift her out of the chair onto the bed, undress her if she couldn't undress herself and eventually pry her legs apart if they were locked so he could slip himself inside her? Does someone—an aide—help her get on and off the toilet at home? She said she lived alone. So maybe someone comes in during the day, and also gets her ready for bed at night, and is also there in the morning, to help her get out of bed and onto the toilet and washed and dressed. How does she teach, if all the rest is so? Someone could push her to class, pick her up after and get her home or to her office or the library or wherever she needs to go, and shop and even cook for her. Her parents might help out a lot too; relatives, friends. She might also have a motor cart or motorized wheelchair. Maybe the building she lives in is just for the handicapped, so everything in it is much easier for her. Ramps everywhere, wider doorways, lower toilets and mirrors and sinks and stoves. But he's probably carrying this too far again, he thought. It can't be as bad as he's making out, or it could be but he doesn't think it is. Something more about it would have come out in her conversation with him, indicating how bad it sometimes is for her. Or in the way she moved; some involuntary motion in her face or hands or legs, as the book said. Spacticity—or contractions; he forgets what the difference is, if there is one—which many people with the disease have, not just the worst cases, and can be very painful. Maybe she took some powerful pills that reduced all these symptoms for the night, so she could get through the party without losing physical control over certain parts of her body. Pills, or a drug in any form, which she can only take sparingly, like steroids. She had no speech problem either, which hits a lot of people with the disease, and no sudden fatigue, nodding off, things like that. It can affect the brain—"intellectual deficits," was the way the book put it—and memory. But she was one of the brightest women he'd ever spoken to: sharp, witty, articulate, and also funny and lively. She can't be in that worst category, he thought, and he bets she's able to do most things on her own like cooking and going to the toilet and showering and dressing. Just call, he told himself. One date—what the hell's that? And he wants to know more about her and also how she manages with the disease. But more than that, a lot more. Her brains, yes, and her looks, and he was definitely attracted to her in a sexual way too. If he doesn't want to see her again after that first time they get together (of course it can be the other way around too), he'll make it clear it has nothing to do with her illness. Not that she'll believe him—he can just imagine the things that go through her head, sitting in that chair. But maybe, if he acts convincingly enough—if he does a good job acting convincingly, he's saying—she will. So he called. She said she was happy to hear from him; he said "Same here, talking to you again, and I'm sorry I wasn't able to call sooner, but I won't bother you with all the reasons why I couldn't." They talked about a number of things for a long time. A play she'd seen. He'd heard mixed things about it, he said; what'd she think? and she gave a devastating review of it and also of the audience who for some reason thought it was participatory theater and he asked what she meant and she explained. "You ought to print that," he said. "The whole review, word for word in the act way—the exact way; I don't know where that came from—you said it. Of course: act: theater." Then he said "Listen, we should meet, what do you say? It's what I originally called for," and she said she'd love to. What would he like to do? Coffee, lunch, movie, hour in a museum? "A movie," he said. "That way we wouldn't have to talk, for we obviously have nothing to say to each other." She laughed, said "Does seem that way." Oh, I'm glad she laughed, he thought. That was such a dumb remark. She's making me look good. But he better be more careful with what he says from now on. Think, you idiot. Don't just say the first thing that crosses your mind. "Actually…" she said, and he thought uh-oh, she's having second thoughts because of what he said, "does breakfast interest you? I love breakfast out on weekends, if it's not too early, and I know a good place around here." "Then let's do it this Saturday, whatever time you want," and she said "Sunday's a better day for me this weekend, do you mind? Or we could make it the next Saturday." "How could I mind? Come on. Sunday's fine, better for breakfast." They set a time when they'd meet in her building's lobby. "You'll recognize me, right?" he said. "If not, I'll be wearing a rose tattoo in my lapel," and she said "I'll look for it," no laugh this time and he knew he'd made not so much a dumb remark but one that didn't make much sense if you didn't get the references. But that rose tattoo one: admit it; it really didn't make much sense. She must be wondering about him, he thought, and he wouldn't be surprised if she phoned him before Sunday—she took his number, "just in case," she said—calling it off. She was waiting for him when he went into the lobby. They said hello, smiled, shook hands. She looked so pretty, hair sort of shining from the light and flowing almost like water over her shoulders. "So, should we go?" he said. The doorman had to open the revolving door so she could wheel herself through. That the right verb for it? he thought. Or "move, push, propel"? Which word do you use when the person in the wheelchair wheels herself? Never thought of it before, and none of those seem right now, so he'll stick with the first word that came to him unless she uses a different one for it. He said outside "You don't have a motorized chair or anything like that? Because I'd think it'd be easier, if you're going some distance and aren't going to be taking a taxi." "I did; a motor cart. But it fell over with me in it a few times—deep ruts or unsuspected slopes in the sidewalk, mostly caused by burgeoning tree roots underneath—and one of those times I broke my shoulder and another time I cracked my skull." "Oh, I'm sorry, that's awful," he said, and thought: funny; he thinks of her shoulders and a minute later she tells him she broke one. And he's constantly reminded how brainy she is and she then says she cracked her skull, though that's less of a coincidence. "Can I push you then?" and she said "I'm doing fine on level ground, thank you. The curb cuts down here are fairly new and smooth, and it's needed exercise for my arms and hands. I could use, if you wouldn't mind, help getting up the hill on a Hundred-twelfth. Unless you want to continue on Riverside to a Hundred-tenth, which is a flat street, and go to the restaurant from Broadway." "No, I'll push you up a Hundred-twelfth. Though the restaurant's between a Hundred-thirteenth and -twelfth, isn't it?—I thought I saw it from the bus. So why don't I push you up a Hundred-thirteenth?" and she said "That street's the steepest in the neighborhood; I doubt an unmotorized wheelchair's ascended it successfully in years." "Ah, it can't be that bad," he said. "And I pushed my father in these for I don't know how long, so I'm familiar with them. Anything to get him out. It improved his disposition—got him away from the house. You know, outside doings and fresh air, and ice cream cones, which he liked. Across the park, up the steepest hills there. Pilgrim Hill, from Fifth, if you know it, and Eagle Hill inside, and not so light a guy in not as light a chair," and she said "If you want, you can give it a try." They reached a Hundred-thirteenth. It's going to be a bitch getting her up it, he saw, but he said he would, so just do it, though next time listen to her. He got about halfway to the top, could barely push the chair farther—he was already digging his feet into the sidewalk—and said "I give up, you were right," and she said "I'm sorry," and he said "For what? My problem—thinks he knows better—not yours," and turned her around and going down the hill he had to grip the handles tight to keep the chair from rolling away from him. Oh boy, that would be something awful, awful, and shut his eyes and shook his head to get rid of the thought. He looked at her as they went slowly down the hill. She had her eyes closed and was smiling as if enjoying the breeze or something: river smells, the air. "Not too cold for you?" and she said without turning around "I always overdress for the damp or cooler weather. I have to; otherwise I could freeze sitting here." He shouldn't have said anything, he thought; just should have let her continue enjoying whatever it was. Maybe being with him has something to do with it also; who knows. At the bottom of the street he started pushing her to a Hundred-twelfth. He knew she could wheel herself, but he had his hands on the handles and didn't know what he could do or say to take them away. Let go and step to the side of the chair, he supposed, so she'd know he wasn't pushing anymore and she'd have to take over? Wouldn't seem right. And it was easy, pushing, and he felt good doing it and she didn't seem to mind. She stared ahead as they went, hands in her lap, smiling again, and when they got to a Hundred-twelfth she said "Hill doesn't look too much for you?" and he said "Nah, it's a snap. But how could two streets so close together have such different declivities, or the opposite word of that—acclivities, I think, but that one seems so...I don't know; unnatural," and she said "It's not one I remember reading or hearing or looking up, but I bet you're right. The amazing thing is that the other side of the street has even less of a slope than this one," and he said "So I guess that's the one you usually take," and she said "Most of the time, if I'm heading downtown, though never if I'm pushing myself. But this one has more obstacles and cracks and in some places isn't as wide, so it's a toss-up." He pushed her up the street and didn't find it steep at all. She pointed out Bank Street College across the street and he said "Oh yeah, I recognize it now. Once had lunch in the cafeteria downstairs, but I forgot it was around here," and she said "The breakfasts aren't bad there either. Someone told me Dean and Duluca were doing the food. But you have to pass through several heavy doors and take the elevator, and anyway, it's closed," and he said "No, I wasn't thinking of it for that. I'm sure the place we're going to is fine," and she said "I didn't mean it that way either." It was with a woman he was seeing who was getting a master's in museum curating; could that be right? School of education giving a curating degree? Her name? Barbara? Beatrice? Bernice? Come on, it was only three to four years ago. It'll come back to him, he thought, if he thinks of it again. Liked her, and she was smart and great in bed and pretty, but another one who dropped him flat—she knew he had no dough and little prospect of getting a good job, so marriage and all that, which they both said they wanted one day, were out of the question—a few days after she met another guy. At the corner of Broadway she said "I can wheel myself from here on," and he said "Really, I don't mind," and she said "It doesn't trigger sad memories of your father?" and he said "I didn't mind pushing him either. I in fact like it. It slowed my pace, for I tend to walk too fast and miss seeing interesting things on the street. And with my father...well..." and felt his throat choking up but managed to get out "Anyway...enough." "The truth is I'd prefer doing it on my own now, thanks," and he said "Of course," and took his hands off and walked beside her. He held the restaurant door open for her and then the inside door while he kept the outside one open by stretching out his foot. "You want to sit in one of the chairs or stay in your own?" and she said "I'm fine as I am," and started moving a chair away from a table and he did it for her, didn't know where to put it because all the unoccupied tables seemed to have the right number of chairs at them and the place didn't have waiters and he didn't see any clean-up people and didn't want to bother anyone eating to ask if he could slip a chair into the empty space at their table, so he lifted it over his head and carried it—"Hot chair, hot chair," he said and she laughed—to a wall on the other side of the room where there were three highchairs lined up and a couple of small tables, one face down on the other. "About your father," she said when he sat down across from her and looked at the huge blackboard above the food counter with today's date and specials, "I want you to know I didn't mean to assume, make sad or probe and I apologize if it might have come out that way," and he said "Believe me, it never entered my head. Now for a serious question: What do you think I should order?" He went to the counter, got their food, she had tea, he went

back for several refills of coffee, they talked almost non-stop:
art, movies, poetry, their families, ancestries, his work and
her work and her postdoctoral fellowship. About her illness—he didn't ask; it just came out—she said sometimes
she's able to walk with assistance, mostly she's in this chair.
It hits her hard and retracts for a short time like that and
she's sorry to say she's always a little worse after. It's a big
nuisance and a bit scary and she's tried and is trying everything there is to arrest it or slow it down—unfortunately
there isn't a treatment to reverse her condition yet. When
she needs help she has friends or professionals or her parents
to look after her or do some of the things for her she can't or
does clumsily and sometimes hazardously, like making coffee and burning rice and toast. He took care of the
check—"Please," he said when she protested, "it doesn't
come to much and because it's self-service we don't have to
leave a tip," and she said "I always like to leave something
for whomever busses our table," and put down two dollars.
"Anyway," he said, "if it did cost a lot I swear I wouldn't
pretend to be such a sport. Though if you want you can even
things up by treating me to dinner some night," and she
said "All right," and he said "Only kidding; it wouldn't be
fair. For dinner, we go Dutch, if that's okay," and was thinking why's he saying this? Does he mean it? and she said
"We'll see," and her expression didn't give either possibility away. Outside, she said she had various chores to do on
Broadway and that she hoped to see him again. He was
about to say "But I already mentioned we'll have dinner out
one of these days," but said "Good, same here; it was fun.
But how will you get down the hill to your building, if you

don't go by way of a Hundred-tenth, and then let the doorman know you're outside and he has to open the revolving
door?" and she said "The way I always do." They shook
hands—he stuck his out first, after he'd said "Good, you got
things under control. So I'll see ya." He wanted to kiss her
cheek—something he almost automatically did with
women friends he says goodbye to—but didn't want to bend
down to do it and possibly bungle it, kissing her ear or hair
and end up discomposing them both, and she started pushing herself uptown and he headed for the bus stop on a
Hundred-twelfth. Actually, the subway would be faster, he
thought when he got to the corner and was waiting for a
chance to cross, and he wouldn't mind getting home sooner
and getting some work in, since weekends were when he did
most of it. Then she was suddenly in his head again and he
turned around to look at her and saw her moving slowly,
hands on the wheels and though the street had only a slight
incline, the pushing seemed hard. Several people walking by
glanced at her and one couple stopped to stare from behind.
A leashed dog tugged to get up to her and she waved at it
and its owner moved his head as if apologizing to her and
pulled the dog back. It must be such a struggle for her in
that chair, almost everything, he thought. Getting out, getting around and back, shopping, just carrying packages,
what do you do outside when you have to take a crap or pee?
Always being much lower down than anyone on the street
but little kids, dogs like that big one before and some possibly lunging at her with teeth drawn or trying to lick her
face, though she might like the friendly licking part of it,
and all those pitying looks from people and she must have

caught several times some of the ones who stop behind her and shake their heads and stare. He saw some of it when he walked with her but less so than when she's alone now. He felt lousy for her also, way her body was slouched to the side crookedly, as if she was in a seating position she couldn't straighten herself out of and which might be painful and what she needed was someone from behind to lift her under the arms to reposition her. She wheeled left to a drugstore. He hadn't helped her off or on with her jacket in the restaurant—didn't think she wanted him to; sensed she felt that anything fairly simple she could do herself, even if she didn't do it that well, was better than getting help from somebody—and the jacket collar wasn't folded down right, one side sticking up and the other was down. She reached for the door handle and tried pulling it open. Held the handle with what seemed like two or three fingers, but the door went back and she let go. Too far away to get a good grip on it, it seemed. She wheeled closer, grabbed the handle with her whole hand now—so the distance problem must have been it—and pulled while she was moving the chair back, but only got it a few inches out. Either the door was too heavy or unwieldy for her or some part of the chair was keeping it from opening farther. Jesus, he thought, why would she go to that store if she knew the door was so tough to open? He looked around and saw another drugstore a block down on the other side of Broadway. But maybe that's the point. It's across this wide avenue, so more difficult to get to—the cars, trucks, curb cuts, good possibility of not making it across on a single light and being stranded on the traffic island, which has no curb cuts so she'd have to wait for the light to change there and not on the protected pedestrian space but in the street—and that store might have a narrower entrance and aisles than this one and a step up while this one—and he looked at it—didn't seem to have any. He bet most of her shopping was done on this side of Broadway and only on the other side when she had someone with her to get her up the curb of the traffic island and so forth. Should he go and help? As he thought before regarding her jacket: does he think she'd mind? She's independent—that came out in their conversation—and persistent, he can see, so he's sure she thinks the less…Just then a woman pulling a shopping cart rushed over to her, said something, they both laughed, the woman opened the door for her, she wheeled herself inside and the woman went back to her cart on the sidewalk. He imagined her wheeling down a drugstore aisle looking for something and finding it but it was too high to reach so asking a customer or one of the store workers…but enough, drop it already, and he continued to the subway station, started down its steps but then thought ah, hell with getting to his work so soon, subways aren't good for thinking, busses aren't much better, or maybe one can get some good thoughts on them but for him his best mostly came on solitary city walks when he put his mind to it, so he'll walk the rest of the way home. He wanted to give himself time to think about her and what he was going to do next. Next, meaning, is he going to call her again? First of all, he thought, how does he feel about her? That should be the only reason he'd call or not. What's he talking about?—he has to call. And he has to see her again also—at least once—so he means the only reason to continue seeing her after the next time. Well, he thought, she's quite nice, very, maybe as nice as any woman he's known. And interesting, pretty, lovely everything, lovely in every way he can think of, unlovely in no way, really; a soft woman—soft is the word for her, just as anger, he supposes, could be the word for him. She's almost exactly what he thought she'd be when he called her the other day: sweet, deep, very bright, refined, and with a good sense of humor—she made him laugh several times with her quick wit and wordplay—so all those things and more and also someone who's interested in or feels the same about many of the things he does, a lot of which he found out today. All that's important. Same religion, even, which never mattered before and which would be a big change for him and might even be a plus; who knows? It certainly can't hurt, since neither of them observes it in any way and their interest in it—hers, from what she said—is mainly for the poetry and wisdom and so forth and sort of *where they come from* and can't escape. She's also eleven years younger than he, which can be okay in different ways including the younger body and outlook and face. So they'll go out for dinner, he thought, just as he told her they would. And if she wants to go to one—he's usually interested if something good's around—a movie after, if there's a way of getting her there, for the theater in her neighborhood had an awful picture playing, he saw on the way up, so it'll have to be one they can only get to by cab or bus. Subways, she said, are all but impossible for her to travel on, with only a few accessible stations in the city and once you've reached your destination you never know if the car doors won't slam shut on the chair and if the people rushing into the train won't prevent you from getting off and then if the elevator to the street will be working. True, if she were healthier and ambulatory and her life, as she cheerfully hinted, didn't look so grim, he wouldn't think twice about seeing her again and again. He would have thought when she showed some interest in him "Boy, am I lucky, meeting someone like her, but she's too beautiful and intelligent and elegant and everything else for her to really become interested in me," and that sort of thing. He would have made a date with her before he said goodbye just now. Maybe for tomorrow night: dinner, movie, something like that. Tried to move it along swiftly, get her into bed quickly. He'd probably really fall for her, he's saying, rather than be so reluctant or hesitant or whatever's the word in wanting to see her again. And do everything he could to make her—he means, help her—fall for him. Not show any anger, for one thing, or any disagreeable side to her, including the fakery he'd need to hide these things, till she was hooked. And that's the goddamn shame of it, he thought. He meets the ideal woman in almost every way—his dream girl, as they used to say—and she has this disease which could be incurable or many years away from there being any help for it, is what she said, and so will conceivably only get worse and where she possibly can't or won't have children because of it and who knows how it's affected her sex life. Though if she didn't have it guys would be beating down her door to go out with her, while now her condition and being stuck in that chair most of the time and all that they might imagine about it probably keeps them away, leaving the field pretty much to him, though he could be wrong on that. So, did he decide? To see her again, yes, though that decision he'd already made before he started thinking of her while he walked, but nothing about what to do beyond that. He'll see her once and then he'll see; not enough? He stopped at a bookstore along the way and browsed but didn't buy, though wanted to, because he was a bit short these days and also had plenty of books at home he'd borrowed or bought and wanted to read, and at a market a few blocks from his apartment he got some things to eat tonight: cheese, half-pound container of coleslaw, couple slices of smoked turkey, two tomatoes and a jar of French mustard on sale and a few loose carrots and a Bialy and roll, wished the liquor stores were open today so he could get a bottle of vodka—he only had a little left at home but nearly a whole bottle of rum—and an inexpensive wine. I bet I'm going to drink while I read and eat tonight till I get so drowsy or even soused that I fall asleep where I'm sitting and then have to drag myself to bed, he thought as he walked up his street. Unless a friend calls before he starts drinking or no more than a couple of drinks into it and suggests something like a local bar for a snack and a couple of beers or a movie. Then he'll probably just drink himself to sleep reading when he gets home. Anything to do with her? Sure, what does he think? even if half the nights of the last few months he's sat in his easy chair and drank and read and ate, all the food cut into pieces he can eat with his fingers off the plate or paper towel on the side table, though he rarely drank so much where he fell asleep in the chair. But why? Because, of course, he was very much touched by her today. Not touched so much as depressed and upset by what he sees as the goddamn misery of her life. He feels miserable for her, is what he's saying, that she has to be stuck like this and then put on this great face at how she's dealing with it, which he thinks has to be fakery on her part so he or who-ever she's with won't be turned off by her dejection and frus-tration and self-pity and envy and everything else she must be feeling. If only he could do something for her, but what a stupid thought. Why so? Because what could he do but continue to go out with her and marry her and try to have a baby with her and help take care of her the rest of her life no matter how bad off she gets? Then if there were some new kind of treatment or miracle drug that'd just about cure her or at least get her up walking, but why even bother think-ing of it?—she's already said. He went into his building, checked his mailbox in case someone had left a note in it or one of the tenants had received a letter of his by mistake the past week and shoved it through his box while he was out, which has happened. It'd be interesting though, he thought as he unlocked the front door and started up the stairs to his floor, or not interesting or curious or anything like that but *something*—as to what he'll finally do about calling her in the next few days. For really, after all his thinking and deciding and deep concern and sadness for her and so forth, he's still not sure if seeing her again won't eventually make things worse for her than not calling. So we're on that again? he thought, unlocking his apartment door. But that'd be two dates since the party and she'd probably think he's getting interested in her. Well, he is interested in her, he thought, going to the kitchen, but there are all these other things. He doesn't need to make a final final decision immediately, right? So just put your stuff away and have a drink earlier than you usually do, while you finish today's newspaper. Then after maybe a second drink, take or give in to a nap, since he could never get any work in and drink at the same time, or nothing any good. And it's also Sunday and midafternoon and he has a lot of sleep to catch up on and probably won't have the time for it after today till next weekend. Maybe, he thought, opening the freezer for ice, when he wakes up from his nap and has something to eat and a cup or two of coffee, he'll be able to sit down and work. He called the next day. She said she was just on her way out and was glad to hear from him but she only had a minute to talk. "A taxi service will be downstairs in five minutes." "Oh, you take those things?" he said and she said "When it's necessary, but I have to tell them it has to be a car with a lot of space in the trunk." "I've always wondered: are they expensive?" and she said "Once you get inside you have to arrange the price ahead of time, but it comes to the same—or on short trips, maybe a bit more—as a regular cab. I have a good service if you want their number." "Nah, I rarely use cabs, and hailing one in the street's okay with me. So, I'll be quick. Dinner tomorrow or the next free evening you got?" They had dinner in a neighborhood restaurant. He'd said in her apartment "We could go some other place further away if you want to take a livery cab," and she said "I'm feeling a little less able today to do things like transfer myself from chair to seat, so I'd like to play it safe and stay close to home." "I can assist you—I used to with my father for years," and she said "I'm sorry but I don't think you know enough yet about my condition for me to

take the chance. I think I've told you: I've broken a few
bones in falls, hence the gnarled nose." "No, I never noticed.
And I won't say 'Let me see.'" He wheeled her to the restaurant, wheeled her back. Had a problem at one corner getting
the chair up a high curb where there was no cut till she said
"Turn the chair tippers upside down but don't forget to turn
them right again or else I could fall backwards on my head."
"My father's chair," he said, "wasn't so state-of-the-artish,
and I remember those accidents." He went inside her building to tell the doorman she was outside and could he open
the revolving door. After she wheeled herself into the lobby,
he said "So, I think you can make it up okay, and that was
lots of fun again, thanks," and she said "Like to come up for
a coffee or drink? My father brought back this wonderful
cognac, he said, from Spain, and I wouldn't mind trying it
myself." "I love cognac," he said, "but how can it be from
Spain?" "Brandy, then? It has a name I keep forgetting.
'Find the door'? 'Fond of Law?' Spanish obviously isn't one
of my languages." "Oh, there are others besides Polish,
Russian and French?" She gave two more she was fluent in
and said she actually knew enough Spanish to speak it but
can't read it well, or not the more literary novels and poetry. "Me, strictly a *touché* of *Français*, from a half year in
France *dix-cinq* years ago, which is why I can roll *cognac* so
easily off my lips. Yeah, I'd like to come up," when the elevator came, "in case I didn't say and the offer still holds." At
her door she said "Would you do me a favor?" and gave him
the key. "Turn it only once to the left and it opens, but
please don't turn it hard because it's a ravenous lock and
short of iron intake, I'm sure, and has already eaten three of

them." "You ought to get the lock cylinder changed," and she said "The super says it's a perfectly good one and that I'm just not turning the key right. He may have a point, what with my hands the way they are sometimes on the harder tasks, which is why I asked you to open it now. One sudden involuntary manual jerk and the key's gone." "Maybe the lock needs a lubricating oil or something. I can bring some for you next time we meet and apply it," and she said "Any help like that to make my life easier would be very welcome." Inside, she told him where to find the brandy, a brandy snifter for him and a plastic mug for her, "since, as I nearly demonstrated in the restaurant, the stem kind have a way of slipping out of my hands." She excused herself to go to the bathroom. "This might take time, so have a drink or two." He got the brandy and glass and mug in the kitchen. When he came back he saw her in the little hall between the bedroom and living room, having trouble squeezing the chair through the bathroom door. "Can I help you?" and she said "No thanks; it's always a bit of a struggle but I always get through. Same in reverse." "Maybe you could get a different kind of door, like a sliding one, or not have any door at all, just a curtain," and she said "And when other people are here?" and he said "Then a sliding door built at the entrance to the hallway." "We'll talk about it later," and she tugged some more and was in and then seemed to have trouble shutting the door. He poured himself a brandy, sniffed it and drank. He heard the toilet flush about ten minutes later, and five minutes after that the water in the sink turned on. God, does she have problems, he thought; every fucking move. What did he get himself into, coming here, and if she suddenly gets romantic with him, what does he do? But she won't try anything like that, he thought, pouring another brandy. She doesn't at all seem the type to make the first move on the guy. When she was well and walking she might have been different. And she has to be aware of his trepidation and just the whole newness of it for him, and that if anything's going to happen it's got to take time to minimize the strangeness of it. So they'll drink, talk some more, and then he should go, maybe kiss her cheek on his way out and say he'll see her, even if he isn't sure he will. He got up to look at the titles of the books on some of the bookshelves and then at the river. Nice view, he thought, seven, or because she's on the seventh, six floors up. Compared to his and the amount of space he has and decrepitude of his building, a great place, and good security. She said she's had it for years—long before she got ill—or first an apartment in the rear and because of some deal she made with the landlord when she moved to the front, the rent's not so bad. No wonder she'd put up with narrow doors and most of the built-in stuff constructed for someone standing up and her having to summon the doorman every time she wants to get into the building. Rather than move, as she said she was eligible to, into a city-subsidized building with studio apartments especially designed for single people in wheelchairs and which might look out on a dreary street or wall. He heard her chair backing out of the bathroom a few minutes later. "Again, can I be of any help?" and she said "Thanks, but I have a system. It's slow but it works, and for some reason leaving's easier than entering." She kept moving the chair

I.

back and forth a few inches till she was out the door and able to swivel around to face the living room. "There," she said, "not such a big problem, just a long time in returning; I'm sorry. I hope you had a couple of brandies while I was missing in bathroom," and he said "Just a sniff or two. I poured but I was waiting for you." He poured some brandy into her mug and gave it to her. "So, where do we sit?" and she said "You sit anywhere you want. But please hold this?" giving him the mug, "so I can wheel the chair near you when you do choose a place." He said "The couch looks comfortable and if I sit on the left side of it I won't have to move the cocktail table for you. But is it really necessary to even have this table? Excuse me, and I probably don't know what I'm talking about, but if I were you I think I'd clear the room of everything but the essential furniture so I could move around freely." "That table serves several purposes for me, like where I put down things like my glasses, books and that mug. And I can also raise my feet on it, which I from time to time have to do. And I want the room to look like a normal one, though I can appreciate what you mean about moving around freely; the thought is delightful. As for the couch, either side is fine for me, and I can always push the table away myself. I work out, you know. Weights, pulleys, a stretch bar and this huge rig called a Murphy press. They're all in my unnormal-looking bedroom and a few of them are bolted to the floor or wall. My hands and legs might sometimes be a gummy or gelatinous mess. But I'm pretty strong otherwise from the waist up and I apparently, according to my physical therapist, have very strong upper arms. So don't try to fool with me, mister. Sorry, just

325

STEPHEN DIXON

lame-joking." "I was wondering how to take it. Let me feel your arm muscles," and she turned serious and said "If you don't mind, and I realize I was the one who first started on the subject, but it just seems too stupid a thing to do, so I'd rather not." "Okay, okay, then I won't let you feel mine. Now that was dumb too, wasn't it," and she shrugged. They drank; she looked away: at her mug, a painting on the wall, and when he looked away, at him. He's losing her, he thought. And don't say anything either about a narrower wheelchair for the bathroom and such. She's sure to have thought of it and the chair she's in might be the narrowest made and she'll think he's too free with his unthought-out ideas or simply doesn't give her brains enough credit. "So, silent period over," he said after about a minute. "I can't stand it," and she said "I agree; it can be so self-generating and unrewarding. How about if we go back to the last good place we left off?" "And that was?...your drink," which he just noticed on the cocktail table. "So you were right about that, of course," and held it out to her. She reached for it, hand was shaking, so she cupped the mug with both hands as she took it from him. "I hate for you to see so many things wrong at once, but nothing I can do," and he said "Don't worry about it; I don't. And wait!" when she was about to drink, "we didn't do this yet, even if we already drank," and raised his glass—"You don't have to raise yours"—and was about to say something when she said "No toast; there's no call for it. Let's just swallow silently and continue our talk or meander at will," and they drank. "I have to put the mug down," she said, and held it out for him and he put it on the table. They talked some more. He didn't know what his

326

toast would have been. Something where all the lines rhymed with "ight" had popped into his head just before he was going to make it. Something like "To the night, short of moonlight, river-filled window sight, may both our lives all our lives go right, and my apologies for this toasty fright," and something with "delight." In a way she saved him from embarrassing himself. And while they talked he thought She looks so good, so pretty, lovely and sweet, way her hair shines, those multicolored light eyes and soft smile and perfect teeth. He was feeling good too from the wine at dinner, three glasses to her one. And now—he poured himself another: "Is it all right?" and she said "Please, you're my guest"—a third brandy and thought No more after this; brandy's strong stuff and awful in the morning. And after he poured for himself he held the bottle up to her and gave that expression and she said "My poor stomach, and there's tomorrow and work and its preparation to think of. And one's plenty, the way you poured, and see my mug?" and picked it up and held it at an angle so he could see inside: it still had some but was now spilling out. "Oh damn," she said, and he said "Why? It missed the rug," and wiped it up with his handkerchief and she said "You can leave that with me to wash," and he said "Nah, I'll hold it to my nose on the ride home and think of my wiping the brandy off the floor." And their knees were touching—he'd moved his closer to hers so they would and she didn't pull back...and because of all of this he leaned forward to kiss her lips. First, after he'd folded up his handkerchief so the dry part was out and put it back into his pants pocket, he took her hand and held it while they talked, both of them darting looks at his hand holding hers, and smiling. Then he brought her hand to his face and kissed the knuckles and she said "That felt nice but I bet doing it to the other side would feel even better," and he kissed her palm and wrist and she closed her eyes and made the sounds "um, um," and he said "You know, with your eyes closed," and she opened them, "I probably could have stolen a real kiss from you, but I thought instead I'd ask if you'd mind," and she said "Go ahead, it's okay with me," and that was when he leaned forward and she moved a little to him and they kissed. They kissed several times, one after the other. Didn't speak much, looked at each other briefly between kisses some of those times, smiled, but mostly kept their eyes closed. He was able to get his arms around her back and pull her to him and she kept her arms around his neck but without holding on. She was a great kisser—soft lips, sweet breath, just enough pressure, and her lips stayed on his for as long as he wanted. A couple of times when their lips separated she said "Ooh, gosh, whew," without opening her eyes, and once with her eyes open "You're making me dizzy, that was so nice." "Ha," he said and she said "It's true. If I were standing and you weren't holding me like you're doing, I'm sure I'd fall down." "Ha, again," he said, "and I think I better go. It's getting late. I have to also get to work tomorrow, though no preparation—I just go in and do and do." "Good idea, your going," she said. "This kissing was interfering with my breathing and the whole thing was clearly getting out of control." "That's not bad," he said. "I know, I know, they're good, but we both agree just not for right now." "I'll call," he said, standing up. He had a hard-on but didn't care and she didn't seem to notice although it was sticking straight out in his pants. She wheeled herself to the front closet, he got his jacket and muffler from it, looked down and his fly was now flat, and tried unlocking the door. "How do you do this?" and she said "I locked the top one—protective reflex—which I never do when I leave, since I like carrying only one house key. Judging by the position of the bottom lock, it needs to be turned to the right and the top one stays as is." He unlocked and opened the door and said "I mean it, I'll call." "I hope so." "I will, why wouldn't I? I want to. One more kiss?" and she said "Shut the door first?" He did and she put her arms out and he leaned over to kiss her. It didn't work as a big kiss. His body was too twisted, and something about the angle so their faces didn't quite meet. He got on one knee and brought her face down to his and they kissed. "That was better, no?" and she said "The you-stand-up me-sit-down kind is essentially good for thrill-less pecks, like quick out-of-the-house goodbyes. If I could switch subjects? Would you mind, if you didn't call in an indeterminate number of days, if I called you?" and he said "No, call me, anytime you want, but I'll still be calling you," and gave his phone number. "You'll remember it?" and she said it back to him, "and you're probably listed, though it's more probable I won't call if you don't. That's what's happened to me; I'd feel too pushy. Goodnight, and my advice is to go up a Hundred-sixteenth at this hour. It's wider and there's more light and greater car and pedestrian traffic, though another steep street." Problems? he thought on the way home. Really, none. Day to day, that's how to take it, and only at her pace. She says slow, then that's the way to go, and "No no, not the time yet" for whatever, etcetera, and however long, that's okay too. Doesn't work out, then it doesn't, but he tried. She called ten minutes after he got home. "Good, you got back okay. I just wanted to say I had a very good time tonight, which I don't think I told you. That's all," and he said "Oh, it showed, as I hope it did from me. And as long as we're on the phone—" and she said "That isn't why I called, you know," and he said "I know, but it saves me the trouble of trying to get hold of you tomorrow for tomorrow or the next free evening you got ... I seem to be repeating myself with that line," and she said she was free the night after; too much reading to do tomorrow. They went to a movie by bus. She said she could meet him there and he said he'd rather pick her up so they could have time to talk before they saw the movie and he also wanted to see how she managed getting on the bus. "It's quite impressive, technologically, though I irritate passengers sometimes when my entrance holds up the bus or my chair displaces their seats." "Hell with them," and she said "I can sympathize with them if they have to be somewhere on time—a job where the boss won't accept any excuses for coming in late—and are behind schedule, or the bus is. That's why I prefer the number 5 on Riverside Drive. Usually, when I get on, only a few people are on it, and it's a quick trip to Seventy-second Street because it has to stop so few times, so can make up for what it loses on me." Kissing? She offered her cheek when he came in—"Door's open," she'd yelled from the kitchen—and he thought *fine*, because he felt they were going too fast. The lift on the first bus didn't work, but the next one, after several attempts by the driver to lower the outside lip of it, or whatever it's called, did. "You have to wheel me in backwards," she said, "or I can do it myself. But it'll be faster if you do it, and because you're assisting me you don't have to drop in a fare," and he said "Great, money saved, I've nothing against that, and very *gallant* of the Transit Authority." "What I meant was we don't have to pay it now but we're expected to mail it in the envelope the driver gives us," and he said "Sure, I can just imagine most New Yorkers doing that, but okay." "Maybe, he said after the driver had fastened the wheelchair to the floor and given him the envelope, "I can send enough money by check for the next ten fares of my riding this way. Then I can avoid licking and stamping nine envelopes—oh, I see it doesn't take a stamp—the next, nine, or rather, four times, since I'd be paying for you, and it's all on a good-faith basis anyway," and she said "You can do that if you want, but there's always the possibility you'll end up losing on the arrangement and with no way to get reimbursed," and he said "What can I say? If I lose, I lose. So I'm out a few dollars." The other passengers? They watched them through the windows getting on the bus, with no revealing expressions, and once she was settled inside and he was seated beside her a couple of people nodded and smiled at them. After they reached their stop and her chair was unfastened, he started to turn it around to wheel her onto the lift backwards and she said "No, the other way." "I don't get it," he said, and the bus driver said "It's so there's less chances you both don't fall off, and if you do, you don't land on the back of your heads." He couldn't find a seat next to one of the wheelchair spaces in the theater, so he sat a few rows in front of her. He was hoping they could touch or hold hands and do things like look at each other and maybe whisper or mouth or gesture something about the movie or he just looking at her while she faced forward. He did look back a few times but the theater was full and he couldn't see her. After, he said "A bite? Beer?" and she said "I'd rather go straight home. Sometimes it's inconvenient being away too long." "I was just thinking. When I first met you at the party and you went into the bathroom there—you did, didn't you?" and she said "I think so," and he said "Then I presume you had no trouble getting in it. The door was wide enough, I'm saying; you were lucky," and she said "Sometimes I am; most times I don't even try. But what an odd thing for you to think of." "I suppose it shows I'm starting to think of different less ordinary things regarding you; logistics; like that. Nothing wrong with it, I hope. I'd love, incidentally, to invite you to see my place. But it's all up, one long and two normal-sized flights, nothing but landings and steps." "I'm sure you could put me on your back, but I doubt you could carry me upstairs, so for now it's out." On the street, after they'd talked briefly about the movie—"Why do I continue to see his films?" she said. "When is he going to shuck his adolescent fantasies and juvenile humor and grow up?" "I agree," he said—she said she'd like to take a cab home: "Just to give you the complete transportation picture. Though it might not be easy getting one. Typically, if I'm alone, and even if I push up my skirt and flash a leg, ten to fifteen available cabs will pass before an extremely congenial recent immigrant from Ethiopia or Afghanistan or Pakistan or India—very often Sikhs or someone who has a close relative who lost a limb in one of the recent wars there—will stop. And not only will he help me in and out of the cab but he'll wheel me to my building and notify the doorman I'm outside." The first cab he hailed stopped. "He's not from Asia, Africa or the Indian continent so it's probably that you're with me and he knows you'll do most of the work." He helped her slide from the wheelchair to the front seat and then, with her instructing him, he disassembled and folded up the chair and stuck it in the trunk. The cabby stayed in his seat and read a magazine, was a recent Soviet émigré, she determined from his photo and name on the hack license, and spoke Russian with her most of the trip about the beauty of Leningrad and greatness of Brodsky and Blok and ineptitude and corruption and inevitable self-destruction of the Soviet government for good, and she said "*Nyet, nye budet, uzhe slishkom dolgo*," and he said "*Nyet, budet*, it will, *vy nye pravay*, not too long, but still, after, no go back I; it be mess." "Give him a generous tip please," she said when they reached her building. "Even if he didn't lift a finger to help us and is quite unpleasant, I want to encourage him to stop for other sitstills like me." In the apartment she offered him a drink. "I can't have anything—if you'll excuse me, too much fluid already—but help yourself and perhaps get something to eat from the fridge. There's plenty." He ate a piece of cheese on a rice cake and then thought "What am I doing? Cheese; bad breath," and had a carrot and celery stick, washed his mouth out in the kitchen sink, brought in a glass of wine and they talked, sat in the same places as the night before, held hands, kissed, kissed several times, rubbed each other's backs. He put his hand under her shirt there and worked it around to the front. "If you want," she said after a minute of his hand touching her breast, "we can go to the bedroom," and he said "It'd be all right?" and she said "Yes, I have my landlord's permission; it's in my lease. Whatever do you mean?" "You know, nothing about that you'll have any difficulty getting on the bed, off it, and so on, if by 'bedroom' you meant bed," and she said "Ultimately, if you didn't mind the idea, that was my objective," and he said "Then you answered the question I was going to ask." "Not that there can't be difficulties beyond the inconvenience to you of my long pre-bed prep, which I'd do even if I were alone. This, like my liquid-intake limit, so I don't have to get up during the night to go to the bathroom or, to be frank about it, risk wetting the bed. If there did turn out to be a problem—spacticity, for one—I'd try to let you know beforehand it was coming so you wouldn't be too alarmed. If at any point you felt the whole coupling thing wasn't worth it because my physical problems had become a bit too hard to take, don't worry, I'd understand." "Somehow I don't—" "Let me just finish please? If it were the other way around—you in the chair, I able to get to my feet—believe me I'd be somewhat anxious too, particularly after all I've just said and the rather programmatic way I put it." "I'm not anxious," he said, "and I like the way you didn't coat it. Or I'm a little anxious, but only a little more than normal for a first time. What I'm really thinking though is what problem can be so bad that can't eventually pass? Okay, maybe some, but let's forget it, hope that none emerge, and go to bed," and he stood up. "My bed prep," she said, and squeezed his hand, rubbed it against her cheek while he ran his other hand across the top of her head, and went into the bathroom and shut the door. He sat down, heard water running, toilet flushing, her getting off and then back on the wheelchair. He looked at the artwork on the walls, furniture around the room, thought things like So, this is it; shouldn't be bad; he's sure she's got everything under control, done this a number of times before, and once they start, shouldn't be any missteps or anything they can't get back to. Relax, she's very affectionate, sensitive, she'd never bring him in to it if she thought there was a slight chance it could go wrong. About fifteen minutes after she went in he said by her door "Excuse me, everything all right?" and she said "Couldn't be better. I'm sorry it's been so long. Some things I have to do in here take their own time," and he said "I know, I'm not getting impatient; just asking. If you need anything, though I don't know what that could be, let me know." He got another glass of wine in the kitchen, looked out the window there at the river and lights of New Jersey and followed for a while what seemed like a big jet flying north, thought if he was ever going to work here, since she probably works in the bedroom, this is where it would be: small typewriter table over the radiator under the window, window sill for his coffee mug and paperclips and such and a second chair pulled up for a thesaurus and writing paper and other supplies. In the living room he looked at the titles of books in a different tall bookcase than the one two nights ago. If these were his, he thought, few to throw out or give away. He thinks the ones from the other night were like that too. Five, ten in this bookcase at least he'd like to read, and maybe one day he will. He should borrow one he's been looking for in bookstores a long time, before he leaves. He knocked on the bathroom door a minute later and said "Excuse me, but do you think I should just get into bed?" and she said "Is it getting too cold out there? The bathroom, because the radiator's almost as large as the one in the bedroom, is a hot box, and because of some malfunction the super's always promising to fix, it can't be turned off." "No, it's comfortable here, very pleasant. I just thought...I don't know," and she said "Do what you want. But I won't be much longer and I'm coming out fully dressed. So maybe we should both start with our clothes on, something I'd like tonight, would that be all right?" and he said "Sure, anything." "Did that seem peculiar, my request?" and he said "No, I can understand it. And I should also wash up before I get into bed, so forget what I said." He heard her coming out a few minutes later. He'd just poured himself another glass of wine, quickly drank it and rushed back to pull her chair the rest of the way out of the bathroom. "Right or left?" he said in the hallway, and she said "Bedroom; left," and he pushed her into it and turned on the ceiling light. Double bed neatly made, nothing in the room, it seemed, out of place, and he was right: a long table with an electric typewriter, lamp, books and articles and a ream package of paper on it, another tall bookcase filled with books and stacks of manuscripts and piano music, some exercise equipment taking up a quarter of the room. "I should also work out with things like this," he said. "A gym would be okay but they're so expensive and time-consuming to get to," and she said "A couple of these machines you could possibly use." "You mean I'm not in such great shape," and she said "No, you look fine, strong, big forearms, and the right weight. I meant 'put to use,' if you ever feel like it and I'm not working in here." "I wouldn't mind; thanks. And excuse me," and he went into the bathroom. Make it short here, he thought, and peed, saw a portable toilet seat standing up between the commode and bathtub, washed his face and hands and took out his penis again and wiped the head with an already-wet washrag, then thought Ah, come on, and wiped the shaft and dried the whole thing with a face towel and folded it the way he found it and put it back on the rack, rinsed his mouth, checked his nostrils and ears for hairs curling out—one or two in one of the ears, but don't worry about it—and went back to the bedroom. She was sitting on the bed, holding on to the wheelchair arms, still in all her clothes including her sneakers. Ceiling light was off and night table lights on either side of the bed were on. There didn't seem room for her to get around to the other side in her chair—exercise equipment in the way—though maybe she could squeeze through or there was a switch somewhere for both night table lights. Now that he took a good look at the bed it seemed larger than a double—queen-sized, probably—and also specially made or just set up for her: mattress lower than normal and, from what he could make out, even with the wheelchair seat. "So you made it okay from the chair to the bed," and she said "For this transfer I use a sliding board," pointing to it leaning up against the night table beside her. "And in the bathroom—the board too?" and she said "Grab bars and toilet seat arms help me get aloft, which you may have noticed when you were in there," and he said "The special seat, yes, but not the bars. Where are they?" and she said "In the wall and on top of the tub rim." "They work okay then, bathtub isn't too far from the seat?" and she said "Sometimes, like with the sliding board, I forget to use them right or I just slip up, and then there's a problem." "What do you do if you're by yourself and this happens?" and she said "Didn't we talk about this before? Maybe it was with someone else. I work it out. If I can't, I phone someone for help. You might be lucky enough to join that list." "Okay with me. But from the bathroom? I didn't see a phone." "Then, if I'm on the floor or have hurt myself, it's a big problem. Thank God it hasn't happened often, and I've almost always got myself up somehow or out of the room." "Have you had to stay down or hurt in the bathroom for very long?" "A few times." "You could get a phone extension there. Why don't you?" and she said "I've thought of it and I probably will. Please sit next to me?" He did. "And for the time being, don't ask anymore questions?" "I won't." They started undressing each other.